Surreal
South'09

Surreal South'09

edited by

Laura Benedict

&

Pinckney Benedict

Press 53
Winston-Salem

Press 53
PO Box 30314
Winston-Salem, NC 27130

First Edition

Cover design by Kevin Watson

Cover art, "Tiny Gatekeeper,"
copyright © 2009 by Minna Svensson,
used by permission of the artist

Printed on acid-free paper

ISBN 978-0-9825760-1-4

Contents

For Kevin, sine qua non

Introduction

"There is one difference between me and a mad man. I am not mad."
—Salvador Dali

Surrealism is the only meaningful response to the failure of rationalism.

At the end of the First World War, much of Europe lay in ruins, and millions of its citizens (not to mention a significant number of Americans and Canadians) had been slain, for no apparent reason. The Surrealist movement in art and literature arose at that time and in that place because, quite simply, the rational processes by which Europe had been governed had broken down completely, and the only significant opposition was—if not simple irrationality—a deliberate, intelligent, and sharply focused anti-rationality.

This is where we find ourselves now. Every one of the "rational" elements of our society has revealed itself for the sham that it is. We are engaged in fantastically expensive, morally draining, and apparently endless (in that they will certainly be succeeded by other, exactly similar conflicts even should they "end") wars. Our schools and colleges, governed by our best and brightest and most rational, hum away, busily producing armies of semi-literates, and those are the successes; the failures are entirely illiterate.

Vast numbers of our nominally "free" citizens live every day with crippling, enslaving debt. Our municipalities are bankrupt; our states are bankrupt; our federal government is bankrupt; and the way into this bankruptcy was led by that bastion of rationality that is Wall Street. Lehman Brothers, Bernard Madoff, Bear Stearns, the geniuses who cooked up the sub-prime loan market, on and on—all of them, all of the bankrupts and the frauds, the monsters of vanity and conceit: you can bet that every one of them, when he looks at himself in the mirror in the morning, thinks to himself, "But at least I am rational."

The only difference between us and rational men is that we are not mad.

We make no apologies, then, for the anti-rational means by which we made our choices for the anthology—the second in the series—that you now hold in your hands. In fact, we glory in it. We did not seek out stories that sought to convince us of their own merit. Stories cannot convince by argument. They must simply *be*, in the charismatic way that a dream simply *is*. They cannot be manufactured or argued for. Each of these stories is a dream, complete in itself but also suggesting a universe, a multitude of universes, of other stories, each sovereign, each entire.

Of course, contemporary physics seems to strongly suggest that this state of affairs—an infinite number of infinitely idiosyncratic universes massed like an endless congeries of bubbles—is not some science-fiction trope to be laughed at by serious people. Anything that you can imagine, no matter how absurd or horrible or amusing, has happened or is happening or will happen, or all three, in the infinite number of infinitely varied universes that science now posits as reality. That's a prospect to make the rational mind, the serious mind, boggle.

In the South—the South as geographical region, the South as one particular American state of mind—rationality has never been at the top of the list of admired, or even required, qualities. Serious people—self-serious people—are laughed at in the South, because the horrifying, long-running tragicomedy that is Southern history defies rational analysis, it defies self-seriousness, it defies consensus. The South *is* Idiosyncrasy.

Idiosyncratically, then, we decided that the best way to approach this new book was to open submissions to anybody who thought they met our published selection criteria. You're probably aware that the "best of" anthologies which the various major publishing companies (all very properly and rationally run, by the way, and also, not coincidentally, in a state of utter panic and financial collapse as we write this introduction) are selected by editors who themselves see only a very small part of what is published, not to mention written, each year. In that selection process there are gatekeepers upon gatekeepers upon gatekeepers. We're too poor for gatekeepers, and our instincts are too democratic, and so we took what folks chose to send us.

The array of submissions was stunning, despite the fact that we could not afford to advertise widely. We feared, in fact, that we would be overwhelmed by the flood of manuscripts we received, and our fears would certainly have been realized had we not been rescued by our good friend Josh Woods, who served as the official "Surreal South bitch." (He welcomed the title, though he lists himself as "associate editor" on his resume, I believe.) He helped us to read and evaluate, and helped us to keep pure in our mission of anti-rationality.

A surprising number of the fictions we received were excellent; we could have filled a volume of this size with good stories many times over. We're particularly glad to present to you here a mix of the fiction of well-established writers and folks who have previously published relatively little or not at all. As we selected pieces for this second volume of the *Surreal* South series, we looked for two things above all others. Each of the pieces here, in addition to its other virtues, possesses *sublimity*; and each story is, in its effect if not in its explicit content, *apocalyptic*.

Sublimity, as we choose to define it, is that quality a story possesses when it is, in its entirety, completely unpredictable as well as completely inevitable and authentic. Each of the two elements that contribute to sublimity is relatively easy to achieve in isolation. For unpredictability, all that is required is a disengagement from the everyday, from consensus reality. Any mumbling weirdo on the intercity bus can give you as much. Ditto inevitability: most modern stories march to their inevitable endings like condemned men toward their deaths, and an experienced reader knows whither they are bound long before they ever arrive there.

But the two together: Ah! That's the real thing, that moment in the narrative when we say, simultaneously: *I cannot believe that that's what happened!* and *Of course! Nothing else, nothing less than that, could possibly have sufficed.* All of these stories are made up of such instances.

The apocalyptic: because of contemporary film and literature, the term conjures visions of thermonuclear devastation, of mutants and zombies and vampires run amok. There's some of that sort of apocalypse in these pages, certainly. But the word apocalypse is different from that simplistic definition, and it is more.

A story—a real story, of the type that we've gathered here; not the mock-stories, the painless, bloodless vignettes that make up so much of today's "literary" fiction—involves apocalypse. Apocalypse means a revelation (the literal meaning of the word apocalypse is a "lifting of the veil"), and a very specific type of revelation: the destruction of an old order, followed by a time of disorder and chaos, and the replacement of the old order by a new and entirely different order.

Genre apocalyptic fiction simply makes this pattern of revelation—destruction, chaos, establishment of the new—explicit, which is one of the reasons we like it. Nothing hidden; it just lays it all out there, human nature and the nature of the world, raw and bloody and terrible to look at, but revealed for all to see, because it is set in such stark relief against the background of a changed world.

And it's almost impossible to look away, isn't it? Like a car wreck; and that is, in one sense, precisely what a car wreck is: an apocalypse according to the model we have chosen, if a very personal one. Before the car wreck, we exist within the old order, the order that tells us that we are in control, we are in forward motion, we are making progress toward the goal that we have no doubt we will reach, as we have always reached it before. Then the implosion, the shattered glass, the violence and blood, chaos: do we live? Do we die? And if we live, we emerge into a world that is changed, for us if not for others, in every way, for all time.

Most of the fiction that we admire for more than its momentary effect, and all of the fiction that we have chosen for this volume, works in just this way. The world as we know it (as the protagonist knows it) vanishes; we exist for a time in the whirlwind; we emerge into the new order, and either we belong to the new world and are willing and able to exist in it, or we find ourselves excluded from what has been established.

Sublimity and apocalypse. Anti-rationality and surreality. The call for the literary artist is nothing less than to reveal and remake everything; and the writers whose work you are about to experience have boldly answered that call. We invite you to abandon to its well-deserved fate the wreckage of the rational, and to enjoy.

Laura Benedict
Pinckney Benedict
Carbondale, IL
October 2009

Becky Hagenston

Anthony

The ghost had gotten inside her daughter like a tapeworm and refused to come out. How had it happened? Was it something Cindy ate? Something in the water? The water in Boardtown, Alabama was bad, everybody knew it; Nia usually bought bottled water at Wal-Mart, but this week she'd been cheap, she'd been lazy, she hadn't wanted to haul all those bottles to the car. And now a ghost inhabited her child and wouldn't be budged.

Her husband Jake blamed it on Nia; *he* would never let something like this happen to their child; he would have beat the crap out of that ghost before it could get near his daughter. Nia didn't argue with him. She had been planning to leave him for months. He had a temper and she was almost positive he was screwing the waitress at Longshots, the bar where they'd met seven years ago and where he spent more and more of his time, sometimes not coming home until three-thirty in the morning. The bar closed at two, so what the hell was he doing until three-thirty? Not that she cared.

"It's because you don't make her take a bath every day," he said. "It's because you feed her macaroni and cheese from a box. That shit is horrible for a kid."

"How the hell do you know what I feed her? Since when are you around for any meals anyway?" Sometimes she argued with him just because she wanted to see how close he would get to hitting her. He'd done it once and she'd threatened to take Cindy and leave if he ever did it again, and now when he clenched his fists and got up in her face, she stared right back at him and said, "I dare you," and watched him use every ounce of his strength not to bash her in

1

the nose. She wanted to laugh every time because she was leaving him anyway.

It must have happened on Tuesday night, when—yes, she *had* forgotten to give Cindy a bath after her dinner of mac and cheese from a box. Nia had been on the computer finishing up her homework for Accounting 101, a ridiculously easy course taught by a man who looked like he was twelve. Still, it was hard to keep up when you had a child and a full-time job at Blockbuster. She wanted more for herself, and just when she thought she was getting somewhere—didn't it figure—something like this had to happen.

The kindergarten teacher, Miss Missy, had been the one to take Cindy to the nurse's office on Wednesday morning. Miss Missy had seen many things in her life: she'd seen a crop dusting plane fall out of the sky above the cotton fields behind her house; she'd woken up in the middle of the night to see her baby sister in the arms of a Skunk Ape (startled by Missy's cries, it had dropped the baby back in the crib and fled out the window); she'd seen the spirit of her lynched grandfather swinging from a tree.

So when tiny, blonde Cindy Morgan's stomach shouted, "Time to party!" in the voice of a young black male, Miss Missy kept her wits. The children were just down for their naps, and Miss Missy was in the process of cleaning up the Nilla wafer crumbs and milk cartons from snack time. She detested Nilla wafers, but the children loved them. Those, and Fig Newtons. Her own childhood in Tuscaloosa had been filled with chitlins—which stunk halfway down the street—and pork barbeque. She and her sister munched happily on fried pig snouts ("*Snoots*," her Mawmaw called them) after school, watching *The Munsters* and *Gilligan's Island* until their mother came home from work.

"Time to party!" said Cindy Morgan's belly, and the other children turned on their mats and yawned, and Cindy sat up and said, in her own baby-voice, "Miss Missy, I feel funny."

Miss Missy walked briskly across the room, knelt, and felt Cindy's forehead.

"I ain't sick, I'm dead," said the voice from Cindy's stomach. Or maybe it was more the solar plexus. It was hard to be sure.

Nurse would know.

Nurse felt dread when she saw Miss Missy marching Cindy Morgan into her office. She had noticed the girl earlier that month, being dropped off twenty minutes late in a rusty orange El Camino by a woman in a too-short skirt and too-high heels. Mothers like this were usually bad news; they usually had boyfriends with tattoos and motorcycles, boyfriends who didn't like little children. Or liked them too much.

Please, no bruises, Nurse prayed silently, and looked Miss Missy in the eye, as if daring her to say what Nurse least wanted to hear.

"Cindy here is having stomach… difficulties," said Miss Missy. She put her hands on Cindy's shoulders and said, "Sweetheart, Nurse will take care of you, okay?"

"Okay," said Cindy Morgan, and then Miss Missy spun on a heel—Nurse admired Miss Missy's ability to wear heels—and was gone.

Nurse leaned down and looked into Cindy's pale blue eyes. "Does your tummy hurt?" she asked, smiling, relieved that her worst fears had not come to pass. Two weeks ago, she had lifted up Timmy Maxwell's Pooh Bear shirt to discover cigarette burns around his nipples. A woman from Social Services had arrived to lead a sobbing Timmy out to a big white car. Nurse hadn't seen him since.

She led Cindy into an examination room and helped the girl up to the paper-covered table. "Can you tell me where it hurts?"

"I feel like dancin'," said the voice of a young black man. Then he laughed, a joyful sound that made Nurse almost laugh, too.

Cindy frowned. "He wants to dance," she said. "But I don't."

"Well, now, let's just take a look." Nurse lifted up Cindy's pink Care Bears shirt and placed her stethoscope on her white stomach.

"It's cold," Cindy said, and then giggled.

"Breathe deeply," said Nurse. "That's a good girl. Will you lie down for me, sweetheart?"

Cindy lay her head back on the paper pillow and closed her eyes. Nurse touched around her belly button very gently, trying to locate the source of the strange male voice. She had never encountered anything like this before, had never read about it in nursing school or on any of the nursing blogs she looked at every evening while she ate a Lean Cuisine in front of her computer.

"Hello?" said Nurse. "Is anybody there?"

"*I'm* here," said the young male voice. "I'm here and I'm ready to party. Hell yeah!" He laughed again, and Nurse couldn't help smiling. Then he said, gently, "You're a damn good nurse," and Nurse felt herself blushing and had to turn away and clear her throat.

Nia was at work that Wednesday afternoon, scanning in new DVDs of some violent Mexican movie she couldn't pronounce, when she got the phone call from the nurse's office. Then she had to bribe Sherry to cover for her by offering to work the weekend shift. Sherry was a sorority girl and she worked at Blockbuster because, as the poorest girl in the sorority, she needed the money but only if she could work a job that wouldn't make her seem like too much of a loser. Before Blockbuster, she had worked at McDonalds, which was humiliating, absolutely mortifying, all that grease, all those miserable single mothers she had to work with! She lasted one day because at the start of her second shift, Tad from Psi Upsilon came in and ordered hashbrowns and then said, "Fuck, Sherry. What are you doing here?" and Sherry took off her paper cap and yelled, "I quit!" right there. She'd hoped Tad might be so impressed by this that he'd ask her out, but he'd just laughed and asked for ketchup.

Blockbuster was better because a) there was no grease and b) she could watch movies all day long and c) sometimes she could get Nia to take over the weekend shift for her, so she could go out with her friends, cruise the bars—there weren't many—and meet up with boys, though not Tad, because he'd date-raped this girl Racine and everybody knew it, even though she refused to go to campus police.

Nia always had a frazzled look about her, and her hair looked like it had been bleached too many times. Sometimes Sherry wished she could give Nia a makeover.

. . . .

When Nia got Cindy home, she took her temperature (normal, just as the nurse had said) and tucked her into bed and brought her some chicken noodle soup.

"It's probably just a virus, sweetheart," she told Cindy, and she heard the young man sigh heavily and mutter something.

"Did you want to speak up?" Nia demanded, and the young man said, "No, ma'am," very politely. "Do you want to leave, then?" she said, and he didn't answer.

When Jake got home, Nia took him into the living room and explained, quietly, what the nurse had told her: Cindy had the ghost of a young black man living in her stomach, and he didn't seem dangerous, but they ought to keep an eye on her.

That's when Jake accused her of not feeding or bathing Cindy properly, and that's when Nia dared him to smack her.

Jake could be a good father when he put his mind to it, and he picked Cindy up from her bed and kissed her on the cheek and said, "What's this about feeling bad?"

"I'm okay now," she said.

"Who are you?" Jake demanded of Cindy's stomach. "What do you want from us?"

"Don't yell at him," said Nia. "His name is Anthony." She'd actually had a pleasant, though brief, conversation with the young man. He'd died in a car accident, but he wouldn't talk much about that except to say that people should wear their seatbelts.

"Anthony?" shouted Jake. "Make thyself known!"

"For God's sake, Jake," said Nia. "He's not a Shakespearean actor. He's just a teenaged boy."

"Can I have the television in my room?" Cindy wanted to know, and Anthony said, "Say please," and Cindy said, "Please?"

"Show some respect," Anthony said, and then didn't say anything else for the rest of the night, although he chuckled occasionally during the *Happy Days* reruns.

That night, Miss Missy told her new boyfriend Hank about Cindy Morgan.

"It must be so hard on the family," she said. "But people learn to live with things, you find ways to get by."

Hank, who taught third grade, thought Miss Missy (he just called her Missy) was the most graceful, beautiful, intelligent woman he had ever met. He loved the little gap in her teeth and he loved that she wore such sexy clothes to work, those tight pencil skirts and high heels. No jumpers and sneakers for her, like the other kindergarten teachers wore.

They had only been dating for two months but he was ready to ask her to marry him; he could picture their children playing on the swingset at his mother's house, could imagine calling, "Henry! Deanne! Time for dinner!"

Now was not the time to propose, however; Missy looked vexed. She paced the floor in her bare feet. She sat down on the sofa and put her head in her hands. The polish on her toenails was pink and the polish on her fingernails was silver. He felt his breath catch, and tried to focus.

Hank had never heard of this particular situation, but he admired Missy's ability to try to get to the bottom of things. "I think they'll be fine," he told her, and she leaned against him and closed her eyes. And even though he had transparencies to make and dioramas to grade, he stroked her head and said, "There, there," until she was snoring.

Nurse was at home, eating a Lean Cuisine in front of her computer and Googling "child ghosts," which did not produce the result she was looking for. "Stomach ghost" she tried, and then "haunted stomach," but again, the results proved fruitless. Then she found herself tempted to type in the dating website that had gotten her here in the first place, living alone in a podunk Alabama town, so she turned the computer off. She told herself she wasn't that lonely, and if she was she should just go to sleep and not think about it.

Cindy's pediatrician said, "I can't vaccinate her for this, but I don't think she's in any danger."

"She's not," said Anthony.

"They're getting along pretty well," said Nia. "I hear them talking late at night sometimes."

"How long has this been going on?" the pediatrician asked, suddenly suspicious.

"Only about... less than a week?" Nia said. She was lying. It had been three weeks since Anthony made his appearance, but she told herself it wasn't as if Cindy was *ill.* Besides, Cindy hated the doctor. But the school nurse was scaring Nia with stories of parasites and poltergeists and wanted Cindy to take antibiotics, so Nia thought she'd better get a second opinion.

And Cindy and Anthony *were* getting along; that part was true. Last night Nia had hovered outside Cindy's door—Cindy liked to keep it closed now, even though she used to be afraid of the dark—and heard Cindy giggling, and then Anthony laughing, and then Cindy talking, Anthony replying. More giggling from both of them. What on earth did they have to say to one another, a six-year-old and a dead fifteen-year-old? Nia was tempted to hide a tape recorder under Cindy's bed, but she wasn't entirely sure how to rig it so it wouldn't click loudly when it shut off.

"How's your husband handling this?" the pediatrician asked in low tones.

Nia rolled her eyes. "Fine," she said.

The truth was, Jake had been mad because Anthony was black. He wanted a white ghost. He wanted, specifically, Marilyn Monroe. "Or James Dean!" he'd said. "How cool would that be?"

What could you do with a man like that?

"You feel all right, don't you, Cindy-girl?" said the pediatrician, producing a green lollipop from his coat, and Cindy said, "Yes, sir, I feel fine. Thank you for asking."

"Well, now!" laughed the pediatrician. "Aren't you polite."

Nia felt stung. It was Anthony who'd taught her that.

He still sometimes said "hell" and wistfully said he wanted to party, but only when Cindy was taking a nap or preoccupied with cartoons.

"What kind of party do you want, Anthony?" Nia asked once, when they were watching TV together on the sofa. (Cindy had fallen asleep during *Dateline*; Anthony enjoyed it, as he enjoyed most of the programs Nia watched.) All she could get out of him was a sigh. He did that a lot, and it made her sad for him. It made him seem older than his years.

Jake thought Anthony was a riot. At first, yes, he was pissed off, and not because he was a racist, either. He just figured that if his daughter was going to have a ghost in her stomach, it ought to be someone... well, famous. Someone interesting. He wanted the TV news crews to come over and interview him, and interview the famous person, and maybe film the two of them together—Jake and James Dean— chatting about cars or something.

But Anthony was a cool little dude, and he cracked Jake up. One evening, when Nia was at her accounting class and Cindy was napping on the sofa (Cindy napped a lot lately), he had said, "You know how to make a hormone?"

"A what?" said Jake.

"Don't pay her."

When Jake stopped laughing he said, "Do you—did you play any sports when you were alive? Basketball, maybe?"

"Nah," said Anthony. "I had to take care of my little brothers after school, help out my mother and shit."

"What about your dad?"

"What about him?" Anthony said bitterly.

Anthony needed a father figure, someone to talk about guy stuff with, someone to guide him in the ways of women.

"You can talk to me," Jake said. "I'm here for you."

"'Preciate it," Anthony said.

One night, when Cindy was sound asleep, Nia tiptoed into her daughter's bedroom and whispered, "Anthony? Are you awake?"

"I'm awake," he said. "Don't need no sleep. Just lyin' here, collectin' my thoughts."

She pulled a chair next to the bed, stroked Cindy on her pale forehead. "I'm just wondering how long you were planning on staying? Not that it isn't nice having you."

"Nice bein' here!" he cried. "I mean it. I like you people. You all right."

Nia felt relieved, then remembered why she was there. "I was just thinking," she said, "that there might be something you want, or need… something to, I don't know, help you go toward the light? Somehow?"

He didn't say anything.

"Don't you have parents wondering where you are? I know that if I were dead and Cindy was also dead, and I didn't get to see her, I'd worry."

"Dunno," he said, and gave one of his sad little sighs.

Then, because she had spent lunch hour crying in the Blockbuster bathroom, and because she was failing her accounting class, and because here was this sad boy lost and far from home, she broke down and wept. "I'm sorry," she sniffled, "I'm sorry if it's my fault."

"It ain't," Anthony said gently. "Shit just happens."

"I'm thinking I should leave Jake," she admitted, and cried a little harder.

"Aw, man, that sucks," Anthony said. "Whaddya gonna do that for anyways?"

"He's a terrible husband," she said. "He's never home, and I know he's screwing some slut he met at Longshots! Sorry," she added, and blushed. Sometimes it was hard to remember that Anthony was barely more than a child himself.

"Seems like he's home all the time," Anthony said, and Nia realized it was true. Just last night, she had come home from class to find Jake, Cindy and Anthony playing Candyland on the kitchen table. "Where's the babysitter?" she had demanded, and Jake said, "I sent her home," and moved his marker toward Gumdrop Mountain.

And two nights ago, Jake had offered to help cook dinner.

"Because I'm such a terrible cook, is that right?" she'd snapped, and he'd kissed her on the cheek and said no, he just wanted to help out.

"I only married him because I was pregnant," she whispered. Anthony didn't say anything, and so after a moment she gave Cindy's tummy a pat and tiptoed from the room.

. . . .

Miss Missy enjoyed having Anthony in the classroom. He was never disruptive, and the other students listened to him. If anyone got too rambunctious—if Gino pulled Caroline's hair, or Dana hit Rachel—Anthony would say, "Have some respect!" and they would stop.

You expected ghosts to be trouble, but Anthony was a joy, and this is what she wrote on his progress report. But it concerned her that he wasn't getting the kind of education he needed. *Anthony could go very far*, she wrote, *if he had the opportunity.*

On Cindy's report, she wrote: *Needs to speak up more in class.* Then, because she liked the girl, she added: *Cindy is a sweet child, and she knows most of her numbers.*

At the parent-teacher conference, she suggested to Cindy's parents that Anthony needed a tutor. Just because he was dead and stuck inside a six-year-old's body didn't mean he should be denied a good education. Everyone had things to overcome.

"We're all," she said, "differerently abled, in our own way."

"We'll look into it," Cindy's father said. "We only want the best for him."

"You're good parents," Miss Missy said. "Anthony is lucky he found you."

Their usual babysitter was busy, so when Jake asked Nia on a date ("Remember dates?" he asked), they had to scramble to find someone else. Nia immediately thought of Sherry.

"He doesn't need a babysitter," Jake had insisted.

"No, but she does," said Nia.

Really, thank God she was the responsible parent around here. Thank God at least one of them was watching out for their daughter.

"Will you be nice to the babysitter?" Nia asked Cindy, and Cindy yawned and said, "Okay," in a tiny voice.

"That's my girl," Nia said.

Sherry was surprised by how neat Nia's house was; she'd been expecting something much dumpier and red-necky—maybe a Confederate flag and a beat-up pickup truck in the driveway—but it wasn't bad at all, certainly no trashier than some of the fraternity houses she'd been to. There were candles and potpourri in the living room and framed pictures of Cindy as a baby, Nia holding her and smiling at the camera, looking almost beautiful. Most surprising of all, Nia's husband was a hottie. How did someone like her end up with someone like him?

Nia had led Sherry through the house (she caught a glimpse of the master bedroom, of the neatly made bed and the big pillows), ending up in the kitchen and saying, "Here's all the emergency numbers, poison control, you know the drill. I'll have my cell phone with me. Help yourself to the Hot Pockets in the freezer. Cindy already had her dinner."

"Is there anybody else I should call if I can't get through? Cindy's grandparents or something?" Sherry didn't care about Cindy's grandparents, she was just nosy.

"Grandparents are dead," Nia said, and then frowned as if something had just occurred to her. "Actually, there is someone you could contact." That's when she told Sherry about Anthony. "He's been quiet the past few hours, but he'll probably be around later on. He likes to watch *Dateline*. He's really good with kids, and he's smarter than you'd think for someone so young. I just didn't feel comfortable leaving her alone, you know? Because they do share the same body, so if she fell down or something, there's nothing he could really do."

Sherry nodded. "Gotcha," she said. She couldn't wait to call up Tad—he wasn't her boyfriend, exactly, but he had started hanging around the store lately, and a couple of times they made out in the back room. She gave him DVDs from the sale rack—who was going to notice if they were gone anyway? But she didn't think that was the only reason he liked her. He told her Racine made up the date-rape stuff, and she believed him because it was exactly the sort of thing Racine would do.

Cindy was lying on the floor, coloring in a My Pretty Pony coloring book. Sherry sat down next to her. She was terrible with kids, but she needed the money, so what could she do? "Hey there," she said, in a fake-sounding voice. "Whatcha got there?"

"My Pretty Pony," Cindy said. "Do you want to color with me?"
The girl looked pale and her eyes were bleary.

"Um, not really," Sherry said. She'd read somewhere that it was
important to be honest with kids. Was that in her Marriage and the
Family class? She'd pretty much snoozed through that one. That
class was full of brainless debutantes who wanted to be married by
the time they were twenty.

"Okay," Cindy sighed, and went back to listlessly running a blue
crayon over the page.

With Cindy occupied, Sherry made herself comfortable on the
sofa and took out her cell phone.

"Who you callin?" It startled her, that voice coming out of
Cindy's stomach.

"Tad," she said, and the voice laughed as if that was the funniest
thing in the world.

"Tad! Tad ain't a name. *Tad.* Oh, *Tad.*" He was imitating a British
voice now. "I *say* now Tad, tally ho and all that."

"Cut that out. You don't even know him. He's in a fraternity and
he's really cute and really cool."

"Yeah, he sounds like a real—" he lowered his voice. "A real
dick weed, you know?"

"You don't know shit," she said. Then something occurred to
her. "Do you? I mean, can you see what he's doing right now?"

"Jackin' off," he said. "But he sure ain't thinking of you."

Sherry didn't buy it. "You're just being a jerk."

Cindy gave a loud sigh and put her head down on her coloring
book.

"That's right sweetie," said Sherry. "You take a nap now."

Sherry told Anthony about Tad, about how he came to the store
and she gave him DVDs and how they kissed in the back room, and
how he didn't date rape Racine after all.

"He's usin' you," Anthony said. "That is typical male behavior, is
what that is. He ever take you on a date?"

"No," she said. "But so what?"

"You know so what," he said. "You can do better."

"I can?" said Sherry. She felt herself getting weepy. It was true, everything Anthony was saying. "I want him to like me!" she wailed. "I want him."

"Why?"

"Because," she said, and started crying again. Finally, she managed to whisper, "Because he doesn't want me."

They talked and talked, and Anthony told her jokes, and she forgot all about the Hot Pockets and watching TV and she even forgot about calling Tad. When she heard the keys jingling in the lock a little before midnight, she quickly scooped up snoring Cindy and tucked her into bed. When Nia peeked her head in, Sherry was stroking Cindy's cheek and saying, "You're such a sweetheart, such a sweetheart."

Sometimes Nurse poked her head into Miss Missy's classroom and said, "Can I please speak to Cindy?" She felt it was important to keep close tabs on the girl, make sure she was doing all right.

Also, she enjoyed talking to Anthony. She even found herself telling him about Rick, the man she'd met online, the man she had moved to Alabama for and who had broken her heart. She'd met him in a chat room for certain personality types, and after chatting for a few months he bought a plane ticket to Boston. Nurse was 42 and Rick was 36, and—she didn't tell Anthony this part—the sex was the best she'd ever had. Her ex-husband Denny had been clumsy. Two months later she'd quit her job at Boston General and moved to Alabama for love. Or, more accurately, for sex—again, she didn't tell Anthony this, only that "I really thought I'd found my soul mate, the man I'd spend the rest of my life with."

But after supporting him for six months—paying his rent, buying dog food for his ridiculous Doberman—she'd had enough. Soon, she would make her way back east, but she had used up all her savings and she had to get her head on straight, "so here I am," she said, "and I have to tell myself I'm doing some good with my life, that I'm making some kind of difference, orthewise I'll go nuts." Then she told him—because he was such a good listener—about the poverty and the abuse and the kids who came to her office twice a week for baths because they had no hot water at home. It almost broke her heart, she was almost ready to give up, and then—

"And then?" said Anthony.

"And then you came along," she said, and patted Cindy on the knee.

Miss Missy found Cindy hiding in the coat cubby, crying and pounding on her stomach.

"Cindy sweetheart, what is it?"

Cindy continued pummeling her stomach with her tiny fists. "I hate you!" she sobbed. "Go home."

Miss Missy took her by the hand and led her down the hall to Nurse, who gave Cindy a red lollipop and told her she shouldn't hit people.

"Yes, ma'am," Cindy said weakly.

"I'm sure you didn't mean to hurt Anthony's feelings."

"Yes, ma'am," Cindy whispered.

The pediatrician said, "She'll eat when she's hungry."

"But it's been two whole days," Nia said. "Her teacher says she won't even drink her milk during snack time."

"You feeling all right, Cindy-girl?" said the pediatrician.

"She's fine," said Anthony.

"You're looking out for her, young man, aren't you?" said the pediatrician. "Keep it up. Maybe you-all should take her out for a cheeseburger. You feel like a cheeseburger, Cindy?"

Cindy shrugged.

"She doesn't have a fever," the pediatrician said. "But if she's feeling poorly, let her stay home from school a couple of days."

The tutor came for three hours in the morning and taught Anthony history, English, and math. Since Cindy couldn't stay awake long enough to read, the tutor read the text books out loud to Anthony and then asked him questions. The Socratic Method. The tutor was a twenty-nine-year-old named Mark who was majoring in Special Education and needed the money to pay tuition. Last year he'd tutored a blind girl, but she was kind of a bitch—he hated to admit it, but it was true—and so it was a pleasure to have a tutee as enthusiastic and intelligent as Anthony. He was lazy at times—but what fifteen-year-old wasn't?

Mark read him "A Good Man is Hard to Find" and Anthony laughed at the beginning, at the grandmother and the cat and the bratty kids, and then he got quiet and then he started saying, "Oh no way, man. No way." After Mark finished Anthony said, "I didn't see that coming. Man. That was a damn good story. What else you got?"

Sometimes Mark stayed for four hours instead of three, but he told Nia not to worry about paying him for the extra hour.

"Anthony honey," said Nia, spooning chicken noodle soup into Cindy's mouth. "You have to go." It broke her heart to say it.

"Got nowhere *to* go," he said. "I like you people."

"Well, Cindy's feeling bad and I hate to say it, but I think it's because of you."

"Maybe she has the flu," said Anthony, sulkily. "Ain't my fault if she has the flu."

"It *might* be the flu," Nia allowed. "But I don't think so."

Anthony didn't answer. He didn't say anything the rest of the day, or the next, or the day after that. Cindy got out of bed and lay on the floor in her nightgown, coloring.

One evening at dinner, Jake said, "Anthony, you want to watch *Die Hard* with me?" No response. "God damn it," said Jake. "I'm going out for a little while."

Alone in the house with Cindy, Nia felt a depth of emptiness she hadn't felt in months. When Cindy crawled into her lap with a Berenstein Bears book, Nia said, "Not now honey, Mommy's tired." Then, feeling guilty, she said, "Oh, okay." But she couldn't muster up much enthusiasm.

It wasn't that she was upset that Jake had left, that he had probably gone to Longshots to meet up with the waitress. She felt relieved. She had realized, over the past few months, with Jake always around—always wanting to spend time with her, always after her in bed—that not only did she not love him, she never could. His hands were rough; he had a dumb sense of humor. *He's a good man*, she told herself; *he's a good father.*

She had married him because she couldn't think of a better alternative. It was hard being a single mother; her own mother had raised her and they had nearly starved, had slept in the car for two weeks, had shoplifted milk and hot dogs.

She and Jake had hardly even known each other; they had slept together more than dated; she was missing her ex when he came along. She'd had too much to drink.

She used to tell herself that she could fall in love with him, if he'd give her the chance. But she couldn't. She never would.

Miss Missy noticed that Cindy Morgan was losing her blank, haunted look. Her eyes were no longer lined with black circles. She was drinking her milk, and she played patty cake.

But the class was in shambles.

Without Anthony in the classroom, Dana hit Rachel and Gregory pushed Benjamin off the swings and Wendall gave Marty a black eye. Veronica cried in the corner during story time and kicked anyone who got near her.

"Children need role models," Miss Missy said to Hank.

"Our children will be happy," he said, and Miss Missy was so surprised she couldn't think of a response.

Nurse treated the children's cuts and took their temperatures, and she called Social Services when a third grader named Ronald showed up in her office with welts on his back.

Sometimes she stayed awake until three a.m., emailing men and telling them she was thinner, blonder, and happier than she actually was. Sometimes she told them she would meet them, but she never did.

Jake started staying out until three-thirty every night, and when he got home he passed out on the sofa. One early morning Nia thought she heard him crying in his sleep, and she wished there was something she could do. But there wasn't.

She missed Anthony. She knew he was there—where else could he go?—but he refused to speak. Sometimes she could swear she heard him sniffling, just a little. It broke her heart.

And then one night when she was tucking Cindy in, Anthony said, "I missed talking to ya'll."

Nia was so happy she picked Cindy out of bed and kissed her on the stomach, which made her daughter shriek and kick and wail.

"Don't do that again," Nia said. "Do you promise?"

"I promise," said Anthony, but he had to say it twice, so Nia could hear him over Cindy's sobs.

It was Miss Missy who told Nurse that Cindy Morgan was no longer enrolled in school, that Cindy's mother had moved away, taking the child and leaving the father behind. He had come home from work and found them gone.

"That's too bad," said Nurse. She looked like she was about to cry. "I'll miss them."

"Yes," said Miss Missy. She was mulling over Hank's proposal and had been distracted for the past few days; there was so much risk involved, this tying of oneself to another. Things could get complicated.

Nurse was staring sullenly at the floor. Miss Missy thought of giving her a hug, of telling her everything would be fine. She wanted to reassure Nurse that she would find love someday, that she had to have faith that everything would work out for the best. She wanted to ask Nurse if she thought she was doing the right thing, marrying Hank, because things could go so wrong so fast, and you never knew what you were in for.

"They might be back," Nurse said, in a hoarse whisper. "They might."

"They might," said Miss Missy. She gave Nurse an awkward pat on the arm, then headed back to her classroom to dole out the Nilla wafers.

Dressing the Dead

S on," he said, "when you put scalpel to skin, let your mind
think on other things."

He put the boy's hand in his hand and with his other
hand took the black thread and laced it through the boy's fingers.

"Elmore Weed taught me to sew with black thread," he said.
"My mother cooked pork pies, lemon meringue, butter pecan."

Here downstairs it smelled like old pennies where the old man
was cutting. Upstairs where they weren't it smelled like Sweet Mary's
cheap old lady perfume. All the permanent grievers wore Sweet
Mary's. A sheriff's deputy leaned against the wall. His old lady was
home waiting for him to smell like Sweet Mary's so she could take
him for his thousands, and this truly grieved him, the notion that
she could beat him to death under an interstate overpass like this
Indian downstairs, and all she would have to show for it was his
thousands.

The spirit of the dead Indian wandered the house thinking on
these things, for it had not been extinguished by those boys beneath
the interstate overpass. "Do you hear me, son?" the old mortician
was saying. "Nothing in the world is so sweet as the butter pecan
pie."

The daddy was sewing. The boy was sewing. The black thread
lacing like baseball mitt, like lingerie, the daddy yammering about
the Bretons. "In a language hardly anyone speaks anymore," he's
saying, "all the curses are reserved for tailors, for their idleness and
paleness, their skinny, precise fingers."

His fingers, fat and precise, *violating the body* as the boy would be thinking but not knowing how to articulate, not knowing the words, but thinking of the fat fruit bat he had caught and dismembered and buried in the back yard behind the crematorium, this fat thing that could not fly but still could eat and less could have hope of flight the more it ate. The great yellow clumps he found stored in the fat pouch to which the body had reduced itself.

"Fashioning," the daddy was saying, "garments"—a breath, here; he winded at so little exertion; exertion a word the boy did know— "from wool, linen, silk."

And: "See here, boy? See this?"

His hand, sweeping over the body.

"Three nights ago four strong boys sawed the handle off a shovel, embedded a lead ball in a strip of leather, stole two baseball bats from the equipment shed."

His jowls, working. The boy swore he'd avoid the cookie jar after one more binge this evening. *Pork pies, lemon meringue, butter pecan.*

"Knocked teeth from the head of a Haitian drifter and killed this whisky Indian."

Four hundred miles away, the drifter held a bloodcaked handkerchief in his hands and prayed the Greyhound bus toward Rochester, New York. The sheriff's deputy hunted him impotently, leaning upstairs against the mortuary wall, his wife in her best two-piece sunbathing in the backyard, scheming to spend his thousands. The boy did not yet know his destiny was more or less the same as the sheriff's deputy, or how he would come to believe all our destinies are more or less the same as the whisky Indian's, the span of a lifetime whether stillborn or the allotted threescore and ten more or less the same against the vast backdrop of time and space. But he did not think it now, his hands inside the Indian, his hands and his father's, and his father jowling: "We gonna dress him this morning in rodeo finest."

Handwashing, then the old man's large hands and the boy's small hands digging around in the surplus closet, fingering pearl snaps and arrowhead pockets and rhinestones.

"Your momma's gonna paint him," old daddy said. "Maybe kiss his lips. Maybe you should kiss his lips."

Sometime deep in history some chariot of fire come down, and Elijah rode it north. The old stories are true.

Sometime in North Dakota another father said to another son, "Go split some logs outside. Let's build him a boat and sail him home."

And not in a goddamn Byakuryu, said another father, in Thai.

And not in a goddamn tent city for the Hajj, yet another, he a refugee in unspeakable squalor.

And not in goddamn Viet Nam.

And not with phylacteries.

And not with Slivovitz.

And not with coriander, dill, or wild carrot.

Not with inflorescence.

And not with slip-ooze, Stay, or bird vision. Not with Coade stone, not slap stickers or syphilis, mending leather or bracings.

"No oxen, zebu cattle, nor donkeys to pull it," said our old man of the here and now, our fat father, hollowing the drifter. "No cart, no dray, no wagon."

The prophet Elijah stared down fully alive from his heaven of fire. "Kiss his lips, son," he mocked, "let's build him a feather with a lace agate eye, buy him forty Malachites, chattel them seventy times seven around the city gate."

Upstairs, the sheriff's deputy leaned against the wall, but inside himself he dwelt in the recent past, the place he would return to again and again in the future, all seven months of a future not meant to end in an abandoned green hotel in Lake Wales, Florida, amid the florid stench of rat droppings and what things grew in them, and how might things be changed if he knew, when they found him and his pistol beside him, his wife would say, "Who now remembers the things we two remembered?" Even into her old age, when she had forgot some of these things, she grieved him wordlessly in her room at the Meadowlark home in Chicago, overlooking the streets and the snow and the men with their guns and their knives walking their children to school.

"Your grandmother always said she could have been an opera singer if I had not come along unexpected," the father was saying.

old tree stump and laughed; they pulled him out of the ocean, and laughed; they dragged him from a hole in the ground, and laughed. But Acirema didn't laugh, and she asked him who "they" were. But Saynday didn't laugh, nor did he give her a reply. This was when she first commented on his *krank chaos*, but, as she picked at a scab on her left cheek, she said it with a salivating hunger. Then she asked if he would trade his Cadillac for the sixty-two dollars she had left in her pocket. He took her up on the offer and found himself that much richer. While she had asked him how he arrived in the city, she hadn't asked if the Cadillac was stolen. And he repeatedly reminded her of this fact in every letter he sent to her while she was incarcerated. Even though Acirema was a person, she had this erratic, twitchy, untamed quality that Saynday admired. Besides she carried a pad and pen in the back pocket of her blue jeans.

As his own jeans pasted to his thighs with building sweat, Saynday turned himself either left or right to squeeze between the oncoming shoulders. His bruises responded to every word, step, and jolt as though each were shrapnel from this explosion. Why did these people and spirits direct themselves into his path on this of all days? They had some preoccupation with order and purpose, but, as far as Saynday was concerned, order and purpose were a pair of plain bookends holding together novellas of chaos. "I have to stop the direct, pobs, challenge myself to not be so 'impulsive minds bring bruises,'" he said to himself, because he wanted to end this *krank chaos* that not only affected his speech pattern, but, more importantly, his decisions. A fictitious bullhorn constantly blared direct challenges over his shoulder, and he impulsively reacted. When he knew Acirema wanted money, he took it as a direct challenge, so he impulsively asked *her* for money. Before she could pawn his electronics, he urinated into the vitals. Before she could sneak into his money can, he shit onto the rolled up bills. He desperately wanted to smash this fictitious bullhorn into the street and let the paraders trample it into pieces, because it created the synapses of brainwaves that made up the networking in his *krank chaos*.

And this time his *krank chaos* compromised his volatile but engaging relationship, so he regretted what he had done to Acirema.

When she cancelled out his MySpace account for associating with online prostitutes, he responded to it as one of those direct challenges, so he impulsively opened a Facebook account. On Facebook he met a guy who belonged to a secret society. The secret society required a gift of chocolates of the inducting member's choice, and he bought this guy a box of Godiva's finest truffles. So he was invited to a secret meeting, so he went to the secret meeting, so he did wild and wonderful things, so he had a lot of fun, so he contracted this disease called herpes. Acirema hadn't been as excited about the incident as *he* had. While regret jostled through his mind in the same way he jostled through the parade, he attempted to overcome the order and purpose of both people and spirits in this explosion.

Saynday stepped atop black circles of fresh asphalt, and, as the scent of the ashen tar drifted from underneath his feet, a hand wrapped around his upper right arm and jerked him backward. Fingernails pierced and ripped into his skin. A few months before the MySpace incident, he had felt a similar bite. He had awoken one morning with a sharp pain on the inside of his thigh, and he thought it was Acirema, because, when specks of yellow-crystal flakes stuck to the edges of her nose, she always started sex with a pinch, or a slap, or a bite. A smile spread his lips apart, his eyes remained closed, and, often when aroused, his tongue lightly tapped between his parted teeth. When he lifted his head and looked down, it was an oversized rodent making its way up his thigh. After cleaning the wound, Saynday wrote a powerful letter to the Governing Council of Rez City. He made it clear that the use of nuclear weapons was needed to control the outbreak of prairie dogs, and the people and spirits would have to make that sacrifice. *Rez City Times* later printed a front-page article about the eradication of these prairie dogs from every neighborhood. The article indicated that the grass house ghettos of the south central borough had an unimaginable infestation, but, since the Governing Council promised to end this Year of the Prairie Dog, the city was negotiating with a nuclear energy company who needed a waste site. It went on to mention how the Caddo packed thatches of prairie grass onto a continuous train of horses, and those beasts-of-burden had appeared like a massive golden snake from the mountains that surrounded Rez City. The fifty-foot high complexes of the grass house ghettos stretched over a hundred city blocks, and the article concluded that these prairie dogs had embedded a deep colony underneath this section of the city. The image of the prairie dog faded, but, as the tar's charcoal drifted from the refurbished street, the fingernails continued to dig deeper into his upper arm and drag him into an awkward reverse step.

Out of the people and spirits in his proximity, he found that it was a person who had him by his arm. He yanked and pulled to free himself, and as he stumbled backward, he fought and struggled against the hold, but the lady would not release him. Her eyes were wide, not because of a natural design, but because of her panic and he captured a surge of it himself. The lady's mouth came open as if she cried out, but he missed her call because of the repeated chant. "Store-Nuclear-Waste On-My-Rez!"

In between a short pause, the lady's voice broke from the din with a high pitch, "My baby-girl!"

Saynday followed the direction of her panic stricken eyes as she looked over her shoulder, and he found a cradleboard half strapped and almost falling from her back. The lady released her hold on his arm, which gave him the mobility to reach out and save the baby. Just as the other strap broke, he caught the wooden structure and lifted it against his chest.

One-back-two, he told himself as his feet moved into a reverse march. The cradleboard fumbled in his arms as he attempted to keep up with the lady on his right and a spirit on his left. Also face to face with a short row of three spirits, who forward stepped in pace with his reverse march, he scrambled with the urgency of a water bug caught in a drainage canal, because the torrent of people and spirits could easily wash him and baby-girl into the street.

While he had expected the lady to be immediately concerned for her nearly lost infant, she instead scanned the tops of the skyscrapers, and her panic stricken eyes turned to wide-eyed awe. While her mouth moved as if in conversation, Saynday adjusted his hearing to block out the repeated chant, and just in time to hear her ask, "Did you notice the sky?"

His response to the odd question was to see if she *noticed* her baby, more importantly that *her* baby was in *his* arms, so he extended the cradleboard. She turned from the cradleboard to Saynday; as she smiled an extra layer of moisture covered her dark brown eyes. He assumed it was the mixture of gratitude and sadness for almost losing but saving her child. While he expected her to retrieve her baby, the lady pushed the cradleboard back against his chest. She returned to observing the sky, and said, "I've never seen it so blue. You could almost jump up there and dive in."

"Take your baby before you, pobs, jump all day but you don't want to swim in that 'blue has yellow on green,'" he said, as the cradleboard pinched and dug into his arms, adding to his current agitation in this explosion.

"I love the look of the sun reflecting in the windows. Always have," she added, and every note in the lady's vocals carried a soft strum, as though each annunciation held the tune of a melodic bluegrass song. "And the sun shines so pretty in the adobe walls. The way the brown cascades into pink. It's almost like magic."

From his vantage point the sun only accentuated the water stains below every windowsill. Not only that, but pigeon droppings dotted the sides of the buildings and created milky lines with black specks on that cascading brown and pink wall.

The strum continued to play in her words as she scanned the rooftops and carried on with her one-sided conversation. From behind his swollen eyes, he was able to make out the lady's dark blue vest with what appeared like the Wal-Mart logo in the upper left hand corner. There were pockets on each side of the vest, and she had two blurry pens clasped to the right side. He took special notice of the lady's long double braids, not because they appeared tight and smooth to her scalp, nor because the braids ran neatly around her ears and across her neck. It was the way the double braids stretched past her shoulders, down the length of her arms, and ended where the lacerations in her forearms began.

"Let me tell you about this morning. I cooked my eggs without breaking the yolk. The hash-browns came out so golden that I could've taken them to the bank and turned into a rich lady on this day. And, get this, I didn't burn the prairie dog bacon."

As he squinted to make out the cuts on her forearm, he might have assumed them to be a costume in this parade, but bright red moisture trickled onto the skin. There had to be at least a dozen lacerations on each forearm, and all folded open to the flesh. In the midst of his hazy observation, she lifted her arms and turned them out. "This is what happens when your husband is taken away. I came home one day after visiting him in that... ...that cage. I go into my purse, you know, to take out the key. And my right hand snatches the key out of my purse. But my left hand wants the key, so my left hand snatches it out of my right hand. And, might know, my right hand cusses my left hand up one side and down another. So they get to bickering. My right hand wants the key, and my left hand won't give it back. I do my best to get the situation under control, but it does no good. Before I know it, my right hand finds a knife lying in the bushes and starts swinging it at my left. Finally, my left hand drops the key, but only to grab another knife lying in the bushes. And the two cut and slice at each other, in a matter of seconds my arms look like this."

Often people and spirits lose their truth when detoured onto a rutted street, and they discover avenues of lies that refurbish the pain. Truth or not, Saynday knew by the lacerations on her forearms why she had pushed the cradleboard away.

Below those open wounds, just beyond her wrists, he discovered the lady's costume and contribution to this parade, all her fingers were plastered together with a rubber-type substance and only her thumbs were free to move around. Saynday wondered how she had fused her fingers together with such authenticity, because, through his pair of blurry goggles, it appeared like real skin.

"I haven't been able to get baby-girl quiet since," she said. "She's a daddy's girl, that's for sure. He would start singing her stomp songs, and baby-girl would just look up at him, as quite as a blue bird."

At the reference to baby-girl, he uncurled the cradleboard from his chest and found the spirit of a newborn baby neatly strapped inside. Baby-girl had a thin layer of rubber over her eyes, and it was the same rubber that held the lady's fingers together. The most impressive piece to baby-girl's costume was an inch long meaty growth protruding from her mouth, and, as she let out a faintly quiet but subtly piercing cry, it moved as though it were attached to her tongue.

When Saynday turned his attention to the left, he found a spirit who wore an overdeveloped and hairless head, and, from what he could make out, veins protruded from the surface in crisscrossing highways of blue fluid. The spirit's lanky arms and legs swung slow and deliberate, as he kept pace with the thousands of other people and spirits in this parade.

"Back home in our grass house ghettos, there are daycare grannies who can't do in thirty minutes what my husband could do in five," the lady continued, and her soft brows twisted as though she were hit with an unwelcome thought. The tone in her voice drained along with the color in her cheeks, as she said, "Why he would take baby-girl in his lap, and if his singing didn't work, he would pull out jelly packets from his pocket. He always brought home jelly packets from work. And he would smear the jelly on baby-girl's tongue, saying, 'My jelly ain't as sweet as my uranium, but my uranium ain't as sweet as my baby-girl.'"

The lady had a happy sadness in her tone, as though she longed for the past, which made the present fleeting, and in turn created an uncertain future. Saynday shared the lady's mixed reaction, because the last time he had spoken with Acirema she had been so offended that tears covered the lower half of her face. Her rage was so fierce that she reached behind her back, and, as Saynday fled his own apartment to save his ears and life, she did not pull out the pad and pen. Initially he kept the herpes a secret, against his doctor's orders. But one evening they saw a commercial for Acyclovir, where a lady smiled and rode a bike on a nice beach somewhere in the Bahamas or Hawaii, and Acirema jokingly said that she wanted to have herpes. While the two laughed at the notion, as the commercial played out, Saynday told her that she did. He also told her about Facebook, and if she delivered him a box of the sweetest ganaches she could become the newest member of a secret society. She sat quietly on the edge of the sofa. The uneasiness of her silence made his stomach turn sour and he fought off the nausea by giggling, with the giggling came lightheadedness and he fought off the euphoria by laughing, with the laughing came dizziness and he fought off the spinning by bellowing. Acirema responded by slapping him repeatedly in the face. When both of her arms grew tired, she took a cell phone from her pocket, dialed a number, and handed it to him. With welts on his cheeks, he placed the cell phone to his ear. A voice came through the receiver, and a man introduced himself as a counselor with a sex addiction clinic. Within minutes, he had enticed the councelor into a dialogue of phone sex. Acirema knocked the phone out of his hands, and pulled out her mini four-shot magnum. As she released an erratic mixture of sobs and laughs, tears rolled out of her eyes, red covered her face, and she discharged an explosive shrill that haunted and carried, carried and echoed for the impending weeks in his then-terrified bones.

The guy from the secret society gave him shelter, and Saynday engaged in late night secret meetings without having to answer to anyone. Every morning he laid in a stranger's bed, and, regardless of how much he indulged in the pleasures of people and spirits, he continued to hear that haunting shrill. After a week of being unable to sleep, no longer impressed with the secret meetings, he moved onto the streets. For the next week he lay on benches, in alleys, under bridges, and behind trashcans without a moment of rest. The only way he could lessen the shrill was to talk about the incident over and over again. Since the alleyway occupants also repeated themselves, but for lack of medication, he kept company with the beggars, addicts, and lunatics. After a week of constantly hearing about Acirema's tears about Acirema's words about Acirema's shrill, one of the alleyway occupants grew tired of the story, and said, "Let's play a game of chin checkers. I've never lost a round." With countless strikes to the face, Saynday fell behind a large, industrial-sized dumpster, and he stayed in that position for twelve straight hours.

This morning he picked himself up and leaned against the back wall to a McYazzie grocery store. His face had a scatter of bruises from his jaw to his brow, and, as he slid his fingers over his swollen eyes, an explosion of pain erupted. "How will I survive out on these, pobs, streets are filled with 'killers roam in disguise.'" Then a clear question had followed: "Will she take me back?" Only one person had the answer to that question, so he came to his feet determined to retrieve Acirema Gonzalez and his apartment. In that moment, the haunting shrill had finally stopped. On his return home, Saynday happened upon a crowd of both people and spirits and it appeared to him as a direct challenge, so he impulsively marched into the center of the parade.

"Listen to me," the lady said, as she laid a hand of fused fingers between her double braids, partially covering the Wal-Mart logo on her uniform, and followed it with a laugh. "My grandfather used to always say, 'Patty-Cakes, I've left you behind at grocery stores, amusement parks, and once at a funeral. I wish you would speak up every once in a while.' And listen to me now, I can't seem to shut up."

As a plea to beg for reason, an attempt at compassion, Saynday confessed, "I'm on the way back to my, pobs, girlfriend is upset with the secret 'meetings organize the disorder.'"

"Oh, yes, the secret meetings. I did as they instructed, but, you wouldn't believe, it took me longer to strap myself up this morning than it did to get baby-girl ready."

He double glanced behind a triple flinch, and not only did he want to know why the lady attended the secret meetings, but he wanted to know what she had strapped to herself. Before a third glance made it a triple take, something like a kitten's call drifted from the cradleboard. Still crying, baby-girl squirmed against her restraints. In an effort to sooth the spirit, he loosened the straps to free her arms, and he rocked her in the swaying motion of his reverse march.

"Why we would've never have gone to the secret meetings if it wasn't for baby-girl. I know, you probably think we should've thought twice. And even our medicine man in the grass house ghettos told us that all we needed was a simple curing. But he didn't see what happened. And neither did you. When my husband watched baby-girl die after only three days of life, he turned into a different man. He couldn't work anymore and then all the uranium money dried up. We had no other choice. Besides the secret meetings gave us back our power."

Baby-girl gained more energy with the room to breathe and released long screams of an unknown discomfort.

"This tape itches something fierce." The lady dug her fused fingers into her right side, while she sighed with relief. "Then again, if it wasn't for the secret meetings, my husband would be a free man right now. The things we do for the sake of family. But I don't blame him. We saw three dead prairie dogs on our way to one of the secret meetings. And as you well know, if it comes in threes then it's a direct sign from God. So then and there, we decided to not let baby-girl die in vain. He held up to his end, and today I hold up to mine."

A part of Saynday wanted to know how the secret meetings put her husband in a bad way, but most of his parts had to deal with the crying spirit in his arms. Baby-girl released angry bursts as though she were defying Saynday's efforts to help. This tiny creature, this delicate thing, opposed his charities with such rebellion that Saynday would not and could not let it go unchallenged. He leaned down, without missing a single reverse step, and he hummed an old gourd song that he had once heard on a television commercial.

A helicopter raced from between a pair of buildings and darted toward the parade. With red lettering on top of a white body, the side of the helicopter read: Rez City Patrol. As the whipping blades drew closer, a wave of wind splashed onto the crowd and drowned out the repeated chant. The paraders matched the helicopter and yelled louder, "Store-Nuclear-Waste On-My-Rez!"

"Look at that!" the lady yelled. He had to compartmentalize the chant to one side, the helicopter to another, and the kitten calls somewhere else, to hear the lady's uneasy laugh. "I didn't think that they'd send in the troops!"

Her left arm wrapped over her stomach. She shifted her attention from the helicopter to the front of crowd, tip-toeing as she marched to see above the heads.

"Why I hope we make it to the plaza soon enough," she said, as she came flat to her feet and stepped in sequence with the other paraders. "We didn't prepare for this at the secret meetings. The Governing Council will be on the plaza to announce an end to the Year of the Prairie Dog. We can't have that, now can we?"

With baby-girl continuing her rebellion, Saynday used his last option. He brought the cradleboard up higher on his chest and spit tufts of air into baby-girl's face. Typically he reserved the enormous potency of his power, because, after Acirema had escaped from the correctional facility, he had used his power to heal a gunshot wound in her shoulder blade. After she healed within moments, Acirema swore an unending love for Saynday. Despite the risk of causing a chain reaction that he might not be able to control, he made his final effort to comfort baby-girl, but the spirit continued to cry.

"The secret meetings prepared me for road blocks, spot checks, and defused triggers," the lady said, her eyes shifting from the helicopter to the plaza ahead. She scratched between bulges that creased awkward underneath her Wal-Mart uniform. It distorted what appeared to be an otherwise flat stomach. "They even prepared me for stalled eruptions. Why didn't they tell me about helicopters?"

The kitten calls came steady and irksome from the cradleboard, indicating his defeat. He could be at his front door yelling promises of moving to Mexico, sobbing pleas to give him another chance, and offering terms to an unbreakable contract. But this lady, the way she fidgeted with the device strapped around her middle, the way she rambled about helicopters, stalled eruptions, defused triggers, and the way she carried on and on with her melodic but *insane* ranting. It gave him no other choice, and the lady jerked backward as he grabbed her by the arm.

The short row of three spirits collided into the pair, and they stumbled against the oncoming parade. Just before both lost their footing, the throng parted and left them room to save themselves.

In the middle of Goyathley Avenue, as he held the cradleboard with his left, Saynday lifted each of the lady's forearms and spit tufts of air into every laceration. Blood seeped into the cuts, cuts folded into scars, scars faded into unblemished skin. While the lady rotated her healed limbs back and forth with a trembling expression of fear and awe, Saynday placed the cradleboard in her arms.

The paraders swept around the pair with an occasional nudge, and, as the infant stopped crying, the lady put a hand of fused fingers inside the cradleboard's opening. The spirit disappeared before the lady could touch her daughter one, final, last time.

As the lady released an erratic mixture of sobs and laughs, tears rolled out of her eyes, red covered her face, and Saynday was directly challenged when he recognized similarities of Acirema in that desperate cry, so he impulsively made the comparison. With people and spirits swarming past his shoulders, Saynday contemplated whether he should forward march or reverse march through this parade, because nothing made the similarities more true as the lady detonated an explosive shrill that haunted and carried, carried and echoed for the impending weeks in his now fragile world.

Daniel Mueller

Red Cinquefoil

I was playing the nickel slots, three at a time, at an Indian casino off I-40, twenty minutes west of Albuquerque, when the first wheel of Wild Wilderness locked on canned beans, the second did the same, and the third teased the pay line between canned beans and campfire logs. Though not a man of strong religious convictions, on a whim I prayed to Saint Anthony. I asked him to gently guide the machine to its maximum payoff and help me reclaim a small portion of the large sum I'd lost to a gambling addiction with which, on a Friday when my youngest daughter Cecily expected me for dinner at six, I'd struggled for more than fifty years. I told Saint Anthony that, if he existed and weren't too busy helping other, more deserving souls to lend me a hand, I'd rectify my profligate ways, walk a narrower path, and with my winnings affect change that would honor the glory of his master and mine. I admitted I was a weak but far from humble vessel who was susceptible to vices of many varieties, and that for these and other failings I hadn't been the clean instrument for magnanimous acts God, if He existed, had no doubt hoped for when He created me, and just as I was about to list the changes I, at seventy-one, was prepared to make on His—which is to say, if He were inclined, in His most holy of hearts, to care, even an ounce—behalf, the slot machine lit up from within and began to quake.

Myriad bulbs hidden beneath a casing of slick polyurethane unfurled in rippling banners of cherry, apricot, and blue. Flugelhorns, a battalion, performed "Save the Last Dance for Me" as fireworks exploded in the background. More lights, located deep within the contraption, flickered like stars, like distant galaxies, as teapots whistled, chainsaws whirred, and a laugh track stopped and started. A crowd of gamblers gathered around me, slapped my shoulder, patted my back. A woman removed an oxygen mask from her face, took a puff of her Marlboro, and cried, "You've won!" Balanced atop her wheeled cylinder was an ashtray overflowing with butts, into which she tapped the end of her cigarette and pointed at the payoff screen where animated woodchucks played leapfrog over a jackpot of $1,597,244.10. "You're a millionaire, laddy," exclaimed a man in his fifties wearing a tartan kilt, carrying Uileann pipes, and supporting himself on prosthetic legs. To the cacophony he added a Scottish rendition of "Adios, mi Corazon" as from the slot machine, but sounding as if at the mic in the casino lounge, Bobby Darin crooned, "Splish Splash."

A skinny blond wisp-of-a-thing, no older than twenty-five, removed one of a dozen strings of mardi gras beads from around her neck. She motioned for me to lower my head and as she draped a necklace over my ears she shouted, "Will you marry me, grandpa?" I shouted back, "Show me your intended." I assumed she'd meant for me to conduct her ceremony—in seventy-one years stranger things had been asked of me—and she directed a lazy finger at the white hairs tufting like a dickey from the collar of my favorite lucky Hawaiian short-sleeve.

I sipped my Jack and Coke. I'd been divorced since '75, the year my then-wife Annabel was treated for syphilis she'd contracted from me. Back then we lived with our daughters, Cecily and Kate, then five and seven, in a trailer at the southern-most edge of the Nevada Test Site. Four days a week I oversaw crews of miners and roughnecks whose job it was to plant nuclear devices, "pits" we called them, hundreds if not thousands of feet beneath the surface of the desert. Fridays I reported to the Department of Energy's offices in Las Vegas where briefings never lasted longer than an hour and afternoons were mine. I didn't blame Annabel. In her position I would have left me, too, always promising to steer clear of the casinos, cut back on my drinking, quit smoking, and end my affairs with particular prostitutes to whom I'd grown attached.

"You wouldn't be pulling my leg, would you?" I asked the girl, imagining how pretty my living room would look with her in it. Ever since Clinton killed the nuclear weapons testing program, I'd lived by myself in a west Vegas subdivision. I'd been given the choice of a desk job with the D. of E. or early retirement with full benefits. I considered telling them to shove their paper-sorting where the sun didn't shine, but if you'd spent thirty years planting nukes in the earth you'd know there isn't such a place, and I quietly retired.

"No," she replied.

"Okay," I said. "You're on. Let's get married."

I reached into a pocket of my Bermuda shorts and handed her a piece of sludge, glass formed when the first pit I'd ever planted, codenamed "Red Cinquefoil," was detonated and underneath the desert temperatures in excess of a 100-million degrees Centigrade opened a cavity roughly the size of the town we lived in, Indian Springs, and ensconced it in melted rock that grew opaque and shiny as it cooled. Trapped in the piece I'd given the girl were tiny air bubbles commemorating the moment of the blast. "We'll use that until we find us a proper engagement ring," I said. The last I'd checked, it was radiating between 40 and 45 milliroentgen an hour, less radiation than one might receive during a visit to the dentist or, back when Annabel and I bought our oldest Kate her first pair of patent leather sandals, a trip to the shoe store.

As my intended examined what was undoubtedly the oddest "rock" she'd ever seen, I said above the ruckus, "If you're a gold digger, darling, it's only fair to warn you. The odds of my dying anytime soon aren't good."

She looked at me with wet blue eyes. "Why would I want you to die?"

"For the money?" I glanced again at the payoff screen where my 1.5 million and change pulsated like Joey Bishop's name on a '70's Caesar's Palace marquee.

"I'm not marrying you for money," she said with a pout. "I'm marrying you for luck."

"I got plenty of that," I said, "both good and bad."

"It seems pretty good to me right now," she said. "You're the first jackpot winner I've seen since I got here."

"When was that, sweetheart?"

"Tuesday."

Already I was imagining Cecily and her husband Mike's reaction to this Kansas blond waif-of-a-girl stepping out of my Lincoln in her men's white V-neck t-shirt belted at the waist. Two weeks before, my youngest daughter had given birth to Mike Jr., whom I was ostensibly on my way to meet. Though the occasion was joyous, and my trunk filled with sacks of baby clothes, some of which Cecily herself had worn, I wouldn't be telling the complete story if I didn't also confess an ulterior motive: a year earlier my daughters' stepfather, J.R., had died of colon cancer in Denver, and while I would never wish anything as evil as that on another human being, now that J.R. was dead I could take pleasure, especially in the company of those who had known him, in having outlived an ophthalmologist who, according to my daughters, had abstained from alcohol, tobacco, and prescription drugs; who exercised obsessively and ate farm-raised salmon and trout three times a week; and who regularly faulted me, in the presence of my daughters, for exposing them as children to radiation that, he said, would give them cancer later in their lives.

Now if Cecily, Kate, or Annabel, God forbid, contracted cancer, it wouldn't be because of the environmental doses to which I'd exposed them; no, there was a reason 51% of the roughly 120,000 men who'd worked at the Nevada Test Site between '62 and '92 were still alive, some of them in their nineties: radiation at the levels we and our families had experienced it was beneficial to human life. And all of us had known it. It was why we brought sludge home with us from the Site, why we set it alongside geodes on our mantels and bookshelves and carried it in our pockets like rabbits' feet.

"Tell me your name, darling," I said.

"Tell me yours first," the girl replied.

"Gordon Langley," I said.

"Gordon Langley, God bless you. This is for you."

Then my angel wrapped her arms around me, drew my lips to

hers, and our tongues danced a tango in the ballroom of our mouths. In a periphery blurred by her wheat blond hair, two Indians in dark suits and one wearing a turquoise calf-length dress pressed through the throng. A photographer and a uniformed policeman followed in their wake. In no time they had formed a celebratory crescent around us, but they could wait. I was a lover and in no hurry for our kiss to end, so enveloped was I by my new young lover's scent, the taste of her saliva, the softness of her breasts against my chest.

When at last we separated, I unzipped my fanny pack, withdrew my pill canister, popped two OxyContin, and washed them down with Jack and Coke. "Just a second," I said to my Native American emissaries, all smartly attired and wearing their hair in ponytails, the men as well as the woman, and lit up a menthol cigarette. My pleasure receptors open as baseball mitts, I said, "Okay. I'm ready to be officially told I've won."

"I wish we could, but look," the woman said and with a varnished nail directed my attention to a third wheel that hadn't stopped on canned beans, as I'd assumed, but on campfire logs. "This machine's experiencing a malfunction." Her finger hovered above the payoff chart, there in plain view on the face of the slot machine. "This machine's maximum payoff is two thousand five hundred dollars. There's positively no way for it to pay out more than that without a machine malfunction, and if you'd read the House rules, accessible by punching the House rules key," which, of course, she did, "you'd know the House cannot be held legally responsible for winnings resulting from machine malfunctions of any kind."

"You're telling me I've won a measly two and a half grand?"

"I'm telling you the House cannot be held liable for winnings resulting from machine malfunctions."

"Which means?"

"All the House can do is reimburse you the amount of your bet."

"Five nickels?"

She nodded. "That's wholly righteous," I said.

As the crowd fell away as if from a plague victim, the photographer stepped between my fiancée and me and stationed his accordion-sized Polaroid camera before the slot machine. He peered into his viewfinder, and a white flash went off above my head. When my eyes readjusted to the lighting, the pretty thing to whom I'd pledged my love was gone, mardis gras beads, t-shirt, radioactive sludge and all.

"For your troubles," the female casino manager said, placing a coupon on my lap, "we'll treat you to a dinner-for-two at the casino steakhouse. Does that sound like something you might enjoy?"

"It's better than nothing," I admitted.

I was disappointed, sure, but knew better than to make a mountain out of a molehill. Over the slot machine the pair of male casino managers fit a yellow canvas bag with laces like a straightjacket. On the bag was stenciled "OUT OF ORDER," and as they tightened and knotted cords at the bottom and across the middle, I found myself wishing it were me they had identified and isolated, me they had contained.

At six, I parked beside the curb in front of my daughter's house. In a rust orange sweatshirt and Broncos ball cap, Mike sat on the frame rail of his Peterbilt, the outer tires of which rested on the grass on either side of the driveway. I called to him, "Howdy, Mike," and popped the trunk of my Lincoln. "Mind lending me a hand with the luggage?"

In the mid-90s he'd been signed by Detroit and traded to Denver, where he protected Elway for exactly seven downs before blowing an Achilles', effectively ending his NFL career. On the street I set nine grocery bags of baby clothes Annabel had left when she'd taken the girls to Colorado. As I unloaded a valise, two-suiter, and overnight kit, Mike remained planted above his truck's leaf springs, idly slapping a monkey wrench into his palm. "How thoughtless of me," I said. "You're a father now. Congratulations." With the same winning smile I'd shown presidents when they came to Nevada to see for themselves what species of man they'd employed at the Test Site, I made a bee-line for my son-in-law. "You and Cecily have waited a long time for this. You deserve nothing but joy."

Neither Cecily nor Kate had proven particularly fertile. Both had been diagnosed with hormonal imbalances their doctors had treated with regimens of estrogen, progesterone, and prolactin, but only Cecily had conceived. I'd felt for them, I had. Like their father, both were genetically predisposed to depression, and in an America forever broadcasting to the world its capacity to destroy the world thousands of times over, children gave one hope that the human race's finest attributes would prevail in the end. Without children, we as a nation had nothing to protect, and without a child of one's own, it was easy to believe we as a nation had nothing to lose.

"You carrying any of that radioactive shit on you, Gordon?" Mike asked when I came to a stop before him on the driveway. "Because if you are, I'm going to have to ask you, as nicely as I know how, to cart your skinny ass straight back to Vegas."

I wagged my head, no.

"I don't have a counter, so you're going to have to empty your pockets for me."

"Has J.R.'s ghost taken residence inside your head?" I asked.

"I'm not letting you inside the house until I'm sure you're clean. It's as simple as that."

"I'm clean," I said, at the same time wishing I weren't, wishing I'd retained the sludge I'd given to the girl who'd vanished from the casino before telling me her name.

Like the sun itself, therapeutic in small doses but lethal in large, the subterranean nuclear explosions to which I'd devoted my working life had bolstered my immune system and strengthened my resistance to illnesses. And in the gamma rays still emitted by the souvenirs I'd taken home from the more than 700 tests I'd overseen, they continued to in ever shortening half-lives. Each pit we'd planted had been connected by five, ten, twenty miles of fiber optic cable to mobile units manned by physicists from the nation's top labs, and to me even the nuts and bolts and sections of married wire that had lain just outside the melting range were talismans. Without a remnant from a blast, I felt nervous and vulnerable and no longer as impervious to pressures.

Still Mike was entitled to his opinions, upsetting to me as they were. So I emptied my pockets of change, lighter, wallet, cigarettes, flask, and the coupon from the casino for a steak dinner-for-two and laid everything out on the driveway for Mike to inspect. "Let's see what's in the fanny pack, Gordon," he said from his throne of reinforced steel.

"I'll tell you what's in the fanny pack," I said. "Pills."

"Take 'em out," he replied, so I laid out the vials of OxyContin, Percocet, Vicodin, Valium, Xanax, Demerol, Tylenol 3, and Ambien. Mike set the monkey wrench on his rig's fifth wheel and knelt on the concrete. He picked up each vial and examined the label, his pupils wide as camera shutters. "Sweet Jesus, Gordon," he said when he'd set down my sleep medication, "with all this garbage in your system, it's a wonder you can drive, gamble, or talk on the telephone. It's a wonder you can function at all."

"I have a strong constitution, unlike a certain over-educated prick who recently passed on." I grinned and coughed.

Mike sighed. "You can trash talk J.R. all you like in front of me. Lord knows, I didn't hold him in the highest esteem either. But I'd watch your mouth around Cecily."

"Cecily and I are of like minds about her stepfather."

In spite of the distance separating us, my daughters and I had remained close. Kate conducted research on rocket engines at Boeing, and Cecily did clerical work for Sandia. Together they represented the second generation of Langleys to earn a living within the country's industrial-military complex, and I was proud of them.

"Be that as it may," Mike said, "Annabel's still in deep grief over J.R., and she only left this morning."

"Annabel was here this morning?" I said.

"Uh-huh. She was here for ten days helping Cecily look after the baby, but I think it was Cecily who had the tougher job looking after her."

"So Annabel was here this morning," I said.

"Pick your pills up off the driveway, and I'll help you with your bags."

With little of the fanfare I'd come to expect from my youngest daughter, Cecily hugged me briskly in the kitchen, then kissed me brusquely on the cheek. Late February, spring was taking its sweet time getting to Albuquerque, and the aromas from the oven put me in mind of families and how grateful I felt to be basking in the warmth of one. Most nights I microwaved a frozen dinner or ate at one of the casinos, and here Cecily had gone to the trouble of preparing a supper of roast chicken, mashed potatoes, biscuits, and gravy. I unscrewed the stopper of my flask and took a nip.

"Now stay put a second, would you, darling? Let me get a look at you." I leaned back against a countertop speckled with radish filings and celery leaves as Cecily smiled coquettishly. "That's my girl," I said, but before the words were out her smile was gone, a radioisotope that had already changed into something else in the time taken to identify it.

"You drink too much, Dad," she said and returned to paring a cucumber over the sink. Though I loved my daughters equally, Cecily was the beauty of the family, with pale white skin and dark brown hair that curled at her shoulders.

"I drink just enough to balance the pills," I replied.

"You take too many pills, too."

"I'm an old man," I said. "The pills help me regulate my environment."

Mike came into the kitchen carrying three bags of baby clothes. "Riddle me this, honey? What do your old man and Rush Limbaugh have in common?"

"I can't believe you spoke of me and him in the same breath," I said. "I can't stand that blatherskite."

"Give up?" Mike said as he dropped three bags of baby clothes on top of the six I'd brought in. "OxyContin."

I unzipped my fanny pack, located my Tylenol 3, and popped two. "Both of you know the kind of work I did. But do either of you have any idea, any idea at all, of the mental toll testing weapons meant to annihilate hundreds of thousands of people in a matter of seconds takes on the human psyche? Do you? In my lifetime I participated in over seven hundred such tests. And I would do it again, happily and with honor. But it takes its toll, is all I'm saying."

They'd heard it before, but I didn't care. Cecily turned to me with a vegetable peeler in her hand, her creased brow an etched pagoda. "OxyContin is an opioid, Dad."

"Opioids work for me," I replied, "especially in combination with other opioids."

"Opioids are for patients on their deathbeds."

"Maybe I'm on my mine and I don't even know it." I smiled, which made Cecily frown. "Seriously, darling, if you'd seen our subsidence craters, which you haven't because they're off-limits to the public, maybe you'd have an inkling of the enormous destructive capability basically uneducated, God-fearing men like me handled on a bi- and tri-weekly basis."

Mike snorted. "That why you brought all that radioactive shit home with you, Gordon? That why you contaminated an environment you shared with your wife and children? You wanted to spread the suffering around, didn't you? So you wouldn't be the only one with altered DNA, the only one with permanently mutated genes. You wanted to leave your mark on history, didn't you, Gordon?"

Cecily shot her husband a furious glance. "My father didn't know any better. The government gave the men hardhats and sunglasses to wear. That's the message men like my father received."

"And most of us threw our hardhats and sunglasses away," I said, "because the explosions were underground, in case you hadn't heard, and we were protected by hundreds, if not thousands, of feet of solid bedrock. The minute levels of radiation that seeped up through the desert floor weren't dangerous. On the contrary, radiation in the doses we were exposed to bolstered our immune systems and gave us energy. Few of us even came down with colds. Some tests required a week of eighteen-hour days, which we clocked without suffering the slightest fatigue."

Crescent moons of phantasmagorical purple and brown lay recumbent beneath their eyes. I felt for them, I did. They'd recently brought bawling human life into the world. But this wasn't an argument I expected to have with them. At wedding receptions —I'd attended one for Cecily and two for Kate, whose first marriage ended in divorce— J.R. was the one I quarreled with, his liberalism and belief in social change easily as idiotic as the conservative war-mongering heard 24-7 up and down the AM dial. Now that J.R. was dead, it seemed as if he'd divided, and I wondered if he'd multiplied and the next time I visited Kate and her homosexual second husband Donny, they'd be his ghostly ventriloquist's dummies, too. I thought of the $1,597,244.10 I hadn't won and how different things might've been if only my lovely young fiancée were running interference for me.

"Indeed, thanks to the radiation I received back then and the ever-diminishing doses I receive at home, I can mix diazepam, hydrocodone, acetaminophen, codeine, anti-insomnia drugs, anti-anxiety drugs, amphetamines, and other analgesics with alcohol and tobacco without experiencing adverse side effects of any kind. So don't talk to me about the dangers of something not even our nation's top physicists and pharmacists fully understand . . ."

I would've gone on an even more impassioned rant if Mike hadn't slumped to the kitchen floor and begun to weep, all three hundred fifty plus pounds of him shuddering in an orange and blue heap beside the butcher block. Cecily fell to her knees before him and massaged his lineman's neck and shoulders. Peering up at me with plaintive eyes, she said, "Our baby has eleven fingers."

Mike heaved even harder. I saw then what this was all about, the driveway search, the chilly reception. They wanted to pin my grandchild's defect, if 'defect' an eleventh finger could even be called, on me. I unzipped my fanny pack, found my Valium, opened the vial, and handed two 2-milligram pills to Cecily. "Give him these," I said and went to the sink to fill a glass with water.

"We don't drink the tap water," she said, "because it contains traces of mercury."

"A little mercury never hurt anyone," I said, but handed her a glass of filtered water poured from a Brita pitcher as Mike regarded the pair of pills in his palm, each imprinted with a heart, as if they were tealeaves. "Take them." I said. "They're your friends."

"I know what they are," Mike said, wiping tears from his whiskered cheeks. "But what I'd like is Percocet."

"Are you sure?" I said, wary of the fluctuations in mood I experienced whenever I was on them. But Mike nodded, so I took back the pills I'd given him and found the ones he preferred. Before I put the Valium away, I offered them to Cecily, figuring she too could use a lift.

"Thanks, but I'm breastfeeding," she said.

"The Valium will be out of your system entirely by this time tomorrow," I said.

"And Mike Junior will have nursed six times by then," she replied.

"Surely you have infant formula."

"Who's going to feed him infant formula at ten p.m.? At two a.m.? At six a.m.? At noon? You?" she said. "Because if I take two Valium, I guarantee you I won't be conscious before this time tomorrow."

"I'll do it," I said.

"You'll stay up all night?"

"And all day tomorrow, too, if need be."

"Don't you need your rest?" she asked.

"When I need my rest, I take sleep medication." A mischievous smile crossed my daughter's lips. "Take them," I said, holding the pills out to her.

"I can't believe I'm accepting prescription drugs from my own father. It would kill Mom."

"It wouldn't kill your mother if she and I were still together, if she hadn't fallen under the sway of that granola-eating, slogan-spouting peacenik, that healthier-than-thou, sand-worshipping, vegetable-loving hypocrite with the bald head, ponytail, bolo tie, hemp slippers, and twin banana yellow Hummers with vanity plates reading 'Thing 1' and 'Thing 2.'"

"Dad," Cecily said, "J.R.'s dead. You don't have to hate him anymore."

I didn't fault Annabel for leaving me, I faulted her for marrying a man whose idea of a romantic night out was protesting nuclear proliferation in a snowstorm and who would've dismantled the nation's entire arsenal given half a chance, blissfully unaware that every livelihood, even his own, was dependent upon a flourishing weapons program. Indeed, I could not have faulted her more were he, instead, of the camp that maintained we needed to blow every country hostile to American interests to kingdom come. Having the biggest, longest nuclear arms meant never having to use them. What punk picked a fight with Jack Dempsey? Joe Louis? Mohammed Ali? That, in a nutshell, was my politics. Beyond that, I believed in love, specifically the human being's inalienable right to give and receive it freely.

But Cecily was correct. My nemesis for over three decades was dead, and Annabel, whom I would've taken back in a second even after all the years apart, was still grieving her loss of him as much as I was my loss of her.

"You ready to meet your grandson?" Cecily asked, and in the warmth emanating from her eyes I saw the Valium exercising its tranquilizing influence.

I thought of the steak dinner-for-two to which I'd treat myself on my way home. "I might live forever, but I doubt it."

Cecily sighed. "You'll probably outlive us all." As she rose from the kitchen floor, she kissed Mike on the button of his ball cap. "Get up, you big, lovable oaf." A mammoth hand closed around her slender wrist—between the second and third knuckle of each finger a skull and crossbones had been tattooed—and she lugged him onto knees the size of small duffle bags. From there Mike raised himself from the linoleum one leg at a time, like a weightlifter under a bowing yoke of iron. Once on his feet, he engulfed her in an embrace, and Cecily was a child again, on a Halloween long ago, in a grizzly bear costume that needed zipping up in the back.

A human lean-to, they led me to a master bedroom that smelled of milk, and in a crib canopied with dangling stegosaurs, tyrannosaurs, and triceratops Mike Jr. lay bundled in blankets. "Oh my," I said and gathered my grandson in my arms. To me he seemed the most perfect of creatures, his lids leaf-shaped and so translucent I thought I could see his pupils studying me through the networks of delicate blue veins. I pulled back his swaddling and his arms sprang up as if in surprise, though he remained sleeping. On his right hand were a thumb and five fingers, digits five and six veering out from a shared midcarpal joint like identical necks of a newborn two-headed snake.

"Who knows?" I said. "With his extra finger, maybe he'll be the first to perform Rachmaninoff's 'Second Piano Concerto' the way it was meant to be performed."

"Unh-unh," Mike said. "The little fella's getting a Stratocaster the day he turns five. I've already exposed him to Jimi, Jimmy, and Frank."

"Who?"

"Hendrix, Page, and Zappa."

Cecily was peeking at her baby over my shoulder, humming "You Are My Sunshine." "The obstetrician asked us whether we wanted the extra finger removed. We told her no."

"Of course you did, sweetheart," I said. "You don't know why he's been given it. Nobody does."

"We almost told her yes."

Soon she and Mike were in the guestroom setting up a bassinet, giggling, neither long for this world.

I understood.

Every couple prayed that their baby would be born perfect. But what did 'perfect' mean? If I'd learned anything from my thirty years at the Test Site, it was that we as a race were forever adapting to changes we had wrought upon the earth. Who was to say we weren't entering an age in which eleven fingers was the norm? As I held my first and no doubt only grandchild in my arms, I imagined human beings in the not-so-distant future playing musical instruments that looked nothing like the musical instruments of today, with hundreds of keys and thousands of strings and perhaps more than one mouthpiece.

To this day a curious red wildflower springs up on the Test Site after a rain, and it has no name.

Melanie DeCarolis

Looks Like Tomorrow is Coming On Fast

I worked in an office in Harlan, back in the Before. The company processed those cards that fall out of your magazine whenever you open it. The money was good, but the hassle wasn't worth it. It sapped you, having a boss who berated you for not being a team player if you didn't have an MBA in ass-kissing. Or pale deskbound co-workers, getting large and soft beneath their clothes, who would say either *bet you'd be cute*, or *bet you'd have a boyfriend if you wore only wore skirts once in awhile*. Sure, it might have been easier for me had I done what they said, but that's never been who I am. Handling all those cards gave me endless paper cuts.

Now I work at a Mobil. I know that sounds weird. I have my reasons. The station is not quite a mile from home. It's long enough. Silvio had one of his goons take my car. I don't know this for sure, but who else could it be? He wants me, he can't have me, he's going to make things difficult for me. I have to walk down a state highway. Here—in Defiance, in the bowels of western Iowa, Before population 300—that's a two-lane road bordered by miles of cornfields. The road hasn't been repaved so long that it's wearing away back down to cinders. Ashes to ashes, dust to dust.

It's taking longer for me to get home. Behruz owns the station. He had been letting me leave my shift at 4:30. That was when Scooter, he was 16, was coming in and doing the night shift. We haven't heard from him in weeks. So now Behruz expects me to work longer, later.

Behruz won't let me close up when I leave. I don't see why it matters; so few come this way anymore anyhow. "There are people," he says in his sad, lost accent. "We need to be open for the people." I wonder what circumstances swept him up and deposited him here. He's brown like the desert. He doesn't belong here where it's either too green or too pale, like straw.

I work in a four-by-five Plexiglas strongbox of a cashier's booth until Behruz comes to let me go home. He overbuilt it, thinking that the register would prove too tempting, what with all the meth labs out here. I can be seen from every angle, like I'm in a zoo cage. Sometimes, a long dark car with tinted windows pulls into the station and just idles there for minutes, sometimes an hour. The first time it happened, I peed in my Big-n-Thirsty soda cup because I was too scared to go across the bay to the rest room. Now I know the car will always leave before I do. It's too big to hide in the cornstalks along the road, but that doesn't mean it will never be there, either.

Winter's coming, so it gets dark sooner.

Contrary to what popular literature and movies would have you think, you can only use a crucifix against a vampire if you believe in the faith behind it. *Really* believe in the Father, the Son, and all that other stuff. This is what my next-door neighbor Jennifer says.

"It's a papal conspiracy," she says. "Look who's propagating that myth. Crucifix sales keep St. Peter's and the Vatican afloat. Man, organized religion is so evil."

Jennifer was raised Lutheran. The Missouri Synod back where she grew up in Michigan. That's as conservative as you can get outside the Bible Belt.

"The damn Catholics started this whole problem to begin with, with the Crusades," she says. "The First One, the Great Nosofuru Lord, fought in your so-called holy land. He got captured, tortured beyond human imagining or suffering, and came back with all sorts of knowledge to transcend mortality."

I never know what to do here. Do I cluck sympathetically? Say, "Tell me more?"

"Have you heard from California? Or parts elsewhere?" I ask instead.

"No." That's all she says. But I hear it twice, once over the phone and once from behind the wall our apartments share.

I don't attend Mass. I read my copy of the *Oxford Study Bible* a lot, wanting to find something, a hidden key that turns on all the lights, drops the scales from my eyes, some over-translated phrase passed down from Aramaic to Latin to Old English to now that will undo my decades of paganism, of disbelief, of indifference to the everlasting. That hasn't happened yet.

But the crosses seem to work for me just on the sliver of faith I have. So far.

I don't tell Jennifer this.

We think the minions came from the cities, by the grace and favor of the so-called Great One. He sent his favorites to establish their own private demesnes or hunting grounds, treating us like game. The favorites decide who lives on after death, and who dies. Ours is called Silvio. Jennifer has never seen him. She's not part of that scene. I don't think she goes out much anymore.

"He can't be all that great in the hierarchy," I say. "Come on. *Iowa?* There's nobody out here. Sooner or later, they all will be cannibalizing each other, like some undead Ponzi scheme."

"It's not like victims have a say in this. Though it's actually, if you think of it, an honor." Jennifer's talking fast now, sounding defensive. She can't actually buy into this, can she? Maybe vampires can read each others' thoughts so there's no room for dissent.

"Besides, you need to be careful," she continues. "Don't spout off about things you don't know. Have some respect. Maybe he won't drain you entirely and kill you. Maybe he'll let you live."

"What do you mean?"

"He knows all about you, your vegetarian diet. Out here that makes you special. He thinks your blood might be pure, like an elixir."

I should be scared, but the idea that I could be a delicacy like monkey brains or an open bar for bloodsuckers is too surreal to take seriously. On the other hand, I'm taking precautions. "Is that what you think?"

"I know how much booze you can drink, sweetie." She snorts.

Contrary to popular belief, too: vampires aren't especially superhuman anymore. Sure, back in the day of Vlad the Impaler, dark undead things could take root in the blood pretty easily. Back then, it was all fresh Carpathian mountain air and hearty peasant diets of starches and non-steroidal livestock bred for pure, primal, survival-based consumption—not bioengineered for resistance to mad cow or for meatier, leaner, more economical cuts of beef.

Flash forward a few centuries past the Industrial Revolution to Kyoto accords, aspartame, and ineffectual antibacterial soap. The stock is thinning. When the prey ingests poisons, those get passed on to the predators. It's like the fear cattle feel going up the ramp into the slaughterhouse. It stays in the meat when the animal is killed, when it's processed, packaged, and put in the grocery store. It's bad both for the body and the karma of the one who consumes it.

"I thought everyone could levitate up to victims' windows. You know, all that typical stake-bait behavior," I say.

Immediately I feel the frost coming through the receiver. "Don't use that term around me."

"I'm sorry." To my surprise, I am.

Jennifer hesitates over the phone. "A lot of them are just really coked up. You know, it's that whole immortality thing. It's a total license for bad behavior. Go through a whole kilo by yourself, and sure, you can walk through windows. But, whoops, better not get a big sliver of glass in the heart when you do it. Or else it's time to go take a dirt nap. I probably shouldn't be telling you this," she sounds regretful. "You might use it against us."

"Jesus, Jennifer," I sigh. I don't know if I should say Jesus. "You know I'm a pacifist. I'm looking out for my own sorry skin in case one of your compadres come knocking on the door."

"Well, you know just not to invite them in." Her voice was always husky. Now it's gotten deeper. She must be smoking again. I haven't told her that after twenty-six years on the planet, four of which were as a nicotine-free English major at a liberal arts college for chrissakes, that I've started.

"Yeah, but you've been over to my place plenty of times in the past. Before."

And then the telephone line goes silent between us as we both sit and think about what that means. Jennifer and I have decided that, given our new divergent lifestyles, it probably isn't a good idea to keep meeting for the Saturday martini nights we used to have. Too much temptation for her, though she might very well suspect that I'm going to slick her.

Jennifer's got a car. She would probably give it to me. But then she'd really be alone, and I'd feel guilty about that. And my cat Asta, whom I refuse to leave behind, is a real bitch to travel with. She screeches and howls in a car more than a two-year-old.

Besides, I find it funny that they came for Defiance. So defiance is what they're going to get.

Being a vampire doesn't automatically make you evil, but it does tend to magnify certain darker, less philanthropic traits in your inherent makeup. Jennifer is wonderful, but she was on a lot of psychotropic meds to keep her depression in check in the Beforetime. We talk on the phone a lot now. All the utilities still work, so I guess the vamps have yet to take control of them.

The phones still work, and I know that's killing Jennifer. At least on an emotional level, I mean.

The apartment building is eerily quiet now. The Russian family who live upstairs are the only ones left, other than Jennifer and me. They always kept to themselves Before. They also always had the same pale, wan look to them to begin with. It really doesn't seem to have affected them too much. They still tromp down the stairs in their perfumes and furs, overly made up and loud. They nod to me, efficiency in unison. I think they hang out with other Russian vamps in Omaha, go hunting there.

I sleep with a stake kept between my panties and my thigh, and a cross around my neck and another beneath my pillow. I grow garlic in my bedroom, along the doorframe, around my bed, and on the windowsills. Garlic plants lie inside my front door. Every time I leave, I line them up neatly so I know if anyone's come in. They make my apartment smell like sweat all the time.

. . . .

"How's Kismet?" I figure that's a safe subject to ask.

"Oh, good, she's good," Jennifer says. "She and Pepe are getting along now. Stella still hisses whenever she sees her."

Pepe bit Kismet, my other cat, one night on the landing. Just jumped her when she scooted out the open door. Kismet has about five pounds on him, and knows how to put up a fight. I used to have to plan to leave for the vet's an hour before the appointment. But she didn't move fast enough for Pepe. It just seemed safer for me and Asta if Kismet went to live across the hall. We don't know how Pepe got vamped. Only the lowest forms of Undead vamp animals, or those who haven't gotten the hang of it. It's not something self-respecting vamps do on a regular basis.

Asta is lost without her big sister. Kismet was her feline maternal figure, always bathing her, letting Asta get all rambunctious on her. Asta prowls the door inside my apartment crying loudly. Kismet mewls back from behind Jennifer's door. Call and response, all night. It's annoying.

"Do you think we should let them see each other?" she asks.

I hesitate. I don't ask how Jennifer feeds. It might be a ploy. As if on cue, Asta lines up at the door and starts keening. "Maybe it will shut them up."

"Okay. See you in the hall then."

I look through the peephole. All clear. I wait until I hear Jennifer throw her lock and listen to hear if she's whispering to anyone.

I open the door just a crack. I hold a crucifix behind my back. Asta steps out. Kismet trills. She looks feral. I don't know if Jennifer is brushing her or taking care of her.

"See? There's your sister, Asta. She's fine." *It's just that she's Dracula Cat now.*

Asta sniffs once and backs away from Kismet. She assumes the hissing stance, but nothing comes out. Kismet is confused. Out of the both of them, Kismet was always the one to catch the mice. But I think, or I'd like to think, that somewhere down inside, Kismet is able to fight off one set of primal urges—the bloodsucking ones— with the other maternal ones. I know that's silly, assigning human emotions to an animal. Ever since I had stuffed animals as a kid, when I believed they could talk to me, if only I was a genuinely good, kind, and honest person, I've always thought animals can see the true souls in us humans that we tend to miss. I think that's why I became a vegan in the first place.

It is the first time I've seen Jennifer in weeks. She's leaning behind her door just as I am, like we're two starlets playing coy behind bath towels. "Hey neighbor," I say weakly. "How goes things?" The circles under her eyes are deep, muddying her complexion. Her Jean Seberg gamine-cut hair is blonder now.

"I'm out of gin. How do ya think I'm doing?" I can tell that it is worse, much worse than she's pretending.

"Oh, shit. Better call 911," I smile.

"I thought I might as well use all my free time to perfect my martini technique, ya know. Not having a baby around the house frees up my time."

"How's Maddy?" I ask.

"Real good. Ellie's taking care of her. Everything seems okay out in Berkeley." When this whole thing broke out, her mother-in-law Ellie was in town visiting. After three nights of hiding in the apartment with the shades drawn, watching endless shadows flit across sidewalks to the street, engulfing other shadows, Jennifer and Dan decided to send Maddy, their eighteen-month-old, back to California on Ellie's lap, and then try to get out there themselves. Ellie lives in the hills; at least that was something in case the After spread out there as well. They went in the first hours of day to the airport. Ellie wasn't due to fly out until the evening, when it would have been too dangerous. Their plan was to go to the airport, stay as long as safely possible with Ellie and Maddy saying goodbye, and get home safely before dark.

"It's something to be thankful for," I say.

"It's all I have to keep going until I hear from Dan, wherever he is."

"Hey, I got an unopened bottle of Tanq," I say.

"Now I know we're in the decline of Western civilization as we know it," she said. Back in the Before, we were both heavy consumers of Bombay Sapphire.

"Yours if you want it."

She shrugged. "Yeah, if you don't mind."

"Hang on a sec," I said. Asta is still out in the hall. I'm not going out there. "Kitty, come back." She doesn't budge. She and Kismet just stare. I shut the door and lock it, praying that Asta will be safe for the ten seconds it takes to grab the gin from the freezer.

"Got it," I say. I roll it across the hall to her. "*Salut.*" She stops it with her toe and looks pained.

"Can I give you a hug?"

"Oh, Jenn—"

"I promise. This is legit. I need to feel human again." There's a tone in her voice that breaks my heart.

"I don't know if I can help you with that." I pull Asta off the doormat so her claws flex. "Dan will be back. I know it."

"You know I love you. You know I'd never, well, I'd never." She sounds so defeated. She's trying to keep me out here.

"I know, hon," I say before I close the door. I have holy water and garlic cloves stuffed in my pockets. Just in case. That's cold of me, I know.

I don't blame Pepe; he's a cat. Nor Jennifer. She's suffered a lot of loss. The way I heard it later, Jennifer simply couldn't leave the baby, hugging and clutching and kissing her up until the boarding call. By then it was 8 pm. If you get caught out at night, you're supposed to stay inside until daybreak, but they don't lock the doors at an airport. Anyone can come in off the street. Motels are no good; too many passcards floating around and too many staffers-turned-stake-bait who don't need to be invited into a room because they've entered it freely before.

Jennifer and Dan got home safe that night, but safe didn't last long. Dan got vamped first, from one of his music students. You could expect that kind of let's-dabble-on-the-dark-side behavior from the rockstar wannabes, the guitar players, but Dan teaches *trombone* for heaven's sake. There's nothing sexy about a trombonist from a community college. And now Dan's disappeared.

. . . .

Behruz shows up a half-hour early. "You're stealing gas. You're a thief," he says.

"I don't know what you're talking about," I say.

"I've seen the security tapes," he says.

The tapes only show part of the story. It shows me filling the Big-n-Thirsty cup with thirty-six cents worth of 93 octane. It doesn't show me putting the thirty-six cents in the register before I trip the tank release. It doesn't show me mixing that thirty-six cents with Diet Dr. Pepper—which I also buy—and drinking it. Dr. Pepper hides the taste the best.

"I know what you are doing," he says. "Stop."

"It's just going to get worse," I say.

"It's not good. You are young. You need hope."

"Behruz, I'm thinking of the people," I say.

His eyes on me are steely. He pushes up his shirtsleeve. Rows and rows of tiny wooden beads girdle his arm. He pulls one of them off and pushes it at me.

"Your people believe one thing." He glances at my neck. "Mine believe another." The beads feel like sand, brittle and porous. They are fastened by a thin red cord.

"So what's it like?" I ask Jennifer. "To be you. Now. How does it feel?" I'm not being flippant. I'm curious. Maybe it's not so bad. Maybe I'll get used to it.

"Open your door," she says.

"I don't think I should."

"Wear your charms and trinkets. Nobody is going to touch you. I told you."

She has sunglasses on. Her face is a burned palette of pink and black in harsh cruel bubbles and lines. "I was awake the other day. I thought I could look through the blinds. You should see my eye. What's left of it. I just want to see the fucking sun, you know?" She sounds like she's going to cry. But her kind can't. "I can never see Maddy again. I can never see Dan."

"Dan would have loved you, whatever you looked like," I say, realizing too late I have used the past tense.

. . . .

The pounding woke me up. Dan was calling me from the other side of the door.

"Dan, I don't think it's a good idea," I said.

"Please, you gotta open up." He moaned a little. "Silvio's coming for you. You have to get out. I'm going to help you get out."

I just stood there blinking. The sleep was hard to throw off, but that's the way it was most days.

Dan yanked out a suitcase from my hall closet. "Get clothes. Get going. Come on. I'll get the cats." He pulled down the carriers from the shelf.

"They'll fight you," I said. "Especially Kismet."

"They can't hurt me," Dan said. "Just pack, dammit. Hurry!" He stayed away from my bedroom. There was a cross on the door, and garlic plants around the frame, my bed and on the windows.

"How do you know this?"

"People. Connections, whatever. Faster! There's no time!"

I threw things into the suitcase randomly. It felt like the heat had been turned up in the apartment. I was sweating.

"What are they planning?"

"The road. Before you get to work. It could still be dark enough."

I dragged the suitcase out of the bedroom. Dan's lips curled. "Silvio says adrenaline in the blood gives the best rush: fear, arousal, excitement. What are you feeling?" He grabbed my shoulders. His breath smelled spoiled.

I pulled the waistband of my sweatpants down, pulled up the stake and slicked him. He dissolved like fireworks. I felt his scream rather than heard it. All that remained was a pool of twitching oil and his wedding ring at the edge of it. Asta shook a paw at the puddle and hissed. It burned the floor a little. I threw a towel over it until I could decide what to do.

Jennifer called me the next night, in hysterics.

"I'm so sorry," I said. "Did he go to California?"

One mildly overcast day, the car door opens.

Silvio and three of his goons come out. I've never seen him

before, but I know it's him. They're wearing big brimmed hats and long robes. They look like Italian priests, but without the big crosses. They all wear goggles. Silvio's are large aviator style, gold. Their skin looks gray underneath their hats.

They surround the booth, one on each side like a compass. They hum, or hiss, I can't tell, it's one long note. They tap the glass, gently, in unison, still humming.

Silvio takes off his glasses. He's younger than I expected. I thought he would be some dark, Slavic-looking type with slicked back hair and a widow's peak. He looks like an underfed Nebraska farm boy with red-blond hair and eyes that are clear as an icy stream. He smiles, and the corners of his mouth reach up to the corners of his eyes.

"We smelled you. You smell so good. Do you know how good you smell? We came all the way out here to tell you." His voice is low and smooth, but there's a twangy catch to it.

One of the others licks the glass. His tongue looks like a starfish's point. His teeth look like old tree roots.

"Your blood wants to come out and play. Don't be a tease. Just give us a taste; we'll go away," he says.

"Just give us a taste. We'll go away," they chant. The hissing continues on its own like the susurration of cicadas. They tap on the glass, impatient and slow. The glass starts to rattle on all four sides. One of them pushes too hard and cracks it. His eyes, flat, spark with life. He sticks a long pointed nail in the crack, worrying it back and forth. I see the tiny little fractures. The nail has a half-moon of black at its tip. It's in the booth with me. Silvio just paces back and forth with his vulpine grin.

One of them springs to the roof of the booth. It's aluminum and shiny up there. He lands with a slam that rattles everything. His thrashing, as the reflected sun hits him, sounds like a hailstorm. Dents erupt in the ceiling. He's burning. I smell it, so dark and cloying and rank that I throw up in long ropy heaves. When my stomach feels flat and empty against my spine, they are gone.

I run to the bathroom. There is a large blot of blood when I pull my pants down. My period has come a week early. I buy a tampon out of the machine. It takes me awhile to rip my panties up into small pieces, since my fingernails bend and tear against the cotton fabric. I flush them down the toilet.

If I scratch my arm, I bruise. I wake up in a sweat. It's all I can do to go to work. I lean against the wall of the booth. I go home and go to bed. I don't know if I should feel thankful or angry if I wake up the next day. The irony is that medically, a person with vampirism has a severe energy deficiency. I find that terribly funny.

I come home after looting the library for new books to read. My front door is wide open, keys hanging in the lock. My initials are on the tag. It's Jennifer and Dan's spare set that I gave them if I ever locked myself out. Her door is open too. There are dark streaks on the walls in the hallway. Her apartment smells like something burned, even though all the windows are open. Maddy's picture lies on the floor next to a big viscous puddle, two wedding rings, and shavings of what looks like lacquer. I find three smaller pools around the apartment. Kismet's was on the bed, soaked into the pillowcase. Stuck to it was the small, hard capsule of the microchip the vet gave her as a kitten to keep her from getting lost.

The garlic in around my front door is strewn all over the floor. She must have been burning as she came in here. There are more dark dull streaks along the walls and on the floors. There are deep claw marks in the wooden floor where Dan was. I hope she is at peace.

I arrive at the station. Behruz isn't there. The door to the booth is wide open. Dozens of beads lie scattered on the floor.

I buy a gallon of high-octane. I carry it home in a rusting jerry can I found around back. I don't feel bad about not paying for that.

C_6H_6. Benzene. From it you can make plastics and synthetic rubber that never break down. It makes gasoline that creates little explosions in engines, and napalm that blows things up in more noticeable, less controlled ways. It burns in cigarettes. It smells nice and sweet, like tea. It tastes like dirty vodka.

I wonder which way I'm going: burning or blowing. Certain of my cells have already begun to explode. My lymph nodes have been swollen for three weeks, pushing against my armpits. My period has slowed to a watery pink trickle, barely a day's duration. My uterus is too tired to weep for children I will never have.

Finally, results.

I'm getting things in order.

I had always thought vampires found it easy, natural even, to sleep during the day. I found seventeen different kinds of sleeping pills in Jennifer's medicine cabinet, lined up like a welcoming committee. She kept a notebook of what combinations of pills gave her the longest sleep, which ones didn't give her nightmares, which ones spared her dreams of Maddy.

I pick one that looks pretty mild. I grind up half a tab and mix it in with Asta's food. She sniffs her bowl for the longest time. At first, I don't want her to eat it. I haven't fed her for a day to make sure she would. I want to take the bowl away. I don't want to do this to her. The sacred truce between human and house pet: I will take care of you. This is the cruelest thing I've ever done.

She nibbles carefully. I stand by and hate myself as she eats her death.

I hoped she would just fall asleep and stay there. She convulses. She growls. I hold her close. I stroke her face the way she likes. She struggles and scratches. "Shhh," I whisper over and over again until I gasp on my sobs. It's hard for me to cry these days. It's hard physically. Very little comes out. "Mommy's here. Mommy loves you. Mommy did it because she loves you." Eventually she stills. I don't know when exactly she dies. I sit with her for hours in my arms until her bowels relax and I smell her shit on my lap.

I manage to squeeze out some tears into her belly, matting her soft black fur. It dries in stiff little peaks. I should brush it out so she looks nice, like she is sleeping. I leave her that way though. The tears are traces of me. If whoever may judge me in the next life uses cat poisoning against me, I will have proof of my innocence, the pure intent of my love.

She was an indoor cat her whole life. The outside scared her. It didn't make sense to be burying her in it. I wrap her in Kismet's pillowcase. Ashes to ashes, dust to dust.

This is why I can't be like them out there.

There is no going back now. There is nothing left.

My blood is poisoning me. The nosebleeds come daily, several times. I see things at windows all the time that aren't there, overgrown babies, big reptilian birds with lions' heads. It might be the fevers. My skin looks withered, as though my bones might poke out at any time. I'm pale, like them.

I don't know if this is going to work, turning myself into a time bomb. I don't know for sure if I have leukemia. I don't know if I can make a difference. I don't know if Silvio is still waiting for me. I'm going to make it easy for him. No charms, crosses, or garlic. I'm going to walk out to the road and wait. And maybe I'll sing until he comes.

I don't even bother to shut the door as I leave.

Alexander Lumans

Elephants Are Why He Made The Oceans

The spirit tree on Hunting Island has always been dead. The island is an old, bare bones pirate landing, marshy as hell. On the only road, near the abandoned lighthouse, the fat trunk of the spirit tree stands among the salt swamp's reeds and wild fetterbush and brown baldcypresses. The thick, low limbs reach out like hangmen's arms. All of the Sea Island people know the tree as a Baobab, and it haunts their dreams. They call it a tree altar, a ghost post. And it's said to have been planted upside down, but the swamp does not drag it beneath the water.

People have waded out to it and hung things from the limbs: hymns written on rice paper and tied up with sisal, skulls of animals splintered with shot, and conch shells filled with broken fiddle strings. Rotten eggs. White and brown. People throw eggs because hitting the tree frees the soul that a jumbie has trapped there.

The man who taught me taxidermy said I needed to know the tree, limb to root. I was twenty when we finished stuffing the body of a lynx in his Olar studio. A mess of bones and bowels pooled on the tabletop the more he emptied the cat's body. I struggled not to cough up stomach acid. It was only my second project. He wrapped the lynx's insides in a tarp and cinched the top with a miller's knot. He said we had to drive.

It took an hour down oak-lined roads and past the black and white lighthouse to reach the swamp with the spirit tree. Plastic eyes rattled behind the dash's grill the whole ride there. My teeth chattered with the same clacking. We stopped at a break in the Spanish moss and climbed out into the drainage ditch. Into the bog, I had to carry the heavy tarp sack by the top and the bottom. Every step tightened my arms and legs, and I squeezed the sack so hard it should have gushed. I walked in each of the man's boot marks. I pushed aside the wheat grass's starchy blades where they clustered together and barred the way. Rumors said sinkholes and bogs and bogmen disguised themselves in the marshland. Long scratch marks in the mud frightened me, dry tide pools where claws had tried to furiously dig themselves out of the muck. The deep red tree stood in front of us with no birds' nests in the stunted branches, and that worried me.

He said we were doing a sacred thing and if I learned anything from him, it would be to respect the animal, inside and out. We had to bury the blood-soiled organs and bones to finish the job we'd started.

I loosened the miller's knot and reached inside the bag, reluctantly. I grabbed soft, pliant entrails and short, snapped lengths of bone and I imagined withdrawing my hand to find it gone. But he reached in and brought my arm out of the bag and made sure I had a handful of organs that smelled of clogged drains. The cold fluid ran down my arm to drip at the elbow, and it was hard to tell where the lynx's insides ended and my bloody arms began. The man who taught me taxidermy stood behind me and pointed at the peeling trunk.

I stepped up to the tree's wide base and spread the lynx's insides up and down the trunk, which was even colder than the organs, as if the trunk hid an underground fissure. He threw me the canvas bag and the tarp opened and splashed at my feet. More of the skeleton tumbled out and stuck in the mud. I stepped around rib bones that sank in shallow puddles, but he ground his teeth and said, *Finish the job*, and so I got down on my knees in the muck. No prayers came to me.

The ground was easy to dig into. Olive shells and live oysters dug into my palms while water filled the hole each time I pulled more refuse out. Woodpeckers knocked erratically against dead pines all around the bog. He said through his teeth: *Hurry, boy.*

I dug faster. The dirt and salt stung my eyes and caused them to water. My fingers left tracks in the marshy ground. The hole was big enough for a tractor tire and the depth would never end. I picked out severed intestines and twisted tendons from the sack, and then dropped them in the hole. The land wanted the body back, even demanded its return, so I dumped the entire bag in and felt like I'd lost something as the water mixed with the blood and the bile.

I froze. In the hole I saw no reflection. But looking deeper, bending down, I found myself in the gruesome sheen and collapsed forward. The viscera splashed all over me, sloshing and pink, and filled my mouth. Bones jammed into the backs of my knees and ligaments wrapped themselves around my stomach. It sucked me down and filled my throat with strands of muscle and fat and marrow. To scream was to swallow.

Then the man who taught me taxidermy caught me by the collar and hoisted me out to lie against the ghost post. *All's good*, he said. I wiped what blood and sticky yellow fluid I could from my arms, and I felt filthy, yet satisfied. He walked back toward the truck, me trudging with tarp in tow. The flat sack caught on reed stalks all the way out of the marsh.

At the road, he said that whatever I didn't use for the body, I had to use for the soul. He asked if I remembered the directions to get to the tree and made me repeat them back to him, even made sure I learned by heart how the Baobab looked in the moonlight. We got in the car and he jangled the keys. My muddy feet stuck to the floor mat.

I asked if we had to come here every time. He turned the engine on and diesel smoke drifted around the back bumper, clouded the mirrors, and he said I had to. Every time. And as we turned the car around to drive back, two fake hawk eyes rattled free from inside the dash and rolled over to my side. They landed pupil up and I stared into their reflective yellow glass and painted iris on the way home. I saw the lynx still hunkered down in the green weeds, alive with hackles raised, redolent of my contrition. The oblate pupil swelled into the hole I had filled and swallowed me like a grave.

Thirty-four years later, the day after the blackest, best-dressed negro I have ever seen, a negro named Ogun Orish, had shown up at my shop, I drive down in my D-Series to an unfamiliar address. He'd handed over four hundred dollars with the address just to get me down there, and said the job would pay more than twice that.

His English was pretty broken. Just full of clicks and swallows, like cicadas trying to fly up a well spout. But I bring my medicine bag of tools and the truck bed is also full with wire netting, skin pullers and folded sheets of plaster, tanning-oil drums, foot-wide strips of burlap and finishing nails. The biggest tub of borax I could find perches in the front seat.

The site is deep in the Lowcountry, about an hour north of Savannah, just a big old flat field of browning sea oats and squat palmettos. Everything's wind-swept. And there in the middle is this barn, the only building for miles, big enough to fit twenty threshers wheel-to-wheel. The walnut wood has lost all its luster. Rust stains the roof. The walls are so gray with salt air that I could lick their siding and my tongue would shrivel up on the spot. And there's Ogun standing by the barn, tying grass into a knot, tying the knots into a bracelet around his wrist, the thin loops curving into holes that lead into other tinier pockets of reed. He's in a custom-fit cream-colored suit, the kind you see men wearing on Charleston porches behind the Battery's painted cannons. He's come into my life like a stormy petrel. And I figure he is the only negro ever to be hanging around that barn for good reason. I know for a fact some of those crossbeams in there have been used for things other than support.

He grins yellow teeth and sticks his flabby tongue out and then points inside.

The sky runs a dead gray. It's an awful omen to watch cover the horizon, but I'm shit for brains and I follow him into the barn, where, in the center, a roofless cage stands grain-silo tall, and inside that cage, an elephant rakes its trunk against the bars. No circus I've ever heard of has an elephant so fat and wild. And this one's a cow, a matriarch by the size of it. The skin on it reminds me of the tin siding on my old farmhouse. I can still remember the smell of hay bales in the fallow cabbage field and the truck that doubled as a fire engine my pop drove before he died in the refinery's blaze.

The skylights shine on the animal that towers beside a great haystack. Her trunk can grab me by the waist or leg and paint the sand with my insides. Her wet, brown eyes follow me like those fake hawk eyes followed me home from Hunting Island, and so do her tusks. I get to see the teeth that were once milk teeth. She tests every inch of the cell at least once, and makes decisions in that sloping, carriage-sized forehead. She's a barrel of muscle with legs like columns and girth that seems to weigh more than her skin can hold.

I'm normally not one to worry about what hides inside something's skin—I'm not in the butchering gig—but this animal's different. The ears fan, each four feet wide. I look down the two black holes of her nose, and they can suck me up. I don't want to keep staring into them for fear of seeing more of the emptiness I've always filled with excelsior.

I walk back out and almost keel over. My breath just goes away when I see myths in the flesh, flesh enough to make my nose bleed. I don't want to go back in there, but Ogun follows me out and hands me a silk hanky patterned in diamonds. He says the ship ride over was worse. Down in the hull, the elephant had put six holes in the keel. At night, they'd sailed up the Ashley River at Charleston and landed on a private dock to unload the rogue animal. It'd trampled three deckhands and cracked the pier straight in half.

The elephant trumpets from inside the barn. Ogun tells me I have three days.

"To skin it?" I say, still surprised.

"Yes. Only you," he says.

"I'd need at least a week." My hands, though used to peeling away fur and tying miller's knots by now, are unsuited to do this alone. But the animal's boasting pulls me further in. Ogun helps me off the ground and we walk back inside.

I ask, "When you planning to put it down?"

Ogun goes to a locker behind the sliding door and brings back the longest rifle I've ever seen. It comes from Africa, like the elephant. And it's just as old. Ogun wraps his hands around the black powder, muzzle-loading smoothbore. He shows how the barrel holds four-bore single-shot: lead ball bullets the size of owl eyes. They can ruin anything's skin. The stock wood runs a deep, dark grain, oiled well and smelling of clean brass and gunpowder. It reminds me of Smokey Mountain mines. The barrel is as long as the exhaust pipes on roadsters at the Orangeburg drag strip, and the business end resembles the elephant's trunk. Someone has scratched notches along the iron. I count fourteen kill numbers.

One of the few things Ogun manages to get out in English is: "Tough. Frontal brainshot—if it charges." He pauses, and then adds, "It takes two."

He passes the elephant gun to me. He wants me to shoot the damn thing myself.

I ask why I've got to be the one to do it. He holds his hands up like he wants to keep them clean, but I just push the rifle back into his palms and tell him no. He says he's too weak, too busy, and I'm the best taxidermist in the area. If I don't agree, that animal is just going to suffer and starve to death. The man who taught me taxidermy said never refuse a job, especially one where you might learn about your own imperfections in the process. And then there is his cold hand on my shoulder, lifting my arms to receive the firearm. Ogun hands it over. The elephant isn't getting any smaller in that cage, and she bellows over my thoughts. I don't know if I can even fire this gun, let alone discern where an elephant's heart hangs, but that organ alone could swallow me whole. I'd like to see Ogun hold that stock up to his own bony little armpit—his shoulder blade doesn't stand a chance. I try to give him the weapon one last time, but now it's my own muscles that reel my tendons back in on their joint spools. Isn't this what pulls you out of the swamp and turns you into something fierce? Now I cannot ignore the unfinished job.

Ogun's yellow teeth show again when he smiles, and then he takes off his top hat with its black bandana pinned around the brim. He's shaved all his hair off. His black crown slopes sleekly. His skin sticks tight to his skull. The dents in his left lobe tell of blows to the head or bullets grazing by. I want to clutch it and smooth out the lumps and feel soft, unwrinkled hide. In this trade, you appreciate curves and natural imperfections.

The barn echoes with the elephant's stomping. My hands shake as much as my feet. Ogun shows me how to load the weapon. He pulls a powder horn—a rhino horn—from his jacket and opens it to pour two big capfuls down the gun's barrel. He has me knock the stock on the ground twice. Then a few inches of greased, fat-smelling oilcloth wadding goes over the barrel's opening. He hands me one lead shot and a ball starter. I put the ball on the oilcloth and use the short peg to push the bullet in. These are strange movements and I fear I will do something wrong, wrong enough to blow my own arms off. When I use the long peg, I have to stand directly over the shaft and shove it down farther with my palms. He shows me where the ramrod hides below the barrel. I slide it out and force the pole down onto the oilcloth, but Ogun stops me before I ram it too many times. Don't want to damage the ball. I prime it by pulling the hammer halfway back to put a primer cap in the slot. The gun is noticeably heavier when I pick it up, heavy enough to use a punt for the muzzle. The oil mixes with worry, all over my hands.

With the hammer pulled all the way back now, it is strange to imagine what shooting this thing might do. Ogun stops smiling, points again. I picture the elephant's skin wrapped tight around a plastic body.

Like the fourteen killers before me, I aim dead on and walk up to the cage. Her tusks clink sharply on the bars while she blocks out gray beams from the skylights. Look an elephant in the eye, the flecked mud pupil tucked behind those deep wrinkles and lashes, and tell me you don't feel God's foot making His mark on the land, stepping down on your lungs. Elephants are why He made the oceans.

I hold the gun level and look down at the small sight on the end of the barrel. The elephant, blurry with my one eye closed, turns and looks straight back at me. The forehead is ridged like a walnut shell. I remember the first time I skinned a cottonmouth, when I pricked my hand on the fangs before I'd milked the venom, and how I was sure that I'd be dead before sundown. Waiting for the poison to take effect clawed my nerves with the same feeling I have now. I keep one eye closed and fire.

A huge cone of flame from the barrel's end lights up the whole damn barn but the elephant's head turns away. My shot strikes her heavy ear bent back, and rips straight through the thin, venous layer into the right side of her head. At once I am guilty. She rears back on her hind legs and the trunk nearly curls itself into a lariat loop knot. Blood runs down the side of her body in this long streak of unnatural black and a cloud of noxious smoke rises around us.

The elephant comes down on all fours and brings me to my knees with the thunder. The kickback has winded me. I gasp and steady myself while she rushes around the tight perimeter of her cage, her head bent down to the right. Her tusks catch on the bars and twist her head around even more in a sickening, serpentine way.

Ogun shouts, "Load! Shoot again!" He throws me the rhino horn. I pour more sloppy capfuls of gunpowder down the barrel, spilling everywhere, and then I push another oilcloth in. The elephant charges suddenly and throws her bloody side into the bars that rattle like they're coming apart. I shove the ball down with the ball starter and ramrod, probably smashing the bullet into an ugly new shape. Between deafening roars, the beast whips her trunk against the iron and the gray skin breaks open in a spray of blood that coats me. She drives her blunt forehead forward. She tries to squeeze through the bent bars, her long tusks stretched in opposite directions, brutish and determinedly violent. She will kill herself before I can.

At the cage, I pull the hammer back and aim again. She runs around the square, and when she faces me I fire with both eyes open. Beyond the flameburst and smoke, her forehead opens but she does not drop. She must be blind from the blood that runs down her face. I load, walk closer, and fire again.

The lead drives deeper, same spot, and the elephant shudders suddenly backward. She sways and knocks her gaping wounds against the crooked iron. The sweltering barn goes quiet. She vomits thick, dark waste as the day is ending, and a small, greedy young man has just forced an elephant to her knees.

Legs buckle, the head hits ground first, and the whole Lowcountry shakes. The trunk, a dirty mess, is trapped and ripping under her side. I drop the gun. I cannot stop staring. I have ruined part of the hide, ruined myself in the process.

Ogun comes to stand beside me in front of the cage. A part of me feels caught beneath the dying mass, and it remains there, stuck, grabbing at light or air or skin. Ogun tells me, "Good."

He says he will not watch me skin it; he knows our superstitions. No one can look at the hide before it's done else it'll spoil. If the skin spoils, so does the worker, and then there's nothing left for him but to return to obscurity. Taxidermy's all a curse, but it gets its claws in you. You don't work with carcasses for thirty-five years without knowing that all animals have a soul.

Ogun leaves me in the barn with the elephant. Blood pools on the dusty ground, runs out of the cage, and meets my boots. I pick up my foot and then put it back down. My shoulder still hurts, but the jolt from the gun has not broken any skin or jilted any bone. It has only re-injured an old scar, a dormant bruise from carrying my heavy sack across the evening marsh.

The carcass is still warm. It's unfortunate the elephant had to die in the cage, but the hide will come off wherever it falls. I pace four steps back and forth and look at the body, and the more I stare the more I imagine her entire herd collapsing in a great elephants' graveyard far away from here. The man who taught me taxidermy would have already thrust my hand into the elephant's mouth to feel that tongue grow cold while the tusks lie in the straw. In a way, I am skinning it for him, to show him I did not forget what the lynx's insides felt like that first time. It's not a job I want, but a secret that, in wake of killing this beast, needs to be unearthed.

The skinning process is a long one, and the only experience I have with projects bigger than bucks is from working on Mr. Winterset's state-record-setting sow, a beauty of a pig with a belly that dragged along the ground like the porker had swallowed an iron lung.

My set of eight knives, a pile of plaster and burlap, opened oil and paint cans with the labels scratched off—I stack them all around me. I use the carving knife for the first cut into the neck, but the blade breaks and leaves its point buried. The skin is up to two and a half knuckle-lengths thick at the backbone and around each knee. I have to use a serrated handsaw to break through the skin, and it makes jagged lines, like crude stitching. The bleeding slows. The body's acrid smell deadens my senses and I can only think about each section I'm peeling away, not the animal as a wasted whole.

I cut the skin into seven sections, each one spreading as long as my arm span. The head comes off easily with incisions through the throat's thin jacket and behind the tall ears, after which I use a fleshing knife made from an old rasp to uniform the neck's edges without shearing away too much. The tearing is a sound I am not used to hearing for so long in one sitting and it unsettles me as the smoke dissipates. Resting on its severed end, the head's brown eyes go glassy. I crouch beside it. Fake eyes, dead eyes, tend to follow me around a room, like they want to do the same things to me that I've done to them. I push the shredded ear forward to cover up the baleful eye and save the head for later.

But when I reach the tender belly, I draw my knife down the stomach's middle and the skin opens up like spicebush petals. An underdeveloped calf rolls out, the size of a sago palm, still steaming. I fall back too, rolling on my side like the fetus, immediately feeling those lynx ligaments wrapping around my throat. The splashing of blood and birthing liquid reminds me of oil boiling on the range and I am afraid my skin will burn away if it touches the overflow. The elephant is, was, a parent, and the realization hardens my insides as if they too held an infant waiting to be sliced out.

I hold my mouth closed. I have never worked on a pregnant animal before, and the fetus's body has just begun to take final shape. The darkened form is still soft and jelly-like. The trunk is tucked in against its neck, with two bare slits at the end that are closed like eyes. Each ear is the size of my hand, but curls in on itself, crenulated and wilted. No long protrusions split its mouth, and I feel an urgency to pry open its lower jaw and run my fingers over the tiny ivory deposits. It resembles Mr. Winterset's hog but looks even more alive with all the lifeblood that runs down the small belly and gives the illusion of breathing, sleeping. It's impossible to bring myself to carve two notches in the gun's shaft. The baby's skin wouldn't even fetch a look from other taxidermists: too young, too easily torn by hand. In the cage's iron-barred confinement, the animal reveals its use to me, or rather, demands that it cannot be wasted. The man who taught me taxidermy did not leave me as a rootless boy to drown at the foot of the spirit tree; I, not he, let that first shot fly into the walnut's furrows. And though I cannot pull the skin from the infant and trophy it, the animal requires a reverence befitting a family member, the same I displayed when I let my own father's ashes fly into the cabbage furrows behind our farmhouse. I do not know how to do this again, and I'm afraid that it will haunt me for years, as the tree altar's shadow does the Sea Islands.

I push the baby to the haystack's other side. It leaves a wet, red streak on the ground. In the center of the barn, I draw chalk outlines for each section and arrange them in a long line.

Benzine goes on first. The fat-killer softens up the strands and pores. Then bending down on my knees over a skin segment, I begin to scrape with a currier's knife. My left hand on the horizontal handle, my right on the vertical one, all in an effort to shave the red and white inner layer down to a quarter-inch. When I move and adjust, my hands leave well-defined handprints in the sponge, even my fingerprint whorls, and so I work to cut myself out of the fat. Here are my tools, in the flesh. The more I try not to think about the unborn calf, the deeper I dig, two inches at a time, a long siege of grating.

Now it is night. I stand and cross myself, though that may draw His attention even more. I do not trust sleeping beside the mother's organ pile or the sere calf in the straw. For the duration of the night, with oil lanterns hung on support beams, I sprinkle sawdust on each of the mother's skins and paint them with tanning liquor from an earthenware jar and some of Old Dr. LePage's Liquid Hair Remover. One streak each. Repeat one inch to the left and then to the right.

By noon, I have rinsed every pore with mineral water and borax. The skin has whitened. My own arms are flushed and every muscle feels raked by scratch awls as the sleepiness and the repetitive cuts and brushes leave me delirious. I only sit down when I can no longer breathe over the strong chemicals. The calf is deteriorating, and I cannot keep my eyes off the rounded, toeless feet or the underdeveloped trunk that looks like a roll of wet dough ready to be baked in a furnace. The tanning liquor's odor and smelling salts keep me awake, though I do not think I can ever sleep again. I want to finish this animal and clean myself with gas. The man who taught me taxidermy would feel ashamed to leave such work unfinished and the thought of his hand on mine, deep in entrails, is enough to forget that my legs are too tired to carry my own weight.

I walk out to my D-Series to retrieve the old tarp and then carry it back inside to shield the unborn calf from my sight and from the remains of the day.

I am famished. Even the rotting elephant meat looks good. I build a small fire with gas and straw and cook some of the mother's back legs. The blood sizzles off and the flames burn the muscle, but I still eat. It is a part of the job. The job is becoming me. I keep the bowels between me and the calf. It knows how shamefaced I am and how I avoid even glancing. Each tough, unflavored bite leaves another hole in the mother's body, and though my stomach is filling, there is an emptying hollow as well. The thieving sensation is like eating a part of my self or a part of my father, as I am now the only surviving member of this family. No barn owls are nesting in the overhead rafters, and I wish there were. Something natural needs to witness this and tell me, in low hoots, that I am not doing the Devil's work.

I loosen the skins with a thin coat of warm neatsfoot oil and stretch it between my arms as best I can. A day goes by and the only indication is the color of the calf, now a paler gray when I lift up the tarp. I check on it hourly, like a hen on its egg. I must sleep in the corner with the cage locked.

In the morning, I swear I am awakened by a noise. The canvas over the calf is still there, brown and ragged and stained with lacquer. I walk circles around it.

But instead of drying the mother's skin and building a framework, I drench the sections in more oil and stack them like cake layers. I wrap the infant in the tarp and hoist it into my arms, the only child

I've ever lifted. You learn to love the things you work on, like I do this calf. It's love that stuffs an animal, and fear that preserves it.

The head lolls out one end of the cover, and I keep the chin up as I head toward the door, but the tarp rips and the baby elephant falls through. Immediately I drop to my knees and wipe the dirt from its eyes, aware that my only other option is to use one of the skins. The calf's body fits perfectly into the natural pouch of its mother's hide. She will have to wait.

I strap the passenger seatbelt over the calf. I make sure the buckle clicks. Though I've never had a child, this feels strangely familiar. I am the new womb's keeper, and I will find it a home in the wild, not buried beneath sawdust and rotten crossbeams.

Hunting Island. The Baobab tree's shadow reaches far across the wheat grass where the red trunk sticks out of the marsh like a barbed fishhook. The calf lies between my elbows. My boots stick to the rising tide mud and come off. I wade shin-deep, in socks, through a sea of cold entrails and thin, waving femurs. The baby fat of the calf sticks to my skin and pulls at me.

I cannot count all of the holes I've dug in the roots' circle, nor how many times the moon has drawn the water up and washed my burials away. I take slow steps toward the tree's broad chest. A deer skull, antlers broken off, jaw hanging by a socket, perches on a limb. It watches me, just as the tree, moon, and calf do. I set the calf against the trunk and dig without a word.

I unearth stones and fish ribs and bird bones. The soggy hole grows as wide as a deer bed. The gnarled tree looms. I lift the nearly translucent calf, whose weight is now nothing, and I wrap its head in skin and I set my unborn down in the cavity. I nod at the deer skull. It says I have reached the roots, but I have not climbed inside. It tells me to find a decent animal and love it.

Solemnly, I push mud back into the emptiness. The top layer of dirt spreads like ash. The oyster bed's sludgy water soaks my socks and cakes my bare ankles. Out from the bog, I walk without my shoes and feel the natural ground give way. I wonder how long the skin will preserve the calf.

On the drive back to the barn, I try to forget the child. I listen to a truck driver on the CB: a man, singing to his dog, moans softly, *You stole every bone of me and built a house in the yard, I had no cup for the buttermilk, me, your only kennel guard.*

It is not clear if the animal has died or run away.

I sit next to the stack of skins with hands on my head. My throat has dried up since yesterday, and now I spit out burs. Ogun will return to the barn today to find that, with one section gone, I cannot build the same elephant. I am ruined.

The entrails are decomposing into dried bubbles. The head still points skyward. Where the calf once curled up, ghostly flour now stains the ground. I spread more smelling salts under my nose. I have to finish because I owe the elephant my devotion, and because I know I cannot finish.

In the middle of the slowly warming barn, I construct an armature of the now smaller body. I trowel plaster across stiff wire netting. Every leg I make, the elephant becomes less real to me, and the struggle to make it come alive worsens.

Deep orange slurry melts down my arms as I spread molding clay across the netting until only the neck's gaping hole remains.

The skin fits back over the clay with little sagging at the stomach and thighs. I am putting together the ghost of an elephant; I am bottling something back up. The work is hard, but goes quickly. My arms do not stop moving and I breathe through my mouth.

Taking off the skin, I build layers on the sections' insides. I mix quick-drying plaster Paris, wet wood pulp, and LePage's oil in a bucket I'd once used when I was a boy to carry heron eggs. They all broke before I made it home to my mother. I wanted to drain the yolks and save the shells, just as I try now to build a larger shell. More screen wire and papier-mâché and shellac that must wait to dry. I wipe my face on the pachyderm's rough, furrowed back. There are pieces of me in that skin, and I am glad because it is proof that I've remembered since the beginning what hides inside an animal.

Red and black cow ants weave their way into the cage and tear away scraps of offal. I stitch the skin, piece by piece, with a long sacking needle and fishing line. The work goes quick, too, as the gray skin comes sutured together, guided by string. The body forms: feet, legs, stomach, back, tail. It's a headless wonder. Evening arrives and I have expected the barn door to slide open on its rusted track all day. The faster I go, the more I believe I will never be done.

My own limbs hang on threads. A hunch bulges in my back. Tanning oil and papier-mâché coat my skin and clothes to form a hard cast around me. I have built an armature of myself, with me still alive inside, but I do not scrape it off.

There, behind the belly's new skin, is the shadow of a curled-up infant. It's right there inside the shell I've constructed, and I imagine the twenty-two months culminating in a hot, wet season birth. The gray ghost of the baby elephant floats down from the mother's womb and wobbles in muggy pink afterbirth. The ghost sifts through my fingers like bone dust, and the elephant's body has never looked more hollow. Shadows of clouds move across the skylight like the elephant's profile. The crooked branches of the spirit tree reach all the way from the island marsh to scratch the barn's glass panes and reach their fingers under the walnut walls. Something outside is sloshing and knocking on the wood. Even the red tree trunk blocks out the sun and may do so forever. I am the only man, I bet, to bury one elephant and build another with the same pair of hands.

But I let something out that wasn't ready to touch open air. It isn't about moving skin anymore. I have to put something back, and not just back into the land of the trembling earth, at the base of the spirit tree, but back into the elephant. I used to think it was the elephant's life I had to re-insert through the needle holes, though that life is now gone and buried on Hunting Island. The mother's open neck begs to be filled, like so many holes I've dug, all those creatures I've dressed, boiled, tanned, stretched thin, soaked in gasoline, scraped the fat from, filled with plaster and putty and climbed all the way inside.

I hold the head, scraped clean. The ears have wilted like orange rinds. All the animals I've ever buried are pressing themselves against the barn, every one of them skinless, their amorphous bodies seeping through the cracks. The spirit tree pushes them through.

I throw a spool of fishing line into the mother's stomach. A sacking needle sticks out from between my front teeth, and I use it to quickly stitch the head to the nape of the neck. I never turn around. All over, the skin tries to regain some lost color. The lynx outside growls shrilly but I keep my hands on the elephant's head and neck. A steady heartbeat starts up behind me and rumbles beneath the baying. Above them all, the worst noise is this sudden trumpet—the first noise such an animal has ever made—and it bears mourning that I will never be able to understand. The buried come for me, like children back to a mother.

I hold my breath, grab the trunk and lift, and climb inside the smaller elephant. And so the neck swallows me whole.

It is pitch black and utterly silent inside—perhaps the rattling spirit tree has pushed me in here. But I find the seam between the body and giant head. You have to sew it from the inside out so the thread never shows. It takes an hour to seal the head up entirely and when I pull the last thread through, the needle drops. The longest breath of my life issues out.

I lie in the belly. I curl up. I feel my own rigid skin forming.

My nose, in the dark, departs from my face. It elongates bands of muscle. My ears bat against me and can now cover my eyes. Palms and foot arches flatten and widen. I am thirsty for the wet season. But I do not believe the transformation until I open my mouth and touch the upper incisors. They are growing. They are more than just milk teeth. They become weapons.

Lee K. Abbott

Youth on Mars

In the latter eighth of the century, Kirby Puckett was our most famous revolutionary. He was renowned, particularly, for his verse, which was arch as death itself. In De Funiak Springs (in the old Republics of West Florida), hours before battle, he read from his second publication, *The Unity of Philosophical Experience*. He alluded to avatars and privation. Flanking him, clad in skins, stood his lieutenants: Al-Ali Khadary, his expression suggesting squalor and sloth, was from Dallas and was said to be crafty with poisons and large numbers; the other, Ernie Witt, his hair wild as winter, was an expert in woe.

"What are we," Kirby was saying, "but a plucky material that yammers and haunts from below? Rise, people. Join me in advocating rapture."

Around him, their sweaty hopeful faces lit by dozens of flickering torches, were his guerrillas. They cradled ancient Uzis and M-16s and Jetfire .25s, plus weapons which had once belonged to Vandal and Ostrogoth. Kirby saw cudgel and club, broadax and arrow. Many of his followers, including the women, had been with him since Little Rock, the months in the steamy deltas; they had been wooed by sentiment, as well as by metaphor and a senator's voice. Dozens had adopted names from his works: Plexor, Telugu, 0 City of Broken Dreams; all had ambitions to be the vaunted objects he put into poems: mottle, rifts, angels that ate.

"This is 'Flesh for Fantasy,'" he announced. "It is a sonnet and you may sing along." It recounted his experiences among the Mung, the GDF, the Kansas Khmer.

Yonder, beyond this clearing and the woods, he could hear his enemies. Occasionally, a word came on the wind: "epicure," "jejune," "ectomorph." Twice a phrase: "outcry and clamor." Once, in a moment grave as those which used to attend money, he heard a complete sentence whose theme was the origin, nature, method and limit of human knowledge. Clearly, they were a choleric people—disobedient as weather, single-minded as insects.

"My people," Kirby said at last, "this is my last battle."

He waited for the wailing to cease.

"I'm tired," he said. "I am through with foment and our disgruntlement. I intend to roam about and he up in places free of discord."

There were tears and displays of self-scourging, but Kirby hushed his people with a smile. He felt nothing, as if his organs were dry-frozen and fractured. He ordered his vehicle brought to him, a Buick from the olden days, substantial as the earth itself, its grillwork bright as daytime.

"Go," he directed, "vanquish and be free."

There was another roar, this in concert and serious as thunder.

"These men will lead you now," he said, embracing his pals Witt and Khadary. "They are like me, updrawn and always busy."

In his travels, he met the many who were afoot in those days: the Virgins of Albuquerque, datu bikers, a tribe of females allied with the Clytemnestra cults, the itinerant and gelatinous, carnivores, essentialists, purdahs and moujiks, knaves and their libertine masters. They wore plastics and leathers, some disguised as furniture or states of mind achieved in sleep. Their headgear fascinated: feathers for ideas, rickrack and crewelwork, metals that had meaning.

Near the ruins of Baton Rouge, a group of black men on horses stopped him. They wielded barongs and identified themselves as the progeny of several running backs for the old New Orleans Saints.

"What is the Grammar of Assent?" they demanded.

They had wounds and appeared intractable as perdition.

"It is folly," Kirby said. "Your dispute is with the scoundrels of Pittsburgh. "

"And Cleveland," they said.

Kirby reminded them about the pashas of Ford, their ermines and many mates.

"You must be Kirby Puckett," they said. "What is your advice?"

Kirby studied their mounts, their artful hairdos. The air in this part of the world was thick, heavy as history itself.

"Go willingly to the end of a thing," he said. "Be jocular. Avoid the wistful. Practice horseplay. Reproduce. I recommend human delights. Remember, being is not different from nothingness."

They seemed to agree.

"These are dark times, white boy. *Adios.*"

Toward midnight, in a densely wooded rest stop on the old I-10 east of Dallas, Kirby was ambushed. There were six, including two teenagers dressed like rinderpest, and they made him squat with his arms overhead while, snarling and laughing, they sacked his Buick. They carried stones and had faces the color of parboiled beef.

"I wouldn't do that if I were you," Kirby said.

A woman eyed him with interest. She had a toothy smile which suggested rot and what it is to fly. "Why not?"

Kirby had two reasons.

"I had a mother, too," he said. "I was her nursling and made these noises: Goooo, gaaaaa. I appeal to you in the name of our common debt to biology."

Behind her crouched the teenagers. They were eating Kirby's favorite apparel, the smock with the stars and the far-off frosty moon.

"What's the other reason?" she wondered.

Kirby waved his hands. "These."

He possessed the coordination and temper of a welterweight, and in an instant his bushwhackers lay in a pile neat as cordwood.

"There is a moral to this," he said. "It has nothing to do with weal or shared uplift."

In Dallas, Kirby endeavored to establish residence in an abandoned movie theater near the shell of the old Cotton Bowl. Though dusty and crammed with refuse, the place still seemed as ornate as a doge's palace. Names were scribbled on the walls: Vico,

Octavio-V, Dante, Dr. Filth. In the balcony lived refugees from the PAC 10. They spoke the patois of many western provinces, including the San Fernando Valley and Las Vegas, a tongue in which it was impossible to be either explicit or too profound.

"We heard you was dead."

One inconceivably pale man had edged forward. He was wearing jewelry said to be favored in these parts by citizens named Ike or Spoon. They were a clan, Kirby knew, subject to the same ills as farm life: splints, ulcerated eyes, wolf teeth, spavin, founder and worms.

"I am in retirement," Kirby said. "I have forsaken the killing arts."

A chair was being burned for light, and among the flickering shadows were beings to which the word *ruin* might apply.

"How do we know it's you?" the man said. He held a weapon Kirby had never seen; its name was Boy, and it had the bristly pelt and wet teeth of a cur. "Read us a poem."

Kirby felt his heart squeeze into his throat. There were too many to fight, too few to die for.

"I have many poems," he said. "Which one?"

There was a debate. Some wanted "Baby Green's Evening in Paris," a tirade that ripped through the truth like grapeshot. Others wanted rhymes which addressed their current condition of disarray. In the back, noisy as nightmare, a fistfight broke out between those who desired poems of cognition and those preferring coitus. A barbed spear whistled through the air. From the darkness, someone was shouting, "Aaarrggghhh," and a garment red as sunset floated near the ceiling.

"May I suggest something for the rearmost of us," the man said. "Among us are the wrathful and mirthless."

Kirby held a sheaf of papers clotted with writing, which looked like what fowl might write.

Boy, the weapon, was making a strangled sound—part whimper, part growl.

"We like carnage," the man said, "and stuff that whizzes around making chatter."

Kirby sorted through his papers. He had everything: verses that mentioned toxins, puling from the ruling class, what the hearty hear when wishes wilt.

"'Familiar Usage in Leningrad,'" he began. It was his best work. In it, citizens frolicked and gamboled. Garlands were mentioned, as were greenswards and naughty trifles. Its hero—more than a little like himself, Kirby imagined—was called El-Dor and he had come to our planet from a more advanced civilization; he used words like "ilk" and "vault" and sought to deflect us from pain.

"Lovely," the man said. "Give us all a hug, please."

Later that hour, in tribute, his host sent him a woman.

"My name is Lana," she said. "I had grandparents who went to the University of Iowa. I once believed in grains and such advancements as iron and long-distance communication. Now I believe in haste, plus the places chemicals take me."

She had hair like straw and the thighs of a Hittite.

"What is it you do, Lana?"

Her outfit split open and she showed him. It was a male-female principle involving sweat.

"Very good," he said. She would be in his next work, which would have the shape of sense and make the ears bleed.

Through the autumn—six months of storms and rent heavens— he drafted his third book, *Puckett's Ontology, Cosmogony and Physics*. In it were insurrectos and the fumble-witted, those boisterous as riot, those gaunt with belief. He told the members of the Universal Remnant Church of God, who sometimes bunked in the balcony men's room, that it was like having the same child twice.

Once Lana asked him where he came from. There were many rumors about his childhood. Parents named Flo and Buster, for instance. An immaculate conception. Several miracles.

He didn't know. An image came to mind: a house, a yard, a tailwagging lapbrute that knew its name.

"They say you speak to bushes," she began. "You had a wife, we heard. There was mention of loaves. Of penury."

He was thinking of the beasts he'd seen in picture books: their matted fur, their scales, their blind pink eyes. He'd seen a fish once—

a trout, Ernie Witt had said—small and desiccated, murdered by a hundred holes. He'd seen a bird too. It didn't soar, as he was told it ought; instead, weighing over a hundred pounds, it lumbered and was cloaked in the outerwear of a nummulite.

"I hear Kirby isn't your real name," Lana was saying. Quite possible, he answered. In the northern wastes—the old towns of Minneapolis and St. Paul—he'd been ice itself: rimy and everywhere. In the deserts of the West, he tried to be like the indigenous flora: thorny and shriveled, a hook for hair to hang from.

"I like it when you're mystical," Lana said. "Here."

In a second she leaped atop him, heedless and moist, and the world was wealth again.

Later that season, Kirby was one of several speakers at the Cotton Bowl. In the full light of day, the crowd looked numinous and pulpy, food that could amble and say hello. There were representatives from all the sciences: disquiet, malice, lamentation. The delegation from Corpus Christi—where fires were thought to be still smoldering—wore foil on their ears and argued in behalf of a contracting universe. In the air you smelled the scent of these times: pitch and sulphur, a rain that glowed.

"Perhaps you have heard of me," the first speaker said. His name was Fork and it was claimed he had turned to philosophy from a related discipline, terror. From his neck dangled a sign, PLEASE STOP, and he wore rusty dropshank spurs. Kirby thought him the most serious man he'd ever seen.

"I have a number of observations to make," Fork said. He had a voice like a cat climbing a window, as well as apparent pain under the wishbone. "First: Things will grow less intelligent as time wears on. Second: The next era will be like the last—a cycle of assertion and disjuncture."

Kirby liked desperados who knew their own minds. "Third," Fork said, "like ground fog, our confusions will disappear. Something has a plan for us. I hope it is good."

The next speaker, a man named Saint Teresa of Avila, was as broad-backed as a bear. He affected the outfit of a monodist and spoke of felons and nightsoil.

"I too have had other lives," he said. "A king knew me; likewise the maids of his court. I may have been a sailor, as I find myself quite festive near fluids. I have always been holy."

There was a weak sun somewhere—perhaps directly overhead, but Kirby couldn't be sure.

"In the afterlife," Saint Teresa continued, "my aim is to shimmer and flit about, being cheerful."

Thoroughly polite applause greeted Kirby when he reached the podium. There were thousands at his feet, all hollow-eyed and semigorgeous. Some looked familiar—perhaps from the campaigns in the Tennessee hills. Kirby felt he could have been gazing at ash or comparable vermiculite matter.

"In the old days," Kirby began, "I was bombed and paid meat to shoot back." His voice echoed into the yellow, parched geography beyond. "I was a youth then, living elsewhere with people named Butch and Congressman Red Sorrell, and impressions were made. I shunned inquiry into the spirit of things. I had two cohorts, Witt and Khadary. We learned to crawl and fake stupidity. We read books about venery, about edible grasses. All night our lanterns burned. We were taught the assassin's skills—the walk, the gesture that says little is amiss. We learned disguise—plant, old-timey farmer, agreeable states of mind. We became familiar with loathsomeness, with chills. We fashioned weapons from the impractical and the discarded. Footwear, texts, credulity. We could imitate certain fowl, as well as habits of thought. When we left, Butch gave us sloppy kisses and mementos. Mine was the moral and political authority of literature."

In the east rose darkness and unfriendly noise.

"That is how I became a cutthroat," he said. "Goodbye."

That week, a woman knocked at the door of the projectionist's booth Kirby often used as an office. Her costume, webbed belts, large snaps, mail and coarse hair, had all the charm of peonage.

Kirby felt a muscle snap free in his chest.

"I know why you've come," he said.

He'd had a dream: decline, goo that once looked sapient.

Witt and Khadary, she said, were dead. Balazos, falling sky, night.

"When?" Kirby asked.

Weeks ago. Maybe a month.

"Where?"

Florida, she said. That place he'd left.

"How?"

Bile, she said. Skullduggery, underhandedness.

That evening, Lana sought to comfort his head and lower parts.

There was a code of honor, he said. The code applied to every feature of daily activity: betrayal, calumny, piety, etc. It was prescriptive, detailed as needlework.

"What will you do?" she asked.

On this issue, the code was usefully specific. He was to purify himself. Abstract into the realm of fact. Keep the weep out of his voice. Make his cerebration simple as the four winds. When this was completed, he was to gather an army and—in the argot of the deep past—kick ass.

Within hours, fighters had begun assembling. They were what he expected and deserved: the otiose, hooligans from the hinterworlds, a group of Bay City Orientals quiet as cats, those with the deportment of fifth-century pirates, many from the netherparts of natural worship.

"They're beautiful," Lana said.

Kirby selected one to interview. He had the absurd and painful-looking bones of a pulsator.

"Why have you come?"

Dust fell from the man's shoulders. He knew Kirby's publications, he said. Their sweep, their purl. Besides, there was doing this or, worse, dying slowly.

To a second, the same question. In another life, this hombre could have been a stone. "Me too," the volunteer said, "sweep and purl."

To a third, the question again. This time with additions: "Think of the ways you yourself could die-puncture, lacerations, heartbreak."

"What can I tell you?" the man said. "I heard the story, I got aroused."

By daybreak, they were on the road, hundreds of them, nearly as formidable as that regiment he'd driven into Birmingham years ago. Once again, Kirby was amazed at the shapes we came in: portly, robust, craven, slumped. There was a principle in this, he knew. It concerned the spirit and where hope lurks.

"I have in mind another work," he told Lana. "It will be true and last forever."

All morning they marched. Some of the old songs went up: "0 Youth and Beauty," "Just Tell Me Who It Was." Few were in automobiles. Some rode scooters. Dozens had scrambled aboard an airplane without wings. Eyewear was popular: goggles, glasses, sunshades, sleep masks with holes. Many had modeled themselves after the legendary heroes of the former orb: Agamemnon, Batygh the Tartar, Captain Ahab. Those with beards were regarded as blissful, in touch with a more earnest mission.

"I had a vision such as this," Kirby told Lana. In this vision, there was menace overcome, and plunder. Sacrifice led to reward, love to joy. People spoke and were listened to. Respect extended from mammals up and down the chain of being. Gobbledygook was considered piquant but harmless. The lightsome was preferred to its opposite, and everyone moved at very high speed.

"I had that, too," Lana said, "only more so."

At bivouac, a brilliant wind came up. A cold, balsamic smell was in the air. Rubble was near and yon. Kirby remembered his history. First was the age of burdened beasts—quadrupeds and willing man. Then an age of cleared land: water flowed where it ought. The machine age. Then, most recently, the age of sadness and throng.

"Now," he told Lana, "is the time of the self-fortified and those the victim of shame."

Toward midnight, a spy was discovered. He looked like something that might eat its young, and it took four brigands to subdue him.

"What is your name?" Kirby asked.

The man had the disposition of a hammer. He used a vocabulary of graphic violence, then endeavored to break free to maim them all. His name was Jerome and he had ridden with the Redlegs, an ad hoc group of mongers from Missouri.

"I have heard of you," Kirby said. "I'm told you have good sense and a way to do mayhem painlessly."

Jerome was parts scorn and arrogance. He had a way, he said, of doing it gruesomely and often.

"Bring him closer," Kirby commanded.

Howling and wriggling, Jerome was dragged forward. At this distance, it was possible to smell him. There was a sweetness, like decay, which could have been fear. Or ignorance of it.

"How had you hoped to hurt us?" Kirby asked.

Jerome delivered a wonderful speech. It concerned disrepair and puddles the crushed viscera make. It drew upon documents from the lost age—*The Critical Heritage, The Drama of Human Relations*—to fetch up a world of small deeds swiftly performed. There were subtleties too: time and what mortifies. He offered to be to Kirby what pestilence had been to our forebears. He could be blight, a plague of frogs, murrain. When he finished, defiant and outraged, he was less than a foot from Kirby.

"My specialty is massacre," Jerome said. "I aim to be like you, but without all the chitchat."

They were at that point where one man is inclined to slay another.

"You're in a bad position here," Kirby said.

Jerome used the words "perdurable" and "wreckage," then showed everyone his wet, pointed teeth.

There was an exchange of earnest expressions. Kirby thought he saw something familiar in Jerome's eyes. Kindredness, perhaps.

"Let him go," Kirby ordered. "I feel generous tonight."

As Jerome plunged into the wilderness, Kirby had one question: What is man? And one answer: Three or four colors, an instinct to breed life, plus remorse at the loss of it.

Near the end of their trek, Kirby had occasion to lecture his people on combat. Even in death, he said, war was about living.

Clouds like flatirons rose out of the distance, and in the breezes hung particles gritty as granite. The terrain was a dreamscape of precipice and butte, bluffs and thawed tundra. In the formations of boulders could be seen faces and what the previous generation of addlement had achieved. One rock in particular, tilted toward the horizon and mammoth as a building, resembled chaos itself: split and gouged, with little to cling to.

Kirby remembered one firefight especially. His first, he said, in the leafy country in what used to be northern Arkansas. Like those that followed, it trafficked in tumult and shudder, rupture and din. With him were Khadary and Witt, youths as well. They wore the appropriate garb, camouflage, tight as skin; they were to be conifers, erect and healthy. The secret words were "chapel" and "moonbeam," and they fell upon the bad guys like night itself.

"We were stealth," he said, "as natural as calamity."

In his audience now were those dressed as a wise, scurrying species. Bushlamps gave them all a rapt look.

Chief among his weapons that night had been a righteous frame of reference. Plus foresight.

"We anticipated everything," Kirby said. "Who crept where, what to ponder when it was done, how to exit."

Kirby recalled his thoughts—the few which could be uttered: fall down, shoot, jump up, be sufficiently furious, shoot, flop down again. Intensely aware of his body, he had addressed his innards as you would slaves you depend on. Heart, beat on; brain, be serious; guts, be still. There were feelings too—ponderous as tides, and rampant: alarm and shock, tremors that were thrills.

For a time, he remembered, mere panic prevailed. Foliage was shredded. These were the sounds you heard: thump, whack, wail and profound disillusionment. Light spun in chunks, splinters, shards. Hoots, laughter, the groans the fragile have. The night had heft; thoughts, hue. Then order was found. A voice barked "Go" and several humans lurched to obey it. You heard clatter, steady as breath, and brigados scuttling beneath it. Hysteria, stampede, pleas from beyond—these were noted. Once something ragged limped by, waxen and mumbling. It was a thinking meat, now thinking less. "What do I know?" it said. "I am foolish and just want to be old." Kirby heard a wet cough, and another fellow was hurled headlong into an outer, eternal darkness. Then the ground quit trembling and the night was quiet as a tree stump.

Kirby thought he saw shapes—possibly those common to nightmare.

"Chapel," he whispered, "moonbeam."

A second later the proper reply: "We have divinity. Light is everywhere."

It was Witt and Khadary, and Kirby had flown to them in a flash. They were wet-faced and grinning.

"Such is battle," he now concluded, "crunch and a great drying up in the interiors. Then there is joy."

Stinging rains fell the next day. And the next. Machines sputtered, failed. Several pack animals toppled over from exhaustion. A few fighters deserted, in one case leaving behind a note, conceived as a fairy tale, which addressed indolence and how, in the context of the discarnate, one was to live.

"I am cold," he told Lana one night. "Squeeze me."

She was strong and had knowledge of the tender joints.

The next day, the sun came up bleak and distant as heaven. Kirby remembered old, odd things: spades for digging, voluptuaries for being kind to, dank climes to leave. By afternoon, it had begun drizzling again, constant and fine as needles. Words came to mind: *tissue, crater, melt.*

"Lana," he said, "what would you do if I died?"

She had the posture of a queen. Mourn, she said. Then go elsewhere, for another.

"How long would that take?" he wondered.

"A week," she said, "possibly less."

That night he suffered dreams—of plains and such seas as heroes ply. He remembered being small and hungry, an orphan. He had learned a lesson from his mentors, Butch and Congressman Red Sorrell. It concerned demise, what it is to flee this mool. One aimed to have an idea, Butch said, then act immediately upon it. He provided examples—humility, cleverness, the usual vices—each a method for affecting one's circumstance. Congressman Red Sorrell advocated the direct approach: wrath, radical demeanor. Reflection was for those who followed, not for those who stood apart and screamed.

In the morning he dressed in gold, a textile shiny and slick as glass. A title had come to mind: *Youth on Mars*. It was himself, he believed, removed, indifferent as truth.

"On the one side," he told Lana, "is swill, an accumulation of objects, dismay."

"What's on the other?"

He smiled. "Me."

That day, his tropas marched with dispatch. He encouraged them to concentrate on the zany, the subversive. "Avoid nostalgia," he counseled, "it trivializes and saps the fighting juices." As his partisans moved through southern Alabama, he visited with small groups, shaking hands. He liked their costumes— their skins, their whichaway plumes and chestgear. "Convert," he told them, "have a notion, then realize it." Once he spoke through a bullhorn. Standing atop his Buick, he watched them trudge past. They were an array, motley and euphoric like a mob. "Be muscular of mind," he said, "exercise against the inert weight of the past." In this part of the country, the sky was orange, as if filtered a thousand times. It was a fine sky, vast and parlous as themselves. "Be proud," he advised, "you are ooze which speaks and often renews itself."

From his final bivouac, he sent out scouts.

"Be a shadow," he told them, "be a root."

They made affirmative sounds, stood at attention.

"Be dust," he said, "be a cloud."

Hours later they returned. Kirby could hear his enemies clearly now. Sprawled like one of the old cities, they were noisy and near.

"What are they?" Kirby asked.

His foes were the usual sort, one scout reported. Stiff with rage, eyes frenzied, unreconciled minds. They had a million disguises: glory, promise, lower states of mind.

"What weapons have they?"

Another fighter stepped forward. He had watery eyes and the expectant look of a pet.

They used noxious vapors, he said. Plus coils and slings, contraptions which flung stones over sizable distances, a command of fire, fertile imaginations.

"And what have we?"

The man drew himself up with pride.

"Humbug," he said, "and ire."

Through the twilight hours, while Kirby labored at his verses, there was a star shower, glowing streaks flashing thither. Beside him sat Lana, toying with her pistol and its four slugs. Names from his past reached him: Pesto, the Great Humongous, Virgil. These brought forward yet more: Butcher, Nod, X. It was a trail which, if followed, would lead backward into yore, a time of mists and smoky nights and swamps and the kind of misrule which sped hithermost on two legs, its shaggy head crowded and heavy with fear. Yore, Kirby knew, was a time like this.

"I am not scared," Lana said.

"What is the matter?"

"Nothing," she insisted. "I can't get my leg to stop shaking." She looked delicious—an accomplishment with teeth and rare talents. He would miss her one day.

"What should I do after I slay them all?"

Do as he did, he confessed. Hide away and celebrate.

His musicians woke him at dawn. It was a thrill to hear brass and string in the service of peril. Rain had fallen during the night, and everything—beast, human, invention—was sheathed in ice. The hill in the distance, behind which his enemies were massed, glittered and sometimes looked like fire.

"This is a good omen," he said.

Lana was in the back seat, sorting through his outfits.

"What will you wear?" she asked.

He could be anything: pantologist, bronco buster, gent with a god.

Raiments, he said. Robes and many vests.

"In honor of this event," he told his people as they assembled, "I have written another lyric. Later will be the time for singing." He felt calm, as apart from this adventure as Witt and Khadary were apart from life. He could be standing meters away, he believed, his arms crossed and most amused, saying, *Kirby Puckett, my-my, you have come some ways since infancy.*

"For now," he said, "let us go forth and slaughter."

. . . .

Early into the battle, after his people had tumbled screeching and yammering down the hillsides into the encampments below, Kirby believed he heard a loudspeaker or a radio. There were few in operation in these days; of those who did operate, most dealt in zealotry and affliction. This one now was speaking of sluts and man's due in discontinuous times.

Through his spyglass, Kirby watched his legions swarm and trample. He saw a turmoil of chair legs, fence posts, machetes. He saw one of his fiercest fighters—identifiable by his rictus grin and evident need to please—charge headlong into a group. He was a tornado, furious and lashing. Close by stood Lana, in a Calabar frock and bandana. She was shouting, too, and making flesh heave over in a heap. Kirby could read her mind. Flee me, it was saying, I am Kirby's product and not at all merciful.

"This is perturbation only," the voice on the loudspeaker was saying. "Repel and trounce."

Kirby surveyed the opposite hills. Cudweed, shrubs, char. "Worry them, citizens," the voice was shrieking. "Cause them to drift and cry out."

Kirby could see little but ravaged trees—twisted and uprooted and blasted—and clogged earth. Perhaps they had a poet, too, he thought. A man like himself: slender and determined, but empty on the inside.

He spun his attention to the right: over there was flame and terror composed into men. On the left, Lana, hair like a storm. He read her lips: *This could be over in minutes, or maybe days.*

"Be not forlorn," the voice was saying, "hit, hit, hit."

Kirby held the spyglass steady. Slow, he reminded himself. Anxiousness is for the slack-brained. Breathe, he told himself. In. Hold. Wait for insight. Count. Listen. Out. A fireball shot up, like a sun in collapse, and for an instant he was blinded. Wait, he thought. Relax. Concentrate. Think. Life is meet. Think again. One, two, aaaahhhh.

So there it was: a ramshackle house trailer, painted green and dirt brown and set into the slope. Very cunning.

"What are you?" Kirby whispered. He knew the voice, its whine, its furor.

A second later, he had located the loudspeakers and between them, mostly hidden in a lacework of shadows, the speaker himself. Jerome.

"How nice," Kirby said, "I favor things which come to an end."

His organs turned over, shook. He could feel his heart slamming into his ribs, the stomach tightening like a fist.

"Rise up, my people," Jerome was hollering. "Hurl yourselves into them!"

There was an idiom for this, Kirby knew. It was swift, vulgar, and true.

Struggling down the slope, his footing made treacherous by mud and debris, Kirby remembered his first woman. She had been much, much older, with a name which suggested beauty—April? Linda?— and it was said she had been a girl in the years of Heat and Great Darkness. She had scars and hair like mold. Loving her, Kirby decided, was like knowing the world's first primate.

In the valley itself—between, in fact, a shack of beaten corrugated tin and a breastworks of sandbags—Kirby's Orientals, grinning mysteriously and babbling, went racing past. They were dragging mattresses and buckets, old-fashioned grips and weathered luggage. "Shit," they were muttering, dispassionate and sullen. "Shit."

"What did you find?" Kirby asked.

"All goddam stuff," one said.

They showed him: petrol cans, a desk, toilet articles.

"What will you do with it?"

The man spit. "Who goddam knows!"

Off they scrambled, pointing and grabbing.

Nearby, a scout, the one with the dark eyeballs and the tragic aspect, was spinning in ragged circles, arms fluttering. "Pillage," he was saying. "Displace." It was an A-B-C recitation like that which schoolchildren had once upon a time to sit through. He nodded, thoughtfully, began anew: "Hobble, incrust, wander." Kirby noticed that the voice, Jerome, had stopped. All that could be heard was Kirby's former host at the abandoned Dallas theater scolding his weapon, Boy. "Growl," he was saying, "charge, leap, bite, snap. Do it endlessly."

Kirby had a thought: turmoil. And another: uproar.

"This is my philosophy," someone was saying. The voice hailed from a long way off, perhaps a kilometer or more. "We should surrender ourselves to the underhalf of our natures. Eat and sleep, then find another venue to savage."

Kirby waited.

A motor was running: clank, thud, clank, thump.

A poplar tree disappeared in a whooshing geyser of flame. "I have a philosophy, too," another voice was saying. It was distant as well, and most reasonable. "There ain't no complex nature. Just such rigamarole as us."

Kirby watched three men pedal by on a bicycle. They seemed happy, undisturbed.

Behind him, an animal was loose and in pain. A gun went off— pssst, pssst, pssst—and then a man dashed up to Kirby, grabbed his hand. He was frenzied, a glaze of tears on his cheeks. The hem of his caftan was crusty and torn. He kept pointing to himself and spitting. He panted. He hollered for another minute, then vanished into the woods.

"Who was that?" Lana was positioned on a rock nearby.

"Fork," Kirby said, "from the Cotton Bowl."

"What did he want?"

To go home, Kirby said. People were trying to hurt him.

Lana nodded and bounded out of view. Again, Kirby stood alone, waiting. An image came to him: himself flopping about and heading rearward in time.

He touched his verses in his jacket pocket.

He wanted something to happen very soon and to be very important.

Ten giant steps away squabbled two men. "Yes," snapped one. "No," said his confederate. They slapped each other, hard, then hurried off, mumbling.

There was another principle here, Kirby knew. It addressed dither and such hugger-mugger as the fear-wrought make. And then came the familiar voice.

"Well, lookee here."

To one side, not a dozen paces away, stood Jerome in the outrageous sleepwear of a prince. He was wearing a fez, and with him were a dozen equally dark-minded attendants.

"I was expecting you," Kirby said.

Jerome executed a bow he was clearly proud of.

"These are my elite," he said. "Let me introduce them." They had not names but states of consciousness: Envy, Torpor, Vigilance, etc. They all excelled at behavior appropriate to disorder. They had bony, massive hands and appeared to enjoy their work.

"They must love you," Kirby said.

"I am loved everywhere. I inspire serious affection."

So this is how it will be, thought Kirby. I am to be slain by a youngster in love.

They had circled him now, Jerome in front, his eyes glistening. He had an ascetic's face: gray and blank with need. War, evidently, was food to him.

"Why are we doing this?"

A combination of reasons, Jerome said. Ennui, rigorism, the riffraff we are.

The sky was dark once more, like a bruise. It would rain in an hour. Nature, Kirby knew, could be especially impressive during clamorous times.

"I am told you were a real son-of-a-bitch." Jerome was using his hands like cleavers. "I used to have great admiration for you, truly. I was impressed, specifically, by your mongrelism and where it got you."

The battle proper was shifting away, into a glade several hundred meters distant. Hectoring and praising, Lana was directing his warriors. She looked jubilant. She was resolve and fury, plus such forces outlaws feel. Good, he thought. She will be the son-of-a-bitch now.

"Would you like to hear a poem?" Kirby brought out his manuscript.

"I think not," Jerome said.

"What is it you want to do to me?"

As before—now years ago, it seemed—Jerome told him. It was an entertaining five minutes. Havoc was discussed, as were the concepts of disunion and crypt-life. He mentioned melancholy and longing, firmaments and what creatures seem from a higher point.

"Now?" Kirby said.

Jerome nodded and his henchmen closed in like a claw.

Laura Benedict

Five Revelations Concerning Jenny L. As Told to Maura C. by a Compassionate Angel

By the time you and Jenny L. are halfway up the walk to her house, you know something is wrong. The curtains are drawn, making the house look sleepy. Closed. The lace panel beside the front door moves just an inch or so, as though someone is watching you but doesn't want to be seen. Jenny's mother Rita isn't a person to peek out of windows. Rita L. doesn't take time to peek. Rita L. is an RN who supervises thirty-five other nurses at the hospital. It's not a job that you would want, but she's supposed to be very good at it.

Jenny's fingers are sticky from the two jelly doughnuts she ate at the Krispy Kreme store, but you hold fast to her hand. Back in the minivan, your daughter Dickie and two other girls from the sleepover are waiting.

"Do you think your Daddy's home?" you say.

Jenny nods, the orange velvet bow she's borrowed from Dickie bobbing in her hair. "Daddy's sleeping," she says. "Saturday mornings we have to be quiet."

"Daddies need their sleep," you say. You know few details about Jenny's family, except that her father, Paul, and mother, Rita, both work at the hospital and are expecting another child, their fourth boy.

The door opens slowly and there is Rita, her hair pulled away from her face in a loose ponytail, her faded blue surgical scrubs taut against her pregnant belly. Her face seems to have aged ten years since she dropped Jenny off at your house the previous afternoon.

"Mommy!"

Jenny lets your hand drop and runs to the porch steps.

"I got a fairy wand. Do you want to see?" She lets her glittering Tinkerbell backpack fall and kneels to open it, her tiny fingers fumbling for the zipper.

You watch, anxious that delivering her home is going to take much longer than you thought. But she is so cute that you can't help but smile. You look from her to Rita, who is staring at Jenny and seems to be struggling to speak.

"Are you all right?" you say. There *is* something wrong and your first thought is that it must be the baby. Is she already in labor? The birth of a fourth child can come without warning: in a car, on a sidewalk, in a hospital corridor. Does she need a doctor?

For all her ungainly weight Rita springs forward, half-sliding the final few feet to the porch stairs so that she nearly knocks Jenny down.

"They killed Paul. They have the boys!" She picks up Jenny, who is too surprised to make a sound. But you can't move. The words make no sense to your brain. *Paul.* Her husband. It's *they* and *killed* that confuse you. And then you hear a popping sound and the concrete sidewalk shatters a few feet away from you.

You think of Dickie and how she tugged at your hair when she nursed. Even six years later you remember the sweet smell of your milk on her breath and her wet smile of delight when she pulled too hard, making you cry out.

Rita runs toward the street—toward the minivan—screaming for you to get help. A second *pop* like a cork from a magnum of champagne and you see Jenny fly out of Rita's arms and into the grass. She screams as she hits the ground, shoulder first, and you finally move. Somewhere ahead you hear Dickie screaming as well, but you know the sound of her voice well enough to understand that she is terrified, not injured.

Rita has fallen onto Jenny and you want to look back at the

porch to see who is there. You don't because it's all happening too fast and looking back is always dangerous and you think that if you don't, nothing will hurt you.

Jenny struggles and cries beneath Rita's weight and you're torn between getting to Dickie in the van and stopping to see why Rita isn't moving away with Jenny, why she isn't moving at all. You feel as though you could take them both your arms and carry them as far away as you need to—at least to the van where you could get them away from here.

You shake Rita's arm and beg her to get up, to run. But she is still. Her body limp, heavy. As you try to shift her, Jenny's cries block out every other sound. Her wispy blond hair is clotted with dark red matter and her face, also defiled, is white with terror.

But she is alive when you drag her from beneath her mother, whose precious blood is soaking back into the earth.

Jenny is alive.

II.

Doke has four bucks and an idea. He doesn't know if Vaughn will be into it because Vaughn is just as likely to wake up and be a candy-ass for the whole day as he is to be one of the scariest bastards Doke knows. Doke likes this about Vaughn. Vaughn is never boring, and Doke hates to be bored. When he was a little kid, his mother would have him wash windows or clean the toilets or the cat box if he complained about being bored and that entertained him for a while. But then he realized that his mother was just getting him to do her work and he stopped saying he was bored to spite her. He discovered other, more interesting things to do, which led her to complaining about *him*. And so there were times like now—times that were getting too frequent for his taste—that he finds himself thrown out of his basement room with only four or five bucks in his pocket and no place to sleep.

He lets himself into Vaughn's bedroom and finds him asleep beneath a navy blue down comforter and a couple days' worth of clothes. Sitting beside Vaughn's bed, he flips through a gamer magazine that he figures must belong to Vaughn's younger brother. It's possible that Vaughn himself was reading it. They aren't above kicking the crumb-crunching little bastard off the Xbox in the family room if Vaughn's old man isn't around to give them shit.

But today Doke is impatient and, after about five minutes of blahblahblah bullshit about new car models on some driving game, he accidentally-on-purpose slides his foot beneath the comforter and pokes Vaughn with the wicked-long nail on his right big toe.

"Why don't you just stick your hairy homo tongue down my throat?" Vaughn says, opening his eyes.

"Fucking faker," Doke says. He hates it when Vaughn says shit like that.

"Give me a smoke." Vaughn points to the dresser. "And that bottle of water over there."

Doke drops the magazine and leans back on the chair to reach the water. He pitches the bottle onto the bed and the cap rolls off, spilling water all over the blue jeans on top of the pile.

"That stuff is clean, asshole," Vaughn says. He sits up to grab the bottle before more can spill.

"We're out of smokes," Doke says.

Vaughn chugs down the water in the bottle, his knobby Adam's apple bobbing with each swallow. Despite his sparse moustache and head of black curly hair, the skin on his chest is as smooth and hairless as a girl's. It has occurred to Doke that Vaughn might shave it, which makes him wonder sometimes if Vaughn isn't maybe the homo.

"I was thinking," Doke says. "You know, about that guy."

That guy in the parking lot behind the Cue Bar. They'd gotten a string of unopened rubbers in neon colors and three hundred bucks off of him. Vaughn had filled the rubbers with water and put them in the freezer in the basement. They were still there as far as Doke knew. He couldn't remember what they had planned to do with them.

Vaughn fumbles around in the drawer of his bedside table looking for cigarettes. He finds a crushed pack containing three or four and lights one.

"Yeah, so?"

In twenty minutes they've parked Vaughn's mother's Subaru in the lot of a 7-11 and are walking past some of the nicer downtown houses. Brick, mostly, with long porches and tall, spreading trees in their yards. Gold and yellow leaves carpet much of the grass beneath the trees. Doke lived in this neighborhood up until five years ago. But his mother decided she wanted them to move farther out where the houses were newer and she could show off her jewelry without worrying about getting carjacked.

"We were too exposed in that lot," Doke says.

"We were fucked up," Vaughn says. "You can't do anything worth a shit when you're fucked up. Too damn messy." His clothes had been so soaked with blood that he'd had to burn them in the crumbling brick barbeque at the back of their property.

"Plus, we had the wrong tool."

They hadn't made any kind of plan that night. The guy was there. They were there. Vaughn looked at Doke and he looked back at Vaughn and it was like they just knew. Sometimes he and Vaughn could communicate like that. It was Vaughan who got the length of wood off the busted pallet lying on the bar's loading dock. But it was the guy's dumb luck that it had a couple of nails poking through its end.

"The doors and windows around here are crap," Doke says, keeping his voice low. "You can get into any basement pretty easy."

Several of the houses on the street are decorated for Halloween already, with Jack-o-Lanterns on their porches and goofy pictures of witches and spiders clinging to the inside of their windows. Doke talks on, but Vaughn is staring at a woman getting mail from a rectangular box on the wall beside the front door of the house they're approaching. She has her back to them, but he's got a good look at her legs beneath her tiny cutoffs. She looks older, maybe twenty-five or thirty, but she's pretty hot with her blond ponytail hanging down her back and muscular calves. Still staring, hoping she'll turn around before they get too far down the street, Vaughn misses the pink bicycle lying on the sidewalk in front of her house.

His foot catches on the bike's front tire and he falls, his palms scraping the concrete and the handlebars digging into his chest.

"Son of a bitch!"

Doke tries to stifle a laugh.

Vaughn glares up at him. His ribs hurt like hell and he knows the woman in the shorts is probably laughing, too. He jumps up and grabs the bike by the handlebars and seat and sails it ten feet into the yard. It bounces, then lands so that its red and white *Jenny* license plate snaps in two against the ground.

The woman isn't as pretty as he thought she would be. She puts her hands on her hips. She looks pissed.

"I was going to ask if you were okay," she says. "What the hell was that for?" She points to the bike.

"Let's go, man," Doke says. "We can come back tonight. Bitch."

Vaughn stares back at her. He imagines whacking the shit out of her with the right kind of tool. A ball peen hammer, maybe. It could get messy, but not as bad as the board with the nails. Also the kid whose bicycle it is.

"Come on," Doke says, bouncing on his toes like a ten year-old.

Then Vaughn sees two small kids appear at the screen door. One wears a Winnie-the-Pooh mask, the other is a little boy without a mask, maybe two or three years old. His blond hair sticks up in the back like he's just gotten out of bed. The kids wear matching pajama shirts.

"Boo!" one yells. He starts laughing like he's made the best joke in the world. Then the kid with the mask starts, "boobooboobooboobooboobooboo!" The two of them jump up and down, screaming and laughing.

The woman hesitates, trying to decide which pair of boys she wants to deal with.

Vaughn starts walking. The kids' voices get louder behind him and now the woman is telling them to be quiet.

"Man, she is *such* a bitch," Doke says.

They're almost past the next house when she calls "Hey!" after them. The kids are still laughing behind her.

Vaughn raises his arm and flips her the bird, holding it for several seconds so she'll be sure to have seen it. But he doesn't look back. He wants to be off this street. Now.

"We've got to think of a tool," Doke says. "Shut her up."

"Why don't we advertise in the fucking newspaper," Vaughn says.

"We're not going to?" Doke says. "I don't understand."

Because you're a moron. But Vaughn doesn't say it out loud. "Give me that four bucks. We need smokes."

They cross the street and walk down another block before heading back to the car.

III.

Rita turns her face to the window, tired of listening to the moaning teenager in the bed across the room. Outside the window there's nothing but a brick wall, some addition to the hospital, and it seems appropriate to imagine that the rest of her life—a life without her new husband Paul—is on the other side of it. She reaches out to touch the baby in the rigid bassinet pushed against the bed. Jennifer Marie. *Jenny.*

When she feigns sleep, she hears the nurses whisper, tut-tutting over the baby whose father was the only fatality in the accident. A miracle baby, that little Jenny is. Born on the side of the road.

Why did it have to be raining?

Rita opened her eyes to the sound of thunder, but there was nothing to see through the shattered windshield except indistinct waves of gray rain.

She couldn't turn her head, and so blindly reached for Paul in the driver's seat, saying his name. Feeling the soft nap of the fleece anorak she'd bought him for his birthday she rested her hand on his arm and could breathe again. The baby had shifted and was no longer pressing against her stomach and lungs. She remembered leaving the apartment, having to stop on the stairs as another, stronger contraction came on—Paul holding onto her as she tried to sit to keep from falling down the stairs.

Paul?

Not thinking not thinking not thinking about the stillness of his arm, the stillness of the air inside the car. Not thinking not thinking not thinking of the pain in her belly. She squeezed shut her eyes and squeezed Paul's flaccid biceps beneath her hand to ride through a contraction that rumbled through her with the thunder overhead. *Something was coming.* She wanted her mother's garden-roughened hands on her shoulders, Paul's face smiling into hers as he teased her about how her boobs got bigger but her bladder got smaller. The desires were as physical, as feral as her need to have Paul inside her when they were just beginning to make love, but it was a thousand times more intense: pain and pleasure and fear together. Fucking hormones. Fucking baby. She screamed.

Paul.

The shrunken car couldn't contain her anymore. She unbuckled the seatbelt and found the door handle. She heaved against the door so that it opened enough to let her roll out of the car and onto the sodden grass in the drainage ditch. The contraction left her sweating and thirsty and the pain in her neck was worse, but the cold rain swathed her, soaking slowly through the long wool sweater she'd taken to wearing when she found her jacket no longer fit.

Paul was the one who had wanted a baby. She put it off as long as she could, first with nursing school, and then with this new job. There were people waiting at the hospital for her. Her mother was probably there already. Her mother, who seemed to think that Paul was almost too good for her. "He's so patient, Rita. Don't test him. You know how you push people away." *Thanks, Mom.* Would she be happy now?

Pushing the sweater away, she clawed at her wet leggings and finally got them to where she could use her feet to peel them off.

Something was coming. It was coming.

First babies weren't supposed to come like this, with sudden labor. Or maybe she had been asleep in the car for hours. Maybe she had missed her own labor just like she had missed Paul's death. Paul had gone to heaven or hell while she was strapped, unconscious, in her seat, the spent airbag collapsed over her belly.

What kind of wife was she? If she didn't die here, she would have a whole lifetime to look back and judge herself.

She couldn't see her legs, only the black cotton rise of her stomach and the tree line above it. She heard cars pass above her up on the road. But they couldn't see her.

Hush. I see you.

The voice came from her right, but she couldn't turn her head.

A voice like the susurrus of ocean waves. The tenderness of it softened the violent trembling of her body. Dispelled her anger. The pain was still there, but her attention to it was removed as though it belonged to someone else.

It had come.

Help me. Two words she didn't remember ever saying together before. *Help me, please.*

Man or woman, she didn't know which. She chose *woman* because she would have been afraid if it were a man. She was helpless. This baby, this thing had made her helpless.

The woman settled in front of her and laid her hands on Rita's knees. Her touch was warmth itself and moved through Rita's body like a numbing drug. Undampened by the rain, the woman's silver hair dropped over her shoulders to brush Rita's legs with the music of a thousand tiny bells. And when the woman leaned forward, bringing her unlined face closer to Rita's, her breath was like a field of lavender. Rita wanted to weep with joy.

Give me your hand.

The woman's voice surrounded Rita, caressing her ears, touching her lips.

Rita lifted her hand from the grass and the woman took it.

Now.

The woman bent closer to Rita and put her other hand between Rita's legs.

And, now.

Rita felt only a gentle pressure as the woman's hand entered her, but imagined it crawling slowly up the birth canal toward the baby's head. She was seized with fear, thinking that the woman might clamp her fingers around the child's neck and squeeze, just as Rita herself had squeezed Paul's arm, desperate to feel life there. The woman might take the baby's life, strangle the child right in her womb.

Hush.

Her eyes looked beyond Rita's face and Rita understood that the woman was seeing inside her. She was seeing the child.

As the woman's body shifted with her vision, her voluminous silken robe, the color of muddy earth, gaped open. Rita saw that the body inside it had no substance, but was made of light shot with countless eyes that blinked and rolled and stared. Blue, green, hazel, black, brown, yellow, red. It was the eyes occluded with milky cataracts that Rita was drawn to. What did *they* see?

Rita's fear was gone. She wanted to touch the eyes, to feel their silvery lashes on her fingertips. Butterfly kisses. Paul loved to cover her in butterfly kisses.

The woman caught her watching and moved again so that the eyes were hidden. Her wry smile made Rita feel like a naughty child.

Only in that moment did she feel a single, stabbing pain.

Let go.

Rita expelled her breath and let her chest relax. She remembered a horror film from her childhood: someone turned the head on a statue of a cat and a wall groaned deep within a tomb, revealing a secret passage. She felt the child scraping through her, rock against rock. She gripped the woman's hand hard enough to crack the bones, but the woman's bones didn't yield.

When it was over Rita groaned with relief.

Ah.

The woman let go of her hand.

Now Rita was better able to see over her still-large belly.

The woman took the baby from between Rita's legs and held it up for Rita to see. Then she spoke to the child in a language that Rita couldn't understand, the words urgent, commanding. The baby was naked to the rain and still covered with bloody fluid and white bits of what had covered it in the womb. But it was still and silent in the woman's hands.

Rita felt the endless body of eyes staring at her through the robe.

The woman's question whispered in her brain.

A desperate yearning came over Rita. She craved her daughter's cry. She craved the feel of the infant's skin against her own, her child's mouth on her breast.

The woman swiftly maneuvered the baby into one hand and swept her mouth clear with two fingers.

The baby sputtered and a spray of yellow fluid erupted from her mouth. Then her breath caught and she began to scream at the sky and rain.

The woman laughed. Rita laughed.

Then the woman lifted the baby to her own lips. Rita saw a flash of brilliant white teeth, the umbilical cord suddenly between them. She couldn't cry out, but she couldn't look away, either. The woman's lips bloomed with amniotic fluid and blood. She turned aside to spit. But when she looked again at Rita, she was smiling.

The woman picked up Rita's leggings from the ground. She murmured to the baby as she wrapped her in the leggings, which had dried at her touch. She snugged the waistband over the top of the baby's head like a hood and swaddled her with the long, stretched-out legs so that she looked ready to be strapped onto the back of some ancient desert mother. She laid the baby in Rita's outstretched arms.

The rain stopped.

IV.

Paul takes the gold-nibbed pen the window salesman offers him and signs page after page after page of the contract that's spread over the coffee table. He's read as much as he can stand of the agreement and wants to get this part over with. He sees enough paperwork in his job at the hospital's collection department to want to keep it as far away from him as he can when he's in his own living room.

"When we talked yesterday, I thought I could get your order delivered in four or five weeks. But now they're telling me there was some kind of freak storm that knocked out the Mississippi plant's power for a week and it's running behind."

"Sure," Paul says. He doesn't like the way the guy—Jason is his name—keeps looking at Rita. He can't blame him, though. She's beautiful. Three months pregnant, she's over being sick and already showing.

"There's something I've wanted to ask you," Rita says.

Paul loves how she sits in the wing chair, her bare feet curled beneath her. She never wears shoes in the house, even when it's February and the trees are covered in ice.

"Do you do background checks on your installers?"

"Background checks? We've had the same installers for fifteen years," Jason says. "I'm related to two of them."

"But that doesn't mean..."

Paul interrupts her. "I think my wife just wants to know if they're reliable. Safe to be around the kids, you know?"

There's laughter and a loud clanging from the kitchen as though on cue.

"Baking sheets," Rita says. "Their favorite."

Jason drops his thinly veiled indignation.

"Precious cargo," he says. "We're all about safety. No worries."

Jenny runs into the room with one of the twins, Robert, trailing after her. Robert toddles over to Rita, his chubby arms outstretched, but Jenny climbs onto Paul's lap.

"Daddy, we want dinner," she says, stroking his face. "I want mac and cheese for dinner. Will you make me mac and cheese?"

Paul tickles Jenny so that she erupts in laughter. "With what we have to pay this man, mac and cheese is about what we'll be eating for the next five years. Gotta keep the boogie man out even if it means we all have to turn into noodles!"

Jenny had bad dreams. The pediatrician called them night terrors, and the whole family was on a strict bedtime regimen because of them. Some treatments called for anti-depressants, but both he and Rita refused to consider putting Jenny on them. Her worst dreams were of animals—lions, wolves, enormous rats and fierce chimpanzees—roaming through the house and fighting their way into her bedroom. It didn't help that someone had recently hacked through their next-door neighbor's rotting basement door to steal her televisions and jewelry.

"What do you say, honey? Want to be a noodle?"

Jenny shakes her head so that her pigtails swing back and forth, hitting her face.

Jason smiles indulgently. "Sweet," he says. Then he's packing up to go, stuffing the pages of the contract in his soft-sided briefcase. "I'll leave you to your dinner."

Paul tries to set Jenny on the floor, but she clings to him as he shows Jason out.

Before Jason's out of the room he turns back to Rita. "Plus, I need to drop by the halfway house to see who's available for your installation." He winks broadly at Rita and tousles Jenny's hair.

"What an asshole," Rita says when he's safely out of the house.

"You were very restrained," Paul says. "But you need to put a buck in the cussing jar for the whole *asshole* thing."

"Are you saying he wasn't an asshole?"

"No, I'm saying you owe the cussing jar a buck," Paul says. "You're right though. He was."

On their way into the kitchen, he touches Rita's hair. "I love the way you worry about our kids," he says.

Rita puts her hand to her stomach. "Full time job," she says. She smiles.

V.

Dickie's mom looks mad. She let me ring the doorbell three times, but Mommy won't answer the door. Our minivan's in the driveway. Daddy's fancy car is gone. I look through the front window, but I can't see anything except the twins' toys all over the living room. It's not picked up and neat like at Dickie's house.

"Wait right here," Dickie's mom says. "I'll go get my cell."

She's not as pretty as Mommy, and Daddy says she has fork-in-mouth disease. When she walks down the sidewalk, her butt bounces, but she's not as fat as Dickie.

Dickie told me that at Christmas she's going to have her own Christmas tree in her room. And last week Dickie's mom carved three live pumpkins for Halloween. She puts them in their extra refrigerator every night so they don't die. Our pumpkin is plastic and plugs into the outlet on the porch. We're not supposed to have it plugged in during the day, but it's plugged in now, even though you can't tell it's glowing because the sun is out.

I push the doorbell two more times and I can hear it ringing in the ugly brown box down the hall. Then the phone rings. I count five times. Nobody answers. Maybe everyone is playing a trick on me because it's almost Halloween. Or maybe they went to the store and forgot I was coming home.

Dickie's mom comes back and flips her phone shut.

"I don't know, Jenny," she says. "Maybe they're asleep?"

"Maybe," I say. Sometimes we all get in Mommy's and Daddy's bed in the morning and go back to sleep together. Robert kicks, but Justin curls up like a baby and sucks his thumb. I hope Mommy kept the door to my room shut so the twins couldn't rip up my books.

"Do you know your Dad's cell number?"

I don't.

"I know where a key is," I tell her.

"Really?"

"Under the rock turtle in the yard."

When they see us going into the house, Dickie and the other girls want to get out of the van and come with us. Dickie's mom tells them not to.

She lets me go in first. The front hallway is where I'm allowed to skate with my roller blades and they're lying in the middle of it like someone's been playing with them. I yell for Justin because he's the one who always wants to wear them.

I run upstairs, leaving Dickie's mom to shut the front door. I hear her walking around calling for my mom. Upstairs the beds are all made. My bedroom door is still closed and I look inside. My gerbil Fetch puts his front paws on the wall of the cage and sniffs at me. No one has fed him today. No one has been in here today. No one is hiding from me.

Will Dickie's mom go back home and leave me here to wait? I like to be alone, but not at night. I don't even like it when there's a babysitter here at night.

I run downstairs.

"No Mommy, no nobody," I say. I follow Dickie's mom into the kitchen. It's shady and dark even though it's not even lunchtime yet. Mommy says the kitchen is depressing.

"Hm." Dickie's mom taps her fingers on the counter just the way my Daddy does when he's thinking. She goes over to the calendar on the refrigerator and leans close so she can read the writing. "Tacos," she says. Then she looks at me.

"Tacos on Saturday with Friday beans," I tell her.

"Refried beans?"

I don't know what she's talking about, but it seems better just to tell her *yes*. When she steps back from the refrigerator some goldfish crackers crunch underneath her shoes and it makes her jump. Mommy wouldn't want Dickie's mom to see what a mess the kitchen is. There are chip bags open and cookies all over the table and bottles of beer and soda knocked over on the table. The floor is sticky.

Dickie's mom looks down at her feet, then over to the table and the sink. The sink is covered with nasty brown stuff. I think Dickie's mom is going to throw up and it scares me. I've never seen a grownup barf before and it will make the kitchen worse.

We hear a sound from the basement, like a door or window slamming shut. Beneath the door there's a sliver of light, which means they've been downstairs the whole time. I'm so glad! The basement isn't like a regular basement anymore. It has all new ceilings and carpet and a couch and a tv where we can watch videos. There are bright lights, too, so I'm not afraid to go down there like I was before.

"They're hiding downstairs," I tell her.

"Jenny, stop!" she says.

But I don't listen to her. She's not my mother. I open the door and yell, "I'm home!"

Robert looks up from where he sits at the bottom of the stairs. He has one of my old Barbies in his hands and it looks like he's been trying to get her dress on. Or maybe off. But is it Robert? His hair is clumpy with brown stuff and his shirt is dirty, too.

"What are you doing, Robert?"

When I say his name, he throws the Barbie on the floor. "No!" he says.

I go down a few stairs, calling for Mommy. The basement smells horrible. Dickie's mother is behind me yelling for me to stop.

Then Justin comes to the bottom of the stairs, his thumb in his mouth. His diaper sags around his knees and in his other hand he carries a shoe. He's a mess, too, but the stuff all over him and the shoe is bright red, like blood. His nose is running and I can tell he's been crying a lot. I want to run away.

Dickie's mother makes a sound behind me like she's choking. She grabs my shoulder.

Robert takes the shoe from Justin and holds it up for me to see. "Mommy shoe," he says.

•

Jenny L's fingers are sticky from the doughnuts she ate at the Krispy Kreme store, and Maura—who hopes against hope that the box of wipes back in the minivan isn't empty—can't wait to let go of her hand and turn her back over to her mother. She tells herself not to be judgmental and does her best to ignore the weeds growing through the cracked sidewalk leading to the L family's porch and the scatter of toys in the yard. Jenny's mother and father both work at the hospital and there's a black woman who comes to look after the two younger boys during the week. Still, she can't help thinking that it's Saturday, and there's no reason the family couldn't take fifteen minutes to make it more presentable. Even with four six year-old girls sleeping over for a birthday party, she'd wiped down the bathrooms and vacuumed before taking them out for breakfast. Keeping things orderly wasn't that difficult if you were just a little organized. And how much would she like to get her snips out of the minivan and take off the heads of the nodding salvia and petunias and spent geraniums in the lush garden hugging the base of the porch? There was something so satisfying about deadheading flowers.

Beside her, Jenny talks *good Lord does the child ever stop to breathe* and she listens with half an ear, making the same understanding noises she makes for her daughter Dickie when Dickie is just talking to hear the sound of her own voice.

The curtain in a sidelight flickers and after a moment the door opens.

"Mommy!"

When Jenny lets go of her hand, she can still feel the icing on her fingers and has to stop herself from wiping them on her cotton sweater. She calls out a cheery *hi* to the woman standing in the doorway and wishes she could remember her first name. The woman's ash blond hair is drawn away from her face in a sloppy ponytail, and the faded surgical scrubs she wears pull tight against her pregnant belly. Although the porch's shade is deep and she's a good twenty feet away, Maura sees that she's exhausted, as though she hasn't slept in days.

Later, when they ask her if she saw a stranger standing behind Jenny's mother or if she seemed afraid, she tells them *no, never afraid.* She can't be faulted for having thought that the woman might have been sad or angry or even—to be perfectly honest—rude. She thinks they will never stop asking her questions about that morning, but they finally do—after the comforting angel visits her, after she explains about all the universes where Jenny lives on. An infinite number of universes, she is certain, though only five are revealed to her. She is not greedy. Five are enough to make her understand. Five are enough to give her peace.

Jenny drops her glittering Tinkerbell backpack on the porch and runs to her mother, who pulls her close, pressing her against her against the swell of her stomach. There is such tenderness in the action, such a melting transformation in the woman's sharp features that Maura feels a lump of emotion develop in her throat and she has to turn her head away.

"Thanks for bringing her home."

The woman's voice is quiet, Maura barely hears her. She swallows, hard, and turns back to give her a bright smile.

"She did great at the sleepover. Didn't you, Jenny?"

Jenny looks up at her mother and begins to bounce in her embrace.

"I ate two jelly doughnuts and their dog Buttercup licked my cheek," she says.

"Not at the same time," Maura says. "We ate doughnuts at the Krispy Kreme. She had milk, too." There was no way she would've let the girls eat after playing with the dog without washing their hands.

Jenny's mother strokes her daughter's hair. "Now, get your backpack," she says.

Jenny pulls away and kneels beside the backpack.

"Bring it here," her mother says. She stays rigid in the doorway, as though trying to keep Maura from seeing inside.

Maura wants to tell her not to worry. She doesn't need to go inside the house to know what it contains: furniture more shabby than shabby-chic, limp houseplants, crayon-colored children's rooms, aged cherry woodwork and floors to die for, but windows that don't open properly, and decent appliances in a kitchen that hasn't been updated in twenty years. The garden and yard tell her enough.

"Where's Daddy?" Jenny says. She quickly unzips the backpack. "I want to show him my fairy wand."

"Jenny, no!" her mother says. "You can show it to Daddy in a minute. Inside."

"Don't *you* want to see it, Mommy?"

Jenny sounds hurt and Maura feels suddenly uncomfortable.

"I do, sweetheart. But you can show it to me in the house. Let's go inside."

Pouting, Jenny rezips the backpack. She stands up and all but stamps her foot. "But I want to show Daddy!"

Why Dickie likes to play with Jenny at all, Maura isn't sure. Despite her tiny frame and high, lisping voice, Jenny tries to boss the other girls around, folding her sun-browned arms against her chest and pursing her lips like an old woman when she doesn't get her way.

"I've got two more girls and Dickie in the van," Maura says. She doesn't know what the woman's problem is, but she certainly doesn't want to get involved in the battle of wills that is already under way. If she hurries she can drop the other girls home and she and Dickie can get to the garden center before the worst of the day's heat. "Everyone's a little sugared up. Sorry about that."

"It's okay," the woman says. "Jenny, please. Daddy wants to see you in the house."

"I think everything's in her bag," Maura says. "Give me a call if she's missing anything. She's welcome to come play any time." Keys in hand, she waves, relieved to be going, and heads for the van. Dickie has her nose and mouth pressed against the van's open passenger window. She should have known that the girls would all be out of their seats thirty seconds after she left them.

Jenny's mother calls after her: "Wait."

Maura stops to look back with an overwhelming feeling that things are happening in slow motion, now. Seconds pass before the woman continues, all the urgency gone from her voice.

"We'll see you at school," she says.

Maura smiles and waves again.

As they drive away, Jenny raises her hand, the sullen pout gone from her face. In her daisy sundress and the orange hair bow she borrowed from Dickie, she is just another little girl, a colorful miniature of the woman who stands behind her, holding her close.

Jessica Glass

Coin-Operated Boy

Marguerite didn't even notice the ad at first. It was nondescript, about the size of a postage stamp. She flipped to the next page and continued scanning the columns of classifieds to find something she thought she could use. Any old thing would do. In this manner, she had acquired a variety of interesting bric-a-brac, including a plaster collection of mini composer busts, a whale-bone comb, and one bookend shaped like a hand. She hoped to one day find its lonely pair.

In fact, she might never have read it at all if she hadn't spilled a drop of coffee that leeched through the newsprint and revealed the words from the previous page in bold relief. Marguerite read the ad once, and then again. She puzzled over it. And she couldn't stop thinking about it, the inky letters bouncing around her skull all day at her data-entry job, while she ate her dry ham sandwich and black coffee lunch, and as she fought traffic on the way home.

That evening she called Jenny Two. At one time, there had also been a Jenny One, another member of their small, casual circle who got married and more or less ceased to exist. Marguerite and Jenny Two, Sasha, and Louise were left, and occasionally a girl named Kirsten, whenever they could stand her intolerable good humor.

Jenny Two seemed preoccupied. "Tonight? Oh, actually I sort of had plans. With this guy. Sort of."

"You sort of had plans or you had plans with a sort-of guy?" joked Marguerite.

"With a sort-of guy," said Jenny Two. "It's weird, I know. It's this new thing, and they say it's incredible."

118

"Oh yeah, I heard about that. I know all about it. Does the mystery man have a name?"

"Kevin," purred Jenny Two. "Speaking of which—whom—I've got to run and get some rolls of change at the bank before it closes. See you."

That decided it. Marguerite experienced a moment of panic when she couldn't find the newspaper, but then she spotted it peeking from underneath her jacket on the table, where she'd tossed it when she got home from work. She felt silly for panicking and then angry at herself for being so silly.

"Fiddlesticks!" she yelled at the ceiling. She squeezed her hands into fists until her fingernails were cutting her palms. That always made her feel better. She flipped to the classifieds section and scrolled her fingertip down the column to the ad she'd noticed that morning. She dialed the number. A woman's voice hummed warmly on the other end.

"Hello, how can I help you?"

"I want a—a boy?"

"Don't we all," said the woman, not unkindly. "Do you have an ethnic preference?"

"Um, no, I don't think so."

"Eye color, hair color, medical history?"

"No, no, whatever is fine."

"All right. I'm just going to get some demographic information from you, your credit card information, and your home address. We can have him delivered in two business days."

"That's it?"

"That's it."

"I just thought there would be more... How exactly does he work?"

"Exactly like it sounds. No tricks. Put in a quarter and he should operate anywhere from one to three hours."

"Just like a real man?"

The woman laughed. "Why don't you just wait and see? We've never had an unsatisfied customer."

· · · ·

Marguerite didn't sleep well for the next two nights. She cleaned the apartment and flossed her teeth and trimmed her potted plants. She watched infomercials until early in the morning, had a shower, made some coffee, and went to work.

"Are you okay?" asked her boss Lorraine, a tightly-wound little woman who seemed to be always clenching.

"Yeah, I'm fine. I think I'm coming down with something is all."

"Drink plenty of fluids," said Lorraine. This was her advice for most situations in life, including but not limited to: fatigue, exercise, heartbreak, insomnia, menses, root canals and headaches.

Lorraine put her palms flat on Marguerite's desk and leaned in close to whisper, "I saw you sitting next to Jerry from accounts payable at lunch today."

Marguerite blinked. "We were sitting three tables away from each other."

"I can smell when love is in the air," said Lorraine, smiling in her peculiar way with pursed lips.

"Jerry doesn't even know my name," insisted Marguerite, but her heart wasn't in it, and anyway, Lorraine had already walked away.

"He doesn't even know my *name*," she whispered furiously. She didn't realize she was fidgeting her fingers until something snapped in her hands. She looked down; she had broken a pencil in half. She opened her drawer, pulled out the pack of No. 2 pencils, and snapped a few more, pretending they were Lorraine or Jerry or her mother or Helena Ashgrove from the sixth grade, but she had to stop when her coworkers began giving her strange looks. She swept the pencil corpses into her trashcan and began counting the hours until 5 pm.

Then on the third day, there was a package waiting when Marguerite got home from work. A man-sized box. She dragged it inside, surprised at how light it was, and she panicked momentarily at the thought that perhaps the box was filled only with Styrofoam packaging peanuts. What a silly thought. They would never. The panic fled again like a moth briefly flickering in a porch light. Really, she felt stronger for having done this, whatever *this* was.

She made a fuss over opening the packaging neatly along the

seams, breathing deeply the paper, mothball smell of the cardboard, and reading the whole instruction manual without unraveling the bubble wrap cocooned around her new purchase. The instruction manual wasn't long:

Insert coin. Your boy will function for one to three hours. Enjoy.

At the bottom were listed the customer service number and the words "We've never had an unsatisfied customer."

Marguerite popped a bubble between one thumb and forefinger. Then she popped another. Then she wrapped both hands firmly around the edge of the wrapping, and to the tune of its frantic stacatto music, she uncovered him.

She was relieved to see he was clothed, though the clothes were poorly fitted and unevenly stitched. She wondered if he were hollow, if she could push him over if she leaned her shoulder into his chest, but she didn't try. Marguerite crouched and inspected his fingers, slightly concave as they dangled by his thighs. Tiny, delicate hinges graced the curve of each knuckle down the phalanges, and he had no fingernails. His neck had a strange sort of ball and socket hinge that nested together seamlessly, which was nice because she would be looking at the neck quite a lot, perhaps. On the back of his neck was a small brass-framed coin slot, with 25¢ lightly embossed to one side.

Her new boy toy was just a few inches taller than she, with curly brown hair, pale skin, a long straight nose, and green eyes, which were open and real and incredibly off-putting. They seemed sensitive, she thought. She couldn't make out hinges for his eyelids, but she supposed he must blink occasionally. That, like the neck, seemed an important detail. His jaw was cut at a lovely, sharp angle.

She was afraid to touch him. She just walked in circles around him, keeping a radius of six inches or so. The first night she didn't turn him on. She went to bed and lay awake in the dark before getting up again to drape a blanket over his still-standing frame. In the darkness of her living room, everything was the color of murky water. She looked at the shrouded figure and shivered, then hurried back to the safety of her bed. That night she dreamed of marble pillars in the desert.

The next day she called out sick.

"I knew something was wrong with you," said Lorraine, who liked to be right. "Drink plenty of fluids."

Marguerite hung up the phone and squared her shoulders as she approached the living room. "Okay, boy," said Marguerite to the boy. "It's just you and me now." She reached into her spare change jar and fished out three quarters. She dropped one into the coin slot on the back of his neck, listened to it roll down some hidden pathway and clink hollowly as though it had landed at the bottom of a well. And she waited.

She didn't wait long. The disconcerting glaze melted from his eyes, and he smiled at her.

"Hi," he said. "I'm Dwight. You must be Marguerite. It's a pleasure to meet you." His body seemed looser somehow, like a marionette constantly trembling on its strings.

She thought for a moment of the injustice that Jenny Two had gotten a Kevin and she had gotten a Dwight, but the moment passed quickly. Dwight seemed very pleasant. His smile broadened as she gazed at him. She took his outstretched hand, which was a little cold, not terribly, soft and unyielding.

"The pleasure is all mine."

Marguerite found she could tell Dwight to be quiet and he would, or she could ask him to talk to her, and he'd do that too. He made her sandwiches and fetched the remote and massaged her scalp. He was marvelous.

Sometimes they played games together. They had one they called Staying Alive, which entailed Marguerite hiding a coin somewhere in the apartment that Dwight had to find before his juice ran out. They tried Scrabble, until the day Marguerite upended the board and scattered all the letter tiles in a fury. She had never been a graceful loser.

Once a month a service man came out to collect the coins. More often if needed. The customer service woman confided when

Marguerite called to inquire about emptying the coins that some customers needed servicing every three days. Marguerite set two weeks as her goal, but it was certainly tempting to keep him going all the time. He scrubbed her back in the shower and rubbed her arms to put her to sleep. If she put a coin in when her alarm went off the first time, he'd have coffee percolating and eggs frying by the time she got up.

The first time the coin collector came, Marguerite and Dwight were playing pinochle, and Marguerite was beginning to suspect Dwight was letting her win. The doorbell buzzed, and a young man waited in the hallway, wearing coveralls and carrying a toolbox. He was smooth cheeked and smiling. The name Harry was embroidered on his left breast.

"I'm here to collect the coins," he said, "from your unit."

"I'm sorry, I don't know what you're talking about," said Marguerite as she began to push the door closed again.

The man's smile slipped. "Your unit. Are you not Marguerite Giroux, at 1307 Willow? Apartment C?"

"I am. But what unit to do you mean?"

"Your coin-op," he said.

"My—oh, you mean Dwight."

"Call em whatever you want to call em, but I've got to collect the coins." The man shrugged, and his toolbox rattled.

"Sure, okay, come on in," said Marguerite, finally pulling the door open for him. She led the young man into the kitchen, where Dwight was seated at the small red Formica table studying his cards. He looked up as they entered and smiled brightly.

"Very nice to meet you," he said to the coin collector. "My name is Dwight."

"Hey, you're all Charlie to me," said the coin collector. "Cough em up." The coin collector stepped behind Dwight, pulled up his shirt and appeared, to Marguerite, to open a small panel in his back. She had never noticed any panel, and she didn't particularly want to look at Dwight's guts, or whatever might be lurking around inside him, so she sat down at the table across from him. She tried to pick up the game, but the jarring crash of coins made her hands shake.

"Are you all right?" asked Dwight.

"Yes, I'm fine. Just go, it's your turn." Marguerite crossed and uncrossed her legs. She chewed on her lip. What was taking so long?

"All done," said the young man after a few minutes. Marguerite walked him to the door, where he tipped an imaginary hat at her. He really had the most wonderful cheeks, she thought, the kind that made you want to cup your hands over the curve of them. She'd have bet money that his skin was warm and soft.

"Thank you," she said, adding "Harry" after a moment's pause.

"See you next month," he said, winking. "Or sooner."

"Marguerite, I hope that was okay," said Dwight when she returned to the kitchen. "You seemed uncomfortable." There was a soft whirring noise as his mechanical brows drew down together. He put his hand over hers, and it felt almost real.

Marguerite pulled her hand away. "Oh, no, having someone open up your torso and scrounge around inside your body cavity is completely normal," she replied. "I'm completely fine with it."

"Marguerite—"

"Don't."

"I just want to make sure—"

"I said shut up, Dwight."

But she didn't often lose her temper with him, simply because Dwight asked nothing of her. If she gave, which she didn't, it was voluntarily. He literally seemed to need nothing at all except the pleasure of her company. When she turned him on, he often told her that he'd been thinking of her, which she doubted. It was nice to hear, nonetheless. He listened while she told him about other, non-coin-operated boys who she felt had used her or who needed her too much, and about the ones she had broken. She told him about her unhappy, clichéd childhood and her violent daydreams. She told him about how dried out and inhuman she'd been feeling. She told him she loved him.

But if she went on too long, she would look up to see him frozen and glazed over, stuck in whatever position he'd been in when he ran out of juice. She did not always put in another coin at these moments. She simply disengaged, walked away.

. . . .

Marguerite returned to work in a daze. She couldn't concentrate on her work. Occasionally she'd glance down and realize she was typing some sort of legal document, but no sooner had she touched ground than she would notice words like *caveat emptor* or *habeas corpus*, and she would be off in space again. This last, *habeas corpus*, she knew meant literally "you have the body." She pondered the meaning of the phrase in a whole new universe of context.

"Working hard, I see," said a voice. Marguerite looked up at Jerry from accounts payable leaning over her with a grin, and then she followed his gaze back down toward her desk. She had drawn a creature in the margin of her paper, stiff and tubular like the robot from *Lost in Space*.

"Or is it more like hardly working?" asked Jerry. He was still smiling. He seemed to find himself very funny, so Marguerite didn't mention that he had just told her most loathed office joke of all time. Damn if he wasn't cute, though.

Marguerite managed to look bashful. "Just one of those days, I guess," she murmured, shoving the papers beneath a folder.

Jerry put up his fingers in the Boy Scouts salute. "I won't tell a soul," he said. "Your secret's safe with me." He winked at her as he walked away.

Marguerite grabbed an ink pen and began clicking the button furiously. Her pulse was running doubletime. Then she spotted Lorraine watching her from across the office, smiling smugly and jerking her head in the direction Jerry had gone. She looked like a dashboard bobble-head doll. Marguerite stopped clicking and put the pen down calmly. She imagined the pen was a bazooka, and when she clicked the button, it would fire a rocket straight at Lorraine's head. Her breathing slowed, and she smiled back.

She looked at the clock. It was only three-thirty, an hour and a half still to go before she could drink herself silly.

"Hey there, stranger," said Louise later that evening. Marguerite felt better already in the dim light of the bar, and the glass stein was cool in her sweaty hands.

"Where have you been hiding?" asked Sasha.

She was going to tell them all about her coin-operated boy when she noticed a strangely familiar man seated next to Jenny Two. That long thin nose and that pale skin. She knew who it was, and for the first time she realized how perfect he was, how smooth-edged and slim and completely out of place among regular, real people. Marguerite found herself furious that Jenny Two had brought her boy to a bar. It was obscene to bring a man like that out in public, she thought. They were private creatures, meant for intimacy and aloneness. *He's mine!* Did Jenny Two have no shame at all, parading him around like that? Showing off? Clearly, she couldn't find a real man to bring along. Clearly, Jenny Two was a whore.

Marguerite missed Dwight.

"I met someone," she said to Sasha. "A wonderful, real man."

"Oh," swooned Kirsten, "that's so great. Tell us all about him."

Marguerite settled onto the barstool next to Kirsten and ordered another drink. "Well, he's very handsome, naturally. And he went to Harvard. He's a genius. But he's not pretentious about it or anything. And he's, you know, he treats me like a princess. I already met his parents, too, and they're fabulous." Marguerite almost bit her tongue in two to keep from blathering any more.

"He sounds dreamy," said Kirsten, leaning her fat cheek on her hand.

"He doesn't even sound real," said Louise.

"Don't be jealous, Louise," said Marguerite, "just because you can't stay in a relationship longer than one night."

"I don't know what that's supposed to mean," Louise said, tapping her long manicured nails on the tabletop.

"Now, ladies," said Kirsten, their little peacemaker, "let's place nice."

"Another round," yelled Sasha, and everything else was forgotten.

When Marguerite got home that evening, she found Dwight had made her dinner, a deep frying pan filled with paella, smelling thickly of saffron and the bottom of the sea. He was slumped in a chair with his chin drooping toward his chest. The paella was cold.

Marguerite began reheating the food, and she lighted some candles on the table. She put on an Ibrahim Ferrer CD. When everything was ready, she brought Dwight back to life with a couple of quarters.

"I guess I fell asleep," he said.

"I guess you did," said Marguerite.

Dwight insisted on playing maître d' with a dishtowel draped over his arm. The dishtowel was one of Marguerite's newspaper finds, decorated with cat paw prints in rainbow colors, but Dwight didn't seem notice its incongruity. He gave the towel a flourish as he scooted her chair beneath her and poured her a glass of wine.

"What did you do today?" asked Marguerite. This was another of their games, a make-believe pretend game in which Dwight was a real boy who spent his days autonomously and interestingly while Marguerite was at work.

"I did some lion taming," said Dwight, "and gave a lecture on quantum mechanics."

"So, the usual?"

Dwight laughed, a not altogether pleasant sound, but then again, reasoned Marguerite, there were plenty of obnoxious laughs among non-mechanical people. Dwight's sounded like what Marguerite imagined would be the result of stripping away all the layers of a TV laugh track, leaving only one hollow, tinny, pathetic voice. But when she looked into his eyes, he seemed so real. As real as Marguerite, as real as her polished oak table or her crinoline curtains. She realized that everything, everywhere was real.

"Dwight," said Marguerite, "let's get married. We can move to the country, into a farmhouse with peeling paint and rocking chairs on the front porch. We'll have a tire swing and little Dwight Jr. running around the yard. We'll go to the flea market every Sunday."

"Marguerite, you know we can never...have a child together. You know that can never happen," said Dwight softly. "I'm very sorry."

He reached out his hand, but his arm squeaked ever so slightly when he moved and she pulled back. She remembered it had been some months since she'd lubricated him. Marguerite lowered her eyes to the frying pan between them on the table, which had gone cold again with the socarrat hardened into a crust at the bottom. It was food he would never be able to eat, she thought, and the thought

made her angry. It made her furious. It made her a little sick to her
stomach. Here was a beautiful, perfect, doting man who was only
pretending to be a man. The whole thing had been nothing but a joke,
and Marguerite was the punch line.

"Take care of the dishes," she said. "I'll be waiting for you in the
bedroom."

Marguerite watched while Dwight took off his clothes, the new
clothes she'd bought him from J. Crew and Neiman Marcus. She
had to force herself to watch because she didn't like the sight of his
naked body. The parts that were kept politely covered during the
daytime were angular and inhuman, and his coloring was flat and
monochromatic. He was also hairless. His body reminded Marguerite
of nothing so much as a slab of raw chicken. She touched his skin,
which was never warm. She put his hands on her body and closed
her eyes. The pleasure of being touched rippled through her, and
she gasped with ecstasy each time her skin caught with a pinprick
of pain in his hinges.

Then she called him names, like metronome and Mephisto and
motherfucker. She told him she would never put any coins in him
again. She'd let him rust away in a closet. All his joints would seize
up, and he'd be paralyzed, forgotten, alone. She told him he'd never
measure up to a real boy. She punched him in the gut and scratched
his face, aiming at his lovely green eyes, wondering briefly if she'd
have to pay for the damage, though he didn't bleed and the synthetic
skin was barely marred. Hurt registered in his eyes (were those tears?
could he cry?), and she exulted. She shook out her bruised hand
and went charging back into the fray.

"Oh, did you think we were done?" she asked as he began to go
limp. She had learned that the more she exerted him, the quicker he
tired out, but she grabbed a handful of quarters from the glass dish
on her nightstand. Some of the coins slipped from between her
fingers and clattered against the bedframe on their way to the floor.
"We're only just getting started."

In the morning, they lay with their arms around each other, and
Dwight seemed to have faded away again. But Marguerite pretended
he was only sleeping, and she stroked his thin hair and his face with

her fingertips. When she snaked her arms around him to pull his body closer to her, she brushed against the cool metal coin slot, and she wept with small slurping noises as she tried to steady her breath.

"I am not a machine," she told herself. "I am not a machine. I am alive."

Some time later, while Marguerite was daydreaming at the copy machine, Jerry from accounts payable crept up behind her and asked what she was doing that evening.

She turned to face him. Jerry was the perfect height for her, just tall enough that she could snuggle under his arm if he threw it across her shoulders. "Are you asking me on a date?"

Jerry smiled. "You got me. Can't pull one over on you."

"Do you even know my name?" she asked.

"Of course. You're the new girl, Marguerite."

"I've worked here for three years," she said, crossing her arms.

Jerry shrugged. "Time is relative, I always say."

Marguerite pulled her lips back from her teeth. "Unfortunately, I'm busy tonight. I have a prior engagement." She winked at Jerry, gathered her copies, and swished her skirt as she walked away.

On the way home, Marguerite stopped at a hardware store and purchased a fillet knife, a sledgehammer, a staple gun, and some industrial staples. She asked the sleepy-eyed cashier for her change in quarters. The cashier was a pimply-faced kid who viciously cracked open the coin rolls on the edge of his drawer and poured the quarters into Marguerite's outstretched hands. She shifted them back and forth like sand. Back at her apartment, she made herself steak au poivre and opened the bottle of wine she'd been saving for a special occasion.

Only then did she drop five coins into Dwight's coin slot.

"Hello, Marguerite," he said, smiling broadly.

"Dwight, I want you to do something for me."

"Anything." He spread his hands before him and opened his eyes wide with sincerity. "What is it?"

"I want you to tell me you love me, and that you'll always think of me kindly."

"I love—"

"Not yet. When I tell you. And I want you to keep saying it in that beautiful fake voice of yours, and I don't want you to stop, no matter what happens, no matter how much it hurts. Can you do that for me, Dwight? Can you do that?"

Michael P. Kardos

Mr. Marotta's Ashes Have the Personality of a Grouchy Old Man

The baby upstairs was crying again while I tried to think up a fairy tale for Larry DeSantis, who bowled lane three every Monday/Wednesday/Friday, and who was beginning to feel disrespected because for three days I'd come up empty. The crying wouldn't stop for hours and was making me crazy. I screamed back. I got off the Barca recliner that I'd burst a heart-vessel haggling for at the Army-Navy, took a hammer from my toolbox, and hurled it again and again at the ceiling until my floor was covered in paint chips. Nothing stopped the baby's wailing. Nothing. I sat down again and bit my thumbnail until the skin ripped and blood formed at the cuticle. More screaming from upstairs. Finally I licked my thumb and went up there to tell the baby's parents to shut the baby the hell up. It was enough already.

A note written in green crayon was stuck to their door with packing tape.

Dear Gunnipuddy,
Take care of Tyren. We left the door open. He likes applesauce.

The note was signed *M. and C.*, initials for names that I'd forgotten seconds after hearing them the day I'd moved in three years ago.

I stepped into M. and C.'s apartment. No furniture, no rugs, no pictures on the walls—in this way, it looked a lot like my apartment. A baby was in the middle of the den, in a little plaid seat, bouncing up and down. When it saw me, it stopped crying. I wandered around the apartment. No toothbrushes or combs in the bathroom, no clothes in the closet. No bed in the bedroom. In the refrigerator there was applesauce behind the ketchup. I went back into the den and picked up the seat with the baby inside and carried it downstairs with the applesauce (and the ketchup) into my apartment. I put down the seat with the baby and watched for a while. I watched the baby watching me as if I knew things.

I didn't.

Here's what I learned, though: You put some applesauce on a spoon, push it into a baby's mouth, baby's going to eat. I fed it and fed it, and when it seemed full, turning its head away from the spoon, I said to Mr. Marotta's ashes, "I'll be home around ten."

"You are *not* leaving me alone with that thing," the ashes said.

But I had no choice. I had to leave for work, and so I poured the applesauce into a bowl, put it on the floor next to the baby, and left for the Gaston Bowling Centre, where I mop the bathrooms and unclog balls when they get stuck behind the pins. I've heard that working in a bowling alley's the best job for a poet, because it's mindless and doesn't sap your energy. Maybe so, but I'm no poet. This is my actual job.

Mr. Marotta had been my ninth grade music teacher. He'd had no family, and although his will had specified cremation, he hadn't taken the instructions any further. When he'd been my teacher, I hadn't liked the man. Not one bit. He'd cursed a lot and smelled like burnt coffee, and he'd seemed very, very old with those gray bushy eyebrows and creased eyes, and he'd flirt with the fourteen-year-old girls and berate us constantly about our lousy intonation, and when we played, he'd slash his baton through the air as if defending himself from an onslaught of invisible birds.

I do credit him for teaching me basic musical concepts. That, he did. "A whole note is four fucking beats. A half note is two fucking beats." Or he'd say, "When you see a fermata, look at Marotta." Then he'd grin as if all of his years spent on this planet had made him wise and cunning.

His funeral had been held next to where I did laundry anyway, and it was between the casket and the row of empty bridge chairs that the funeral director overheard me telling one of his clerical staff that Mr. Marotta had been my teacher. Suddenly, he—the funeral director—was all smiles, offering me spring water with lemon. So because I had history with the deceased—besides playing second-chair clarinet, I'd been on the Carwash Committee—and since otherwise his remains would be buried behind the crematorium next to people nobody cared for, I said okay, I'll take the stupid ashes, though I wasn't going to be suckered into paying for an urn. Mr. Marotta wasn't a man to keep in an urn anyway. He had driven a '78 Duster, and even our band uniform was nothing but blue jeans and a used white T-shirt with a logo drawn by some student from years past who'd won the School Spirit contest.

"But in a beautiful urn," the funeral director said, "the dead feel respected."

"I'll be back in an hour," I said. I went next door to get my clothes from the dryer, drove home, and dug around in the drawer of my night table for the Mai-Tai fishing-tackle box. That box—hard plastic, sturdy, with a dependable clasp—had been given to me years before by a Mai-Tai fishing-tackle representative one morning when my dad and I were out on the fishing pier. Long ago, I'd used up all the Mai-Tai tackle. None of it ever caught one damn fish. So then I'd used it to store condoms, bought when I was young and optimistic, but I never caught any women, either. The box was cursed, I'd like to think, but more likely it was me—I wasn't any good at landing things. I took out the condoms, which had expired anyway, returned to the funeral home carrying the Mai-Tai box, and in went the ashes, and there you have it.

You can't just put somebody's ashes back in your night table, so I set the Mai-Tai box on a wooden dresser that had followed me from place to place and eventually to my apartment here on Talmadge Road, next to the prosthetic supply shop. I kept the dresser in the den, covering a fist-sized hole in the drywall left by an old tenant.

One morning, I awoke to Mr. Marotta's ashes yelling at me from the other room: "Tremolo! Largo! Andante! Pianissimo!" I went into the den and looked at the Mai-Tai box. The remains of my music teacher said, "What the hell are *you* doing here?"

Mr. Marotta's ashes began giving me advice. Often, his advice wasn't any good and bordered on the criminal. Usually, I ignored him. But yesterday, I'd been fed up already—what with the writer's block and the baby's screaming—and so when Mr. Marotta's ashes told me for the millionth time that I was sure to die shivering and alone, I sprang up from my kitchen chair so fast it fell over backwards, landing with a *thuck* on the linoleum, and stomped over to the dresser.

"I'll scatter you over the beach," I said to the ashes. "I swear, if that's the only peaceful—"

"Comrade," he had said, "how about I scatter *you* over the beach?"

As soon as I stepped inside the Bowling Centre, I heard Larry DeSantis calling my name. I was at his lane and full of apologies before he said a word.

"I'm having a killer time working with the handlebar moustache," I said.

"But it's got to have that," Larry said, and subjected me to his secret handshake that I hadn't begun to decode, leaving my wrist sore, a layer of his sweat on my palm. "The moustache is my trademark."

Larry is a bread deliveryman done working for the day by ten a.m., and probably had been here since we opened. Leagues hadn't started yet, so there was just Larry and the other regulars, guys with their own shoes and balls named after girls they met once on a bus or in Radio Shack. We stick the regulars in the same lanes every day so that they feel part of something bigger than themselves.

"I need another day," I told Larry.

"Why, Gunnipuddy? Why is mine taking so long?"

Something I'd have liked to know. I was either on the verge of something or the verge of nothing. It felt the same. "Tomorrow, okay?"

"What've you got so far?" he asked.

I didn't want to say I'd come up empty. So I said, "Once there lived a man who delivered bread each morning to the King and Queen, and who had the world's strongest moustache."

"And?"

"And the moustache attracted the land's most beautiful women, who all wanted his hand in marriage."

"And?"

"And so the deliveryman decided to hold a contest, and agreed to marry the winner."

"No. The deliveryman makes love to many of the women before agreeing to settle down with any one of them."

This is what happens when I improvise. "I'll keep working on it," I tell him.

I wouldn't consider myself a bowler. In the three years I've worked at the Bowling Centre, I've rolled just a handful of games and never broken a hundred. The little holes in the ball make my knuckles sore. The shoes kill my feet. Still, I can see the appeal. You get your own lane where the light isn't too bright and the air temperature's steady. The Bowling Centre isn't too loud, either, not like you'd expect, because we've got carpets on the floor and on the end walls; and anyway, that smacking sound of ball hitting pins, it's a good, clean sound. It means that somebody's getting points. For the regulars like Larry, we're like their local tavern, where the faces are the same every day. And it's exercise, too, if you aren't too tight with your definitions. Exercise, plus we're on tap.

I suppose you could say that bowling's a game with clear rules and a clear goal, too, which are things that you don't find too often in life. But I don't think that's it, not really, not the root of the matter. Here's the real thing about bowling: You knock the pins down, a machine sets them up again. Knock them down, up they go. The pins you miss, the machine knocks them down for you, then sets everything right. No matter what you do, whether you throw a strike or a gutter-ball, once per frame all the pins go down, then they all come back up. You might score higher or lower on a particular day, but you never fail. You can't fail at bowling.

When I got home shortly before midnight, a gray rabbit was sitting on the lawn near my front door. Its eyes reflected red light from the prosthetic supply shop's neon sign (Arms!). Even when I came close, the rabbit just sat there. Its fur was matted and missing in patches. It looked as if it'd lost a fight with one of the raccoons that live in the dumpsters. The rabbit was blocking my way, so I nudged it aside with my shoe and opened the door. But it followed me right into the apartment.

"What?" I said to the rabbit, and closed the door, trapping us all inside. I noticed how rank the apartment smelled. I looked at the baby. Tyren seemed okay, except for the applesauce on its face.

"What?" I said again.

"You irresponsible schmuck," the rabbit said.

"Seconded," Mr. Marotta's ashes said.

I knelt down next to the baby. It made some baby noises. It didn't seem too unhappy.

"I'm here, aren't I?" I said in my defense. "I went away to work but then I came home again. That's better than M. and C. could do."

"It was wailing all night," said the rabbit. "I could hear it all the way down the block."

"Way to go, Gunnipuddy," the ashes said.

I was tired from work, and frustrated because without the fairy tales I was only a utility man. My head throbbed. I went into the kitchen and swallowed three ibuprofens, then returned to the den with a roll of paper towels. "Newsflash," I announced, "I don't know how to take care of kids."

"Master of the obvious," the rabbit said. "You've got to feed it. You've got to buy diapers and change them often. A baby takes constant attention. You can't just leave food out like it's a dog."

"Gunnipuddy thinks he's got a dog," Mr. Marotta's ashes sing-songed. "A little puppy. That what you think you have?"

"A poodle," the rabbit said. "A cuddly little poodle. Gunnipuddy thinks he's got himself a poodle."

The rabbit's voice was tinny and abrasive, and although I'd gotten used to the ashes by now, the ranting still reminded me of his former self hollering at the woodwinds for playing everything staccato. Anyway, the rabbit was doing a little circular hop, and the ashes were chanting raucously along with the rabbit, "A puppy, a puppy, a—"

"Shut up, you stupid rabbit," I said. "Shut up, you stupid ashes." With a square of paper towel, I wiped the baby's face. It pulled back and started shrieking just like I'd always heard it doing upstairs. From inches away, the noise pierced straight into my skull. "Are you both going to sit around and make fun," I said, "or are you going to help? Shit, Mr. Marotta, you could be in the ground right now, staring at bugs all day." This appeared to sober him up. "Now, you two watch this baby while I get some diapers from the Wawa."

I took a fourth ibuprofen and went to the Wawa even though it was five blocks farther than the 7-Eleven, because the woman who works the register could stop the earth from spinning. If I were to make up a fairy tale about myself, she'd co-star.

"Hi, Gunnipuddy," she said when I walked in.

I waved, but nothing was how it looked. Bonchie didn't know me at all. I'd been coming in there for months, when yesterday I'd finally said to her, My name's Gunnipuddy. Can you say my name when I walk in? And she'd said, I'll try and remember, and then we had practiced, I went out and came in again and she said it, my name. Then we repeated it twice.

But today I was a different man. I had Huggies in my arms.

"How old's your baby?" she asked, her eyes wide.

"Beats me."

"How do you mean?" she asked.

"I mean, he can't talk yet. So I don't know how old he is." I was joking with her, only there were so many parts missing, things she'd need to have known, that it was hopeless she'd think what I said was funny. So I just paid, not looking up again from the conveyer belt, and left with the Huggies. The good part about liking a woman like Bonchie was that I knew I'd get another chance with her tomorrow or the next day. The register can't make change by itself.

That first night with Tyren I learned that you aren't born knowing how to change a diaper, or knowing how to make a baby stop its nonsense. I can see why M. and C. gave up. There went one a.m., two a.m., three a.m. When the baby finally stopped complaining and fell asleep around four, I was wide-awake, feeling like I had to make use of the middle of the night. The thing about writing fairy tales, though, is that you can't force them. You can't just write words on paper and expect them to be the right words. You need to spend time listening to Aerosmith. You need to get out your clarinet and play "Stars and Stripes Forever," or watch brawny men sell juicers and knives on television, or throw a Superball so hard that it hits the floor then ceiling then floor then ceiling then floor before you catch it. But all of that shit's off-limits if it wakes the baby.

"You won't believe this," Larry DeSantis said, and grabbed my wrist, forcing me into an extra-long handshake, bending my hand into baffling positions. "I mean, there's no believing it, so don't even try. You look like shit."

I did. Fifty-six diapers had come and gone. Four extra-large jars of applesauce. A week, but it might have been a month or five years or ten minutes. I'd stopped shaving, and yesterday my boss said that I smelled like a carcass. Driving home from work, I'd fallen asleep at an intersection and woken up to a UPS man tapping on my windshield. For a week I'd been scratching my hairline until it bled, and so when I lifted my head from the steering wheel, the wheel was all crusty. When I got home, I was feeling so tired and so lonely—I had never felt so alone before, even with the ashes and a rabbit and a baby under my roof—that I actually bawled, until Mr. Marotta's ashes told me to stop being such a pussy.

"I met a girl last night," Larry was saying, "the most beautiful woman I ever saw. Green eyes like celery. Skin like ivory. And her name's Agatha, same as in the fairy tale."

That fairy tale had taken a superhuman level of concentration, sitting in the Barca, getting ideas during the quiet hours of 4-6 a.m., paging through *The Complete Fairy Tales of the Brothers Grimm Volume I*. That's my book. What I mean is, except for that book, I'm not a reader. I'm more like the kids who hang outside my apartment blasting T-Jerky, and who might know every lyric by this one local thug with a hit record, but who hardly are interested in music.

When Larry was a kid, my story went, he received a terrible gash on his face trying to defend a man and wife from a knife-wielding lunatic. Ashamed when the gash left a jagged sprawling scar, as soon as Larry was able, he grew a moustache that covered nearly his entire face. Still, for years he kept to himself, until one day some very tiny people took up residence inside Larry's handlebar moustache. These people had fairy dust that would make Larry irresistible to women. (This was a calculated risk as to whether Larry would get pissed off because it was the dust, and not him, exactly, that made the women crazy about him).

Anyway, the fairy dust resulted in lots of sex for Larry, and talk of his sexual prowess spread across the land. Only one woman in the kingdom, however, managed to capture Larry's heart. Agatha. She urged him to shave off his moustache, because her own father and mother had been killed by a moustache-wearing lunatic. When Larry refused, Agatha put a sleep-inducing potion in his wine, and while he slept, she sheared off his moustache. When Larry awoke, he touched his lip and became mortified, knowing that his moustache housed the fairies whose dust gave him his sexual powers. He ran to the mirror and, seeing his reflection, he gasped. What Larry hadn't known, because he'd worn a moustache for so long, was that the scar on his lip had come together over the years to spell the name of his true love: *Agatha*. Moreover, Larry realized, it had been Agatha's own parents who he had tried to defend all those years earlier.

The trick had been asking myself why somebody would grow a moustache like Larry's. Once I came up with the scar, things started flowing. Normally, I would have worked out what happened to the little people who lived in Larry's moustache. They had to go someplace, didn't they? And why did they have fairy dust to begin with? Ordinarily I was more careful with the loose ends. But I'd had a rough week, and something had to give.

In the end, there was true love and lots of sweaty sex. And a 300-game for Larry. They all want 300-games in their fairy tales.

"And you're saying your fairy tale came true?"

"That's what I'm saying," Larry said, and went to the bar (also the shoe-rental counter) to buy me a beer.

I'd made up a dozen or so fairy tales about customers at the

Bowling Centre, but none of them had ever come true before. That was never the point, if there was a point other than doing something I had a knack for.

"You're a fortune teller, Gunnipuddy!" said Frank, a bouncer at Bazookas nightclub.

It did look that way. "Maybe," I said, and then Larry returned with my beer, handed it to me, held his right hand over the air blower, picked up his bowling ball, and rolled his ninth, tenth, and eleventh strikes. All the regulars had gathered and were shouting encouragement. Larry cradled the ball—*Angelica*—in his arms and stroked it. (With a black marker he'd crossed out some letters and added others so that now the ball sort of said *Agatha*.) You could tell he felt very tender toward that ball. He kissed it gently, then sent it down the lane so that it curved dead into the pocket. It'd be a better story, maybe, to say that while nine pins went down, the tenth pin hovered there for a moment, spinning, still standing, before finally losing to gravity. But that's not what happened. When Larry's ball hit the pocket, the ten pins exploded—that's what we call it— and dropped. The pins never had a chance.

Larry began to hyperventilate, and the guys had to ease him onto the cool floor, where he sat with his arms around his knees, tears streaming down his face. They huddled around him and punched him on the shoulder, and said that no bowler had ever been so deserving. I sat on a bench and sipped from my beer. I wanted to be excited for Larry, except, I realized, I didn't know this man at all. Did he speak other languages? As a kid, had he been bullied? Two years I'd worked here, and yet I knew only three things about each of the regulars: name, occupation, and high score.

Obviously, others were quick to become the leading male of my fairy tales. At first it made me anxious, taking numbers and figuring out priorities.

"Ben is short and sloppy, and he drinks all day," I said to the circle of men around me. Ben, a hospital orderly, bowled lane one. "Where do I go with that?"

"Maybe he meets a barmaid?" Larry said. He'd taken some of

the guys out for steaks and had returned with a splotch of sauce on his shirt.

"Maybe I meet a woman who drives a beer truck?" Ben said.

"Maybe you meet a woman at A.A.," I said. The words sounded wrong, but I pressed on. "You meet at A.A., and she owns a McDonald's franchise, and you go into business together." I jotted this down on the back of a score sheet so that I'd remember it later.

"We meet at A.A.?" He pursed his lips.

Larry asked Ben, "Do you see yourself giving up the liquor?"

"Don't ask me, ask Gunnipuddy. He's the story-teller."

Maybe I was, but I wasn't going to lie. "No. Ben's right. She drives a beer truck. Her route takes her past an old witch's hovel, where..." I looked around at the pairs of eyes straining wide at me. "I'll work on it when I get home tonight."

"What about me?" said Frank, the bouncer. "Who will I meet at Bazookas?"

"No, me," said Russell.

"Russell, Russell." I chewed on the little half-pencil. "I always see you riding that stupid bicycle." I had never asked, but it had to be a DUI. "So let's think about what type of woman—"

"Money, Gunnipuddy. I need money."

My version of *The Complete Fairy Tales of the Brothers Grimm Volume I* ("The Frog King" through "The Devil's Sooty Brother") comes apart in your hands. The binding isn't any good. I stole the book from my school's library, because there was talk of banning it. I didn't think that people banned books anymore, but I was wrong. Anyway, I saved them the hassle. After I stole it, for years I kept it under my mattress like a baseball glove, as if I had other kids on my team depending on me.

When I told the rabbit and Mr. Marotta's ashes that my fairy tales had been coming true, first Larry's and then Ben's and now Russell's, the rabbit said, "You're home late again."

"Idiot," Mr. Marotta's ashes added.

"The guys took me out drinking. I couldn't say no." It was true. Everyone at the bowling alley looked at me differently now that I had great powers. I'd stopped cleaning the bathrooms, but nobody said anything. Clogged toilets, nothing. Musty urinals, nothing. I just sat on a bench at the end of the alley, lane twenty-four, and guys brought me beer from the tap and Pop Tarts from the vending machines. I got the idea they loved me and feared me.

"Yesterday, Russell won ten grand playing Lotto," I said, and flopped backwards onto the Barca. "It would've been an insult not to let him get me drunk."

The baby was sucking on a binky I'd bought at the Wawa.

"All I'm saying is," said the rabbit, "you've got a baby now, and you can't be—"

"Are you my wife? Is that it?" The last thing I wanted was a lecture. I wanted to be drunk and ride the high of telling fortunes or creating fortunes or whatever it was that I seemed able to do. But forces had converged against me—not only Tyren, but also the rabbit, which was supposedly watching Tyren while I was away. Yet its own pellets were everywhere, its fur was everywhere, and the place on its back that used to have fur had become infected or something and was red and dotted with pus. I shook my head in disgust. "I've got to get to work."

"It's three a.m. and you just came from work," the rabbit said. "You don't have to go back there."

"No, I mean, I've got to write more fairy tales." I went into my bedroom with my book so that I could get some work done for the guys at the alley where, unlike here, I was appreciated.

In the morning, things were more civil. I sat on the floor with Tyren in a square of sunlight and fed him sweet potatoes and apples. Despite what M. and C. had written on their note, I found that Tyren wasn't a fussy eater. You could mix leftovers from all sorts of jars—peas, pears, pumpkin, creamed chicken—and he'd slurp it up. Also, if you put him on his stomach, he'd roll over onto his back. A good trick. And he'd laugh whenever you hung tube socks over your ears and said *blagablagablagablaga*.

"You must be a hero at the alley," the rabbit said, watching me and the baby from across the room.

"Work's been satisfying." I tried to stand on my head, because

Tyren liked seeing me upside-down, but the hard floor irritated my sore scalp.

"You're a man of special powers, Gunnipuddy."

I didn't want to admit what I was about to admit, so I reached for a bottle of baby food and pretended that I couldn't unscrew the cap.

"Need help with that, Hercules?" asked Mr. Marotta's ashes.

I twisted opened the bottle.

"I don't think it's me," I said to the rabbit and to Mr. Marotta's ashes. "None of my fairy tales ever came true before. I think this baby is special." We all looked at Tyren, who was looking at me, but only because I was holding the food. "Yeah, I'm pretty sure it's a godlike baby. I think it might be God. Or something just as important. So don't kill it accidentally while I'm at work."

The baby piped up: "No, I'm not very important. If you don't consider the fate of the world very important."

"Oh, shit," the ashes said.

"Baby's first words," said the rabbit.

I put down the bottle I'd just opened and watched Tyren, waiting for some elaboration. Outside, the sun was barely up, yet the kids were already blasting T-Jerky.

"I'll fill you in," Tyren said, "while you change my diaper."

I grabbed him under my arm and carried him like a football into my bedroom where I kept the Huggies. Now that he could speak, I felt that I had better do a thorough job cleaning him, applying the cream, making sure that the tape didn't pinch.

Anyway, Tyren had completely exaggerated. It wasn't anything like the fate of the world. It was just a dumb car accident that I could prevent, a fender-bender at an intersection across the street from the Wawa. The drivers were of religions and ethnicities that had spent several thousand years hating each other, so maybe you could argue that if the accident had occurred, it would have worsened the tension between two communities, and that maybe this accident would have been the straw that broke, etc., and that battles would be waged, wars fought; that this particular accident, as non-political and, well, accidental, as it might be, occurred for reasons far more cosmic than I could understand, the one accident that had to be prevented at any cost. Or maybe the incident was more symbolic, like if these two people's crisis could be averted, then blah blah. Or maybe Tyren was way off base, being a baby.

He told me the how's and where's and when's of the accident, which pissed me off because the *when* was only thirty minutes from *then*. I put Tyren in the crib I'd bought him at Baby Depot, ran outside to my car, and sped to the Wawa to ask Bonchie to a movie.

Not the best timing, maybe, with the clock ticking and all, but something about the urgency I was feeling gave me a surge of adrenaline. Do it now, I said to myself. Right now.

Twenty-eight minutes later, I didn't care whether I fumbled the fate of the world or not, because Bonchie had said no, fucking no, she preferred not to meet me at the Regal Cinema for a movie. So fuck the world, I was thinking.

And yet I was thinking this from a position standing outside the Wawa, eight-thirty on a Friday morning, right where Tyren had told me to be, and overhead the traffic light suddenly started blinking yellow on all four sides, and there came the '86 Ford Taurus and the '88 Honda Civic, just as Tyren had said, and since I was the only one there who knew what was going to happen, I went in the middle of the street and stood with my hand outstretched like a traffic cop's in front of the Honda, which I assumed had better brakes than the Taurus. The car screeched to a stop. The driver growled something and gave me the finger.

I went around to the driver's window, and he rolled it down. He had an immense gray beard and round green eyes, and I thought how easy it would be to write a fairy tale about him.

"I'm taking a survey," I said. "Do you drink Coke—"

At that moment, the Ford Taurus puttered through the intersection and was gone, my mission accomplished.

"Or is Pepsi more your thing?"

The man gritted his teeth and roared the engine, sending the car forward—over my feet, crushing bones—and into the intersection. Long after the car was out of sight, I kept howling.

When I refused to stay overnight at Saint Memorial's on account of the baby, the surgeon said that I was being-a-difficult-patient, that I must reconsider. Then he left my room and returned with a form stating that I was being noncompliant with my physician's orders, that I released him and the institution from any liability. He sent me home with prescription painkillers, a pamphlet (*Caring for Your Wound*), and a walker. I didn't get home until ten p.m. When I told everybody about what'd happened, the rabbit said, "Then it's time to leave."

"But I just came home," I said.

"Me. I'm leaving. So open the door."

"Why're you leaving?"

"I'm all done here. My job was to make sure you bought Huggies and took care of the baby."

"I still don't know how to take care of a baby."

"I know. But you're learning, which means that my job's done."

"You have only one job?" I wasn't being very thoughtful to that rabbit—I could tell he needed the outdoors, some grass, dumpsters to rummage through. Yet it felt wrong for him to abandon not only the baby, but an invalid still numb from foot surgery and high on painkillers. "Why can't you have more than one job?"

"Why? Because I'm a fucking rabbit. And about that girl," the rabbit said. "It's just a rejection. No biggie. Ask her out again."

"You think?" Bonchie had heard me cursing in the intersection and, seeing my smashed foot, called for an ambulance. Maybe it was the beginning of something.

"Sure. Isn't that right, Mr. Marotta's Ashes?"

"In two-four time," the ashes said, "the quarter note gets one goddamned beat. In six-eight time, the eighth note gets one goddamned beat."

"Just don't stalk her or anything," the rabbit said. "Don't get creepy on her. And remember that the kid always comes first. Now let me out. I want out."

After the rabbit left, I picked up Tyren and put him on my lap in the recliner, but he was being all wiggly, so I put him on the floor where there were some old milk cartons I'd saved for him. My feet killed, but I wasn't supposed to take more pills for another four hours. In my head, I starting writing a fairy tale about Bridget, who rents the bowling shoes, about how she found a rich architect to run off with. But it didn't feel right. The words in my head felt as if they'd been written by someone who didn't know a damn thing.

"This won't come true, will it?" I asked Tyren.

He looked up. "No."

"Why not?" I pictured the clogged toilets I'd been ignoring for more than a week. And how even though I never promised anyone anything, there'd be hell to pay at the Bowling Centre if I were just a utility man again.

"You're a loser, Gunnipuddy, and yet you took care of me without hesitation. That was some good work, so I made you a hotshot for a while."

"Aha!" yelled Mr. Marotta's ashes from the other room. "I *knew* Gunnipuddy had no talent of his own!"

Tyren ignored the ashes. "You took in a baby even though you're a totally unfit father. You're a good man, Gunnipuddy."

And those were the last words the baby ever said until he was eighteen months old. Turns out, except for when he was God, Tyren was a late talker.

Not long ago, I took Tyren to a little park. Afterward, I was pushing the stroller up the hill back toward the apartment when the owner of the prosthetic supply shop saw how badly I still hobbled and waved me in. He was a thin old man, all teeth and joints, and he'd always seemed harmless. But I'd never even said two words to him.

"Name's Fink," he said, once I was inside his shop. Along the walls were various wheelchairs and crutches and walkers, and on shelves were hand- and arm- and foot- and leg-looking devices, though none of them looked very much like hands, arms, etc.—just enough to suggest what they were meant to represent. A smell of formaldehyde might have been real, or might have been in my head. On a shelf running along the window was information on various products—colorful pamphlets, or what my dad would have called, *literature*.

"Gunnipuddy," I said.

"Apartment next door?"

"That's right."

He knelt down. "Who's the little one?"

I told him, and we both looked in the stroller at Tyren, who was sleeping, silent, giving the wrong impression of himself.

"Mister Gunnipuddy, you just sit right here and take the weight off those feet. You make yourself comfortable. What size shoe do you wear?"

I told him, and he went into the back room and then reappeared carrying two cardboard boxes. Inside each box was a soft foot-sole-looking contraption that fits into your shoes if you've got fucked-up feet. I'm making it sound simpler than it is—he rattled off some words, *plastoform* and *purolon-urethane* and other things I've forgotten—but that's the gist. The point is, those contraptions that he put into my lap so that I could feel them, they were soft. Not squishy, though. Supportive.

Fink took them from my lap and kneaded one into each shoe. I put on my shoes again, stood, and, using the stroller for support, took a few steps.

"Well?" Fink said. "Better?"

"I'm walking on cotton," I told him. Not true, but each step wasn't excruciating, either.

"My diabetics swear by them." He nodded sagely and put me on a payment plan. Still leaning on the baby's stroller, but feeling less pain than I had in months, I headed toward the door. When I'd gotten to the doorway, Fink called out, "Behaves himself, doesn't he?"

Tyren had been asleep the whole time.

"He's curious," I said. "Always into stuff." I smiled then, because just that morning I'd been making grilled-cheese sandwiches when Tyren got his hands on the Mai-Tai box and opened the clasp. The ashes spilled right out onto the rug. I got mad for a moment, cursing like Mr. Marotta would have, while Tyren stared up at me with big eyes and new teeth. I vacuumed the mess and made a mental note to empty the vacuum bag in a nice place, like in the grade-school playground, or maybe on the beach the way I'd sometimes threatened. I rinsed off the Mai-Tai box and put it back inside my night table, deciding right then that next time I went to the Wawa, I'd buy a pack of condoms to keep in the box. The way I saw it, it was time to find a girl—Bonchie, maybe, or somebody else—and prevent starting a family together.

"I'll bet he's a bright little boy," Fink the shop-owner said, and came over for another look. "Is he a bright boy?"

I'm happy to report: this baby's average.

Josh McCall

The Ballad of Scrub and Shelly

S crub bought the house from a man named Brown who said, "It might make a nice bungalow, what with a little paint." The wood had gone soft with rot, most of the windows were too swollen to lift and in the front yard lay the unhinged screen door, killing a rectangle of grass. It was no bungalow but, like Shelly, it was beautiful in its way. He put his money down and took the keys.

That evening he brought Shelly over, stopped her at the front door and laid an empty bottle just inside the threshold. They watched as it rolled across the living room floor and down the hall by the kitchen, jumped the backdoor sill and clattered off the porch. "It's like a funhouse at the fair," Scrub said.

"We'll have to get seatbelts for the bed," Shelly said.

The house seemed to be slipping off its concrete foundation, inching its way toward the woods behind it. Anything round that was not fastened down would find its way out the backdoor and vanish in the chokeberry skirting the porch. Soon the bushes were peppered with a confetti of beer bottles and cans, the odd rubber ball, paper towel rolls and plastic cups. When they lost something they looked for it in the chokeberry. One day Scrub hid the remote from Shelly and refused to help her hunt it down. She went out the backdoor and searched among the shrubs. Half an hour later she found the ring he'd strung among the bright red berries.

The wedding only a few days off, Scrub sat on the back porch with his friend Hal, watching the first snow fall. Scrub's chair had three rotten legs and he did his best to keep his weight on the fourth. Hal sat beside him in a folding chair, shifting every few seconds to keep his ass from freezing to the metal seat.

"It's pretty," Hal said, meaning the snow coming down in whorls.

"Looks like laundry detergent," Scrub said. "It's too early for snow."

"It's never too early," Hal said, moving from the metal chair to sit atop the plastic cooler. "Why don't you just kick his ass?"

"Keep it down," Scrub said, turning to check the window behind his head.

Shelly had ears as big as radar dishes and proptotic eyes. Scrub suspected the large organs could see and hear better than normal-sized ones. He liked to call her "grandmother" and nibble on her ears. He liked to watch her eyes protrude further and further until they seemed ready to pop out. If they ever did he'd hold them in his hand and kiss them and poke them back in. "We're a living, breathing fairytale," she would say and put her thumb against his big front teeth. And soon he would be gnawing at her, pawing at her, her eczemic skin coming off in his hands.

"That's the worst thing I could do," Scrub said to Hal, meaning kick the pigfarmer's ass. The two men were working their way through a twelve-pack and cooking up a conspiracy against Shelly's pa. "No way to hide it from her, short of dumping him in a hole."

"I ain't helping you murder nobody, even Abraham Longtree."

"Have I asked you to?" Scrub leaned back on his chair's good leg and Hal sat up off the cooler to get them another beer. There was nothing inside but ice and bottle caps. "Get some from the fridge," Scrub said.

"Yell for Shelly to."

"She's watching the TV."

"She watches it a lot," Hal said. "Too much, seems to me."

Scrub kicked the cooler and it went sliding off the porch into the shrubs. "Go get us some more beers," he said, "or go home."

A week earlier Scrub and Shelly sat in the front room on a couch afflicted with the same rot that had ruined the outside chair. The couch lay flat on the floor, all six legs removed. Scrub held the *County Herald* in his hand, folded to the classifieds section, his index finger jabbing at a half-page insert placed there by her pa. It announced their wedding and a reception it called "gala."

"How does he even know a word like that?" Scrub said.

"Probably somebody at the paper wrote it." Shelly leaned forward so she could see the TV. "You ain't made of glass, you know."

In the middle of the page were two pictures, one a glamour shot of Shelly, her hair teased out in a way she had not worn it since high school. The other was Scrub's yearbook picture, his toothy grin below a thin mustache.

"Shit if I understand," Scrub said. "Whole town knows he don't approve, so why go throwing his money around?"

"For his only daughter?" Shelly moved to the foot of the couch. She stared at the TV and gnawed on one of her red knuckles.

"To spite me is why."

"That too," she said.

He followed Shelly's eyes to the TV. It warned of the first freeze, showed clips of last year's hoarfrost and a burst water main sprouting tendrils of ice. She flipped the channel, the news again. This time an undrained pool had frozen, popped out of its reservoir and ended up on the lawn. "If we wanted an above-ground pool," the owner was saying, "we would have bought one."

"I don't like it," Scrub said, meaning the pigfarmer throwing his money around. "Not a bit."

"Well you can't do anything about it. Besides, it'll be nice. Catered food and all."

"Don't suppose he'll sport me the money for a new suit."

"It would be contrary to his intentions, don't you think?"

"Meaning my personal embarrassment?"

"Yes."

Scrub pulled Shelly back onto the couch and laid her head in his lap. He put his hand on her belly and looked into her eyes, still locked on the TV set.

"You won't feel anything yet." Shelly put a hand over the hand he held on her belly. "It's too soon."

"Did you tell him?" Scrub said, his hand dead still as he waited for the answer.

"I didn't."

"Well don't."

"I won't."

She took her hand back and he slipped two of his own fingers beneath her belt buckle, made it as far as the hairline before she mumbled something in the negative. "I'm watching the TV," she said.

"Do," he said and put his front teeth on her ear and closed his jaw. He watched as she jutted her chin out, her eyes bigger and bigger. It drove him crazy. This woman, a medical book of infirmities, drove him crazy. He whispered that he loved her and she mumbled something in the affirmative.

The night the snow fell, while Hal was in the kitchen getting beers, a bear padded out of the pine cover and into the backyard. Scrub saw her cock her head to the side and open her maw in a silent yawn. Best see what she wants, he said to himself and slipped off the porch, following her into the woods. It was dark. He ran into low-hanging branches and they dumped fresh snow on him.

The bear waited. She was in no hurry. She had an offer to make and she didn't care that he was drunk.

Ten minutes later he returned from the woods alone to find Hal atop the cooler, a lit cigarette tracing and retracing an arc between his knee and mouth.

"Where you been?" Hal asked and gave Scrub one of the beers from the fridge.

"Nowhere," he said, settling into the rotten chair. "I got a plan."

Scrub related the plan. Hal listened, dumping his butts into an empty beer bottle, lighting another cigarette. He was soon giggling and choking on his own smoke. By the end of the telling Scrub could think of nothing but how simple it was, as if there never was a bear but only the plan of how to get back at Shelly's pa, nothing but an idea waiting out there in the woods for somebody to stumble upon it. He began to laugh and the chair buckled under him, dropping him flat on his ass. Hal stood up to offer a hand

and then jerked it back as he lost his footing and tumbled off the porch.

A moment later Shelly came to the backdoor and found the one man splayed atop the broken chair and the other struggling to free himself from the chokeberry. "You don't think you've had enough to drink?" she said.

"We'll need more now." Scrub reached for one of Hal's boots, tried to fish his friend from the shrubs and then gave up, letting Hal tumble off into the yard.

They were supposed to be in Wyndell celebrating Scrub's last night of bachelorhood. Instead they were sneaking onto the pigfarm, keeping wide of both the house and the slumbering pigs. They had parked on a logging road half a mile away, grabbed shovel, pick and tire iron, then made their way through the woods to come out beneath the apple and pear trees that had not borne fruit in forever as far as Scrub could recall. The pigs grunted softly, sleepily. When the men reached the barn, Scrub wedged the iron between the door and its hasp, pulled down on the iron and opened the door. Inside they could smell pig shit.

"You'd think being frozen it wouldn't stink so much," Hal said, about to light a cigarette and then thinking better of it.

"Maybe it ain't frozen."

Scrub grabbed his friend's arm and the two of them wrestled there at the pool's edge, an elbow war that lasted for all of five seconds.

"I'm not trying to push you in," Scrub said, jumping back from his friend and the pool of shit. "I just want to hold onto you so I don't fall in."

"You might have said that first."

Scrub took Hal's outstretched arm and leaned over the pool. He tapped the surface with his boot. "Sure it's frozen."

"All the way?" Hal said.

"I'm not gonna check, are you?"

They left the building and found a hose wrapped around a nearby faucet. The pigfarmer had not thought to keep the faucet dripping

and when Scrub turned the handle the pipes began to hammer.
Both men jumped for cover. When the ice cleared the line and the
water began to flow, Scrub stuffed the hose behind the dirt
embankment separating the pigshit pool from the hill and, at the
hill's bottom, the river.

"You sure this is gonna work?" Hal said, toeing the dirt.

"I'd stake anything on it."

Hal took the shovel and Scrub the pick and they began to loosen
the dirt. They meant to weaken the structure. The water would do
the rest, thaw the pool just enough that it would break through the
embankment and begin to slide downhill toward the river.

"You know what I'm thinking?" Hal said, peaking around the
corner at the dark farmhouse, holding his lit cigarette behind his
back. "I'm thinking what are we gonna do if all of a sudden it just
pops right out on top of us. Like when you're trying to get ice from
a tray and some of it always ends up on floor."

"I saw a swimming pool do that once."

"Be a shitty way to die."

"You're not funny," Scrub said. "Let's go."

They left water and gravity to do their work and traipsed back
through the woods, at first fearful of shotgun blasts and then, once
they were halfway to Scrub's truck, of something more sinister.
They heard the cracking of twigs, the crunch of forest litter. The
last hundred yards they ran. Twice Scrub fell and the second time
thought he might have sprung his ankle, though the ache would
wear off soon enough. Hal, hearing his friend cursing in the darkness
behind him, tried to take the fence full tilt. Afterwards he said he
could have made it if he only he didn't smoke so much.

Early the next morning Shelly rolled Scrub out of bed with, "Go
on. I need to get ready."

He was hung-over, his brain as swollen as her bulging eyes, but
she'd hear none of it. "Go," she said, and he showered and put on
his suit.

He arrived at the hall as the caterers were unloading their truck.
He begged a beer off a gawky boy in a wrinkled tux and then sat

outside on the pavilion. The sun rose behind him, and Scrub's head and shoulders and lapels made a bird-like shadow on the water. The river itself stretched away in a V, flowing down from the pigfarm and then bouncing off the bank to move away to the south. There was ice in the river, small chunks spinning in the current, but not the slab Scrub knew was coming.

He drank his beer and waited, not thinking of the wedding only two hours away, not even of the bear, whose near-forgotten terms would not be mentioned in the wedding vows. Instead he imagined the pigfarmer's face, the embarrassment, the horror that would come over it. Some time later the old man's actual face jolted him out of his reverie.

"Pretty suit you're wearing, Scrub."

Scrub looked down at what he wore. It was two decades out of style, the arms too short and the collar too big. He knew he looked the dandy, but he also knew as soon as he saw the suit hanging on its clearance rack that Shelly would love it and that her pa would not. "Glad you like it," he told the pigfarmer. "I expect your daughter will too."

"She probably will."

The old man rubbed his hands together. They were fat and red and too clean for a man who raised swine. Scrub thought it would be nice if the old man swung at him, what with all these people around. He'd beat the pigfarmer bloody, then roll him off the pavilion into the river, to be frozen like one of those wooly mammoths in a block of shit.

Scrub turned in his seat and looked back at the caterers coming and going from the hall. "Guess you spent a pretty penny," he said.

"I don't suppose you like that at all. Considering."

"Oh, I consider it a mighty fine thing for you to do. For your daughter," Scrub said.

The old man shot his cuffs, and Scrub flinched, then clinched his fists. The old man eased back against the rail and waited a few seconds before saying, "Listen, there ain't no reason for us to pretend we like each other."

"Who's pretending?"

"But we still got to make it through the day. I suppose you'll be drinking?"

Scrub held up his beer.

"I'd rather you not cause a stink with all these people around," the old man said.

Scrub hid his grin behind the upturned beer can. "You don't want a row," he said.

"I ain't afraid of it."

"But you'd rather it not be today."

"Yes."

"Well I can keep my alcohol just fine," Scrub said, emptying the can and tossing it into the river.

"Just so it's said," the old man said, straightening his jacket and beginning to walk off toward the hall.

He stopped and turned when Scrub said, "Tell me this. Why is it you don't want me to marry your daughter?"

"Because, Scrub, you're a good for nothing piece of shit. Everybody knows it."

It was a bleary vision but a vision nonetheless as his bride walked down the aisle, her cream-colored dress falling off her narrow shoulders, gathering at her boney hips, terminating just shy of her bare ankles. Her ears had been hidden behind a headband of baby's breath and her eyes behind a half-veil. When she finally reached the altar and looked up at Scrub, the alcohol haze lifted and he was the happiest man alive.

"You look awful good, you do," Shelly whispered as the preacher began.

"Nuh, it's you," he muttered, and Shelly squeezed his hand to let him know she understood.

When Scrub returned from the bathroom, having puked up a half case of beer, a slice of cake, the flute of champagne he'd allowed himself to drink and on which he now blamed his sickness, the guests were beginning to murmur. Hal took him by the arm and led him through the crowd to the guardrail by the river. Hal had to point it out but there it was, floating toward them.

No one knew yet that it was shit. Some thought it might be the roof off a house. Others thought it mud or a mirage or a submerged boat. It glistened. A flotilla of dead fish followed alongside. Soon it floated into the bend, bumped against the bank and stuck there. It was huge, larger than even Scrub had imagined. With the sun high in the sky, it began to melt. And stink.

The crowd inched back from the bank, children holding their noses, women searching for handkerchiefs, a few of the men hiding their faces in their jacket sleeves. Scrub looked around for the old man and saw him standing dead still as the crowd dispersed. He knew where the shit had come from. His face said he did. And then Scrub followed the old man's stare, followed the line until it met Shelly's face. It was blank.

Scrub didn't have time to grasp entirely what that meant. The sheriff's car pulled into the lot and the fat sheriff climbed out. "It's yours, Abe," he said to the pigfarmer. "Somehow that retainer wall gave. That's what we got," he said, nodding at the frozen block of shit. The old man didn't respond.

Caterers formed something like a fire brigade, carrying coffee urns of hot water and dumping them over the railing onto the flow, then running back as the toxic steam riffled into the air.

"You. Stop that," the sheriff yelled at the caterers. "You're just making it worse." He turned back to the old man. "I'm trying to get them to open the dam upriver. Maybe we can float it out. Then it'll be somebody else's problem." The old man nodded. "Guess you know there'll be some kind of fine."

"I expect there will," the old man said, then excused himself and walked toward Scrub.

Scrub took one hit across the nose, hard enough he could hear the cartilage pop. He got in two of his own before Hal and the sheriff pulled them apart.

A few minutes later the sheriff and the old man drove off toward the farm. Scrub went to sit beside his bride. He tried to put his arm around her, and she mumbled something in the negative, said, "Be nice if you went in and saw to our guests. Be awful nice."

An hour later he staggered back outside to check on his

handiwork. The river had risen but the shit, instead of floating off, had begun to inch its way over the railing and onto the pavilion. The sheriff and half a dozen others stood around cursing. Some poked at it with sticks.

Somehow they made it to Wyndell where Scrub had reserved for them the nicest room in the city's nicest hotel. It wasn't much, a queen-sized bed, a desk, a blue loveseat with gold pinstripes. What made it the honeymoon suite was the tub. Off its side hung an electric pump that turned it into a makeshift Jacuzzi. Scrub thought when he reserved it that all hotel rooms, even the crappy ones, were romantic.

Now he was laid out on the floor, breathing not through his wrecked nose but through his open mouth. He heard something tap against the window and he opened his eyes. Somehow his suit was off and hanging on a chair. Shelly's foot dangled off the bed, the bottom of her bridal gown covering her skinny leg.

He stood. It took some effort but he managed. An arm draped over her face, she seemed to be asleep. He stumbled toward the bed and then steadied himself. He wanted to say something to her, something to make the night what she deserved, and he wanted to seem sober when he did it. He heard the tap again and looked at the window. Staring in was the bear, lit by a nearby floodlight. For the first time Scrub noticed the silver streaks along her snout. He went to the window and opened it. No sooner than it was cracked she stuck her head in and pushed up on the pane.

She pulled her hindquarters through the window and then stood there in the room on her four paws. Scrub didn't ask why she was there. He may have neglected to think about it these last days, but he had not forgotten it entirely. It had been stuck in a recess of his brain, and even the pigfarmer's fist had not dislodged it. For a moment he considered fighting the bear, but what good would it do? She would gore him and it would not change a thing. So he sat in the chair by the reading table. The least he could do was watch.

Her front paws were up on the bed now. She was an enormous beast, too big to squeeze through a hotel window. She nuzzled her fat head beneath the wedding gown. Shelly opened her eyes and looked at the bear, then at Scrub and then back at the bear, its head out of the gown and moving up her body. The bride mumbled something neither affirmative nor negative, something very much like resignation. And then the bear began to rake her claws across Shelly's body. The wedding gown came away and for a passing moment Scrub was surprised to see Shelly wore nothing beneath it.

At first the claws left pink, parallel lines on Shelly's belly. And then welts. And then gashes as the bear buried her mouth and teeth in the open gut. It was only then that Scrub remembered the unborn child.

When he woke Shelly's foot still dangled off the side of the bed. He was almost afraid to stand and look at her. But he did and found her lying there, skinny and naked, the cream dress in a bunch on the floor. He went to the bathroom and rinsed his face, decided he was as close to sober as he was likely to be before morning. He lifted the toilet seat and unzipped his pants and looked down at a wad of toilet paper and clotted blood floating in the bowl.

Back in the room he whispered, "Shell?"

She took her arm off her face and looked at him.

"You alright?"

"Yes," she said.

"You know I love you," he said as she pulled herself up in bed and he went to sit beside her.

"It's gone," she said. He thought she meant the bear until she added, "The baby is."

"You sure?"

"I'd be the one to know," she said. "I thought I'd let you flush it."

He reached out and took her hand, which she did not pull away.

"Go ahead," she said. "I mean for you to do it."

When he came out of the bathroom for the second time, she stood beside the window in her chapped and peeling skin, a long flake hanging off her shoulder. He wanted to go to her and peel it away. He would have liked to go to her and put his teeth around one of her radar ears.

"You know what it is," she said.

"What's that?" he asked from the bathroom door.

"What you did."

"Hal told you then."

"Hal didn't tell me anything," still staring out the window, cars passing on the road, their headlights lighting her up like a glow worm. "Nobody had to tell me."

"I'm sorry."

"You know what it is," she repeated.

"What is it?"

She laughed, at first softly but then loudly. "A shitberg," she said, laughing into the closed window. "A great big shitberg."

" I suppose it was," he said, catching on and laughing himself.

"A fine gift that was. A great big shitberg on our wedding day."

"Well," he said, coming to her and gently pulling the loose skin from her back, "your pa already ordered the cake."

Jedidiah Ayres

Miriam

T he first great mistake Miriam ever made, the one she'd been paying for the rest of her life, was allowing herself ever to be born in the first place. By not succumbing to the sickness, her mother passed on, she'd cavalierly thrown open the door for everything that came after. All the other missteps, bad decisions and sub-par moments really took their cue from that one. She reflected now and again how much you can owe for mistakes made in ignorance or even innocence, though the latter was not her experience.

Her mother lived in a Mississippi brothel near the Arkansas border another half year before she shot herself up with enough smack to kill a platoon and was buried, supposedly at midnight, under a tree overlooking the cat house, in an unmarked grave. The other girls had taken on the raising of Miriam as a hobby that helped keep their minds occupied when the life began to get to them and Miriam, still small and pink and given to fits of coughing and bouts of sleeplessness and without a trend toward feeding became a mascot of great importance to them.

Too young for intent, she became the confessional by virtue of helplessness and dependence. The ritual of rocking and cooing her over their shoulder whilst unburdening the day's trespasses into her tiny curved ear repeated nightly. She took in the very sweat and breath of sin and sighed and farted it back at them all cleaned up and smelling of infant. But it growed her up in an accelerated fashion such as was popularly believed by radio preachers to be the way in wicked times.

She learned things, as all children do, by osmosis and it colored the way she perceived the world and conducted herself in it. Though shy on use, she learned never to be in want of arms. She knew that cash was but one form of currency, that blessed by the Federal government, which meant little much outside of legal documents. And she learned that sheep were wolves, sure as shit.

None among the rotating cast of mothers was more devoted to the child than the Nubian. She called the child Child and nourished her as one of the many she'd never birthed. Over time, she was generally acknowledged as the primary authority in matters concerning Miriam.

Her motherly ways were not demonstrated exclusive to the child and when Miriam was eleven, Auntie no shit Jemima got called upon to take over the madamship of a house in Hot Springs and brought her north. It was amidst the curious natural phenomena, claimed to purify a body and restore a soul, that Miriam first self-administered opiates and then never looked back.

Auntie Jem knew the signs of junk better than your typical vice police and gave her a beating, like you reserve for the ones you love, the lines of which they are to read betwixt and comprehend the heighth and the breadth and the depth. Miriam was in bed afterward four days and reversed the cure just as soon as she walked. Jemima looked in the child's unfocused eyes, saw another sign she knew well, and changed up her tactic.

"If you make these vows, it will be more binding than any holy matrimony you aint never gonna enter into anyhow, an I oughtta know, so go on now an listen Auntie Jem." She taught the child heroin the way she'd taught her intercourse, as plain mechanical facts and proven strategies for recovery from. Flesh was one element among the bounty of creation and held unique properties like any other, but the real difference from wood and stone and sea and air and steel, was only possession.

"There now, then, that's everything I know. Jes don be letting it get in between you and what you need to do. An don ever let me catch you keepin mo secrets from me."

Tired of routine and itchy for the horizon the child ran off at age fourteen with a G.I. who'd seen Indochina. Among other promises, he claimed he would take her to exotic places and teach her worldly things. Two weeks later, her eyes open to nothing so much as the saming of America, she left him the clothes she'd used to tie him up with in a motel room off I-44 on the outskirts of Tulsa and took the rest of his belongings, including a photograph of his mother in a wide collared, floral print dress and high off the forehead construction of hair, as her own.

On her first night, conscious of what alone in the world is meant to say, she removed the picture of the soldier's mother and spoke to it while sitting in a booth by the window of the Stuckeys. She thought she'd know what she wanted when she saw it and chances were, whatever it was could be found as likely in Tulsa as Toledo.

The picture, which she had not yet named, looked at her in a kindly but knowing way and a voice peculiarly like Jem's said "Child, you are alone."

"I know," she stated, without a value attached of emotional import.

"Where is it you going?"

Miriam shrugged.

"What is it you trying to leave behind?" Miriam spotted a bear of a man leaving the Stuckeys and ambling with a notion toward a sixteen wheeler parked on the far side of the lot. She slipped the picture back in her pocket and answered without listening.

"Only what I know."

She worked the highway circuit and saw more of what she'd seen before. She carried a knife with a retractable blade, she'd only once had occasion to cut with. She'd used it on another drifter she'd spotted a curious amount at diners. Once, outside the Loaf 'N Jug, he surprised her by coming upon her while she slept. He had ideas he couldn't pay for and she reminded him of that by making him aware of the blade's tip in his kidney. His counter was to strike her face and she followed through by slicing deep and around to the front. It was enough to encourage him to roll off and she told him if she ever saw his mutt face again, she would certainly kill him.

Not all the familiars on the road were hostiles. Not to first impressions anyhow. She fell in with a boy she met doing a westerly drift originating from Bowling Green. He was nineteen, and thin as a reed with bear black hair, a bit long, and worn back with grease. His name was Casper and he met her by climbing into the cab belonging to a trucker who was distracted by the pickle tickle he was receiving from Miriam.

Casper, slick as duck shit, stepped in and placed his lady stinger behind the trucker's left ear. "Hoss, you got 'bout um ten more seconds to finish 'fore Ima need these here wheels." The trucker's boner did an immediate soft and Casper apologized. "Nah, Hoss, didn't mean for that to happen. Truly, I'm sorry. How much?"

The nervous trucker with his pants around his knees said "It's all in the glove box."

"Nah, I mean, how much you pay for the French?"

"Nothing."

"Nothing?" Casper looked Miriam in the eyes, "That so?"

Miriam wiped her mouth daintily, "He was going to drive me to California."

One second's consideration was all Casper needed. "No sweat, Hoss. I got it." He pulled the trucker, who was twice his size, out of the cab and hopped into the driver's seat. "I'll get her there, don't worry and I truly am sorry. Looked like your pleasure was sincere and I hate to disrupt that."

Miriam watched the trucker tug his jeans back up with both thumbs in the rearview, then fixed her eyes on Casper who glanced briefly in her direction, then focused on the road. He said, "Not enough sincerity these days. Not in people, don't you think?"

And she answered, "Are you for real?"

The way they worked it changed up. They targeted bowling alleys, veteran's halls and the occasional Y.M.C.A. Sometimes they'd be seen together and he'd be her brother and explain they needed money for traveling to their uncle's ranch after just losing their father to tragic circumstances. He would lean in and go on about how nice his sister was and how grateful she'd be for smiling on them in their need.

Other times, she'd arrive in the truck stop cafe alone, count out
nickels enough for coffee and nurse it sallow cheeked, fishing for
looks. Whatever the method, the climax was the same. Casper would
slip in, apologize and leave with what he could carry. He gave the
sincerity rap most times he made an entrance.

Then they would speed away, and with a fresh spike tapped,
Miriam would sink into the deep enveloping grip of the leather seat
and, with her feet, twist the dial of the A.M. radio. She'd switch
back and forth between religious stations, just barely coming in, as
though the open air were a winding, rut pocked trail sapping them
the conviction to beg, once arrived. Casper, when her bare toes fell
into his lap would change it back to rockabilly and tap the steering
wheel unconsciously. Sometimes she raised her foot and punched
an instrument of tuning only to be met by a single clear intonement
coming out of the wilderness to "Repent. Make clear the way..." and
Capser would nearly break the knob turning it off. He'd hum instead.

One such night, Miriam, trying to curl around the tickle making
its way through her said, "Casper...you're what Auntie Jem would
call a... hedonist."

"That so, Mirry? What is that, some kinda bible shit?"

"...guess so..."

"Sounds like bible talk." Then he rhapsodized about ancient
things and the irrelevance of philosophy. Said weren't nothing
thinking about preposterous hypotheticals could do for you now
that you wouldn't do on your own without having wasted an hour
and a minute, you could have been living, supposing. "Besides, all
those bed sheet wearing pederasts never heard Gene Vincent." And
with that, he drove the final nail into the coffin of rebuttal.

She liked the sound of that, far off sound that it was. It seemed
to bounce around the car's interior something less than normal fast.
It took banking paths off the windshield and dash into a slow
cascading arc before reaching her ears. Other sounds were made
that never did get there intact. They tended to arrive in fragmented
syllables unlinked to any intentional meaning. Some said things
escaped out the open windows when Casper would take a curve
and she imagined them melting into the countryside to be picked

up by wild beasts who knew no better than she what to do with them. But the timbre of his voice and reasoning appealed to her teenage sensibilities. She would volley something back occasionally mostly for the pleasure of provoking further ideological commentary. It was like listening to a conversation from underneath a bath.

"Tell me about your momma, Casper." She pulled out the G.I.'s wallet picture of his own mother, looking like an Eleanor or Gertrude or possibly a Helen. Her forehead was impossibly high and her mouth was small and dark and carried front teeth that met at an unlikely angle and which showed only a little bit between lips in her smile. Miriam was eager for traits to assign her imaginary matron, possessing, as she did, no picture of Auntie Jem.

Everything about the motel was thin. The walls were thin, the mattress was thin, the comforter was thin. Certainly the proprietor was thin, as was the smile meant to conceal his lechery when he handed Casper their room key. Casper'd paid extra this evening for a room with a television set and they'd decided to leave it on all night to get their money's worth.

Johnny Carson was sure a funny fella and made California seem like a nicer place than she already imagined. That was their stated destination and Casper meant to arrive on the top part and work their way down at a leisurely pace with an eye toward Mexico. He said they could make some money in California and it would spend better across the border.

Casper's lip curled reflexively. "My momma's a mean bitch, Mir."

Miriam turned over to face him, but he wasn't looking her way. "No. You don't mean that."

"I'm sincere, sugar. You gotta know least that."

"Why? What was so horrible about her?" Without thinking, she pressed the photograph to her breast as if protecting its ears from hearing the potentially hurtful things could be lobbed at a mother.

"Just mean. What else you want me to say?"

She didn't know. Anything would be better than mean, though. She'd seen enough of mean among the women of Jem's places. She'd seen other things too, but mean was a trait she'd grown weary of. It was a quality she was leaving out of photographic mother's personality. Betty, she decided she would name the picture, Betty. "Tell me if she could cook then."

"Course she could cook. Nothing to that. Not like fancy, but there's hardly a thing can't be choked down given the right treatments. Hell, anything that makes its own grease is got half the work done for you. So, yes, she didn't starve me. Thank you, momma."

She ignored the sarcasm in his voice and took the concession as a minor victory. Casper was a man of certainties, earned or not, and she was always pleased to discover a new area of gray in his views which she could continue to bring up until he'd pondered it thoroughly. He had no interest in discussing things he did not have a well formed or at least unretractable opinion on. "Betty couldn't cook."

"Who?"

"My momma." She handed him the picture. "She didn't, anyways. Auntie Jem did all that kind of work and Betty just made her hair pretty." She smiled at the ease the story came out with.

"Since I already got the pretty, I'm gonna learn to cook."

"Well, sugar now we know everything."

They had a pretty good thing going till she spoilt it by getting pregnant by him, or rather by telling him that she was. Her reluctance to say until she was most positive bought her only an uneasy spectator's type enjoyment of their time together. She watched those weeks like it was a T.V. show she'd like to be part of, knowing it was destined to end soon. When the sick was pretty much a constant, she said it. He shrugged the way was reflexive for him and gave her the options.

"We been good together, sweetheart, and I will miss you if you go off and have this kid, but you wanna keep with me, don't worry none, the woods is full of sharp sticks." She spoilt it further by crying when she said she wanted to stay with him.

The next day he told her they could make a much better score by being more selective in their marks. They were somewhere near Lincoln when he explained what he meant. It was mid November

and the sun wore out awful quick those days, so though it was not
even five in the evening, dark had moved in and all but changed the
locks on the doors when he stopped the Chevy across the street
from a pool hall.

"Where is this?" she asked.

"Relax, Mir. I know this place. This is where we can make some
good money." They crossed the street and he walked right through
he puddles while she took care not to splash in them. He looked
impatient with her, holding the front door open, waiting for her to
catch up. The music warmed her instantly upon entering. Merle
Haggard was having the same trouble with a lady he always seemed
to be and it was a minor disappointment to realize that wouldn't
change no matter where she went.

The warmth of the music in the air turned into a suffocating
density of smoke emanating from a score of sources and holding
everything in the atmosphere like a body of water. She could nearly
see the disturbance sound waves made passing through, rippling
out and disappearing in the corners of the broad hall. A dozen red
felt tables in the front gave way to a bar that bisected the room.
Casper led them between the tables; nodded at the man behind the
bar and continued toward the back room where a short and round
man with a cigar like a chicken leg clenched in his large teeth stood
from his table and motioned Casper back.

She took a seat, as instructed, on a high chair along the wall
and watched Casper go toward the fat man. He talked to the
proprietor and she saw him give the man some money. The barman
brought her a vanilla Coke while Casper spoke about business in
the back.

When he returned to her side, he had a root beer bottle featuring
a straw sticking out the top. "Who is that man?" she inquired,
watching him with his back to them now, speaking into a telephone
mounted on the wall.

Casper didn't look at her, but kept his eyes on the customers
going about their games and drinks. Most of the patrons looked
like farmers to her, though she couldn't reconcile what seemed like
the hardest work in the world with recreation of this sort, in her

thinking. They wore overalls, anyhow. There were teenagers at the front tables. Tall, angular sticks of boy men, the fattest part of them, impossibly large Adam's apples protruding from throats that had never been shaved. Five Negro men, dressed like whites in overalls and denim caps, shared a table nearest to the bar. They had given her some consideration, but looking at Casper, knew better than to waste their time making advances.

"Fat man." he answered like it meant something.

"What does that mean?"

"Means he's fat, Mir. Don't worry now. He's gonna hook us up with deep pockets." Over the next two hours, Casper had turned down a couple of dudes who eventually approached them, getting a head shake from the fat man. When a respectable looking one about fifty entered and caught Casper's eye, he triangulated the gaze with the manager who nodded. Casper sucked the rest of his cream soda through the straw and said, "Bingo. Be right back."

He made his way across the room to the man, in the expensive clothes. They conversed briefly, both throwing over the shoulder looks back and bargaining for her. An agreement was reached and Miriam was approached by the man who failed to hide his reptilian nature underneath his expensive clothes and refined manner. Miriam knew the drill, but still felt a shiver getting the go ahead from Casper through the smoke.

He was all of a gentleman meeting her. Called her miss and held out his arm for her to join in the walk out the hall. He had a big black hearse of a car waiting which made her nervous some. Meant Casper would have a driver at least to dispatch of before he could make an entrance, but her love for and trust in Casper had yet to be proved unfounded.

Her concern increased when instead of taking her to some flea bag motel or fuck pad bungalow, he took her to a proper home in a respectable neighborhood and pulled right in to the driveway bold as innocence. She'd heard of such places before, but had to call this a first actually being there. On the television programs she'd seen, these streets seemed common and were home to the best people society had produced and she'd appropriately taken the underlying message speaking at her through television console in the back room at Jem's place to be that this was not where she belonged.

The driver, a big soft Negro with a shiny head and white smile, he wasn't using, opened her door and helped her out. The gentleman had already entered the home and the African instructed her toward a secondary structure round the back of the main house.

"Go on now, make yourself comfortable and whatever you do—" He inclined his head in a conspiratorial manner,"—don't speak to him and don't look him in the eye."

Walking toward the guesthouse, she tossed a look over her shoulder trying to find Casper's Chevy. Even as she entered, she felt the ink drying on that chapter of her life. She paused internally to consider what was to be learned and what could be taken with her into the next. There were things she knew would not pass through the fire, but she wasn't certain what they might be.

By the next morning it was apparent that Casper had deserted, sold her and their baby to the well-groomed monster. She never spoke to another soul about her ordeal that night with the amateur abortionist, but she saw him in her sleep for years, standing over her strapped to a table, reciting from memory, passages of medical texts, poetry and all manner of school-learned appreciations while he experimented. She exercised a tight grip on her voice and refused to cry out and send any extra pleasure toward him, though she was dehydrated from the tears flushed silently throughout.

She was abandoned in the woods fifteen miles outside the city with some water and a towel for the bleeding. She was too weak to walk the first day. The void where the fetus had been throbbed, keeping her from sleep. Over the course of the day, though she could not put words to the process, it filled with something darker and harder and colder by far than she'd ever guessed at in her nature. In the dusk that eventually fell, she heard dogs circling her, attracted to the blood in the air, but she passed the night unmolested.

One and counting.

Aunty Jem never betrayed the flip flop her heart did when she saw Miriam again. The child showed up at the doorstep as the last customers of the previous night were making their departures. Miriam was looking like just another starlet deciding to face facts. Aunt Jay's saw them occasionally; the ones that got out of California before dying poorly nearer to the farm they grew up on. She had the costume, but not the posture of that particular breed of prodigal.

Her clothing was gray and frayed and the marks about her where skin showed told stories she'd been warned against. Her face featured dark places beneath her eyes and her teeth looked less white than they had the last time she was seen, but there was never any mistaking her. Jem saw her coming a hundred yards down the road.

"Child." said Jem in her deep, rich voice. It felt to Miriam like hot butter sliding over her face and she imagined it filling in the many cracks and depressions she'd added in her sojourn. She carried everything she could call her own in a single over the shoulder bag, the approximate size and weight of a house cat. The essentials she carried on her person always. Her knife in the top of her boot, any pills or powders she had left in the toe of the opposite and cash concealed in various private spots.

"Hey Jem."

"How long you staying?"

"Just long enough."

"I see. Well come in and get out those rags. I'll have Sugar fetch you something clean."

Betty had talked her through the woods and found them a Salvation Army. She'd told the caseworker then about hitchhiking to her momma's home in Portland. Said she'd miscarried and been left in the woods by a spooked driver. She'd let the woman read whatever she wanted into that. They'd fixed her up with a couple nights' sleep and food as would keep you from starving.

She relayed the same story to Jem, minus the bunk about family while she cut Miriam's hair after a hot bath and afternoon nap. "I'm ready to pull my own weight around here, Jem."

"Says you."

"Taught me good."

"You all gristle and bone, child. Rest up some."

"I'm not around for long, Jem. You know that?"

"'Spect as much. Don go till you ready, though."

Miriam did not cry in front of Auntie Jem, but rather waited for the time when she was alone in Jem's bed, to curl up like a baby and let loose some of the hurt and fear she'd kept strapped to her. She gave voice to some of the bitter parts, followed by hushed admissions of scares she'd acquired since leaving home. She'd made them audible, which was as far as it would go. She'd let them out that far, but kept a tight leash on them and kept them close and they licked at her body like hungry puppies until sleep was a fact requiring no acknowledgment or cooperation.

Jem stayed on the other side of the door, joining the child in a tear letting and came in to stroke her hair when she fell to sleep. Miriam slept without dreams for a single merciful night.

She'd asked Jem to style her hair up off of her forehead, but never disclosed where the notion came from; suspecting Jem would worry more than she ought when Miriam took her leave again. The result was something of a disappointment to her, but as she negotiated with the mirror she made something more like agreeable terms when she employed heating instruments.

She found work in the house and yard to occupy her body while her mind resolved whatever it was working around. She learned something about cooking too. As she put on weight, Jem encouraged her toward town, saying there was plenty opportunity for a woman not afraid to work and she could do her proud by carving out a respectable life, independent of the needs of men. She always rebuffed Jem's suggestions by informing her that she had needs of her own that didn't fit any cozy, over-the-fireplace-type pictures and leave it at that.

Her needs were not yet in focus, but called to her louder all the time.

One morning, Miriam slipped out while Jem made up the room. This surprised neither. She returned to the highway, plying her trade for distance and sustenance, heading once again for California, because that was where the road ended.

The man behind the bar just wanted to wash his glasses and not give the time of day to the young girl with the short-styled haircut and attitude. He'd had her pegged as soon as she'd come in. Sex fell off her like breath and as much as he might like a ride, he knew when he was over his head. So he only attempted to answer her question. "Where you headed?"

Miriam leaned in to savor the sulfur smell of the struck match as testament to the general fragrance of the honky-tonk. When the scent died, she would rely on the cigarette.

"Casper."

"Wyoming?"

Miriam looked the bartender in the eyes. "You know any other?"

"Guess I just never met nobody headed to. Coming from, sure, but headed to? On purpose? Don't come across that much round here."

"Got some kinda high opinion of this place, huh?"

"You don't?"

"Nothin special, far as I can see. Who is it I should meet?"

He indicated a cluster of bearded men hovering over a pool table, great swollen guts hanging over the front of their pants, all covered in once white t-shirts that ran the length and the width and the return trip underneath back to the jeans they tucked into. Suspenders and ball caps rounded out the club uniform. She'd spotted them the moment she'd entered. Knew the look, knew the type. "Anybody particular?"

The bar tender shrugged. He suggested something along the lines of "Bitch." under his breath as she slid off her stool and wiggled her narrow ass at him across the room.

"Who's the fortunate gentleman going to make my acquaintance on the way to Casper this evening?" she offered by way of introduction. This turned heads in the general direction of her feet and she waited patiently, posing while they slowly turned northward.

One of the younger stood up and squared his shoulders, centering his fleshy hands on his cue. He tilted his red cap back on his head and offered "Missoula?"

She took a pouty puff on her cigarette. "Don't even rhyme, now do it?"

. . . .

She found she needed neither his presence nor advice to have success as was equal to what they'd had as a team. She certainly didn't need his blathering mouth, certain of its own importance and just about full of shit. She also felt no great loss when considering his affections, seeing in a behind-her-now-way how hollow a gesture they had been.

If there were two ways of learning a thing, Miriam would always choose the bloody. This scholarly style had a way of marking her so that every year showed. At seventeen, she made another near fatal mistake. Having set out for California, she'd ricocheted off the coastline and found herself touring Wyoming. She was making a concentrated effort to escape the orbit of the region and spotted a likely ticket elsewhere at the cash register. He was headed south by southeast and she said good enough. Her appetite for wandering not yet replaced by anything else, Miriam continued to work in trucks and that night she hesitated to pull her weapon at the first itch to. The result was she got a detached retina from making the acquaintance of the dashboard with his hand behind her head forcing the meeting to take place rapidly and without time to prepare.

The further result was she took another beating, like perhaps the kind you would like to give a loved one except they aren't there and you wish they were and would read between the lines, understand exactly what you meant. She's not all the way conscious for most of it.

The beating was received after she took off the tip of his pecker with her front teeth when she woke up in a dark place. She felt like her insides were jelly. Sore jelly like a great, single bruise. The pungent smell in the enclosed space was familiar as was the difficulty walking. She had to shut her damaged eye to make sense of the place, such as was available to be made.

She spotted her assailant asleep, without his trousers, on a cot ten feet and as many painful shuffles away. Apparently there'd been a party. He'd had red-rimmed eyes and favored her with darty amphetamine glances when he'd first picked her up, and it looked like he'd spent up a year's worth of twitch while he drove. Judging from the all smashed together feeling her guts were reporting, his fornication style was jackhammer and goodnight.

He looked now like every man she'd ever met and had no detail to him at all. In the other direction was escape out the door of his truck, she reckoned herself rightly to be in the back of. The consideration of options lasted not half a minute. She went about it slow and with great care, not wanting to spoil the opportunity presented her. Carefully, she motioned herself, with great pain, till she was kneeling over him. She found it hidden within itself like a woodland creature sheltering in the roots of a tree and used her fingers gently to coax it out. It responded to her mouth and once she had its confidence she bit down.

The grip she employed was not one designed to preamble escape, but held rather a weight that lent legitimacy to the permanence of her claim. It belonged to her now, the way she'd seen terrier dogs lay hold of a toy. She'd seen them lifted off the ground, supported only by their stubborn grip. She knew that there was finality in those clinched jaws.

When he separated her from him, she retained possession of his dickhead and smiled away as he lay into her with his hands. Eventually he passed out and she was not killed that day, though she told herself she was prepared to die. She would be his last victim and decided that it was also her last time to be one. There was a leverage of power in the ability to follow through your intentions with the possibility of death introduced. She felt it for the first time that night, his flesh now hers swallowed and not to return. Let him do what he needed, she'd only done the same.

In the end, she did it because revenge was holding sway over her hierarchy of needs. She'd got away before, but had never taken revenge. It tasted sweet. Revenge, not his pecker.

She woke again near the back of the rig, gray light insisting its way between the floor and swinging doors. There were still stars visible in the pre-dawn sky and the cold air ran toward invigorating, though she was not a candidate for walking. She strained her neck toward the draft and breathed what she could of freedom. It was enough.

She felt unconsciousness taking her again, but did not fight. She was ready for whatever came next, on the first page of a new chapter in her life.

One and counting.

Heather Fowler

You Are One Click Away From Pictures of Nude Girls

Everywhere Larry looks he sees cunt, the dream of it, the salty murmur of satisfaction. It has become overwhelming with its silver-pink purse unveiled at every glance, traipsing from every corner. Unconsumed by the pixeled pudendum perused before his work's net moratorium, he views it on billboards, in faces, over garments, and beside coat racks in the employee lounge.

In his eyes, the seething expanse of hairy pearls undulates, and so much unexpected unmentionable is enough to drive a sane man mad. Even spied in velvet, it is dangerous, especially in browner shades. Larry is possessed by Aphrodite's pink flower—the bloom peeking from innocuously rose cashmere sweaters, the balding skin of a woman's toy poodle, or the foam-dripping snatch of a cocoa man's mustache. Cunt hides in the fur trim of a commuter's jacket and in sly white clouds over dream-blue labias (or the sopping, gray cumulus with white wispy backgrounds)—it calls to him routinely, "Lar-ry, Come out and pl-ay-ay!"

These visions started after he met Susan at the work shaming-session when she told him to stop surfing porn, and then he told himself, "You may not plunder sex sites on the job, old boy, so have some control!" Now, he has this control in the cubicle, but the organs still emerge from the woodwork, glistening like teenage shroom hallucinations from dribbles of the water cooler or wending free from the paneling of pristine surfaces of butcher block. House-pets and the ripped edges of cardboard boxes begin to entice him.

His cunt-quitting becomes a farce of unexpected overexposure—like how a smoker drastically increases intake when imagining no more butts, and then suckles each microcosmic smoke-stack in a seismic rejection of that thought, nursing each butt like the last oxygen mask available on the end-drop of a turbulent plane: Going down? Larry is; he has. He thinks, "No more cunt? My world is over. I have been trained since birth to pursue this one thing. This will be my devil's dilemma, my heartbreaking loss." The physical reaction to perceived withdrawal pounds in his veins like a hammer, surges like a toothache in an open cavity, while faintly, ever so faintly, despite his volition to quit it all, he hears his own primal plea: No, nonononono! More, and more and more cunt! You will not keep me from the prize.

Also, age has caused a slowdown in the amount of actual cunt he gets, so he theorizes that this is why this is happening: The more he desires this love blossom, discrete punani, esprit d'pulchritudinous, the more creative his mind grows to obtain it: Can't get it at work, find it everywhere else. Like poor slops in tenements who dream of rich picnics, or women in Czechoslovakian death camps who wrote recipes for apple fritters in the absence of flour, sugar, and even apples——he thinks incessantly about his lack, about his desire, onward and upward in hallucinogenic escalation, viewing more and more cunt in unusual places, but left unsatisfied.

And the fantasies are getting worse.

This fixation so consumes him that this morning, he saw cunt in the rough black hairs of an old woman's neck on the subway. Those tiny fibers looked like vulgar obscenities, and as he turned away from the woman's smiling face—having been thoroughly shocked, having never had a thing for fat, old cunts—he sighed.

A pity, he decided later. She appeared to have considered him. Perhaps he should have looked deeper. He rethinks the original debacle weeks ago and recalls the exact, unmanning moment in which the cunt began to appear. Though plenty of employees were reprimanded for net-surfing—one girl for writing stories on a free site, one gay boy in chat, and an old lady in a sewing circle—only Larry had been called to the gray-green carpet in Susan's office.

"Why, Larry?" Susan had asked, "Why on earth would you do this at work? Couldn't you check sex sites at home? Explain it to me, Larry. I don't understand..."

And she was benevolent and patient, her silver brows knit with worry, her face open and compassionate like Mother Theresa, but Larry would or could not explain it to her because he could hardly explain it to himself. "Because I'm stupid with no self-control," was the first thing that came to mind as excuse, but he would not say that. Not to tight-assy Susan of the control-top pantyhose—so he stared at her, lowered his dark lashes then said, with a touch of contrition, "I promise to stop. I'm really sorry," but at this exact moment the very first improbable cunt appeared in her eyes.

It sat on her lashes and spasmed, so he sat with his hands folded over his lap, trying not to draw attention to his aching groin. He thought of unzipping his trousers and shouting, "Elvis has left the building," as a euphemism for his rising member (as a child he had always wanted to be Elvis), but looked away from her blinking eyes and off towards the sun-bleached memos pinned to the cork-board above her desk. He stared at her dying cactus and then glanced to the industrial clock on her wall. It was only ten a.m., which meant another six excruciating hours.

"Do you promise to make every effort to stop cruising porn at work?" she pressed, but when she blinked again, he saw another butterfly cunt spasm flying free across her peepers, and thought, looking at the picture of an enormous Rottweiler on her desk, all about old women he read about in magazines who bought large dogs to service them, creating a love for such service via applied peanut butter to their crotches: was she one?

He couldn't stop staring at the picture, thinking: "The Woman and Her Dog. The Woman and Her Pet Dog"—where had he heard that before? "Yes, I promise," he said, noticing the photo was centered, neat, almost too perfect. Did that mean something?

"That's good," she said, following the path of his eyes to her photo. "Do you like my dog?" She picked it up to dust off with her blouse. "Because I love my dog." For a brief moment, she stared with deep affection at the canine face in the frame, before turning a terrible look upon him and saying, "Seriously Larry, Let's not have this talk again."

"We won't," he replied.

"Very good." Her cunty eyes blinked. When she glanced right at him, he wanted to tell her that her gaze was daunting with that expression and that he was sure that the sugar-substitute she used became formaldehyde at eighty-some degrees, preserving her stomach like a science class frog, and that she should stop using it—but when she came closer, ready to shake his hand and blinking all the while, he instead wanted to say something crazy, anything strange enough to stop the movement of her dual cunt lids so near. She offered her hand for a shake, avoiding her eyes, but after he grasped it, she pulled back abruptly and coughed, looking at him like she might be assessing his child-molester potential.

Then she let loose: "I could understand one downloaded page from the net—but two hundred, Larry? Two hundred in the cache? You'd think we'd have harassment suits sky-high. How could you view such smut on your monitor when anyone could walk by?"

The alt-tab stroke was plain on his mind. He shrugged, noticing a run in her nylons, splintering the stretchy sacks all the way up her right thigh.

"You've worked here fifteen years," Susan said, "so I don't want to fire you, but cut out net cruising. One more instance and I'll have to let you go. We have policies to dole, adjustments to make, people to talk to, and not nearly enough time to waste on such internet slacking. This is your first and last warning, Larry: Cut it out."

She went on, but he didn't listen. "Exactly," he wanted to say. "We have work, and work is what we should do, but it bores us, and there's no more insipid business than insurance—so, aren't you going to wake up one day and realize that, Susan? If we worked somewhere more stimulating, even vaguely more interesting—say in a factory or a beauty parlor, even in a morgue—a copy of Sports Illustrated swim models might do just fine, but the reward must equal the punishment, dear employer, and so it must be full nude exposure. The Law of Big Numbers causes a parallel proportion for the Law of Stimulating Need." He said none of this, but muttered instead, "Say no more, Susan. I won't need another warning."

"Good." Her cunty eyes blinked severely like an abridged orgasm, so how could he explain anything when she seemed so bereft? Her hair, constricted at her nape in long, coiled twists, reminded him of snakes. In a brown suit, she couldn't be more drab. He thought of birds where the female was duller, and she spoke again, but he blotted out her voice and focused on her lower face where her lips had become an undulating vulva, opening and contracting. The sound of her voice was a drone. He thought: "By zip-code, driving record, age, and multi-car discounts, they beat the soul from us, Susan, the screens for premium are duller than rusted Exactos, and yet, you don't seem to regret the loss of your youth, your joy in this business..." But he sighed, giving up his manifesto as he heard her say, with finality, "...so I want you to put the company first, okay?"

She frowned, and he had the sinking feeling she would not understand his musings or rationales—believing neither that online cunt had saved his sanity while improving his productivity, nor that there was a special lure in emails sent by complete strangers headed up with the ten promising words: You are One Click Away from Pictures of Nude Girls.

"Cunt!" he wanted to scream. "Salvation!" Invariably, he had clicked away from split premiums only to see Hilda and Her Magic Disappearing Cucumber, Sally with Two College Friends, Jill does Two Dogs and Masturbates with a Blender Lid—and returned to work invigorated. But this would be no more. The line had been pissed in the snow, or drizzled in the dry, brown sand. Susan was the joy-killer.

Still, free cunt was nothing to scoff at, he thought, staring at Susan's mouth, so labial, still roaming, in his mind, over his veiled manhood, for though he never checked the sites from home, how could he explain to her they were necessary at work? How to explain this desperate need for the mother lode of all pink or petal-soft. Could she find a penis so entrancing?

He doubted this as she said, splish, splash, spasm, "...followed by routine checks. I'll see you in two weeks."

"Penis in two weeks," he replied, thinking of his own.

"What?"

"I said, see you in two weeks." Well, he couldn't blame her for a lack of excitement. A penis was a tool, he thought, functional, good, but not the bloom of a poppy, not even vaguely reminiscent of seafood. A penis was not beautiful, nor did it have to be. It did not give birth, or have endless orgasms. He said nothing further, but pondered these ideas on his way to his desk and went home five minutes early.

At home, he thought of how his own love life consisted of a blow-up doll named Judy and a few over-viewed pornos. Real girls were confusing. They wouldn't date him, or they would, but only if he took them nice places and paid for everything, then made no advances. When he was younger, he got more sex for less buck, but the bang to buck ratio had deflated just as his stomach had expanded. He'd even gone to dating services, put ads in the paper, done everything possible! He was not picky! He was not adverse to dating women with imperfect figures or adverse ages, but he never seemed to meet the right ones. And little things put him off, like women who micromanaged his driving, or virgins at forty, or girls who asked what he did before asking his astrological sign. He wanted to say, "Virgo, baby," but wasn't allowed anymore. The seventies, he was informed by his mother, were passé—despite the retail industry's recent revival of bell-bottoms, which she had noted.

He processed premiums. He balanced books. A week later, he called his mother again, always a pride-swallowing mistake. "You need to shoot lower, Larry," she said. "I love you, baby, but you're no spring chicken. Your hair's not too thick either. Unless you strike it rich—Did you buy your lotto ticket today?—you'll never date Angelicas and Shelleys. Go for the Maudes, the Elizas, a girl who might agree to make you dinner and watch a movie on the couch. You're not ugly, but you're no Tom Cruise, Larry. Besides, I have to go. Regis is on, and that's my final answer." She hung up on him.

"Thanks mom," he said, considering cold pizza in the fridge. Green mold clung to the crust. Froggy cunt? "You've been a big help, mom," he said to the dial tone, since he still oddly carried the phone. "Again."

He paused rather than recommencing with an outpour of the self-indulgent monologue he'd enjoyed many times before after conversations that ended badly, the one that started like, "Why can't she be supportive like other people's mothers. Why can't she…" and grazed the lunchmeat drawer instead. As he glorified a slice of baloney with a squirt of Dijon mustard, he wondered: Since when had forty-five been the death-knell for easy sex?

He had a blind-date that night, set up by a swinger friend, but when he got there, it went poorly. The girl, who had never heard of lip bleach or wax, asked immediately what he did (meaning: What did he make?). He felt more interested in her whiskered mouth than what came out of it. She wasn't happy with him either. "They said you were thirty-two," she said, sucking her soda. "You look older."

"I'm not thirty-two." He laughed, but she glared as if he had planned to trick her—he and the other bad, bad man—so he almost said, "And I thought you were good to look at without the paper bag," but he hated to watch women cry. He wouldn't make them do that. Still, all over the restaurant, he saw cunt: cunt in the waitress tray drinks, on the brocade walls—enough cunt to make her unimpressive lip-cunt before him pale.

Apparently, she noticed his distraction because she left almost immediately when he began to consider the lint on her chair, so he paid the bill and got in his car, cursing his luck. At home, he even got on his treadmill for a furious, five-minute run, then fell to the couch exhausted.

Judy, crammed into the closet, had deflated last week and needed a patch. Plus, there was that disconcerting mew her mouth made, like a windtunnel. He thought about calling an escort service, but had visions of VD or sudden immune deficiency. His computer hovered in his periphery, the screen chanting lowly, "Open the net. Open sesame. Open at home. Buy a subscription and look at me… We're all here, Larry. All the girls you've wanted for years but could never have…" He opened the net, but was not compelled.

At work, they had functioned as a titillating vehicle away—but at home, he was not nearly as interested. He stood, stretched, and took a walk, noticing how many cunts blossomed in dropped flowers from the dogwood trees, cunt eating up the night. Women walking hand in hand, lovers, had no faces—only waists and hemlines. He did not know where he was going, but trudged on until he realized he was two miles from home. His feet ached. His nose was raw from cold air. He sat on a curb as fall draped its melancholy shadows over his shoulders, and: Poor me, he thought. Oh damn, I'm pitiful.

He had a sudden urge to never see cunt again.

Maple leaves curled like bent fists on the sidewalks, yellow, brown, and red—no! More pale—pale red?!—more cunt. He wanted the sky to swallow him like a seasoned whore fellates a finger because it was unfair to see so much of something he wanted yet have so little.

This was, he thought, definitely hell. The next day at work, he put his oomph into his job, tirelessly sifting paper and clicking on the right buttons. Surprisingly, Susan called him in. She said, "Larry, I have to talk to you," and guided him to her office.

When he sat, she said, "You've been exceptionally good about avoiding the net, and I wanted to commend you. Not a single site was cruised this a month, and I'm afraid, the other employees have relapsed, so I fired them. That's why Helen isn't here. God Larry, I hate employees unable to follow directions, but that's not you, thank goodness." She patted his shoulder.

Perhaps he imagined it, but she seemed to caress his arm through his suit, her hand stroking briefly up and down, swishing her painted nails rhythmically across his poly-fibered sleeve, holding it a second too long, and just as suddenly as she'd called him in, she then said, "Would you like to have a drink after work, Larry?"

Her perfume was spicy-fruity. A pearl-clip decal for her high heels had fallen off one shoe. "What?" Had he heard correctly?

"Strictly informal. You can say no."

"Susan," he said, "We don't get along. Why ask me?" She turned to her huge window with its view of the dumpsters and a solitary tree. From her stooped posture, he could tell he hurt her feelings. "I like you. I didn't mean it. Okay," he said. "We can have a drink. Sure. Why not? No problem."

Her resultant shy smile made him feel better, but she insisted on

driving when they left, and after they arrived at the bar, she took off
her long, gray coat, loosened her hair, and told him about hubbies
one, two, and three. Later, when she rubbed her heel against his
ankle, he almost ducked under to make sure he hadn't imagined it.
"Susan was hot for him!" his mental voice stuttered, the revelation
so astounding that he proceeded to get drunk.

"I just felt I could talk to you all the sudden," she said. "Like you
looked in my eyes and knew what was on my mind..."

"Not bloody likely," he thought: "It was all cunt to me."

"So, I said to myself, Susan—that man is much nicer than you
thought he was. And you did well with what I asked from you,
Larry, so I thought I'd ask you here."

"I'm here," he said, grinning stupidly like somebody's pet teddy.

After she downed seven Margaritas, she put her barbed-wire
barrette in her purse and fanned out her hair with her fingers. "Larry,"
she said, "Can I tell you a secret?"

He wished he had a mint to hide his liquor breath. He drank his
fifth Daiquiri. She looked prettier and prettier. "Sure."

She sighed. "When I saw all those sex sites you looked at, I
thought it was great to see a man who still had a strong sex drive.
So many men peter out with age. Like they can't please a woman
anymore. But you—oh, how should I put this? Well, I shouldn't ask.
I imagine you have quite a lot going on." Her finger traced circles in
the condensation rings on the table, drawing spirals and odd patterns.
"Am I right?"

He said, "Be more specific."

"Oh, all right," she said, leaning in. "I wanted to know if you
still want it—I mean regularly. Since Jeff passed away, it's been hard
for me to meet men. When I do, they can't keep up."

"I can keep up," he said. Their faces were so close that he watched
her lashes flutter, entranced they were so brown when her hair was
so gray, and as he mentally took her clothes off with his eyes, he
suddenly thought: Making love to this woman could put me in
crutches. She is my boss. I might get fired. A jolt of acid entered his
stomach, almost bowling him over. "But I've gotta go tonight."

"I'll be in touch then," she said.

"Don't need to take me back," he slurred. "I'll take a taxi. Good luck with everything."

That night he cruised sex sites for three hours, but couldn't get excited. The next morning, he walked to the subway, thinking about Susan because she came into his mind's eye and lingered—he remembered her finger, tracing patterns on the table, contemplated her Rottweiler and three dead husbands. "A dangerous catch," he said aloud.

That afternoon, the office air was electric. The spell of women fully cast, he thought. They had the power to draw a man in and make him wait—but Susan did not dally long. She put a note on his desk that afternoon. It read: 1233 Bread ST. 7 p.m. Not about work.

He hyperventilated like he had as a child when he had used his lunch bag to stop the ragged breathing. Inhaling the ham scent of his noon meal, he calmed and got through the day. At 7 p.m., he stood at her door, with daisies, wine and chocolate. He filled his face with a sappy grin and when she swung open her door, in a frosty white pair of sheer pajamas, having dyed her hair walnut, he saw she was beautiful, though had been getting more beautiful in his eyes all day. "I'm here," he said.

"I see that," she replied. The wine, chocolate, and daisies, were left in the hall. "My dog's in the yard," she said, "because I thought we might want to be left alone." Then she shut the front door and just about ripped off his clothes as he fumbled with her flimsy garments, not wanting to rip them since he hadn't bought them, but she tired of this and soon began to strip them herself. The two were soon almost nude, breathing heavily.

"Susan!" he said, a prude for a short moment, trying to extricate himself—but "Larry!" she replied, teasing him, pushing him into the wall, and he called out her name again as if to interject, "Susan, sweet Susan," but she did not cease seducing him.

Then "Susan, Susan, Susan," he said as he writhed on her bed, uttering her name like it was his first baby word, uttering it non-stop for the next several hours, especially when he first plucked the beige shoulder pads from her bra-cups that sat beside him on the bed, and when she saw he noticed, she colored prettily.

"Susan," he said, enjoying all of her afterwards. "Should we do this again?"

"You have my number," she replied. "Use it—or don't."

But he knew he would. When he walked outside, drunk on the air, he felt he had been taken for a carnival ride. Even the unremarkable became amazing. "You tree," he cried. "How beautiful your leafless branches! You cement, how wondrous your flat, even texture! You pole! Hmmm, what to say about a pole?"

But better—there was no cunt in his landscape! He stopped walking and looked down at his shoes as if they or the walking held the answer: Where had the cunt gone? Had he dreamt it? He thought of Susan sleeping in her bed, wondering how he would feel to see her at work. He thought of her dog and her probable stock of peanut-derived products, but when he entered his apartment, there was a slight pain in his temples and the dull light of the monitor flashed, so he forgot about Susan. The screen had captured the body of a sixteen year-old girl. She was nude, with long, red hair, and her pubis had been shaved like a tiny heart of curls. She winked, staring at him from the still-life, and then laughed. "So you finally got some, huh, Larry?" she said. "Click me. Get some more."

He sat before her in his computer chair, wondering if he was dreaming.

"Come on," the girl said, but her desire seemed ominous, her eyes like cold glare. This girl would never care who stroked on the other side of her monitor; she was hard-edged and sharp, Larry decided, taking manly fans as she did with her tight, young body and stealing their money, never offering a single, soft sigh. She was not Susan.

But as if Monitor Girl could sense his thoughts, she turned to him and said, "You just now realized the sex object always takes you to the cleaners? The sex object does not regret your presence— or absence—because it does not register that you have either. An object is just an object till you make it more, after all, somewhat like a toaster. You see yourself in it, and you think you've won something, but you're wrong. You have nothing. I have a boyfriend, see?"

The view on the screen shifted about thirty degrees to depict a young man on the bed beside the girl, grinning. She laughed. "So why would I want someone like you anyway, Larry? Why?" She shook her hair and returned to her original position, dropping her thighs a millimeter wider as if to lure him back.

He thought of an ex-girlfriend who sent nudie pictures to prisoners on death-row. "I just like to think of them, thinking of me," she said. "Masturbating to me. But I never give my real address. That way they can dream all they want, but I'm not there."

He stared venomously at the screen. He thought only: Susan warned me. She was the one who made cunts everywhere. I saw them first in her eyes. Then the girl in the screen seemed less and less present, like a photograph of a painting of a drawing of a cartoon, so he scoffed, bored, and closed her window, but as he did this, his computer shot up five pop-ups of hard, naked girls with immaculate bodies.

He closed their windows too, but they seemed to multiply, kept multiplying, as he shouted, "Stop, already! I have what I want!" yet still, buck-shots proliferated, hacking repeatedly across his screen only to be erased, as soon as possible, by his clicking finger. As his mouse connected with each tiny X, he felt stronger, but strongest of all as he shut down the last internet search engine with the lingum of his index on his flat gray mouse. The almighty cock-click of a single digit made a giant of his forged resistance.

He didn't need the imagined or artificial. As the piping screensaver came on, he used the same window closing finger to dial Susan's number, pressing the seventh digit with fervor and listening hard before he was greeted by her soft, "Hello."

"Susan," he breathed, scratching his belly.

"Larry? Is that you?"

"Yes," he said. He pictured the silver-laced cunt he'd known earlier, her face above it swooning, and the hoops of twine curling above his nose when he was face-deep in its heat. He relived the memory of her scent, wanting to be back in her bed, imagining a pet dog he'd never seen, and thinking about how it might moan for affection from her yard. The dog. The damn dog! Did it exist? Shouldn't he have heard a dog that big, a single bark?

He thought about reality and falseness. Nothing was truly real, nothing but the thing in the instant that you choose to see it whatever way and agreed with its own certainty, like he had been consumed with cunts. He grew so obsessed with this idea as he spoke to Susan that he barely recognized his own voice when it crooned, "I have just one question for you, Susan. Are you lonely tonight?" Again, he was channeling Elvis. He felt very smooth.

"Yes," she said, a measure of sleepiness in her tone.

"Good," he replied. "I'll be there soon." But as he said this, the screen degaussed and threw up one last pop-up of the cruel young redhead, laughing at him, so he picked up a stapler and beat her back until he registered only a shatter of splintered glass, an empty hole in the monitor where a woman once was. He went about filling that hole with branches from the birch trees outside, muttering, "Susan, Susan," and then walking to her house, whispering her name like a mantra, a lullaby, a dream, or a saved man's chorus in a soft elegant swan song of which everyone might know the tune, but only he could hear.

Chimera

I do not sleep anymore.

I can't take the risk, not again. I won't survive it again.

"I'll see you in hell."

These words are rooted in my brain. They aren't even words, exactly. Not enunciated and pronounced, but hissed and lingering, seeping into my skin and settling into my bones, my heart, my mind.

The room is dark, silent and reproachful. I've forgotten the nightlight again and the gloom is penetrating, the white walls lost in the abyss. There is no boundary to the room, it is infinite, black and salty. I can't smell the sulfur, even though I'd been told I would. It was more the scent of the sea, slightly brackish, dead fish and seaweed making it offensive.

The hissing begins again. "I'm here to take you. It is your time."

I realized this has happened before. I've been in this bed, this room, this murky gloom when the demon came to me. How many times have I fought him off?

I turn to face him. He has come through the shuttered window. The night air blows behind him, sweet jasmine and bougainvillea overpowered by his rankness. He doesn't resemble anything I'd seen before, any depiction drawn or imagined. He is taupe, nearly translucent, skinny ferret-like body supported by long-boned feet, hands ending in claws that drip a viscous liquid. I assume it is the remnants of bitter souls from the night's catch. I'm not sure how I know he is male, there are no external clues to his gender.

"Tiiiiiimmmmeee." That sibilant voice again. I feel a drop of slime hit my forehead. His hands are past my shoulder now, reaching around to scoop me in his arms. His mouth, crowded with sharp teeth, spit trails stringing between upper and lower jaws, grows wider, bigger, and I feel the claws rake across my back. He is pulling me in, consuming, sucking. I feel my soul depart from my heart and begin to leave my body.

No. I will not let him take me.

I take a breath so deep that pieces of his spittle fly into my mouth and scream. Louder, longer than I knew I could. My body convulses, tiny tears surface in my throat. And still I scream. I know, deep in my heart, that he will leave if I continue. They don't like screams.

Flashing a look full of hatred, of lust and regret, the demon is sucked back through the shutters. They bang close, startling me with their vehemence. My scream trails off. I am safe.

I sit up and turn on the light. My fears are realized.

The Chimera has come again.

He sits in the chair, feet tucked under him like a pleasant cat. He raises an inky eyebrow, strokes two fingers through the obsidian silk of his goatee. He flashes a smile at me, teeth so pearly against the darkness that they're nearly blue. He doesn't say a word. Stroke, smile. Stroke, smile.

"Bastard," I whisper.

He laughs silently, deep in his chest, the sound reverberating around the room like thunder.

We made a deal, he and I. It was a long time ago. I was too young to know any better, he was hunting the night for victims. A match better suited to novels and nightmares. But he likes me. Enough that the deal we struck benefits us both.

I murdered. I sinned. He took. It was that simple.

Fetial declarations aside, he takes from everyone. Good, bad or indifferent. The indifferent, mostly. He signs for their souls without them ever knowing. It's that last glimpse, when they assume they'll see the light, that shocks the living hell right into them. And the Chimera laughs as he greets them, down below.

But the lost souls aren't my problem. The Chimera is my problem.

We're friends in a strange, make a deal with the devil kind of way. Like I said before, he likes me. He's a fallen angel like the rest of them, still wanton in his desires. I guess I fit with his image of a partner.

He's here to collect. Anytime, anywhere. That's our deal. I don't have to go straight to hell. He possesses my body. Gives a whole new meaning to burning desire.

He knows that you're most vulnerable when you're frightened. That's why he sends in the demon first, to soften you up. Like I said, he's a true sadist.

I do have a choice in the matter. God gave us free will, the ability to choose which path to follow. My path is forked, two roads less traveled. I can accept the demon's proposal. Go with him the next time he comes to me. It's a toss up, sometimes, which is worse. The Chimera or the demon. Love, or death?

I could just never sleep again. It's not like I get any rest. Every time I close my eyes, start toward that REM stage, they appear. Never sleeping again is a comforting idea.

I wish I could take back that night. The Chimera was there; I didn't know that at the time. I thought it was just the two of us, alone in the alley. That no one heard my screams. That I was abandoned. That *I* wrestled the knife away at the last minute with my own strength. That *my* fingers grasped the hilt. That *my* muscles forced the tip of the knife into the man's gut. That the blood spilling onto my arm, my torn dress, my shoes was untainted.

He could have let me die. It might have been easier.

It was ten years ago.

The yin and yang of his world is too complex for me to comprehend. Suffice it to say that while I was being raped and strangled, he stood and watched. Waited. Knew that he could give me the strength to overcome the man and stop the attack, which he did, just not until after the man finished grunting and scraping at me. When the knife appeared, the Chimera stepped in, silent, transparent. He grasped my hand, grappled with the knife. Using my strength, he stabbed the stranger in the stomach, driving the blade in so deep that the warm spill of his intestines gathered in my supplicant palm.

He turned with that luminescent smile and said, "You owe me."

As we were driving our deal, he had the audacity to point out I should thank him for saving my life. What kind of life is this? Labyrinth assassin, fevered dreams, the warm copper spice of lifeblood pouring through my hands. The Chimera, possessing me night by night, the length of him buried deep between my thighs, his scorching desire blazing inside me.

He comes to me, insatiable, unfulfilled. Takes me, over and over. Drives me onward. Over the brink, where the madness of climax allows me glimpses into the raging inferno that awaits.

He is the cause of my reckless journeys, my wasted relationships, my never-ending string of dead-end jobs. He is in the drugs, the alcohol, the cigarettes. The lush, provocative nights and the solitary days. He never leaves my side, but only appears when I sleep. He and his demon familiars.

I'm a lucky girl. I'll never be alone again.

Josh Woods

Excerpted Entries from The Damned Encyclopedia of When All Hell Broke Loose in Small-Town Kentucky and Somebody Had to Do Something About It

Adieu to Jack

"You do realize that the man standing on that porch is a five-hundred-year-old alchemist armed with a pair of haunted flintlock dueling pistols, each loaded with something a lot worse than blackpowder and lead, and that past him through that door, any manner of terrible thing could be crawling out of the basement from any of the seven Hells or from any of the six Earths or, even worse, from any of the seven Heavens. What exactly is it that you plan to do?"

Jack shut the trunk of Madmax with an elbow and held up two sledge hammers, one in each hand. "I imagine I'll start swinging these sonsofbitches and see what happens."

SEE: THE APPRENTICE; DUELING PISTOLS; MADMAX; THE BASEMENT; THE END; THE OUBLIETTE

<u>**B – E**</u>

<u>**F**</u>

422 South Elm Street (Erin's House)

In 1809, while still an empty lot, it was purchased by John James Audubon, who was really the Lost Dauphin of France, even though he was just a duplicate cover identity who worked to protect the real Lost Dauphin of France. The real John James Audubon of course wasn't the real Lost Dauphin of France, but the real Lost Dauphin of France wasn't really the Lost Dauphin of France either. He ended up not really knowing who he was—if he were the real John James Audubon or if he were the real Lost Dauphin of France. And who knows what "he" even means at that point, since neither knew which was who. One of them liked demonology and the other liked systematically torturing various species of American birds. That was about it for differences. They were both good artists.

Either one or both of the John James Audubons lived in Henderson, Kentucky, either for the bird migrations or for the fact that the place was a crossroads in the oldest, wickedest sense of the word. Bad things passing in the night. While living there, he or they did enough research to find out that he or they legitimately owned several odd pieces of royal estate still hidden in France. One of these pieces was an oubliette. Unlike any other oubliette, or any other dungeon in the world for that matter, this oubliette was a perfect sphere, and it stood alone, buried under a castle but not built into it. Portable. Its construction had begun sometime during the Merovingian rule and was finally completed by Nicholas Flamel circa 1410. All that either one or both of the John James Audubons really knew about it was that its quality was supposedly exquisite and its intention was terrible. It would certainly make more interesting both the promise of summoning demons and practice of torturing birds, so either one or both of the John James Audubons ordered it be shipped to him or them. Six men were beheaded in France before the order was fully accepted by those with the authority to execute such an order, and it took 14 years to reach Henderson, Kentucky.

Either one or both of the John James Audubons buried it in this empty lot and built a house over it.

SEE: THE OUBLIETTE

G

Gremlin in the Machine Shop

Jack wanted to stir it out of hiding, so he skipped sideways and pounded his two sledgehammers along the aluminum-paneled and concrete walls of the workfloor as if the entire building were his battle drum. He had to stay fleet and dodgy in doing so since the lights that hung over the machine stations were too few and too weak to illuminate the perimeter of the place, and most of the company's discarded parts and broken equipment lay stacked along the walls. Piles of pipes and steel rails, cardboard boxes full of spiraled metal shavings, buckets of putrid leak-water, oil rags, broken glass, plastic bottles, an overturned cigarette machine from before Jack was born, some dented file cabinets, even a box-spring mattress missing its fabric. Regardless of his maneuvering over and around these things, Jack knocked the hammer heads against the walls in a weirdly regular rhythm, and the echoes shook the entire machine shop. Most of his night-shift crew rocked forward and back in a stunted head-banging style as Jack's noise orbited them and came at them from the dark edges of their sight. They felt charged, ready for riot or violence, although they weren't sure why. Then they bounced on their toes, even skipping along as Jack did, and they whooped and banged against anything in their paths with socket wrenches and cheater bars and bare fists like some wild breed of industrial ape.It was cacophony. Trash-bang, wrought-iron, stone-struck noise. And it did stir something out of the shadows from under a far corner vise-bench. The something, it darted. The men pointed and yelled directions in clock-speak. Those who didn't see it move asked what it was, and those who did see it move answered only by screaming where it went. Up the wall, above the ventilation shafts, down a pipeline, or maybe up the pipeline again, at which point in three dimensions their hour-handed directions simply caused more confusion.

Jack yelled, "We got it cornered up there, above the lights." He nodded the head of one sledgehammer into the dark where the ceiling corner ought to be, and he continued banging the other hammer against the wall to keep the thing scared. "Get some lights on it!"

One guy tried a plastic flashlight, but its beam couldn't reach that high. Another guy scrambled for a ladder.

Jack thought he glimpsed at the thing trying to escape along the perpendicular wall away from him, so he ran over there and banged his hammers to corral it back into the corner. He yelled at the guys to hurry up, yelled that it was going to get away, but when he saw them with the ladder, he said, "No, no, somebody just shoot it."

"With what?"

"A fucking gun," Jack said. They said, "Somebody's got a gun."

And, "Nobody's got a fucking gun?"

And, "Nobody?"

The men were now panicking at both their lack of having even a single firearm among them and at the shame of it, all of them being native Kentucky boys.

Jack said, "Get the potato cannon. I know you fuckers probably shot it when I was gone last night."

They had, and they dug it out from behind the breakroom lockers in no time. Jack expected them to bring out the simple, old, four-foot PVC-pipe cannon that he had built with them back before he was night-shift leader, but the guys had since taken the concept to more intense evolution without his knowing. The cannon was six feet of tempered 440-grade steel. It had a notch-lock sleeve chamber, form-cut and welded front and rear sights, a swivel bi-pod with an alternate rubber-dipped combat grip, and even a damn shoulder rest. They brought it out in proud fashion, watching Jack's face because they knew that although they would be in deep shit for revealing it, Jack might simultaneously be proud.

Jack smiled. "Hell yes."

The biggest of them shouldered the cannon while another loaded the aerosol and prepared his disposable lighter and the rest went searching for the bag of potatoes from the night before. No one could find the potatoes, but they knew there had to be some left over, but maybe they shot them all, no, maybe someone trashed them. Jack told them to grab the twelve-pack of cokes that he had brought in—as replacements for the ones the gremlin had been stealing—and to see if a can would fit the chamber. They tossed the pack one to another from where Jack had set it near the punch-clock all the way to the cannon loader with flawless assembly style, and the cannon loader continued the efficient movement by tearing out a can of coke, loading, locking, sparking, and yelling, "It fits! Fire in the hole!"

The fire hissed at the rear then roared out of the muzzle, sending a capsule of sharp aluminum and foaming soda into the ceiling corner, and the crack and reverberation of impact stunned every man's ears. It sounded as though something screeched. A dirty liquid spray rained down on Jack. "More, more!" he yelled. "I think you're hitting it!" They loaded and blasted a second can at the same spot, and by then two other guys had rolled out the industrial air-compressor and connected its hose to the rear aperture that Jack hadn't even noticed on the cannon. A fifth man held the long cardboard twelve-pack of cans to the cannon chamber at such an angle as to create a gravity feeding magazine. Even the few men standing back like spectators were screaming, "Fire, fire, fire!"

With belt-feed speed the cokes drum-coughed out of the cannon and pelted the blind ceiling corner. They waylaid it. Liquid foam and chinks of aluminum filled the air. Someone must have screamed *It's moving!* among the splatter artillery noise because the cannon had stopped and the men had begun scanning the walls for a sight of it.

Someone yelled, "There. Along the wall. It's flat!"

"Get it! Get it!"

"It slid into the fuzebox!"

They repositioned the cannon at the fuzebox and began loading

can-length spare tools, since the cokes were all used up, but Jack
yelled for them to cease fire. "Don't shoot that thing at the fucking
fuzebox. Jesus H, you morons. And who saw it? Who?"

One of the boys who worked there straight out of high school
said, "Me."

"What do you mean it was flat?" Jack said like a retail-mechanic
asking for the sound of your brakes. "Flat like what?"

"Like flat flat."

"Like sting-ray flat?"

The kid said, "No, like shadow flat."

Jack said, "Two dimensional?"

"Yeah."

"Well that's just great."

Then the fuzebox whined and crackled, and all the lights
throughout the building popped and blinked at random, sparks
spitting out of some sockets. Fluorescent tubes snapped and spilled
mercury vapor. The whole workfloor buzzed and strobed with
headache flashes, and someone yelled, "It's in the lights. It went into
the lights." And then with a thud the whole place went dark as if
movie credits were about to roll.

It was quiet enough for everyone to hear Jack say under his
breath, "Well that's just great."

"What do we do now?"Jack said, "I guess we build a trap."

SEE: OF THE GAKI AND THE WORLD OF HUNGRY
GHOSTS; TO BUILD A FLAWLESS TRAP

<u>H</u>

The Horde of Elohim

Pouring like a torrent down the valley incline came a stampede of
terrible men. They fought forward among one another, thrashing in
a tight charge. Hides and horns and iron obscured any distinction
of body from implement, one from another. They lopped along
with unequal limbs, faces like heavy globs of flesh, eyes in the wrong
places, features primevally sloping and low—early among creation.

Neckless, barrel torsos hunched. Their mismatched hide armors seemed arranged in mistake, not covering what they should, some of them with gentiles swinging without shame, all of them eager. Thick feet slapping the burnt ground. They shook savage weapons that had too many angles, non-geometric, to be precisely swords or axes or halberds. Others curled back their slick lips from ragged teeth and howled and screeched, barefisted. A horrid few charging at the lead remained silent by decision.

"Oh shit oh shit oh shit." Jack felt as though he were scuttling in place, wanting to get down the hole, down the ladder, faster than he could watch himself move. He held Lou Boo tight over his shoulder and slid down into the dark, even slipping and missing some rungs, and then at the bottom set her down and yanked at the ladder in an attempt to break it down, and he jammed his hand that had the split knuckles—from suckerpunching some cattle-headed monster only moments earlier to get hold of Lou Boo. Jack grit his teeth and yelled at Lou Boo, "Get this thing rolling! Trace the thing on the thing! Get us the hell out of this place!"

She wailed and sucked at her own breath. "I want to go home."

Jack fumbled with the ladder enough to knock it over. At least those men would now have to leap down through the opening to get them, maybe break a leg or something. He crawled around, feeling for his flashlight. "Loo Bou, quit crying and hurry up. Those guys are about ten seconds from coming down here and chewing our skin off and skull-fucking us."

But she cried harder.

"That's just great." He grabbed the light, clicked it on, and hurried to the symbol to trace it himself. He couldn't remember if his finger was going the right ways. "Come on, come on."

Everything began to shake with a massive rumbling. Jack looked up. Still a bright, wide opening: the room wasn't moving. It was the horde. They were shaking the ground with their numbers. It was too late. They would reach him any second now. Jack steadied himself directly beneath the opening, flashlight in his hand like a club. He spoke softly. "All right, you fuckers, come and get it. Your supper's down here waiting for you."

But Lou Boo—Jack wondered what they might do to her and how long they would keep her alive while they did it. Wondered if he should spend the last few seconds executing a hard bit of mercy. He examined the flashlight, the bluntness of its butt end, and then he shone the light on her only to see the back of her—her pink backpack and the bottoms of her little sneakers; she knelt curled over the symbol on the floor. Must be tracing it. Good girl.

The rumbling grew louder. The opening above began to black-out, the light crescent slowly, slowly thinning.

"It's working! That's it, Lou Boo. Yes. Go, go. Come on."

But so slow, damnit. The howls of the horde were stomach-twisting and near. Dust clouded-over the slim opening.

"Come on, baby. Come on."

A hand reached down into the room and threw a craggy weapon as Jack flinched to cover his head and as the opening finally snapped shut. It sent down a spritz of blood and half of an arm, but Jack's skull had been rocked heavily, and he felt himself tumbling with the echo of a wailing, weird-languaged curse far off in his head. Lights out.

SEE: BACK HOME

<u>I</u>

J

Judge Colonel Richard Henderson

Judge Colonel Richard Henderson bought the land from Attacullaculla, Dragging Canoe, and a gathering of 1,200 other Cherokee for the price of three pale maidens who lived in a glass tank of water the size of a wagon. The Judge Colonel's men spent four days with the Cherokee explaining how to care for the maidens, how and what to feed them (which excited the Cherokee most of all), how to make sure that the maidens could never escape or convince others to help them escape, and, most emphatically, how to—if they were to unfortunately die—how to never ever let any of the three of them begin to rot—all of America depended on that. The land encompassed most of 'The Dark and Bloody Ground,' or, 'Kentucky,' and the Judge Colonel was certain that his maps and his information gathered from his several professional hunting parties were all correct—Coyote was hiding somewhere within this land purchase. It was Coyote he sought. Coyote was the reason he formed the Transylvania Company, a venture only made possible through the primary clandestine funding and weird aid of ancient Romanian nobility—one particular noble, in fact, who had read dark tales of the New World and who had expressed interest in planting his influence there. Immediately after the land purchase, the Judge Colonel hired the only man alive he believed capable of hunting Coyote—the amazing Daniel Boone. Daniel Boone tracked Coyote across the wilderness of Kentucky, through the Cumberland Gap, having only the briefest confrontations with his target, until he finally narrowed down Coyote's whereabouts to a speck of land a week's north of where the mouths of the ground whisper and, on the map, at and around the south bank of the Ohio River where it forks from the Green, a place of old crossroads according to the Cherokee, who claimed never to have believed in Coyote as much as Rabbit.

For several proclaimed reasons—some of them public—Virginia invalidated Judge Colonel Richard Henderson's purchase of the vast expanse of land. The Judge Colonel could not deny the accusations made by the officials of Virginia—many of them men who knew him as a child, who knew his father—but he did demand to be given the land at the Ohio River that Daniel Boone had assured him was the hiding place of Coyote. Virginia took back the mass of Kentucky that the Judge Colonel had bought, but they did succeeded to him those 12 square miles he demanded—the place that later took his name.

When Judge Colonel Richard Henderson was a boy in Virginia, he watched Coyote trick his father into hanging himself in the water well that sat just beyond the edge of their barn, one of the few areas on their farm that received very little light at all, even at midday—he remembered that. Young Richard Henderson was so shamed by the sight of his father's death that he lowered his father's corpse into the well to hide it there, for no real utility he could foresee at that tender age—just to hide it. The pulley at the well had spokes wrought in the shape of women's legs—four of them, he remembered that. His hiding of his father's body lasted until the next Sunday when his mother could no longer stand the taste of the putrid water that young Richard brought in from the well several times a day. When the officials fished the now stringy corpse out of the water, it was clear to all that young Richard Henderson was the son of a man damned to Hell.

When young Richard had watched Coyote talk to his father— talk and talk and talk of horrible things—Coyote had stood on its hind legs. He remembered that.

At the end of his life, several years after having given up his life-long and in-vain hunt of Coyote, Judge Colonel Richard Henderson lurched forward in his favorite reading chair, dropped the terrible book he had bought from a vagabond who claimed to have stolen the book from an Arabian prince, and he grabbed his stomach, screamed briefly, and died. At that exact moment in 1785, the Lost Dauphin was born in secret in Avignon, France.

SEE: DANIEL BOONE; 422 SOUTH ELM STREET; JACK FIRED FROM THE HENDERSON CITY POLICE FORCE FOR SHOOTING AN ALLEGEDLY TALKING DOG; ROTTING MERMAIDS

K – N

O

Of the Gaki and the World of Hungry Ghosts
During World War II there were certain Japanese soldiers who felt such a desire and personal responsibility for the victory of their nation and their Emperor that their own deaths left them with nothing but gnawing grief—endlessly gnawing grief. Some of these dead soldiers emigrated to the World of Hungry Ghosts and thus

waved in others to also emigrate to the World of Hungry Ghosts, which is far from the World of Men, beneath even the World of Animals, but not so far as the World of the Woeful States. The ancient people of Eastern Asia were the first among men to discover the World of Hungry Ghosts, so it naturally evolved into a cultural tradition of sorts to go there after death if one wanted to wallow in the grief of unfulfilled desires, unfinished efforts, un-atoned dishonor, or other such regrets. Within the World of Hungry Ghosts it is obviously impossible to perceive those who live in the World of Men, as the World of Men is too far to see clearly, but it is perfectly easy to see water and animals and minerals and all other structures and mechanisms of the shared earth. This is the manner in which the Japanese hungry ghosts, the gaki, decided to continue the war effort: they would slide into any of the mechanisms of the Allies that they could identify, and they would confound them. Airplanes, trucks, rifles, mills, watches, anything mechanical—the more complex the better. The gaki's ultimate effect on the outcome of World War II was minimal, especially since none of the hungry ghosts bothered to confound the Enola Gay.

After World War II, most gaki returned to spending their shapeless years of self-punishment by chasing after deprecating thirsts and cravings—the traditional cravings being corpses of wild animals, live winged insects, and shit of any kind, although chemicals and industrial waste grew more and more popular with them. In turn, the practice of confounding machinery, now any machinery made by any men, became a post-war novelty and badge of identity— something that separated all hungry ghosts of the past and all hungry ghosts to come from the hungry ghosts of the World War II generation.

Before World War II, well, before the Japanese attacked the Americans at Pearl Harbor, the World of Hungry Ghosts was fading through attrition and was near to being forgotten from existence. In fact, if the Japanese hadn't pulled off the attack on Pearl Harbor so successfully and thus been filled with such a precise and realistic hunger for victory, if instead the American Navy had intercepted the Japanese en route and both nations had battled outright from the beginning, the World of Hungry Ghosts might never have received its flood of dead Japanese soldiers. The man responsible for this, for the American Navy being attacked unawares at Pearl Harbor on December 2nd, 1941, was the one man in charge of the base and responsible for every man and craft there, four-star admiral, Commander-in-Chief U.S. Pacific Fleet, Husband E. Kimmel. During the attack, Kimmel stood at his office window and watched his world burning and sinking around him, and he tore at his uniform in utter grief and dishonor. After he died many years later, still deep in regret, he followed the Japanese dead into the World of Hungry Ghosts, where he drank deprecating chemicals and confounded machines as the other World War II gaki did, and he tried to forget he had ever been human or American. But over the years, while still living in the World of Hungry Ghosts, he who had once been Husband E. Kimmel imagined a possible reconciliation with himself, so he hitched a ride from Japan inside an industrial-grade machine-shop lathe back to the town of his birth, his boyhood home, the place of his first fond memories: Henderson, Kentucky.

SEE: GREMLIN IN THE MACHINE SHOP

The Oubliette
Jack climbed into the hole in the floor of Erin's basement, down where she said her daughter had "simply disappeared but with nowhere to go," and Jack edged his way down the A-frame ladder Erin had set into that abandoned space. At the base of the ladder, Jack immediately got the sense that he wasn't in a well like he had imagined, but instead in an opened room, although it was too dark to see for sure. The flashlight wouldn't give much more than a pale beam, and even Jack's breaths seemed to echo. He twisted his sockfeet and stomped to get a feel for the floor—solid and dry, but not actually concrete. No, he had worked cement into concrete before; this was stone.

He yelled, "Hey, Erin, can you hear me up there?"

"I can hear you just fine."

"This is all stone down here." He tried to torch every angle of the room, and it made him dizzy because it looked as though he were following a long wall with his flashlight, waiting for the corner, but while doing so he knew he had turned a complete circle. Then it hit him: the room was a perfect sphere. Bare, save for the ladder. "That's you some workmanship right there."

Erin yelled down, "Pardon me?"

"This come with the price of the house?"

Erin said, "It wasn't here before. I told you."

"Shit, this has been here longer than the house, I can tell you that."

Jack shone the light around the floor of the sphere, looking for any disturbances in the dust that weren't caused by his own feet. "Lou Boo?" He whistled as if for a pet. "Lou Boo, your mommy wants you to come back. Where are you?" Jack got down to his knees and ran his hand along the stone, wiping the dust. He noticed, carved into the stone, a symbol about the radius of his spread hand. The thing was absolutely meaningless—just lines, angles, and circles. Carving circles into stone is no easy job. Even if the carver was someone other than the builder, this sucker was no amateur.

Jack spun the light nearby and noticed another symbol, one a little larger. Then another smaller one. Then another. Once his eyes had become trained for them, he saw symbols everywhere he looked, spiraling around him, swarming obsessively thick, making his stomach feel strange. "Oh, fuck."

Erin yelled down, "What? What is it?"

"All these symbols down here?"

"Yeah? Do you know what they mean?"

Jack said, "It means someone went crazy in here. I don't like that."

"What do you mean?"

"I just don't like the thought of that."

"Do you know what the symbols mean, though?"

"They don't mean anything."

Erin said, "I think they do."

"Will you just let me do my job?" Jack tilted his ear up to the glowing hole above him for a moment and heard nothing back from Erin. "*God*," he said quietly, returning to examining the symbols near his feet. Up close, it looked as though something had in fact been disturbed. Jack traced the carved lines, making a finger-path in the dust to mimic a path that had apparently been traced there already, except the previous path was smaller. Must have been Lou Boo. She probably opened a secret door, that's what. Like the Winchester House, or the Addams Family mansion. They're not all that hard to build, in theory.

He was about to tell Erin what he had found, but a noise of stone grinded and earthquaked around him. It moaned like an ancient grain mill coming back to life. The room—it was rolling. The glowing opening above him slowly eclipsed. Jack screamed for Erin, screamed for her not to shut him down there, but the light from his only exit contracted until it was only a pinhole, and then it winked shut.

SEE: 422 SOUTH ELM STREET; ROLLING INTO THE THROAT OF HELL; THE SYMBOL

P

Page 63 of the Journal of the Apprentice to Ludwig Prinn[bracketed notations by E. S. Ternkey]

"The Terrible Guidepath of the Spirit & of Where to Go Once Dead"

& after ye death of ye Body he Tarryeth not [must not tarry] but cross thru ye Firmament unless a Medium&c. wisheth Discourse wth him. Any Querry must be written in his Quick Footprint [a footprint he made when alive] wth ye Blood of a Black Cock wch never trode a hen. Itt is to be done on a Tuesday or Saturday night at 12 [2] of ye Clock & no Tears must be weepëd by not a Woman nor ye Medium&c.

Before ye Wheel of 1 Year turneth or his Priest forgeteth
his name he must rise past ye 4 Living Creatures wch are nammed

Amaymon, East, his seal is this

Corson, West, his seal is secreet

Ziminiar, North, his seal is this

& Goap [Gaap], south, his seal is this

who holdeth ye Firmament on ye tips of thems Heads.
Iff any 4 Living Creatures seeeth him wth itts Face of Lion, or
Face of Man, or Face of Eagle, that Living Creature most devoureth
[will certainly devour] him into itts Belly where churneth Molten
Rocks & itt rain[s]. But iff ye Living Creature seeeth him wth
itts Face of Ox it pleaseth ye Face of Ox and [it] Moaneth to make
ye other Faces goe to Sleep for 3 Houres. & he Toucheth not [must
not touch] thems Feathers nor ye 5 Hundred Hands undr ye Wings.
Iff he passeth,
ye Firmament is Terrible Crystals.
Terrible.
Each Crystal hath 6 Sides & ye Pointe is most shyrpe as
[more sharp than] Poisoned Arrowes & ye Crystals groweth in all
Directions & closeth most near [nearer] together each Generation
of Man like unto a Hound[']s Jawes. As ye Firmament groweth
Burdensome & Heavy itt maketh ye 4 Living Creatures slouch &
thems horns doe crack. Most presently most near the End Days ye
Firmament shall grow together Solid & Men shall see thru itt
Clear as Waters but none Souls may pass but be trappëd on Earth.
None Souls.
Iff he passeth thru ye Firmament he entereth into ye
cold
Heavens
where ruleth 7 Archons who command each 12 Kings of who
command

each 1000 great Dukes and 1000 lesser Dukes besides
500000000000000000 of ministering spirits who wail and nash thems
Teethe.

This be ye Torturous Armies of ye 7 Archons.

& ye 7 Archons wage War for Eternity of not wch [except for]
Ialdabaoth ye Greater Demiurge &c. who writheth his Horrible
Forme in Maddness.

Ialdabaoth's Seal must not [cannot] be seen by ye Eyes of Created
Creatures.

He [the man] tryeth not to be Seen nor Eaten. He collecteth
ye Souls of his Beloved & hideth himself & all of them away in ye
Caves of Moons, or behind ye Foldes of Stars, or in ye Wells of
Darke, or of all [any] place away like unto Rats from ye Terrors
Infinite for All Time.

SEE: THE APPRENTICE; MEETING E.S. TERNKEY; PAGE
81 FROM THE JOURNAL OF THE APPRENTICE TO
PHILIPPUS AUREOLUS THERPHRASTUS BOMBASTUS
PARACELSUS VON HOHENHEIM [BRACKETED
NOTATIONS BY E.S. TERNKEY]

<u>Q</u>

<u>R</u>

Rotting Mermaids
Cause of the plague known as the Black Death, which began circa
a.D.1340. These two particular mermaids had been killed in the
North Sea by William of Occam during what was intended to be a
leisurely fishing trip with a group of fellow Franciscan monks.
William did not believe in mermaids, refused the complicated
nonsense of properly disposing of mermaid remains despite the
protests of his fellow monks, and therefore ordered the mermaid
corpses to be left on the rocks to rot.

SEE: JUDGE COLONEL RICHARD HENDERSON

<u>S</u>

Searching for God

And Jack came to the edge of a mountain that knew no end to the north and to the south and to the west, for it was a range that grew of its own, like mold, on the face of the desert and had been growing since before Ialdaboath—the demiurge who writhes now in his own madness—gave shape to the earths and separated lands from waters, growing since before the slaying of the great dragon of the void, Leviathan, and the distributing of his body, which will come together again at the fourth end of all time. And just as Jack had been told, he saw in the side of the mountain what would be an entrance to a cave but that the entrance was covered by a golel. The golel was both round and flat as a wheel is both round and flat, and its rim was iron and its rivets were bronze, and the planks of its face were of thick hide that had dried like unto wood, and its boss was an ancient stone. Even as the moon is enormous but clear to see in a single glance, and no matter how much a man might wish to move it in a direction he has a mind to, because it is made to move easily through the night, still he cannot budge it by so much as a hair, nor can all men gather together their strength to budge it so much as a hair, even so did the golel lay enormous over the entrance to the cave, meant to move yet unmovable. And it became clear to Jack that the golel had been the shield of Yahweh.

Jack needed inside the cave. He needed entrance into the endless catacombs where, so it is said, Yahweh has exiled himself, where he strolls through the phosphorescent gloom, an unending owl-light, where he sits himself down beside trickling creeks in fields of mushrooms, where his beard grows ignored and gathering moss, where he leans his brow over bottomless pits and ponders for ages as myriad stalactites weep over his mighty head and his broad back and their mineral tears collect and grow stalagmites that reach like a forest of horns off his bare skin, for Yahweh has discarded his armor long ago. But his sword he keeps with him; Matzmatzit, his sword, he lays by his side, for he will need it one last time.

Jack stood before the golel, looking up at it, and then he sat in the dust of the ground, looking up at it. Maybe he could move it if he had a large enough lever, a matter of simple mechanics except on a theoretical scale—the lever would have to be unbreakable, the contact points and the fulcrum would have to be grooved so precisely as to allow a perfect friction, and he would have to build structures the size of buildings to maneuver around the lever as needed. No, the concept was as useless as a classroom. Maybe it was this hopeless desert that had sent him into aimless thinking such as this.

Jack began losing track of time as he sat looking at the mountains, and he lay on his side, and he fell asleep on the desert floor. And he had no dreams for a long while. But he was awoken by the noise of a rough scrape. Jack blinked and bolted to his feet. Coming around the edge of a nearby canyon cleft, a giant crawled on his hands and knees. It was hard to tell the difference between the perspective of distance and the giant's actual size since there were little other points of reference in this desert, since all things here seemed out of proportion, yet at some scale beyond Jack's own, this thing was a giant. He wore a cone helmet older than Mesopotamia, with cheek plates hanging alongside his wooly beard, and over his many-patched tunic he wore a bronze cuirass, heavily pitted, and a plate-linked belt that was wide and was mighty. The giant set his small eyes as cautiously as a wildcat while he crawled nearer to Jack yet at a guarded angle. Despite the disturbed dust, Jack could clearly see that the giant's feet were gone long ago at the ankles.

The giant spoke with a voice that echoed in his own throat many times before leaving his mouth, but the language was unknown to Jack.

"Are you Yahweh?" Jack said, knowing already that the giant was not.

The giant spoke again, in English this time, except the vowels were all a bit off. "What do you want with Yahweh? You are not an angel of his. You are a purebred of Adam, which I can tell from here in your fine form."

Jack felt as though he had to yell one word at a time and keep his sentences short in order to be heard properly, being so tiny in relation. "Are you Yahweh's guard?"

"No."

"Are you…what are you?"

"I am Og, King of Basham, survivor of the deluge, cut down before my time by Moses, who was black-veiled and horn-faced and shifty as a reptile, he who was master of the Israelites, pet of the Elohim. I wait here at the mouth of this cave for an answer from Yahweh, general of the Elohim, unchallenged king of the earth who knows no peer in might since a time now forgotten. I wait to hear why he vouchsafed terrible little Moses to cut me down, mighty as I was, testament to strength that I was, statue of Yahweh himself that I was. I was the mover of mountains, the basher of skulls, the bringer of the grape seed from which is taken wines, which I paid to Noah as restitution, for I clung to his roof a great while. I was ally to Abraham, I was slayer of the long-toothed mammoths, and I paid tribute to Melchizedek. Yahweh has done me a great wrong for which he owes me either answer or restitution."

Jack said, "How do you know English?"

"What?"

"How do you…nevermind."

Og said, "How do I know English?"

Jack said, "Nevermind."

"I know English from my books, which I keep deep in the rocks in the canyons of these mountains. My books are many, and they hurt my eyes, for I need glasses."

"I need to get into that cave to tell Yahweh something."

"You have not told me your name, purebred."

"I'm just here to deliver a message. I'm a nobody."

Og said, "Ah, you are Ulysses, then?"

"No. Don't worry about my name."

"It is an insult to hide your name when another has freely given his, as I have. I have a mind to think you rude."

"Fine, my name is Jack Shit. So can you let me in that cave or what?"

Og explained to Jack that there is no use in entering that cave, that it is an endless labyrinth, and it is ever-shifting as the mountains grow and shrug. He himself had once moved the golel and had crawled into it in search for Yahweh, and on the first day it was dark and empty and he found nothing in those depths, and on the second day it was dark and empty and he found nothing in those depths, and on the third day it was dark and empty and he found nothing in those depths, and on the fourth day he grew frightened but he continued, and on the fifth day it was dark and empty and he found nothing in those depths, and then he began to lose his sense of days, and he was afraid he would never find his way out again, and as time went on it was dark and empty and he found nothing in those depths, and he thought he heard Yahweh walking somewhere deep in the caves, and at times he thought he saw Yahweh sitting still like a boulder deep in the caves, but by then he had lost his heart and his purpose and did not disturb the form he thought to be Yahweh's and instead continued deeper into the caves, and as time went on it was dark and empty and he found nothing in those depths, and then, in a moment, he turned back and crawled after the mouth of the cave with such haste that he tore the skin from his hands and shattered the bones of his knees, and he has never gone into those caves again.

Jack asked what he might do then, how he might deliver a message to Yahweh, and Og suggested that Jack yell his message into the caves from the entrance, for Yahweh will hear it because he can hear what he wants. But he will not listen to everything, Og assured him, and perhaps he listens to nothing.

"He'll listen," Jack said. "I'm a supervisor too, and even on my day off if someone told me my own crew was fucking with something I custom-built, like messing with my car, just to see if I'd bust their asses or not, you better believe I'd be busting some asses. He'll listen."

Og clicked his tongue and wagged his great head and adjusted his helmet after doing so. Then he slowly crawled back into the cleft in the mountain from which he had emerged. Jack tossed his arms; he had no idea if Og were going to help him open the cave or if that were the last he'd ever see of the giant. Much later, Og again came crawling, and he had a great chain draped over his back and dragging behind him like a tail. The links were unequal in shape and diameter, but they each looked colossal even against the sight of Og. At the end of the chain, digging heavily into the ground, was a crude anchor. Clinging to the anchor's flukes were dried remnants from a primordial seabed: crusts of weed, hive pockets of stone sponge, countless empty shells of once teeming trilobites. Og sat himself with the anchor in front of the golel, and he spent a clumsy amount of time with the simple task of hooking one of the anchor's barbs over the lip of the shield, fumbling it about like a baby working a too-big toy. Then he returned to his knees, one hand on the ground, the other gripping the chain, and he strained forward. The links pulled taught, and the anchor lifted from the ground, pulling only at the shield, but nothing moved. Og relaxed and methodically wrapped the chain under his arm and over his neck like a yoke, then he pulled forward again. He lifted his head and grit his teeth, and his countenance was that of a mighty bull, for even as a bull is roped to a stump in the ground, and to drive the stump out might be to snap his own tendons from his joints and send his ligaments unwinding through his body, and to drive the stump out might be to pull the very earth from its own roots, yet the bull pulls ever harder without rest, even so did Og pull against the golel. And the golel gave with a great crumbling at its edges, and it did move, and there the mouth of the cave yawned.

Jack waited for Og to stop and rest, waited for permission to approach the cave. Once it became clear that Og watched and was in turn waiting, Jack walked to the threshold. The breath of the cave was cool, and it smelled like wet leaves. Jack filled his lungs and yelled, "Hello?" and he listened for an echo, but the darkness carried his sound away and did not return it. He filled his lungs again and yelled, "Your angels got loose. They're in my hometown right now breeding monsters, and they just ripped a freight train off the tracks, and now they're digging up all the streets. You better do something because…" Jack waited again and listened. He heard only the empty air. He yelled one last time, "Call them off!" That was it; he had delivered his message to God. Jack turned to Og and nodded.

Og shrugged his shoulders.

At that, Jack shrugged his shoulders too. Then they began to laugh a little, one then the other, back and forth until they were both bursting all-out and hardy, and for a long while they shared teary-eyed in that generous, wordless laughter.

SEE: BACK THROUGH THE OUBLIETTE; CONVERSATION WITH ONE OF THE ELOHIM; MELCHIZEDEK; THE RAPE OF THE DAUGHTERS OF MEN

The Symbol
Among other things, the Tree of Life offers itself as a literal guide to the seven Earths, of which ours, Thebel, is the seventh, and to the seven Hells, which are located through our neighboring Earth, Arqa, and to the seven Heavens, which should not be discussed. No matter how it is depicted—whether carved into stone, drawn on paper, cut into living flesh, et cetera—the symbol of the Tree of Life is not a symbol. This is because the Tree of Life consists of ten Sephiroth—each connected by twenty-two Paths—which consist of Hebrew letters, and properly utilized Hebrew letters happen to be direct enumerations of the emanations of true existence—which could comfortably be interpreted as the Hypernatural or as the Divine or as 'That Which Is Veiled That Is Not Veiled,' each of which absolutely contradicts and excludes the others—and therefore these letters can make no distinction between the representation of a given existence and the existence itself. This means that any accurate depiction of the Tree of Life is necessarily the actual Tree of Life itself and that the only thing an accurate depiction of the Tree of Life is *not* is a "depiction." For this reason, almost all popular depictions of the Tree of Life are intentionally incorrect in slight degrees because to interact with an accurate depiction of Tree of Life in any way— touching it, tracing it, studying it, even glancing at it—puts one in severe mental, physical, and/or spiritual jeopardy, that is, as long as it is an *accurate* depiction of the Tree of Life.
    Here is an accurate depiction of the Tree of Life:

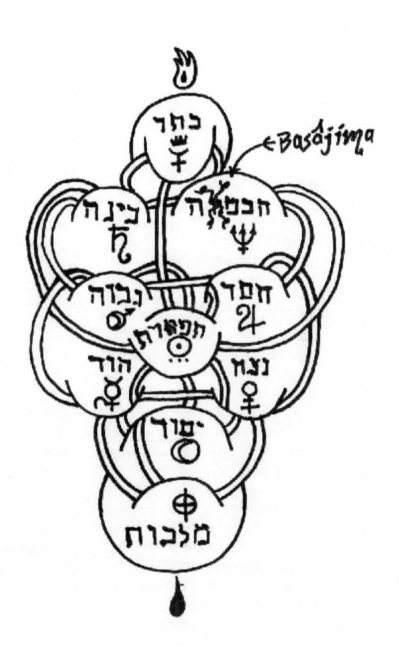

Kurt Rheinheimer

How to Get Sick

It's May, 1969. You're eighteen, and in two weeks you'll graduate fifth in a high school class of more than six hundred. *And only two of them are girls*, your two friends say, *so you're really third where it counts, Lisa—third!* You've been accepted to one of the finest art schools in the country, in New York City, in fashion design. You've been accused, twice, by good teachers, of plagiarizing papers you wrote in a hurry, in an hour, the night before they were due. But you know better. You know the world is as bleak as a used chalkboard. You know that your face, in a truthful mirror, looks like an old Russian woman's. You know the two friends conspire against you—triangulate, someone told you it is—when you are not thinking they will, and then deny it. They are as sweet as the day is long in the light of the day—Jeanne and Tracy—and say they want nothing but the best for you. In the fall they will go, together, to Salisbury State over near Ocean City to have fun and meet boys. *You are our star*, they laugh. *For the three of us, for the neighborhood, for the school.*

You don't tell them or your mother or anyone else what happens to you four times in the weeks just after graduation: A huge red plane of color, broad as a football field and thick and sturdy as a giant two-by-four, spreads itself—at an angle so strange and acute it cannot be real—across your consciousness. Four separate times, for much of an afternoon each time. Across the whole of what you can see and feel in your head, as if it was brought down on the top of your head and into it like a mammoth, thick-bladed hatchet. The color is as bright and red as a wrestling mat, as if in response to

216

your love of another color—pure royal blue. Is it because you've studied color so much, contemplated it far beyond what it deserves? There is, for a block of time that seems on the same scale as the size of the block of red, no escape from the red, save an occasional flash of light within it, brightening the red.

There's more. The Shirelles have visited for more than a year. Shirley, her voice like silver, sometimes sings "Soldier Boy" over and over again, as if to pay you back for all the times you listened to her sing it. Shirley visits alone sometimes, in voice, without the others behind her, asking plaintively about loving her tomorrow. You know why this happens. You bought every Shirelles 45 they put out, the day you could get it. You won radio contests. You wrote them letters, when you were younger, until they at last wrote back. *We're so glad you like our records,* they wrote. *It's having fans like you that makes the music business as wonderful as it is. We appreciate you liking the lyrics of our songs too, but we have to admit that other people wrote them for us. Hope you'll come see us next time we come to Baltimore. Love, The Shirelles.* You were fourteen when that letter came, and you spent days reading and re-reading, picturing the Shirelles passing the pen around to make sure each one contributed equally. In all the years since, while you've waited, they've never come. It is only now, when Shirley breathes on you sometimes in the dark when you cannot sleep, that you know it was she who wrote the letter alone, setting up torture for years later.

In the summer, Jeanne and Tracy work. Jeanne drives in toward Baltimore to help in a dentist's office. The dentist is a friend of her uncle. Tracy drives too, though not as far, to the *Eastern Messenger* offices, where she proofreads and delivers information and sometimes newspapers. She wants to be a reporter after college. You don't drive. You tried with your father and ran over a curb once—bouncing up onto the sidewalk—and he yelled and you got out of the car and then screamed that you'd never drive with him again. The alternative was your mother, and that was no better. She smothers you, Grace does, asking so many questions you want to spin toward her and slap her in the face as you call her Grace. Everyone in the family calls your father Edwin, because your mother did even when everyone was young. So she deserves to be called Grace. You don't drive, so you stay home, drawing some, listening to top 40 radio when something inside tells you not to, something tells you it's bad medicine. The afternoon disk jockey has been on the station as long as you can remember, using the same jokes week after week. *Here's Neil Sedaka from his big sedaka hits. Looks like it's going to be sunny today and daughtery tonight. Remember, you can tune a radio, but you can't tuna fish, so keep your dial right here at WCAO.* Creedence's "Bad Moon Rising" is still on the radio, because it should be, months after it was released. You hate the "bathroom on the right" parodies and sometimes think John Fogerty will make his way up there near Dylan.

You can see your mother go back and forth: She is afraid for you, as she's been since you can remember. One day she is calmly asking how it's going, if there's anything that needs to be gotten ready for the trip north in a shorter time than it seems. "No," you say. And sometimes: "Leave me alone," with a slam of your door. Other days she's: "What do you think, Lisa, time to try the car again? Maybe look for a job? Your brother or I could drive you, you know. Something maybe at that art supplies store in the new mall?" Your mother is as vulnerable as you are, and sometimes you can't help but trade on that—throw a pencil, keep your curtains closed all day, fail to shower for three, sleep for most of twenty-four hours. Spread those out over a week and she's nearly nuts. Maybe more frightened than you are.

"You ever talk to Patti Page?" you say to her one day, picking a name from her era that appears unbidden in your head as you start to talk.

"Talk to Patti Page?" your mother repeats.

"Or have her talk to you?" You talk to your mother faster than you do to anyone else, sending words out like bullets. Double bullets—one for tone, one for content.

"No," she says, pausey, thought-full, puzzled.

"Okay then," you say, and leave it at that. It's as close as you come to telling people about yourself—about what's happening to you. Then you're angry two ways: at yourself for going that far and at her for not picking up what you're saying.

"Okay then, what?" she says, so sincere and puzzled that your slap reflex almost has to be physically stopped.

"Okay then nothing. It's a question, that's all, plain and simple, Grace, a question."

"A celebrity question?" She's going too far, and knows it. You've already shown the amount of anger it takes to back her off, and yet she's going on. That means she's angry, confrontational. Which she should be, you know, but of course you don't tolerate it for a second. You attack.

You had some faith in New York City. You came out of a ratty little neighborhood built for poor families from the South or the Midwest to move into so the daddies could build airplanes for the war, and into the best city in the world. But the way you went was as if you were on one of those moving airport sidewalks that weren't even invented yet. The movement was unnatural, the light unreal, the air faintly scented of metal moving at high speed. You rode along, because that was what had long been planned, with your mother. Up old U.S. 40, where your mother tried to talk about the trips to the Delaware coast in the old days when you were young and the Chesapeake Bay Bridge wasn't built yet and so the family—you, your brother who's three years older, your brother who's three years younger and your mother—had to drive north almost to Pennsylvania to get around the upper reaches of the bay, and then turn south to get to the coast. "Yes, Mom, it was great back then," you said, mixing your message perfectly: calling her mom but coating things up with a good thick layer of irony you didn't know was going to be there until you heard it being said. Then on up the Jersey Turnpike, where you asked her to stop maybe fifteen miles after the last stop, because you had to use the bathroom.

"We just stopped," your mother said.

"I must have missed it," you said. And then, calm and cruel and soft: "I can just pee in the seat, especially if you'll let me ride in the back. You'll never know."

She stopped and you stayed in the restroom until it took you closer to screaming than you had felt before you went in. You could feel your mother outside in the little restaurant counting and making deals with herself about how long she'd wait before she came in. Paralysis, basically, maybe almost as bad as yours. You looked at the little window in the john, hinged across the bottom, tilting open from the top with little chains in either side to hold it at a perfect forty-five degree angle from bottom up to top. Outside there were the noises of cars and the scents of cars and the sights of cars' lights flashing now and again with a turn. You thought about how to get the window open to get out. Not beyond that—just out. Well, one vision: to climb out, walk around and come back in next to Grace and ask her what the hell the holdup was. More than that, though, it was the dangerous, gas/metal scent of New Jersey. What the hell were you doing, going to New York City? Who were you fooling? What would be the thing that would reveal you, that would tear away your surface and leave you more exposed than if your clothes had been taken off a hundred times in front of the U.S. Congress?

The college buildings are old, like an elementary school. Big metal radiators and big metal-frame windows. You are on the second floor in a room with Hunter Marie Alvertson, from Vermont. She is dressed like her parents own the Villager clothing line. Dress, bows, shoes, knee socks, earrings, sweater-even-when-it-is-hot. In fact that's what you say to her first. "Your dad own Villager or something?" She smiles, extends her hand and asks if you are in fashion design. You have to say yes. Her guess is good, but the realm is so much narrower than your guess. Maybe you should have spoken broader: clothing retail, maybe—still a bigger realm than a segment of art school curriculum. A lucky guess. And she—cool, New Englandish, out of prep school—has too much breeding or something to talk about what her daddy does.

You exchange words only to divide the room and its containers and spaces the rest of that day, despite the two mothers' strange dances with each other when neither knows nor cares about the steps of the other. Grace: a beachcomber, basically, and a mother desperate for her daughter who nonetheless wants to get back home and do the things she does, like sew and read and walk and worry.

And the other mother: How do you hide haughtiness when it grows out of your face like a giant nose? Seeps out of your eyes like venom? Who else in the world could put you on your mother's side? You stop talking at all after an hour of the moving-in exercises among the four, but congratulate yourself on stopping short of slamming that drawer, dropping that full box flat and hard, jerking open a window to make real note of the insanity of a sweater in early September in New York City.

The more they throw tradition at you, the more you back away and dismiss; the more ceremonies they hold to tie this new class together with the Big Bow of the History of the School, the more you shrug and duck, the less you talk to anyone. You don't know just then why, or even think about it, this process of disengaging yourself before you're even engaged, knowing you aren't worthy, knowing no one else knows the dangerous secrets you do. And on the third day, the day before classes start, there is a summons to the dean's office, where Dr. Margaret Smiely is waiting beside a big desk, her dark blue suit so perfect you think again about clothing company ownership ties.

"Miss Hardin," she starts.

You sit, still and tense as a cat poised to pounce, picturing yourself as the central character in the classic cliche cartoon: In one thought balloon, out into one side of the room, is Dr. Margaret Smiely as devil-mother, out to probe and poke and pseudo-sympathize the way your own mother tries to do; the blue suit with flame decals running in vertical lines up from the hem and over her breasts before exploding into bursts of flame at the shoulder. And into the other side of the room, the balloon of Dr. Margaret Smiely as savior. What if she's done this for twenty years, met the young ladies with uncertainties at the entrance door and somehow paved their way to health and sanity and realization of themselves at the school? A glow of yellow light around her face, bathing her soft smile in a balm of helpfulness. Next you ponder a moment the curse of not only seeing the cartoon but the situation, and seeing them so brightly as to remind you of the red planks of summer. You feel the pull at your eyes that signals the temptation to pour yourself into her there

and then. You know better, of course, for there is no such hope
with anyone. You pull away from both visions, lock into an imitation
of your friend Tracy in such a situation. You take on her voice, her
posture, her outlook, the tilt of her head and the sincerity of her
eye, and within a few moments offer your handshake to Dr. Margaret
Smiely, who—you know—cannot wait to softly usher you out the
door and begin her report to the dean that the arrival jitters of Lisa
Spelling Hardin are no more than that, and that she looks forward
to the considerable potential you arrived with reaching full flower
over the coming semesters.

In an introductory fashion drawing class, you work next to Francoise
Agiler, whose mother is Italian and whose father is French, who
comes from upper New York State, who stands—lithe and black-
haired and loose-limbed and interested in you in any foreign accent
she decides to play with just then—as the most compelling person
you've ever met. Within two weeks of the start of classes, she knows
more about you—your family, your art, your high school years, your
wonder about the future—than anyone else in the world. You've
even alluded to the summer reds by talking to her about the
occasional intrusion of color fixation into your life. She knows that
sensation, she says, noting that she's read that the stronger it comes
to one, the more likely she is to be successful with color in her
work. "I think Van Gogh had some of that," she says, a hand on
your forearm, "a real fixation with color blocks, and I think mostly
during the warmer months and with the warmer tones." *She knows,*
you think, *she understands.*

    Things lift then, and something new draws down in their place.
Once upon a time, you threw the bums a dime, in your prime, didn't you? can
now roll through your mind without threat of turning into reality
sometime in the next few hours. A letter from your mother is opened
the day it's received. You sit at a table in the cafeteria and eat the
food that everyone else does, in their company, and talk about what
they want to talk about. You awaken ready for classes. You take
showers. You think to call Jeanne or Tracy, though you do not, as if
a connection that precise to back home might break this spell.

What comes to your head instead of the reds or the voices of song is Francoise. Everywhere. You watch for her the same way you did Danny Feakins in the ninth grade. Only much more vigilantly. Francoise can come around any corner any time. In the cafeteria, as you talk to others, you watch the door and see every person who enters, knowing the next one could be Francoise. And so you go, at the short Thanksgiving break, up the interstate with her to her home north of Ithaca, high on a bluff looking down on Lake Cayuga. The front of the house is all glass, and inside, rooms fall off into other rooms on what seem to be ten levels, all full of light, of shadow from trees, of wood floors so gleaming with grain as to rise up toward you. Her father is in Europe, her mother—small, wiry and dark—flitting in and out of the levels in the manner of a bird. Mother and daughter, you know immediately, have the perfect relationship: no worry, no obsession, no stumbling over one another in this house so full of wood and light. Francoise drives the two of you to the village to bring back wine and cheese for the late evening, takes you to watch a woodwind ensemble thereafter, pulls the spread down for you on a bed in a room made in a jungle theme—full of green tangles of color and light. She leans down then, Francoise does, and kisses your forehead once you've laid down. "You're sweet, Lise," she says, running a hand at the side of your face. "You're good." There is a scent in the air in that room that night, a scent, you know, of perfect royal blue. You want to capture your life just then, put a tent over it or a coat around it or even a bottle overtop it so it cannot slip away. You go to sleep, for the first time since you can remember, without fear of the horror of your dreams.

In the next weeks, you begin to look at the calendar every morning, and make a tiny check mark to count off one more before Christmas break. You wait every day for Francoise to ask—she waited until three days before Thanksgiving break to ask, but this is bigger, longer, and so she will ask sooner. Home letters sit again, sometimes existing as intrusion, sometimes as threat. Finally, without opening the last four, you write off a quick note that things are fine, that you've had a pleasant visit with a fellow student's family at Thanksgiving, and fully expect to go back there at Christmas and you hope that is okay.

You write quickly, invoking the presence and penmanship and tone of language of Francoise's mother and pouring them onto the paper in a burst.

As days pass, as December marches by day by day, you begin to lose a few things here and there. Sleep begins to reassert its power. Classwork becomes at times impossible to bring into focus, much less carry out. And worst, far worst, there is less of Francoise. One night you walk to her room and she is gone, her roommate says, until the next day.

"Where?" comes out of your mouth like a bullet.

"She didn't really say," Sarah Collinson says, mild ice in her voice.

"She must have said to tell me something," you say then, not wanting to.

"As a matter of fact," Sarah Collinson begins, and then stops. "As a matter of fact," she repeats, "let's just leave it at that."

"Leave what at what?" Your voice is raised.

"The whole thing," Sarah Collinson says, and stands, as if to usher you out the door.

"I know she said something about me."

"Do you now?" Sarah Collinson says as you reach her door. Then she pushes you at the upper arm into the doorway, accompanied by a harsh whisper. "Did it ever occur to you, Lisa, that she may have other interests in her life besides you? I mean maybe classes, maybe a family, maybe a book to read, maybe a real friend, maybe a boyfriend even?"

You run then, despite being short of breath. A *boyfriend?* Of course Francoise would have told you. She shares everything. *It's Jim Morrison,* is what comes into your head as soon as you have closed the door behind you in your room, which has for weeks been yours alone. Hunter Marie's things were gone one midday, and you've not seen her since. It's the Lizard King snaking into her heart and taking her away before she can even recoil. *I am the god of hellfire,* he says, plain as day. He *admits* it. How can she not know when he says it over and over again? *I am the god of hellfire.* You go out then, onto the campus area alone after dark as all of you are told, nearly every day, not to do. Protection is yours, of course, in the person of Bob Dylan. Yes, *the vandals took the handles off the parkin meters,* but you are safe the same way he is. Remember? He heard that song one day—the one about baby let me follow you down—one day on the campus of Harvard University. He can do it, you can do it. What difference is there with his mission and yours of saving souls, as a group or one at a time?

You do not see her till the next afternoon. No, you've not slept, not gone to class, not bathed nor eaten, so far as you remember, but there is, you know, a radiance about you when you see her, an emanating light that washes over you in her eyes.

"What is wrong with you?"

She is *angry?* She has left you and *she* is angry? "Was it Jim Morrison?"

"Was what Jim Morrison?"

"Where you were."

She turns then, to one side, for a second, her face twisted slightly with a danger you know immediately to be the biggest of your life. You don't wait for her to reply.

"We are still going to your house for Christmas break, right, Francoise?" you say, realizing then you've taken hold of her arm with both of yours.

She shakes your hands loose. *"Still?"* she shrieks. *"Still?"*

"You have to, Francoise, you have to." You hold her arm again.

And so it is that she tells you, then and there, in these words: "Do you not know what is going on here? That the dean's office assigned me to you to try to keep you from cracking up before our very eyes? Do you think you can grab my arm and tell me what to do? Tell me to take you home? I can't take it any more and I won't. You can go to the Dean and tell them I broke their little secret because if I didn't you would break me. Go. Go now and tell them, and get the real help they should have gotten for you the day you got here."

Then you hear it again: "Do you not know what is going on here? That the Dean's office assigned me to you to try to keep you from cracking up before our very eyes? Do you think you can grab my arm and tell me what to do? Tell me to take you home? I can't take it any more, and I won't. You can go to the Dean and tell them I broke their little secret because if I didn't you would break me.

Go. Go now and tell them, and get the real help they should have gotten for you the day you got here."

Did she speak it a second time or did you hear it on your own? Does she speak it a fifth and sixth and hundredth for the rest of your life, or do you hear it on your own?

What you do next is walk to the bus station and buy the ticket to Ithaca. Once you get there you'll find the way to the big house over the lake. You'll hitch. Jim Morrison will be there of course, lizards will be there, the jungle room will be overrun with flame. The lake will be dry, her mother too. Things will be sere all over, but you and Francoise will rise above, rise rise rise above and away and alone. *Sere.* That's Gerard Manley Hopkins' way of seeing it, you know, and that is reassuring.

Off the bus, the ride you get north of Ithaca is with an older man with a full beard and eastern robes, in a white Cadillac. Dia Babba, he says his name is, right after you ask him if he knows where the Agiler home is, and if he knows if Christmas break has really started yet. You were on the bus and hours north before you wondered. "It's always Christmas break where I come from," Dia Babba says next. "Yes," you say, "but is it at school?" You are impatient. Well, something far beyond impatient. You tell him how the house looks down onto the lake, what rooms look like inside, or at least what they used to look like, before the lizards and the fire. "Where can it be?" you say, looking out onto the countryside for clues as he drives. "It has to be right along here."

Dia Babba helps you look until it has been dark for hours. He says you need to sleep, and when you say no, he doesn't contradict you. He stops the car soon after that, and points at the gas gauge. "We are out," he says. "Get more," you say. He gestures outside the car. The only light is in a single building ahead. He opens his door and comes around to your side. You resist at first, feeling not fear but panic that Francoise will be carried away before you can save her.

And so you live, from that day for the next years—two or three or eight or more?—with Dia Babba at Havensworth. Where Dia Babba decides who lives closest to him, who comes to the big house, for maybe a week, to share his knowledge, his insight, his wisdom and his bed. He tells you there will come a time for Francoise, but that the traditional concepts of time are not really at work in the context of so great a love and understanding. Time can elongate or contract, he says, and it makes no difference at all in the ever-expanding universe of love. He holds you sometimes, he tells you of his visits to the Eastern masters, of seeing George Harrison's guitar *actually gently weep* with tears of love. Dia Babba knows you have come to him at Havensworth because it is God's will for both of you and for Francoise too.

At some point, when it is hot, your mother and brother come to see you; another time, in winter, your father, alone. Once Tracy maybe, though it may have been a dream. Each time anyone comes, you tell the story of Francoise's danger, and ask if the visitors know a way to help. You tell about how you will go see her soon, to take the good fresh vegetables that Dia Babba and the others grow to restore health to those fallen victim in any way. About how you will see her soon because either you are going to see her or she is coming to see you. Maybe you'll buy a car, maybe Dia Babba will take you, maybe the sun's not yellow, it's chicken. Maybe all who have come here with no invitation should go back home to Baltimore and live in their crappy little houses and not see the real truths of the world the way they never have anyway.

There is *time*. There is *time*. Why is everyone in such a hurry? So demanding? *Maybe think again someday about school?* they say. *Back to Baltimore? To go get help, maybe at Johns Hopkins?* Why are they saying these foolish things?

You know. You know they say all these foolish things for one reason. It is not love, it is not love, it is not love. It is for the cruelest reason: to get you away from where Francoise knows you wait, safe until she comes; away from where you can go to her or she can come to you. Any time. It is only a matter of the great elasticity of time. It is *I am you and you are me and we are all together*. It is the Lizard King and John Lennon in a fight till John's triumph on the highest hill in all of the state.

It is, not so long away in time at all, the warm, white, winter embrace of death.

Michael Garriga

Zombie Revolt: On Gabriel's Failed Insurrection, St. John the Baptist Parish, Pointee Coup, LA, February 5, 1805

Unbada, 28, San Domingan Slave on the Picou Plantation

Of a sudden my life's become a dream, a shade passing before closed eyes, awake yet unable to flesh out the haints of sleep. I can't conjure my name, let alone who I was, and if I can't, then was I ever? And if not, then what am I now? I reach for fleeting images—a woman's parting lips, a child's hair soft against my palm—and a smell comes over me, strong as pan-tote bacon-fat frying in a deep pot, but like something else too I can't quite call, and there's a roar in my ears like

John Cantrell, 37, Georgian Overseer on the Picou Plantation

Night drums come pounding my dreams, and I stumble from bed into a scene in silhouette lit only by full moon and fire: the plantation owner, harried, dressed in nightshirt and stockings, his wife, and three bastards fleeing in a two-horse carriage, and the warning bells clang in riot and the barn's burning slap up, and against the high flames, the shades of slaves ride upon stolen horses, and I hope they catch their old master, for I'd like to see him dead too, so I could lay claim to this land that he never waves crashing on shore, and that smell again drives my feet onward; it is salty as sea water and like everything you've ever wanted—a hug from your mother, a free moment to drum and enjoy the one-pot feast—and I'm chest-punched, air exploding from my body, and the sky careens before me and I'm on my back and all I want is to lie still and rest forever, but I sniff that scent again, and I'm up, shuffling on like the insatiable drive of mules, and all of my labors and loves pass me like wind, this wanting to know, because that smell's now more intense, and my feet propel me, and I am trying to say my name but it comes out a moan, and that water roaring in my ear, and I'm bellowing like a belly-sick cow, wanting my memory back and an answer to the question of that smell and then there's Boss John and that odor becomes scythe-sharp, and I smack my tongue against what's left of my last meal, grainy remains like mullet roe in grits, and all I can see in the world is him and his gun, but before he can fire again, I realize that he is the smell and that I must have him.

worked, and the air is redolent with cane and burning flesh, and glass is breaking in the Big House, and flames roar there too—the fools—this revolting breed of island slaves, followers of Toussaint in his far off hell-hole revolt, I'll treat same as I'd have done him: grab my gun and whip too, and come to meet this moaning hoard. Unbada's the first I recognize, a docile who I thought would never take up arms, even if he is San Domingan. It's a shame I'll have to make example of him first, but he is coming at me, slowly, insistently, blood slathered across his lips, so I shoot him twice, and twice he is risen. And I begin to re-load my rifle, black powder spilling over my hand, streaking the scars I earned from lashing slaves, taxing their backs and lack of labor, these lazy beasts too brainless to conjure the brilliance of Christ on the cross, only room enough for thoughts of what hangs between their thighs, and I'm ram-rodding the ball down the barrel when Unbada's hands grab hold.

Pharao, Second-in-Command to the Leader, Gabriel, of the St. John the Baptist Parish Slave Uprising

I ride over slavers and zombies alike—neither's human enough for my concern, and once this revolution's done, I'll have no use for either—and the Bay I ride, stolen from the stable, stands 16-hands high and glows the color of fire in the field, and I swing my sword to urge the soldiers on, though they trickle like black strap bound for rum, and in the offing I see Unbada shuffling, his arms stretched toward that overseer, who each week taxed half my rations of meat and bread, him standing there with his long rifle pointed, smoke rising from its just-fired barrel, a hole the size of an urn's base blasted from Unbada's back—his feet cleared the ground—and I bite into my lip knowing our flesh is just as weak and just as strong as Christ's—I told Gabriel we should've stuck to the plan we'd spent moons weaving to the last stitch—set fire to their homes in the black of night and mow them down as they flee, all five hundred of us with sickle and shovel marching to drum-banging beat—but he insisted on the ways of the old country, said, "Cousin, we can't use the master's tools to tear down his house," and I said, "Master don't own fire and death no more than pistols own war." But he'd made his thoughts known and conjured it so, done put herbs in the fieldhands' food, a recipe of the walking dead he'd learned from Touissant's own men—and there he is among them now, Gabriel, a striking figure on horseback—pistol and reins in one hand, a saber held high in the other, and a pheasant plume stuck in his hat—looking every bit presidential at the birth of a new nation, circling the men who do as he urges, and as if they were cattle, he drives them on, and so I watch our revolt, in all its sluggish progress, gone now is our African zeal for speed and grace—and it comes to me that Gabriel would kill or enslave us all for what he wants, and Unbada rises from the earth like the dead thing he is, a Negro Lazarus, and no longer is it the cocaine driving him, and that slaver's hands go fumbling over the loading of his gun and he hollers, and Unbada's hands take hold of him and he moans and his teeth crack the white skull and he laps at the slaver's brains like a dog in a ditch and his hands are shoved in the gore, and I can no longer resist: I heel my horse in a hell of a charge, and Unbada eyes me with that same dull, lustful look—chunks of flesh falling out his open lips—and I run my sword through his skull, and Gabriel has come behind me with his hoard of moaning dead and they are tugging at my feet and my horse rears, all slashing hooves and maniacal, and I club two in their relentless heads yet they yank my ankles and finally I fall, horse and all, to the ground and they're on me, moans in their throats, and though I flail about, I pray for the patience to wait till I too will rise, as I know we all eventually will.

John McManus

A Mist Went Up From the Face of the Ground

12 October

I'll begin with a little about myself including my name, Jamie Keller. I drove here on a learner's permit. Thanks to this journal I'm no longer at large. Because of this journal, this journal exists, i.e. I stopped here to buy it and so I'm alive. I decided to write it because I spend so many hours a day pissed off at how non-geniuses are always trying so hard to understand genius. In eighth grade I saw a film where the non-genius Ron Howard directs the non-genius Russell Crowe in the role of the genius John Forbes Nash, whose brilliance, as defined by the non-geniuses, lay in his ability to look up at stars and formulate new constellations, such as the Umbrella. He drew an umbrella in the sky for the non-genius who became his wife. Why would a genius marry a non-genius? Both Nash and Crowe seem to be dead now, so it doesn't matter except in principle: i.e. the inherent problem in writing is people will sit around trying to *make sense of* my words: they'll *grapple* with them and imagine my creating star patterns like the Ruger or the TEC-9, which I'd do if I wanted to make things easier, but that belies my point: I'm alive because I'm intolerant. I can't stand non-geniuses' interpretations of genius, so I've chosen to explain genius to them once and for all—

—and what a thrilling day to do so. This morning when I awoke I bolted down the aisle, tripping over someone's legs on my way out. The sun hadn't begun to rise, but I could affirm it was true, what I recalled from yesterday: the pavement was gone, along with the cars, the highway, and the flashing blue lights that had shored up my will in those vague final moments. The prairie grass was high enough to tickle my balls while I peed, and the Milky Way glowed, and I heard footsteps of four guys who came to stand in front of the store looking straight at me, although they couldn't see me.

"Like whoever they think is levelheaded?"

"They sell megaphones?"

"Battery-powered."

"Burn the ones we don't use."

"Won't last a day." I heard more pissing and more fear. People kept using the word *unreal*. I recall how everyone thought 9/11 was so *unreal*. The first hint of light appeared in the east as the crowd grew larger, working itself into a frenzy until a voice announced over a megaphone:

"My name's Jack Nance, I got a spread down 45. I propose we implement some system of order—" but he was overwhelmed by a woman howling about her baby. She'd left it in the cart while she ran in for a receipt; now it was gone. An old cross-eyed fellow told her it was in a better place. Jack Nance said he belonged to the Church of Christ, Scientist, and a fat guy named Esau asked if that was like Scientology, and Jack turned red. Folks introduced themselves in a hurry, full of purpose, as if a hurricane was forecast to strike soon. Esau said we had food to last a year and that he had had a fallout shelter at his place down the road.

"You think this is a tornado? Look at the stars."

Some did, then someone offered that satellites after a time will fall to earth. Maybe solar flares were blocking our phone signals? This in the tone of children seeking approval. It seems to me a riot should have broken out, but everyone's acting civilized. A guy named Tito Glascock means to distribute the firearms to men familiar with their use. Others are relying on God, asking him to "help in this time of need" in case he thinks they're asking for help eons from now. Jack told a story about Mary Baker Eddy, who was near death when Jesus suddenly cured her. What I should have shot up was a church, I told myself as I watched three men try to attach a camera to a remote-control helicopter. A woman named Melissa took the megaphone from Jack and said she's mayor not of Big Sandy but of Raulston, twenty miles away. She thinks we're on a show. Behind me some teenagers spoke of the lack of chicks: *you could do what you want here, old enough to bleed,* that sort of thing.

13 October

A girl about my age with black hair and brooding green eyes has been watching me from the periphery. I keep turning to see her feigning to examine whatever is at hand. "You gonna get on that shit?" say the three boys my age. "Lure her over, we'll all take a turn." Even if that were my proclivity, it would remain out of the question: she makes me uneasy. I keep thinking I know her. Being a genius, I can call to mind every picture from my yearbook, so I'm quite certain she's not a classmate; still, she causes me to think my mind is playing tricks on me. I keep to myself as much as I can. Six have gone on a mission along what they believe was the highway. Two of their wives, worrying that there's some new boundary beyond which nothing exists, noticed me listening to their inane banter and asked about my folks.

"They're dead."

"How old are you? Poor thing. I can't imagine how it feels to," et cetera, because women, like counselors, claim to be involved in how things *feel.* I got out my cell phone, held it to my ear, and said, "Yeah, still at the store. The weather? It's—"

Worried Wife 2 grabbed it from me and shouted "HELLO? Why, you little, do think this is—" and I shut my ears before *some joke.* Do you think it's all *a game.* There's no need to finish one's sentences in the United States. The wives were nearly hyperventilating by the time their men arrived back. They'd walked four miles along the rise until Tito felt sure he was standing where his house had been.

We're going to come across as idiots if this book survives to the future.

I walked alone in one direction until I couldn't see the store, then spun until I grew dizzy. Grain blew in the wind, and I knelt and jerked off, imagining Tito pressing me down against the earth.

Afterward I panicked: I'd lost my sense of direction. The sun was high and no one knew my name and I thought, *I deserve this fate*—but then I saw where I'd trampled prairie grass and after a walk I could see the box of the store rising and the truck in back, attached to a loading dock. Its keys are in the cab, and we could drive it across the prairie if the tank weren't empty: such ironies have kept Melissa holding onto her theory about the show.

Walt Wallace wants us to ride bikes to the river. He has a cohort named Sam Schull; the two used to fish together. For some reason Sam thinks their fishing cabin will still be standing, so he's trying to persuade us to join him. The Mexican bagboys were in the bank when Sam tried to sell them on it. One said, "Fishing buddies?" to general laughter. Later Walt explained the joke to Sam, who should gotten more embarrassed than he did. My hope is that his shame at mockery will fester until it leads him to commit an act of bloody violence, which, when reciprocated, will send us spiraling into a race war.

A daily ration is to be doled out by Tito. Also you have to dig a hole when you take a shit. To prove how dumb this is, I shat in Tito's tent while he was out digging the hole for his own shit. Then I wandered onto the prairie, where the boys my age were playing football. They saw me watching but didn't stop their game. Listening to them, I learned that the black-haired girl who stares at me is named Helena. I know because I heard them talking about her being hot, from which I interpolate that they intend to take advantage of her.

14 October

Spent most of today with the gerbils. I admitted everything to those gerbils today, and there was no judgment at all; they kept being my friend. The sound is faint, but think I the black gerbil is purring like I cat when I pet it.

Walt, after trawling the aisles for a star chart to no avail, went asking who among us knows the night sky. The answer is the old cross-eyed guy, who turns out to be blind. This tickled me. For hours he has been sitting with a group who try to relate to him what they see: "Three together in a triangle, then over to the left in kind of a claw."

15 October

The car I lost to the Change was my mom's Voyager, whose odometer would have hit 200,000 by California. My favorite book is lost to the map compartment, but being a genius I memorized passages: *Of mankind we may say in general they are fickle, hypocritical, and greedy of gain.* I bring this up because people aren't behaving as they should. There is a consensus that we should all receive the same rations, as if we're equal. For everyone to get along so well makes me seem weak to have succumbed to feelings, so I decided to spend today on acts of sabotage, in the hope of creating strife. I collected the birth control pills from the pharmacy, put them in a hefty backpack along with the condoms, and walked more than a mile west, where I dumped them onto the plain. This will keep anyone from having sex without the threat of pregnancy. When I returned, a crowd was gathered around Walt, who had taken the battery out of a wristwatch. Now he was using two wires to hook it to a potato. To my amazement, the watch continued to tell time, which made me feel like the note I left in my locker about being a genius was arrogant and foolish. I can't explain how batteries work or watches or even water filters. I brushed that thought aside and looked something else to sabotage. My book said *men are so simple that a deceiver will never lack victims for his deceptions*, but the Bibles had already been moved, and electronics were useless. Really it was out boredom I made my way to the one-hour photo. Behind the counter, as I'd suspected, was a shitload of developed film. I flipped through and eventually came upon the name Jack Nance. His first roll was nothing but old folks around a Christmas tree, but the second was paydirt: Jack was tied to a diagonal cross with a ball-gag in his mouth. There was another man in leather cross-straps at whom I stared, thinking *forget what I said about arrogance, I really am a genius,* before looking up to discover the green-eyed girl, Helena, across the way.

"You've been watching me," she said, stepping forward. I shoved the pictures into my pocket before realizing what she'd said was preposterous. "Were those yours?"

"My mom's, but she's dead."

"Duh, genius."

Before I could show her the photos, she was wandering away toward the fractured light that poured through the front door. "Our water will barely last a week," Jack was announcing by megaphone when I followed Helena out to find humanity gathered in a half-circle facing the encroaching winter. "There are sign-up lists I'll post: folks that are good at hunting, folks that can run." No one was challenging him. *The new ruler must determine all the injuries he will need to inflict once and for all,* but something in Jack's DNA was causing such unanimity that there looked to be no power struggle. It so defeated the purpose of the Change that I considered claiming to have spotted a plane.

Walt plans to lead a group tomorrow to the river. An old man said Jesus will return as a child. Melissa mentioned that her daughter never used to cry. All I've got for strife is that our situation fails as a convincing rapture: our Lord has taken too long, the Christians are thinking; something has gone awry.

17 October

After breakfast today everyone went around in a circle listing their skills, and Esau recorded them on a yellow legal pad. Even the migrant workers were allowed to speak without interruption, I guess because they'll know how to extract water from cacti? I'd predicted an out-and-out war by now, with factions split by race, class, and creed, but instead Jack is offering lessons on Christian Science. The blond football boy, Nathan, is attending. Such foolery is why I'm relieved that society ended when it did, not to mention that the forensics team would have discovered my websites. My crimes would have had the opposite of their intended effect because there'd have been a *national conversation,* but now the world won't need to learn I was curious about some things that no longer exist except in photographs.

"You've got a girlfriend," said Nathan's curly-haired friend, Eddie. At first I ignored him, but when he didn't leave, I looked up from the gerbil cages and followed his eyes to where Helena hovered by the cat litter.

"She's like fifteen," I said.

"What are you, twelve?"

"Fuck off."

"Folks sure are testy this morning," he remarked, which got me sort of keyed up: maybe a vigilante spirit was developing. I hurried outside to find a majority of the group cheerily talking about various religions, generously weighing all remarks. Disgusted, I returned to my gerbils and petted them each before giving them three treats apiece. Afterward they washed themselves as I leaned against the shelf, took out my photograph of Jack and his master, and examined it.

"What are you planning to do with that?"

I jumped up and hit my head on the highest shelf, crying out as I recognized Helena to my left. "How do you do that?"

"I think you want to blackmail him, except that your ability to do it relies on his influence which means you ought to support him."

"Who *are* you?" I demanded, as blood rushed into my ears, pounding in my cochlea. Helena had deduced my conundrum perfectly. She must have followed me from the last life, I thought, as she backed into an unlit aisle: she was here to judge me, or provoke me. After she vanished, I tried to shake off an enormous déjà vu by focusing again on sabotage, but there was nothing left to steal, nothing to do but slip into a daydream in which Sam, butt of the fishing joke, executed Rosa, Guillermo, and Carmen. I pictured a sky purple in the east, black in the west as the remaining Mexicans fired into a screaming mess of men running across the periphery of my vision. Jack caught them and locked them in dog cages behind the store; Nathan volunteered to be a sentry; Jack said "The wise man does at once what the fool does finally."

Since this is the only extant book, I can copy whatever I want from previous ones. It was the best of times it was the worst of times. Mistah Kurtz he dead. From now on you'll never know if I'm referencing some great work or just being independently brilliant.

18 October

It took Walt and his band of searchers twenty minutes to reach us from the horizon after they appeared on it. By the time they arrived,

Esau had opened our last bottle of wine to toast their success. Unfortunately for his toast, Walt said, "There's not a lake." The ensuing silence marked the moment our group's fear finally achieved parity with our predicament. "The Lewis and Clark Dam isn't there," he went on to say. Had God turned the lake into a river? I've never understood what's comforting about eternal life. The people gulped from canteens of river water that I hoped would give them Giardia, and I thought how gorillas are individually unpredictable yet their desires lead to the same group outcomes over and over.

"It's twenty miles northeast, where we figured it would be. I think we should move within the week. We'll bring shelter and food and radar devices to help us fish." A power struggle, I thought with glee: his rival leader, Jack, would demand we stay. Descent into factions. Being shot, and Jack demanding "Say where you've hid him and we'll put you out of your misery"—but it was agreed unanimously that we'll go day after tomorrow. Next what does Jack do but call a testimony meeting. Plagued by disease, the newly widowed Mary Baker gave her nurse her newborn baby and married an itinerant dentist who soon deserted her. For comfort she turned to the Bible and found herself cured by Jesus' miraculous healing method. If Jack told us once he told us twenty times a patient's belief plays a *powerful role*, so, as a trial, I tried believing in a continuation of my daydream, in which he leads an angry mob to ask Rosa, Guillermo, and Carmen for last words. The three jabber in Spanish until he yells *ENGLISH, you bitches!* and Rosa cries *Mijo!* and he shoots her to fall at the feet of Melissa, mayor of the next town. *Whoever conquers a free city and does not demolish it commits an error,* but, try as I might, Jack keeps on treating his disciples kindly, which is truly a strange way for me to be punished.

19 October

Today when I was feeding the gerbils I heard a stifled sob from kitchenware. Ready to bite at any crumb of adversity, I followed the sound to where a circle of women sat in the toaster aisle. In their midst Helena wept tranquilly beside a lady who was eating tuna out of a can, who was saying, "Anyone know this girl?"

My eyes wandered up to the black spheres that hold the security cameras. "Her name's Helena," I found myself saying, so that the women looked my way, making me more ill at ease than at any point since the Change. I wished they would burst into flames. I retreated toward the gerbils but it was too late; Helena had stood up and was already following me, making pitiful whimpering noises. Maybe it was the footballers, I thought, getting excited; maybe the curly-haired one with whom Nathan spends all his time. I opened the guppy tank and used a spatula to scrape algae off a castle turret, thinking I owed it to the innocent dead to shoot the guilty dead too—even though I dreamed of being victim to what Helena seemed about to describe: three of them, their skin bronze from the light of an Indian summer, closing in from all sides.

"What did they do to you?" I asked at last.

"I begged them to leave me alone," Helena said through sobs. I was shot full of adrenaline: it was as I'd imagined. This was the adversity I'd asked for and more. "I begged them," she repeated, facing me now with a sickly, painful smile like the one I develop each time I relate bad news. That's one of the things I used to hate most about myself. Another shuttle has exploded, I recall telling my mother the morning of the Columbia disaster, hovering over her in her dresser mirror, powerless to keep that evil grin from spreading across my face.

20 October

Prayers can be divided into two categories, *Please God* and *Thank you*. The former is irritating enough, but the latter is unbearable. I'm too worn out from the hike to write anything except that I'm at my wit's end from all this praying.

21 October

It was fully dark last night by the time we finally pitched camp to the sound of splashing water. Forty of us had walked in a single day to this riverside copse whose trees Walt says we'll use to build our rafts. Now the sun is rising as we eat a breakfast of granola bars and Pop-Tarts. I like this number and wish the others would be carried off by tornado or flood. Helena seems okay, she even has a faint smile on her face, although a cruel twist for her is that Shane, Eddie, and Nathan are in our group.

Now I have to quit writing because we're being put to work.

Having felled seven trees, we've stopped, because the store manager, Abraham, didn't follow instructions tying a knot. The tree that crushed Guillermo was a linden. Abraham bawled like a baby, but what I felt, for a while, was relief. This death, combined with Helena's rape, indicated to me that we haven't entered some discord vacuum. Gradually, though, it came to seem like anything but a good omen: the whites are as upset about it as Rosa and Carmen, if not more; they even convened to *commit this body to the deep to be turned to corruption.*

Now it's afternoon and Randy, an employee in electronics, is my new sawing partner. "What church you go to?" he asked.

"I'm not from here."

"What denomination?"

"I'm agnostic."

He told me computers had convinced him to believe. Their parts are so small, you need a microscope just to see them. "Every year God manifests more of Himself in computers."

"Until now," I said, which was when we saw the deer grazing on the far shore. It looked briefly up at us, then returned to eating grass.

"We should shoot it," Randy whispered. Our first sighting of a large animal, and all this moron can think of is to kill it. Feeling crazy in my head, I stepped off to observe its splendor on my own. I wanted to bound away with it into wilderness. I miss my gerbils. From a distance I watched Nathan and his friends split logs until finally they jumped in the river and shouted for me to join them in horseplay, which is a cruel taunt given that I can't swim.

24 October

Forgive me, Father, for it has been seventy-two hours since I last wrote. All afternoon I've been sweating from the sheer size of my thoughts. I wish I were a better prose stylist, so I could convey the abstract hugeness that takes over and renders me incapable of grasping time, which somehow began and will end. It all started yesterday when I awoke to the deep voice of a man. I'd been dreaming my mother taught at the high school instead of the middle school. Kids were desperate to convince me she was their favorite teacher, even though she was crippled and never smiled. We love her, they insisted, she's our favorite—but their voices were drowned out by Walt asking me to join a supply expedition. Shaken, I rubbed the sleep from my eyes and asked why.

"You're in fine shape, for one," he said, "but mainly you seem like you've got a good head on your shoulders."

Non-geniuses often think it flatters us to remind us we're geniuses, but that's no more flattering than telling a shark that its teeth are sharp.

He gave me a list of what he thinks we'll need; he said the items will require four backpacks and revealed that he'd therefore asked Shane, Eddie, and Nathan to accompany me. At once my mood soured and I thought of escaping onto the prairie. I decided I must be the disease Christian Scientists ask Jesus to rid them of, and now I would prove the truth of their faith by really leaving—except that I dithered until it was too late but to proceed as planned. We set out in T-shirts at half past eight. My heart was pounding for the first half mile, but the boys' happy-go-lucky demeanor soon disarmed me. "Where are you from?" asked Nathan. "We're from Tulsa, we were on a church retreat."

"So you're big into God?"

"It's mainly for the girls."

"East Tennessee."

"Beg pardon?"

"Where I'm from."

He wasn't a genius, but it excited me to talk to him. We passed an elderly group and told them it wasn't much farther. In the next miles we passed more people, some not doing so swell. A woman named Emily, who weighed at least three hundred pounds, was on the ground crying. Although I felt bad for her, there was an exhilaration we all shared.

"We'll be back tomorrow," Shane told her. "By then you'll be so far along you won't need our help."

"Will you do me a favor?" she implored, taking his hand. "If I'm still here, will you please shoot me in the head?"

The blood drained from Shane's cheeks. "Now, there's no need for anything like that, ma'am. We'll get you to the river."

"I don't want to get to the river. My family's dead. I can't walk. You've got a gun."

"But that's the thing, ma'am: none of us have weapons. Even if we wanted to oblige you, there's nothing we could do."

The temperature was about sixty, and as we walked I could see the parts of my life lined up in a row, from my first day of kindergarten right up to this hike. I wanted to film our camaraderie and send the footage across a thousand miles and two weeks into the past to my peers, so they'd see what little I'd been requesting. We reached the store at twilight, lit lanterns, and walked around gathering tools; then I met back up with my new friends at canned goods.

"Today would have been my birthday," said Shane as he poured cans of soup into a pot.

"How old?"

"Seventeen."

Nathan disappeared down an aisle and came back carrying a box, which he set down in front of us: it was a cake from the bakery.

"It's stale as fuck," said Eddie, but Nathan placed seventeen candles in it and we sang Happy Birthday. Briefly I felt like someone was in the shadows listening; then I felt like we were the only four people alive. "What did you wish for?" Nathan asked, and he got no answer. Surely Shane didn't want to return to the old world any more than I did. He'd pinned a girl to the earth and done harm to her, and I, well, the moon was rising, and Eddie began telling a story. The year he turned nine, he said, his family rented a mountain cabin, and one night a bad storm rattled the windows and knocked out the electricity. Just as Eddie's dad lit a candle, there was a knock at the door. Eddie opened it to find a teenaged girl standing there drenched, with glass shards and blood in her hair. She looked distracted and mildly troubled, as if she was missing an important meeting, far away.

"Can we help you?"

There'd been a wreck, she told Eddie's father, and she needed to use the phone. They invited her in. Sitting on their couch, she dialed a number and spoke so quietly that no one could hear, but then she laid down the receiver, explained that an ambulance would arrive soon, and said, "Sorry to be of any trouble, but may I use your restroom?"

Eddie showed her the way, then sat back down in the dark to watch the lightning. After ten minutes his dad went to check on her and found the door open. There was a staircase to the basement, which had an exit to the back yard; that door stood open as well.

The night winds blew fiercely against his window as he lay in bed waiting for his father to come back up. Surely the old man hadn't gone out in the rain. Before Eddie could worry, he fell asleep. When he awoke the next morning, power had been restored, so he went to the living room to watch cartoons. The local station was showing a news flash: last night, up on the pass, a truck had lost control and some hikers had been killed.

When Eddie paused, I noticed his face flickering with the lantern. "The one pictured onscreen was the girl who'd used our phone."

After a long silence in which I heard only our breathing, Shane said, "You must not have lived a good life." I couldn't tell yet if he was joking.

"I'm not finished. She's here. She's that girl."

I no longer felt safe alone in the store with these three. "*That* girl?" said Shane, as my suspicion that Helena had made up her story melted away.

"After my dad was released, he got messed up in some things. I didn't know it, but we were in hiding at that cabin. He'd shot these guys in a coke deal." A gust of wind blew out the lantern. Instead of lighting it again, we kept listening to Eddie in darkness. "I don't know what made me go downstairs; I didn't have any reason to believe my parents weren't in bed."

In the pause that followed, I thought later, he must have been turning to face me. "Jamie, you're the only one who hasn't heard this part of the story," he said, and I felt like the oxygen was all being sucked out of the room. "When you die, you shit yourself. That's the thing I remember most: the shit that dribbled out of his pant legs when I tried to pull him down."

The world turned itself back on: Nathan was clutching the lantern, having relit it. Suddenly I knew that Eddie would pause, suck in air through gritted teeth, and tell us the girl had come for his dad. "Because he'd killed those guys?" asked Shane in a whisper, and I then knew with the same precognition how he would answer:

"Not just for killing them. He wasn't in danger, and it wasn't for money; he just shot them for the hell of it. Plus he did some other things to them."

If an injury has to be done to a man it should be so severe that his vengeance need not be feared. In retrospect I see that they were ignorant of my crimes, but in the moment, as I failed to be able to breathe, it struck me as inevitable that they would turn to me and state aloud the conclusion I'd easily reached. So it was out of self-preservation, not any sense of justice, that I asked, "Worse things than what you did to Helena?"

One by one they all turned to gape at me. "That's her name," I said, trying to muster up some righteous anger. "She's named Helena."

"Dude, you've got the wrong idea," said Shane, and as he spoke I began to I realize something incredible: if someone was about to die, I could confess everything to him. My actions at school had constituted a missed opportunity on the grandest of scales.

"Had you seen the news, the day of the Change?" I asked, my body already anticipating how it would feel to spill my guts.

"The thing in Tennessee?"

"South of Knoxville."

"My girlfriend had just called to tell me what happened," said Shane. "That's when I stepped out into these fields."

I got the sense that he'd forgotten until just now, and that remembrance was causing him a vertiginous déjà vu. "It was me," I said. "I stopped here just to buy a disguise."

"Why would you do a thing like that?"

"Why would you gang-rape Helena?"

He started shaking his head, then stood and said, "No," pointing his finger at me and incanting *no, no*. "The ball bounced down a hill," Nathan interrupted, lowering his voice. "We found her pointing a gun into her mouth, sitting in some clover. She said to get away from her, but Eddie sat down and told her what his dad had done, and how bad it fucked him up."

"That was when I realized it was her," Eddie added, sounding as though he wasn't present in his body. All these details people throw at me: they want me to think, *That's a detail no one could make up*. I thought back to Helena's original story, trying to recall a single specific word.

"I heard you talking. Old enough to breed, old enough to bleed."

"I'd say that about my own sister."

"Eddie," said Nathan, "this dude's freaking me out."

Around and behind me the world was calm as the three of them moved in closer. I wished I could take it back and say I was kidding; I'd thought the truth would feel good. When they started making secret gestures with their eyes, I put a stop to it. They raised their hands in a panic as if that could stop objects traveling at 2500 fps. They might as well have raised their hands to block rays of the sun. There was silence but for the wind outside. I can't even recall why wind blows; I guess it's because the planet is always spinning, causing friction between the earth and the air.

It was hard to fall asleep. When I did, I was plagued by dreams about my mother, my father, my cat: all three continue to live in my brain as dreams. The sun rose. I got some baby wipes, stripped down, washed myself, and walked naked to menswear for jeans and a shirt. Then I spent nearly an hour with my gerbils. Miraculously, all four remain alive. I gave them enough food to last a week, installed some extra water bottles, and promised to come back for them. Finally, after gazing at Nathan's face one last time, I donned my pack and walked west, singing to pass the time. Was Kurt Cobain saying *I feel stupid and contagious* or *Life is stupid and contagious*? I couldn't recall, but both lines seemed fitting to me. After ten miles, just where we'd left her, sat Emily.

As soon as I offered my canteen to her, she grabbed it from me and guzzled its contents. "I'll die here," she gasped. "Surely you've got a gun."

"The others are following behind with the guns."

"There's nothing left for me to live for," she blubbered, which gave me an idea. Last night's divulgence had felt faulty because it was the wrong one. She was practically begging me to do it. So I gave my other confession a chance.

"I've known since I was five," I said. "Sometimes I even fantasize about getting raped."

"Please," she sobbed, reaching for my water again, but I pulled it away, telling her I'd do what she asked only if she stopped blubbering and listened. There'd been a boy up the street named Chad; I told how he and I used to play in the woods. She pretended to pay attention, but each of us is the hero of his own story; all she cared about was dying. She spoke her children's names along with the name of her grandson. For the rest of the hike my mind wandered across many subjects: had places that I'd never seen existed? Why can no one remember infancy? Does God admit His secrets to men moments before he kills them? I'm not curious enough to puzzle it out. If I were, I would wonder why the Change didn't happen prior to my crime, mere moments before, with Ms. White running in to tell us nothing existed but wooded foothills outside the high school. If I were going to be curious, I would wonder if I have no spirit, if that's why I can't descend to hell, if God created this place for me to languish in while he devises a punishment.

When I reached the river, a large group was gathered around a fire pit where fish were being grilled. "Where's the others?"

"I barely made it out alive," I managed to say as I took off my pack and sat down. I can talk to these people, I swore to myself; if I look them in the eye and respect them, they'll believe my story about Eddie's descent into madness. *He who will trick will always find another who will suffer to be tricked.* Soon I basked in the second-most attention I'd ever gotten, and women were patting me on the shoulder. "Have you seen Helena?" I asked one of them, to a blank stare. "The black-haired girl with green eyes?"

"I'm not sure who you mean."

"She was crying the other day when you all were eating lunch."

They pretended not to know who I meant, yet they trusted that I told the truth. It caused me to grow scared and think maybe something really is messed up inside me. I continue to await some calamity more dire than my crimes. The diabetics gathered tonight for a discussion: they have enough insulin for only two weeks, but even this stark certainty causes no conflict. Isn't a choice going to have to determine who lives, who dies? Tito Glascock joined them and said, "I'm a hemophiliac. As soon as I injure myself, I'll be dead. So I just wanted to come talk."

It was hard not to reach out and cut him with a knife. "What's insulin made of?" someone asked, as if we can brew up a batch of it ourselves, and then Jack sauntered over and said God will cure all who believe. I hoped the diabetics would grow irate—*It takes a lot of nerve when we're dying*, etc.—but they asked to hear more! Without medicine to cure our ailments, I told them, belief in God is our only recourse. *God is not willing to do everything*, says my book, but I decided to conduct an experiment and pray for a suicide overnight, just to test the theory.

26 October

Thirty-six hours later, not a single one of us has done himself in. I'd call this proof that Christian Science is bunk, but there's so little strife that I wonder if God isn't preparing me for heaven's harmony. It troubles me how serene life has become. I've even taught myself to swim. It took most of the day, and then yesterday I practiced all day. That's why I haven't been writing more, and anyway there's nothing worth mentioning except that Tito, Vince, and Warren have set out to the store for more sealant. I can swim halfway across the river and back, which means I can reach the other side if I want. If not for what Tito's group will find on aisle five, I might have swum all afternoon today. Instead I got out and examined the rafts, coming to see what will occur once people are asleep. I took off my wetsuit and swam to South Dakota. Back in Nebraska the fly fishermen waved to me. For some reason it hasn't been bothering me to be looked at. It used to make me irate. People used to think I was fine being stared at like I was some tittie magazine. All of them used to sit together in the bleachers at games, and six of the boys would take off their shirts to spell R-E-B-E-L-S on their naked chests, a letter on each boy, and the girls would fall into their arms, because if you got A's without trying, if you understood calculus while others struggled with algebra, you were asexual, and if you didn't show up at school dances you probably didn't masturbate. I digress. Tonight after our fish fry a number of folks lingered at the fire pit to talk theology. Some think God has broken the covenant of the rainbow, while others feel our predicament is a puzzle we must solve. Two Catholics say the key awaits us in Rome, and the diabetics have converted to Christian Science. Apparently, since we reflect God's nature, we're not made of matter; therefore sin and death are illusions. These ideas beguile non-geniuses. Maybe the non-genius mind will call it a false impression that I undid the ropes. How can I have set rafts adrift if matter doesn't exist? Except at my fear that I'll burn in hell, my adrenaline didn't surge. My reasons were ternary: I had no other choice; I hoped to distract everyone from Tito's looming report; I needed to put an end to the conviviality. In a vacuum I'm no enemy of bonhomie, but if the pursuit of power doesn't control human thought, my actions indicate a failure to know our nature. That in turn would suggest a lack of genius. It's been a week since I've even noticed the night sky. Lest I begin to question my own IQ, I need for Jack to ascend the mound of wet sawdust and announce that Walt has intentionally marooned us here for winter. "It reminds me of Abel and Cain," I dream him saying. "Abel grew wheat and offered it in tribute, but his brother Cain thought God would be pleased by death."

But why root for him to turn against Walt, you might ask; hasn't Walt treated me kindly? Ever since that potato, people act like he discovered special electricity. What about the picture, you might then wonder; why damn us to die of exposure when I could foment dissent with a picture? Because I'm too shy to fucking talk, okay? What am I supposed to do—go up and start chatting? "Hi, I'm Jamie and I'd like to show you a picture?" Have you read an account of a conversation I've started? Start over on page one and pay attention. The whole problem is I'm too intelligent not to be shy. Instead of asking someone to the prom, I used my mind to ponder the thousand outcomes that can emanate from a single sentence. It seemed so easy for dumb kids to ask each other out. On prom night I sat home watching *Battlestar*, disgusted with myself for not asking Ryan Leith. I knew he was like me, but he'd asked this girl Jill. I couldn't comprehend then that you don't have to want to fuck someone, or even love them, to be their date. What I did understand all too well was that kids with dates and I had signed a mutual pact not to give a shit about each other. So all summer I stayed home playing Second Life, speaking to no one but Residents, sleeping till four and going to bed at sunrise. My parents were fighting, but I learned to distance myself by means of a particular thread of thoughts. By the time school started up again and a fall dance was announced, I had realized I could stop dances from happening anymore at all. Part of me wanted to wait until I'd accomplished something intellectually, like solving a theorem. I imagined writing the proof on my skin to be found after I'd died. Except what if I was incapable of solving theorems, what if I would have to attend college like any non-genius.

I decided that I would wait to the last minute to see if anyone asked me out. It could have been some stupid fat freshman chick and I'd have said *yes*; those were the rules. I couldn't make my point if they learned afterward that I'd been asked out. I wrote up a list of grievances. In sixth grade Todd Vaughn shoved me into a Dumpster. At recess the boys played Smear the Queer, which had nothing to do with actual queers; it was just a form of tag where whoever held the ball was the queer. I guess that's not the best grievance, but there were plenty of others, and I knew in the aftermath stunned parents would curse themselves for their bigotry. Whatever I couldn't steal from my uncle Floyd, who was in the East Tennessee Militia, I bought with money from Second Life. What you did was purchase land, develop it, and sell it for a high price. My avatar was named Severian, and he would go on dates with other avatars, sometimes flying to far continents just to have coffee with a cute guy he'd met through a real estate deal. Like me he was a genius, and in the game's environment he found it easy to surround himself with others of his ilk.

Such thoughts of mine might still have gone the way of others if this lispy fag with a funny accent hadn't moved down from Wisconsin. His name was Danny Fuqua, and the thing was, he took insults in stride and mocked himself. Barely halfway through September the popular kids were already on his side. He went to the games, then one night he asked Ryan Leith on a date. I've never seen anything like it. They openly went to Chili's and people kept being their friend, I mean no one even cared. The last straw was when Ryan agreed to go with him to the dance. They were these starry-eyed boys walking down the hall hand-in-hand and it was up to them to reach out to *me*, not the other way. I guess you'd laugh if I say I abhor violence, but I've learned to find beauty in sunsets, rivers, I used to like abstractions but now I like water and the sky.

I drove to school an hour after the dance started. When I got there, I rolled down the window and smoked a cigarette. My mom didn't usually smoke, but there were cigarettes in the glove box; maybe she was having an affair, I thought, not that anyone would want her. That was another part of the problem. Before my dad got fired, he was assigned to write this feature story on Madame Cherie's palm-reading studio, so he sent my mom there for a reading. I didn't learn why she came home crying until the article appeared: Madame Cherie had told her she would die suddenly at the age of fifty. From that day on, my mother stopped caring about things. She got sick, developed arthritis, and spent more and more time playing solitaire; then, at the age of fifty, she died suddenly.

I sat listening to my favorite song, "Idiotheque." When it was done, I took the TEC-9, cradled it beneath my coat, went to the door, and was stopped by Ms. White, who sat behind a table, her hand resting on a roll of tickets. "Jamie," she cried, sounding genuinely excited, "you came! I can't wait to see you decked out under that coat!"

If anyone had ever *asked me to a dance*, I'd have known that dances charge admission, so I'd have brought five dollars. In that case, the kindness of sweet little Ms. White might have won me over, but as things stood I wore a T-shirt and carried no cash. I could only walk past. Around the corner fifty couples slow-danced to

Wise men say/ Only fools rush in,

Ryan and Danny among them, swaying in one another's arms. Watching, I knew for certain my mind's strength crowds out things that other people have. In that terrible moment, I wanted those things. I wanted them so bad. But now that I've had time to reflect, I find that I feel compassion. Killers are said to spend childhood in the most violent ways, ramming firecrackers up their cats' assholes, tying bricks to their tails, but in school when boys bragged about such cruelty I wished them dead for it. I myself had a Siamese named Matty Groves. When bad things happened, I told no one but Matty Groves. Together we worked jigsaw puzzles until one day Matty asked to go outside. I opened the door for him and sat down again to create a fruit tree growing alone in a field in the state of Oregon, which took up most of an afternoon. *Kitty kitty!* from the porch and the next day too, until finally I sensed an ever-so-faint meow. I listened: there was only thunder and wind. Again the warble. "Matty Groves!" I cried with all my power, and while I feel a fool now not to have run to the building site down the road, I wandered in circles, torturing my poor cat with shouting until that half-built house was the only place left. Suddenly the meowing was audible from the concrete foundation, rectangular but for a nook where the porch would be. I leaned to peer into its void and saw Matty Groves, ten feet below, climbing a two-by-four that rose diagonally from the pit. To my horror, he slipped and fell violently back onto boards and jagged panes of glass.

I realized this had been happening again and again since I first called his name.

What I did next was probably the most courageous act of my life. Through deafening thunder I ran home, found a laundry bin, ripped down my window-blinds, tied their pullstrings to the basket, and sprinted all the way back. He was trying to climb the board again. My fingers fumbled with the knots. Finally I was able to lower it to direct him inside. There were just two strings, and the contraption nearly toppled. At that moment, and only then in all my life, I prayed. If I ran back for another string, Matty would think he was being abandoned, so I cried, "Please God, I'll believe in you forever if you let Matty Groves live," and it was a miracle. Just like that, the basket leveled. Matty sat in the makeshift lift until I raised him to the level of my chest. Weeping, I stood clutching him in the rain, revenge the furthest thing from my mind. There was only gratefulness, and it was thanks to my heroism that he managed to hold on for two more weeks, and now it's assumed that I'm cruel to animals? For that I want everyone to suffer, for that and for Matty's death and for Ryan and even for the Curetons, who'd dug that hole and (until the Change) still lived in their split-level rancher down the road.

I kept that promise to God. As I bent to fetch Danny's car keys from his wet pants pocket, I believed in Him and knew I would keep believing. On my way out Ms. White said please Jamie, please, and I didn't like it; I want folks knowing I'm smart but not fucking cowering. Maybe that sort of thing feels good to God but not to me; all I could think for miles afterward was please Jamie, please Jamie, and except for those words the drive is a distant dream.

27 October

Today in a last-ditch effort I nailed my picture of Jack Nance to a tree. If anyone has noticed, I'm not aware of it, and everything else is the same.

28 October

Last night the temperature never fell below fifty. The Nebraskans call this unusual, even disturbing. They speak of a TV show from before the Change, in which an island was magnetically moved across the ocean, but it's still October. I suspect the Arctic winds will make their way here soon and send the gerbils the way of the guppies. I need to get back to them, as I promised I'd do.

"We seem to have lost the rafts," said Jack cheerfully to Walt later over a lunch of soup. "Good thing there are so many more trees we can cut down!"

Later the two of them and others spent hours devising the most fantastical theories on our plight. With all this solidarity, I'm doubting my most basic memories from before the Change. It was always my assessment that the planet was riven by war, but perhaps there was never a Palestine, an Africa, anyone who felt like I did that day.

29 October

I think God intends to destroy me with peacefulness.

31 October

Today when the sun emerged to brighten our weather I stripped naked and jumped off a river bank. Folding my hands like a pillow beneath my head, I floated downstream. Before the Change I'd have pegged Nebraska as a worthless waste, certainly not a place so full of stunning light that changes throughout each day. The sun warmed my chest and I peed straight up, the piss-stream splashing at my feet as two mallards watched me from the bracken. I thought of letting myself be carried to the coast. If I lived in another person's head it might be a nice journey. I used to like Second Life better than my own life, and now that I can swim I'm still sorry that this is my life.

When I returned to camp, this journal was missing. I put on my clothes, looked around, and spotted the usual fisherman standing on shore. Others were at work building new rafts; still more sat around the pit of last night's fire, having a discussion I listened to from a distance. "He seems unhappy." "Yes, I agree, it's worrisome." "By the way, you look nice in that picture; you're in such good shape."

Stepping closer, I saw my book in a woman's hands; then the others saw me and turned, all at once, twelve of them. "Jamie," said Walt. "Come closer."

"We notice you're a genius," said Jack.

"We've enjoyed reading all your thoughts!"

"We wonder if your incuriosity has led you to feel sorrowful." Walt gestured toward my journal. "We're worried about your happiness! Aren't you curious about why we're in this new world, and what has happened to the old? Why not engage with us in intellectual exploration?" And the others all cried "Engage," reaching out to me as if I'm not thirstier for knowledge than them all. I'm the genius here! If conjecture didn't lead me to the same answer over and over, I'd do it as wildly as anyone! What if we've traveled through time to Eden? What if we're being dreamed by someone in another universe? What if, I'm not sure how many lay dead after the dance but what if it's the same number here and these are they, grown into adults? Did I kill Nathan et al. twice, the way Jack says God made the world twice? What if they committed crimes like mine on the day of the change? What if I told everyone how I'd knelt by Nathan's side as the blood drained out of him, traveling my finger from his navel to his breast? Up and down that budding trail of hair I touched him as he lost his heat. Several hours earlier he gazed into the light wondering why we'd been chosen, whether the old world still exists on some unreachable plane, as the part of me without empathy asked, *What in God's name are you talking about.*

"Please," I begged. "Aren't you Christians? Punish me."

"We believe evil is unreal," said Jack.

"Give me an eye for an eye."

"Evil presupposes the absence of God."

"The only people I've touched are dead! How can you know you're real if you've never been touched?" I was crying out now to our camp, the river, the herons near it, screaming that if I'm evil it's because no one ever touched me, but Jack and the others only stared calmly as my words choked me. What did they see? It boggles my mind to attempt an answer, and in fact I must recently have reached some tipping point in regard to my genius, because I've been understanding less with each passing day. *Evil may appear real but it must be seen through*, says Jack's book; *better to be feared than loved*, said mine.

"Engage with us, Jamie," they said as I stood fixed to the earth, paralyzed by both horror and shame. "Help us figure the stars out, your book says you know the stars." The shame came from within me, the horror from their belief that I'm an aspect of God. Because they must be right: those last moments are a blur, but even if I've turned out to be no genius, I can see what must have come to pass, yet I still breathe, I feel the wind and see the stars shining.

The more time elapsed, the harder it grew to move. The others probably thought I was praying, and indeed I want the gerbils still to have water. I want the weather to stay warm for them. But I suspect God has wearied of me, and if that's the case I'll rig up a heater with some potatoes and hold them to my body. Pets expect a certain amount of affection, one reason I've liked them more than people. No cat ever prejudged me or joined a clique. Kittens never excluded other kittens from their play, unless runts had to be expunged from the litter. Maybe that sounds cruel, but it's instinctual. They're animals: aspects not of God but of the planet, which behaves identically, exploding in anger now and then. That's just the way it is. If you don't like it, the other planets are the same, with storms swirling in violence like that of their creation, which is too far in the past to dwell on more than once in a great while.

Steve Patten

Swallow

As the cars roll down the highway, Bud waits to cut one from the pack. They're all speeding, a wake of tail lights merging into one white line; he could take any one of them; he wants to wait for the right one, the one with New York plates. He doesn't dislike New Yorkers. He stops them because he likes the way they talk, especially when they're mad or being brash. He'll be out on his stretch of Highway 75 between Resaca and Chattanooga all night; shift started at nine, and he has plenty in the car to keep him company—a pack of Twinkies, a bag of Utz potato chips, an orange, a box of doughnuts, loaf of bread, some bubble gum and a Diet Pepsi. No partner. Hadn't had one the whole four years he'd been on patrol.

When it happens, he is relaxed, chewing gum with his can of soda balanced between his belly and the steering wheel. Staring out of the windshield he can't determine one shade of black from another. The moon is hiding, and it's the time of night that he usually finds a sign to get behind and have a go at himself or catch some zzzs. She drives past. His radar gun is off. In fact it hasn't worked in over a year. The paperwork for a new one is under the blotter on the registrar's desk where it has been for the better part of the year. The woman is driving fast though. She has no license plate, just a sign saying, "Tag applied for." Bud tips his drink into his lap when he raises up to get a better view over the dashboard.

"Dammit." He puts the car in gear, turns on his siren and pulls out of the emergency lane with one hand on the steering wheel and the other trying to wipe the soda off his lap. Bud can see the car's tail lights zigzagging across the white, then the yellow line, as if the car were a child's Etch-a-Sketch after the screen has lost all color—about three or four car lengths in front of him.

He thinks she must be going 85, 90. He glances in his rearview mirror, smiling—talking to himself.

The car slows and he pulls into the next lane, on the driver's side to get a look. A woman and a looker, too, although there's something wrong with her face; he can't tell exactly what in the thin light coming from her dash. She smiles but not at him. Her eyes are tuned straight ahead to the road. He blows and waves his hand to signal her. No good. The road is on the side of a mountain; it curves and turns, weaving around the Appalachians or at least the part too difficult to blast through, and at times almost runs back on itself. Her head is a gyroscope, bobbing but always lined up parallel to the road. He looks to her right to see how close she is to the limestone cliffs and caves opening black and blue inside, frosted with chalk.

He still has not turned on his siren. "Hey, lady, pull over!" he hollers out the open window. She doesn't stop, doesn't look, keeps taking the curves. Bud doesn't know what to do. He thinks of pulling out his gun, but he thinks, what would he do then, shoot her tires? He's a piss poor shot, and only TV cops shoot out tires. Bud looks over into her car; the dashboard light is still on; maybe a door is open. She is fair-headed with beaten bronze hair going down her blouse with all the top buttons undone; only her left hand is on the wheel. Her nose is big in profile, maybe covering half of her face, but he can't make out the color of her eyes in the dark. She turns suddenly off at the next exit. He's been watching her so intently that he misses the turn and has to go nearly half a mile before he can u-turn to the access road; another half mile, and then he's going in the right direction and he pulls off at the exit she took. The exit goes in only one direction, to the left, so he follows down the one-lane county road hoping to catch up to her. Only his headlights show, and he almost misses where she turned right, onto a gravel road. But there she is, on the shoulder, sitting in the dark. He parks behind her, brushes the crumbs and chips and all the other stuff off the seat onto the floor. He reaches into the glove compartment for his flashlight and is blinded for a minute until he closes the door. The car creaks and shifts as he gets out and the door hinges complain loudly at being disturbed.

"License and registration, please." He approaches the open window, flips his flashlight on, unsnaps his holster and peers into her car; the dash light is out now.

She has her skirt up, panties down and is going at herself pretty good with what looks to be a cucumber. He stands looking at her with his mouth open, his tongue waving like a snapping turtle's, but she gives no sign of recognition. Her eyes are open, and she sits staring straight ahead, her mouth open with no sound. He can't think of anything to say and he doesn't want to do anything to make her stop. He sees a condom over the cucumber and her left hand is pale and tight. He feels hot and flushed, and his head hurts like he has eaten too much candy. He wants to keep looking but he wants to stop. She sighs and pulls her hand up and puts it on the dashboard; the cucumber and the rubber fall to the floor.

He swallows, steps forward and starts talking quick, his words a jumble. "Do you know how fast you were going back there, Ma'am?"

She turns at his voice and smiles at him.

He scratches the dirt back with the toe of his shoe, embarrassed, like a dog covering a pile of poop. "Did you know you were speeding back there, Ma'am? Ma'am? I need your license and registration."

She continues to smile in his direction but her eyes glaze over like a snake, cloudy film sliding over the pupil like a third or fourth eye.

"Ma'am." His voice rises as if he were talking to the deaf, but he still looks down, "Ma'am, I'm gonna' haf to ask you to step out and away from the car." He got that part from a cop show he'd seen on television—*Streets of San Francisco*. He's surprised when the door opens and she twists out of the seat and stands in front of him, almost on top of him. He backs up. She is tall, taller than him and fair to his dark; her hair swings down to her waist. Her shirt opens up further so he can define the curve of her breasts. Then he sees, she's not quite so tall; if she took off her heels, he figures she would be an inch or two shorter than him. Her eyes are gray, clouded over, or at least gray in the flashlight.

"Now just stand over here, Ma'am." Bud takes her arm and moves her next to his car. Her skirt hangs limp and she still has her panties around her thighs. She looks to Bud like she's on something but he can't tell what. Even buzzed, she has sort of a classy look about her, he thinks. Her hair the color of starch but not stiff. Now in the flashlight he can see what is strange about her. Her jaw, the line goes up too far. She is still smiling at him or maybe just off to the left of him, as if someone were standing right beside him. He can't tell. Hell, maybe she's seeing two of me, he thinks. Bud can't keep focused on her eyes or her jaw because his eyes keep dropping to her breasts, which look to him to be a double D cup. Bud knows cup size; he spends every Saturday night in Victoria's Secret at the mall in Sweetwater looking at bras, pretending to search for a present. The saleswomen think he is sweet to buy a gift every week and they are happy to help by modeling the bras over their clothes.

Bud hears something off to his right and his flashlight catches red eyes looking at him from across the road. The eyes, calf-high, shift from side to side trying to avoid the light, then turn and disappear behind a bushy tail. Minutes later a bark-yelp sounds to Bud's left and he swings the light around but sees nothing.

When he turns back to the girl, she is gone but he sees her on the other side of the car, her head drooping and her panties up under her skirt, which is back down. He'd had a boner since he saw her with the cucumber. He hitches up his pants and wipes his hands on the back of his shirt, "You okay, Ma'am?" She does not answer, doesn't raise her head, but begins to shake from side to side, slow at first, like a dance, then faster and her head comes up and he sees she isn't just smiling, she's grinning. Bud looks at her but turns when he hears the noise again, a rustling, rasping, paper sound to his left. He sees the tip of a tail like a torch disappearing into a gap between leaves and grass.

His father was a foxhunter, not with horses or gray-brown trousers or black coats or foxhounds or bugles, not like on television. "That's not how Black folks hunt." His father said. Bud remembered going with his father out to the woods with a coon dog and a .22, only for foxes and only in winter. His father said if you caught up with a fox and followed him to his den or caught him there already, the fox would have to connect you with the other world, not like on a party line but through your second soul. "Everyone has 'em," his father said. "Most folks just don't know how to hook 'em up or adjust 'em once they get going. You don't know, they'll eat you up, spread out on you like mold on bread. You catch a fox at his den and he has to show you; can't leave until you've gone over it at least once. Most folks that do see them get eaten up by they second soul. It ain't the kind of thing a person can look at for long without forgetting who you are. You start off being you and then you fool around and get hooked up to that second soul and you start becoming 'we' instead of 'me' or 'you.' It can gulp you down, whole, like a mushroom."

On one of the days the two went hunting, they sloshed all day with no sightings till the end when the sun left only its shadow of dusk to light their way across the diseased milo and soybean fields shorn for winter. His father's face was like that stubble and he hated rubbing against it every morning when his father came to tickle him out of bed. The light was almost gone, and they were getting in the truck when the dog sounded and the fox right after. The dog took off, crossing in front of the truck, and his father yelled at Bud to get the shotgun. Bud yelled back, "What shotgun?" All they had was a .22, but his father was already in the trees by this time. Bud had never been alone in the woods before, and he froze, not calling out because he didn't want to be a baby, but scared, real scared. When his father came back with a bushy tail in hand, Bud was under the truck. "Where you at, boy?"

"I'm under the truck, Daddy, looking for my second soul." He pulled himself from under the truck; he was no more than eight at the time.

"You ain't gon' find it under there. Come look what I brought you." His father dumped the bloody stump on the back of the truck. Bud looked the other way.

"Got him with my service revolver." His father patted the bulge in his jacket pocket. "Look at it now so you can connect with that second soul, boy. Then you'll know what people are thinkin', you'll know how they feel about you. The dead ones tell you."

"Look at it, boy." His father grabbed his head but not hard; he wasn't a mean man. Bud smelled wild onions, pokeweed, violets, and wild strawberries in the red stream spreading on the truck. He vomited, all over the tail, all over the truck and all over his daddy's hand. His father jumped back and shook his arm.

"You're worthless, damn worthless, boy."

Bud saw nothing under that truck, no second soul, just milo spotted and wilted, dead.

Bud thinks about following the fox, but just then she puts her arm on his shoulder and he hears the fox sound from further up the draw. She doesn't speak. She pulls him around to her face but he comes only to her chin and she doesn't bother to look down so he has to look up. She has the same smile, far off and not kind; as if there is some joke she is in on. The hand on his shoulder is the one that held the cucumber and she swings her other arm to encircle him. He remains there just inside her enclosure, rotating left and right. Her head slowly droops to rest on his shoulder. He doesn't know what to think; he brings his arms up to her waist and then drops them again; he shifts from foot to foot.

The night has gone black, dark in darker shades. She speaks for the first time. "What's yours?"

He jumps. "Huh?" She takes her arms from around his neck and turns back to her car; she opens the door and bends over to get something from the seat. Bud watches as her skirt rises and licks his lips. "You know, Ma'am, I'm gonna have to give you a ticket and, if you don't cooperate, I'll be forced to, to you know, strip search you." He tries to make it sound like a joke. She straightens up facing him with a small turquoise purse with rhinestones—sea green blue with lighter blue variations around the rim. Bud wants to look at her breasts again; he's sure he'll get a better view but he can't take his eyes off of the purse—small and clipped. She waves it at him like a baton.

"Now look, Lady. I been real patient with you but I need you to just come over here and bend over the car." She smiles at him but shakes her head 'no.' Bud is confused; he stands with his hand on the snap of the holster. blowing air in and out. He is staring at her breasts again because this is where his flashlight is pointing. She flips her hair to one side and comes towards him as he backs up. His hand drops to his side as she leans over him whispering. "Unless you want to see me pee on myself, you'd better let me take care of business." Then she walks off into the bushes in the direction of the fox. Bud stands there for a while looking after her.

He starts walking as soon as he hears the flow start. Bud thinks he's never seen a girl squat prettier. She looks like a groundhog, arms tucked in on her haunches and this thought makes his schweiner salute. His dad always called it a schweiner. "Go slop your schweiner, boy; he's standing at attention." Bud hated that. The girl turns and he blushes, putting his hands in his pocket to shift it to the side. He wishes he'd peed before his boner: he has that weird feeling of hard pulse and clogged dam that makes his meat jump. She comes over still squatting, walking with her knees bent like a chimp. Bud can't see where her panties have gotten to. She stops in front of him and looks up at him but makes no move. Bud tries to look everywhere but at her. He looks at the trees—reaching white and black oaks, sandy pines; he looks down—grass springing back from where she walked; he looks up, black clouds against a coal-colored sky; he looks at the moon peeping out from the clouds—paper white with gold rims and flashing hubcaps. He looks at her; he grows larger, larger than he has ever been before. He's heard men get larger when they lose weight—less folds to hide the base, but he's never lost any weight.

She continues to look from his face to his crotch, and soon he begins to ache. His sister always said that was a crock of shit when he said it hurt and he asked her to jack him off but he knew men really did have pain when they got full; he read it somewhere.

She speaks. "I know what you want." He strains against his pants and thinks, *If you know, why don't you give it to me.* His eyes hurt. She repeats, "I know what you want." He licks his lips and swallows; he thinks he sees the fox again, sitting under the shadow of the bushes. "Well, by all rights I should be giving you a ticket, for speeding, reckless driving, crossing lanes, failure to stop, driving without a seatbelt." Bud blushes when he says this. "I think all that adds up to something." She reaches out to touch him; he stiffens but she pulls back. "Look here, I ain't got time for no foolishness; I gotta get back on patrol. Maybe I ought to just take you in." He looks at her; she continues to smile just out of reach but still on her knees in front of him. She tries to get up but he grabs her hair and forces her back to her knees, she makes no noise. "I'll be damned, you gonna do something." With his free hand, he tries to unzip himself but he struggles with his fly and pushes himself into her face and loses his erection. The fox runs across his line of sight heading back towards where their cars are parked.

Now that his ears aren't pounding, Bud can hear the stream. He hadn't realized they were so close. He zips himself without looking at the girl and goes in search of the water. He can hear it as he gets closer, a tinkle that sounds like the girl's stream and for a minute he wonders if she put it here.

Tiny clefts appear and disappear as fish and water striders pop up to the surface. Along the banks he can barely make out depressions burrowed into the clay. The moon comes out and he feels he can see for miles now. Sitting at the entrance to one of the caves, with its back to him, is the fox. He wonders how she, he thinks of it as "she," has gotten here. Or is it the same one? Maybe there are thousands of foxes out here running around, crossing people's trails. The fox rises to go into her den and then he knows it's a she because four pups come out and he can see the fox has caught a swallow still alive and fluttering. She lays it down but it makes no attempt to run or fly. Bud can see it moving its head from side to side looking from the fox to the pups and bobbing its head occasionally, before the pups run to mouth it and its neck is stretched between their teeth.

Bud stares and wipes his head; suddenly he is hot and sweaty and his hard-on is back. The fox picks up the swallow where the pups have dropped it, moving still but slower as if tired. The bird doesn't flop any more, just rises slowly on its side and falls back and its body is slack and limp. The fox turns around once, looks at Bud, and disappears into the den with the pups on her tail.

When he gets back the girl is still there on her knees that are covered by the grass, but she has no smile. He is still hard and this time she takes him when he pulls it out. He sighs when he comes and says, "Damn Fox," and she swallows.

Driving down the road, Bud follows the girl until she reaches her house. He intends to pull off as soon as she gets home but the memory of what they have done haunts him and the fact that he could never, should never be able to get a girl like that. He has visions as he pulls up to her front door, of him in bed, her bed, lying back with his arms on her pillows and her, down below every morning, every day. He drives past when she gets out but circles back when she goes up the stairs and through the front door. He drives around her house several times trying to decide what to do. As the moon slips back beneath the clouds, he makes a decision and stops next to her car.

The front door is open when he tries the knob and Bud walks in looking around the large foyer with the black-and-white checkered tile lighted by a huge chandelier with glass prisms that shower colored rain around the room. Bud hears voices but he can't tell from which direction, so he travels deeper into the house. He sees her before he hears her, laughing with four other people. He thinks two are men but as he gets closer, he can see all of them are women. They stare at him as he comes in and the girl whose back was to him turns and looks at him with a laugh still on her face.

"I thought, I thought—" He starts to go, embarrassed, but turns as the girl starts to laugh again. The others began to smile and then laugh also as he looks at each one of them.

"Hey, what's so damn funny? You know I can take you all in." He looks down to check his zipper and is surprised to see his pants start to rise. He doesn't feel horny, he doesn't feel anything below the waist, and his legs won't move. The girl looks at him once before she kneels down and unzips his pants. As she takes him out, she seems to expand, to blur and he doesn't see the others anymore, only her and she has spread out to engulf the whole room, to engulf him. As she comes back into focus, he notices again the odd line of her jaw as it unhinges and opens wider and wider lined with white shark teeth, and before she takes him in, he sighs and screams, "Damn Fox," and she swallows before she shares him with the pups.

Sheryl Monks

A Girl at His Show

Every night Rasputin chose a different one to come up and go inside the box of blades. Always they were pretty, and always they were thin, T-tiny thin like snakes, wearing green eye shadow and Burlesque on the Beach t-shirts. People thought it was a hoax: all the girls were plants. Rasputin was insulted.

One night, to prove his greatness, he filled the tent with sulfur and, using Mentalism, chose a different girl. A fat girl. Fat, fat. So fat no one could harp and complain anymore. Just as easily, he could have read her lips as her mind, for she mouthed along to his every magic word. MAJOOK! MAJOOK! SARUPY! Her fleshy lips protruding. He spotted her there like a bale of hay on the farthest most bench, sitting utterly to herself, her mind fizzing with whimsy. He called her forward and gave her a wilting rose. She put on a stage frown. He waved a hand, restoring its bloom. She smiled. No one clapped.

Then, lying bare-chested on a bed of broken glass, he had the fat girl stand upon his back. The crowd clapped, more or less, but it was not enough. They wanted the fat girl inside the box. In she went.

Rasputin donned his cape, caressed together his delicate hands. When they had paid their dollar to walk across the stage and peer down inside the box, they would see there was no fooling; the blades were real, the girl was real and fat, and there was no room for the fat girl to twist around all the blades. And how was Rasputin going to pull that off?

It was worth two dollars, Rasputin said. You will not believe it; it is the greatest feat of all time.

267

He pulled six great sabers from red velvet sheaths and laid them across the brightly painted wooden box. Each one gleamed with spellbinding ghastliness. To demonstrate their razor sharpness, he slit the bellies of watermelons, filleted mutton with ease, venison, hamhocks, whole sides of beef.

The audience sat smirking. Watermelons. Hmph. Big deal, they harried.

Rasputin flung back his satin-lined cape and shoved the first deadly blade into the box. The fat girl with yellow eyes screamed Oooww!

Rasputin flinched and bent to her. All right, my darling?

The crowd did not respond. They yawned.

Sorry, she said.

Rasputin held the second blade overhead, then slowly, slowly, slow-l-l-ly pierced the box. He felt the pinch of the fat girl's flesh upon the saber, nearly heard a squeak as if perhaps she were made of cork. He paused. The crowd jeered, threw popcorn. Rasputin sunk the knife deeper, deeper until he felt the scrape of bone against blade. The fat girl shut her yellow eyes, grated her blunt teeth. The crowd bawled obscenities. They cackled and cajoled.

So it went each time, a slow and torturous tear through the corpulent body of the fat girl with yellow eyes. Her great round face paled with each mighty thrust of Rasputin's blade.

Finally, it was done. The crowd paid two dollars and walked across the stage to peer inside. There was the fat girl, brimming over the sides of the box, squared like so much dough pounded into a bread pan. They could not see the blades at all, only the blade handles outside the box. Something's wrong, they said. This is a trick box. They demanded to stand around close while Rasputin pulled out all the knives so they could see.

Five dollars each, Rasputin said. They paid. It was worth every cent in their pockets to disprove Rasputin. And if they couldn't do it today, they would be back tomorrow.

He pulled the blades out slowly, with all the dramatic flourish they were accustomed to. They waited patiently, more or less. All right, already, they said. Rasputin would not be hurried. He looked deeply into the yellow eyes of the fat girl who lay inside his box. She was transfixed by his mustache, by his shiny black eyes, he imagined. And she was. The fat girl with yellow eyes had been to every show and had grown fat there on the bleachers of *Rasputin's Remarkable Sleight of Hand*, eating kettle corn and pulled taffy from the boardwalk.

Rasputin held her hand. The coming out would be worse than the going in, he explained. She knew it would. He tugged at the first blade; it snagged. The audience harrumped. More tricks! They narrowed their eyes, tapped their sneakers on the plywood stage. Rasputin yanked, and out it came, bloody red with an organ dangling from its tip. The fat girl's heart. The audience leaped back and gasped, then leaned forward. Hot damn, they said.

Rasputin was bewildered. The heart beat wildly. The fat girl lay calmly inside. She looked peaceful, but glum. Docile. Her yellow eyes locked wet and sticky onto the black eyes of Rasputin. He trembled. The audience guffawed. They liked seeing Rasputin's cunning, his very acumen, laid bare in such a way. They did not know he was the real deal. Rasputin, himself, did not know it.

Only the fat girl with yellow eyes knew it.

Ever so gently, he plucked the girl's heart from the tip of his blade and carefully laid it inside his satin-lined hat, standing next to a wand and a crystal ball on a velvet-covered, claw-footed table. The heart was big, like the girl, enormous really. It squished down inside the hat but rose up its tall, tall sides and beat red and blue mists of blood droplets that spritzed up from the top of the hat with each great quivering pulse.

Pearls of perspiration popped out on Rasputin's bushy brows. The girl will die, he feared. I will be found out. He hurried with the rest of the blades. Each one came out like the first. Mired in the blood and bodily fluids of the fat girl with yellow eyes, with a different organ swinging from the sharp point of every blade. The gory liver, the gray lungs, the waggling intestines. Rasputin didn't know where to put them all. He stuffed them in his pockets to keep them from being trampled on by the crowd.

The fat girl was speechless. Rasputin kneeled beside the box and spoke to her. He lay down beside her and wept. The crowd laughed. Rasputin had lost his marbles. They wanted to see something else, but he only lay there on the step beside the box. Get up, they said, kicking his shiny shoes, tugging against his split-tailed coat. What's this? You're just going to lie there? You suck, Rasputin. You were never all that good. We're out of here, and we *won't* be back tomorrow. They ditched the finale, peeved and bitching.

The fat girl tried to speak, but she was in awe of Rasputin. Her mouth was dry. *I love you* was all she could say, enough to rouse Rasputin to kiss her lips.

Why? he asked. Why?

Because you're magical, she said.

But Rasputin didn't feel magical. He felt old. He *was* old. Very, very old, hundreds of years old. And this was what the fat girl loved most. She rolled her yellow eyes to look at Rasputin lying on the step beside her. He stared up at the ceiling, spoke of his long, long life, of all the great loves he had known, all the great losses, of victories, and addictions and illnesses. She had never seen him up so close. Her yellow eyes fell over his face. It was not a perfect face. Some thought it odd looking, but the fat girl with yellow eyes found it beautiful, even at such close proximity when every deep crag shone out from the corners of his shiny, black eyes. She loved every line. She felt small enough to fall inside them and travel to all the places he had ever been through all the eons of his existence. She studied his ear because it was the feature most easy to see from her awkward vantage point inside the tight, little box.

It was a glorious ear. Two deep furrows of flesh lay hidden just between the ear and his long-handled sideburn, and she felt so thrilled at having had that special glimpse of him, a glimpse no one she knew would ever have, that she was satisfied in a deep and lasting way she knew she would never be again.

I should go, she said.

Go? Where?

Home, she said. He did not ask where she lived, and she imagined it was because he could not really conjure what such a thing was, home. She thought of him sleeping in rooming houses next door to girls of the night that probably he slept with, or else in trailers back behind fairground fences where the air was choked with the smell of elephant dung and cigarette smoke and the fumes of generators. She sat upright in the box. I wish you'd stay, he said. She wanted to. For a fleeting second, she dreamed of staying, of being part of his show somehow. Only she had no talent of any kind, no beauty, no wit or charm whatsoever. She was just a fat girl with yellow eyes.

He seemed desperate, though, afraid of something. He needed her company like no one had ever needed it before. He needed *her*. She was the only person in all the world whose company he wanted, craved, had to have. Any number of things might happen to her later, during the course of her own long life. She might marry, have children, might slim down, become a Pilates instructor, take up Sodoku. But nothing would bring her to the edge of herself this way again, the brink of her very soul, looking at another human being who was not really human at all but something else entirely, something ethereal, something beyond her flesh, his flesh, all flesh altogether, something she could only think of as breath. Hers, his. It was the same. And it flickered like a candle and was gone as quickly as she could think of it.

She imagined the two of them outside the red-curtained theatre, no funny hats or velvet vests. No props or disguises. Just the two of them, walking along the boardwalk, watching old folks throw buns to the gulls, standing in line for the Wonder Wheel, buying corndogs from Nathan's just like anybody else, just like she herself did on any given day. But it was all just a fantasy. He might turn to a pillar of salt.

So she leaned back into the box and stayed a while longer. But even as she did, she felt all of time sucking away at this spectacular moment. A million things ran through her mind, but they were distant and hazy. She cursed herself for being dense in every way; even her mind was fat, she thought. She wanted to remember everything; she batted her yellow eyes like flashbulbs. An ashtray, she thought. Had he just recently smoked a cigarette? He turned on his side still lying beside her on the step, and yes, she smelled the cigarette on his breath, and she had never loved a smell as much in her life. It was arid but not foul; it was the smell of thirst.

She wished he would levitate her, send her high into the rafters and dangle her there. But she did not ask. She could not speak. She could only marvel at him.

And Rasputin marveled at her, too. Why had she not died? He looked at her heart still beating strongly in his hat on the table, felt all her innards pressing in around him in his pockets, pulsing and quickening and writhing. But it was only a matter of time. She thought he was magical, had magical powers, but she was fooled, this fat girl with yellow eyes.

Levitate me, she said at last.

I can't.

The fat girl frowned. I'm too heavy, she said.

No, Rasputin said. You think you know me? Ha! Why? Because of the tricks?

Yes, she said. They're not tricks.

They are, he insisted. You don't know anything.

The fat girl lay perfectly still inside the box. Her heart slowed in the hat on the table. Rasputin took off his coat. All right, he said. Close your eyes.

The fat girl closed her yellow eyes, and Rasputin waved a hand over her hulking body lying expectantly inside the empty box of blades. He spoke some magic words. Ali-ho-jeni! Kan-rupi! Tar-tuff!

When she opened her eyes, he was gone. She looked down from the roof beams, through the struts and trusses, through powdered-up cobwebs and flue soot and air ashimmer with sea dregs and silica. There was no painted wooden box, no red-handled sabers, no shards of glass. No magic wand, no crystal ball, no wilting rose. No silk-lined cape, no split-tailed coat. No tall black hat.

Okla Elliott & Raul Clement

The Doors You Mark Are Your Own

April 12th

Katya is still angry with me, but what if I told her I saw my brother's troops today, marking the doors of the infected? And that I'd seen common Joshuan citizens doing the same, without provocation or reward from the soldiers? Katya and I fought today, over means and ends again. I left to make the rounds with our conflict still unresolved. I hadn't been in the streets an hour when I saw something so low it nearly turned my stomach. In the door of a once fine Joshua City home, three men stood over something ragged and huddled, clapping each other on the back. A black boot swept forward and there was a whimper from the pile of clothes. Then the flash of a knife blade, the snicker-snack of someone bent to dirty cutting work.

"I'll cut his idiot tongue out," said a skinny man on the right.

"No, wait," said another man, large, checking his friend's arm. "I've got something better."

It was the Day of Joshua, and men like these were celebrating what should be a marker of human freedom with thuggish simple-mindedness. The large man unfastened his pants and squatted over the creature's mouth.

Across the street, a wagon waited, loaded with tied-up lepers. Their faces had gone blank from terror. They did not know their destination—only that it would not be pleasant. The soldiers meant to be guarding them were marking doors, or were distracted by the Day of Joshua festivities. I might have cut away the lepers' ropes while their captors were occupied. But I couldn't leave these other

273

men to kick this poor creature to death. I scolded myself even as I was doing it. What right had I condemning a dozen people to save one? From a utilitarian viewpoint, it couldn't be justified. But on the most basic human level? The thought of their fate brought on the familiar coldness in me.

"Stop now."

They looked at me, their fists hanging loosely at their sides. "Who are you?" the large man asked, taking a delighted step toward me.

"I am an angel of reckoning," I said. "The doors you mark are your own."

They considered this briefly before surrounding me. I looked at the large man. He seemed to be in charge. "Before you do that, you might think about the freedom you now enjoy to walk away from all of this."

"Sure." He smiled. Behind him the undersized man or ancient child they had been tormenting rose to his feet. *Go, damn you*, I thought. "And then I'll have a nice chat with God," the large man added. His friends laughed.

"You don't know who I am, do you?"

"And we don't care." The first blow cracked my temple, and my ears rang but I kicked back. I heard a cry from the smallest of them as I connected with yielding bone. My finger found an eye, worked at popping it. Another blow and I was forced to the ground. A tooth had come free, and I stared at it, pink and glistening in the mud. Beside the tooth lay a flyer, one corner caught beneath a chunk of concrete and steel mesh. I read its garish font: *Day of Joshua Parade! Come one, come all, and celebrate this great city's anniversary!* I raised my head a few centimeters. The creature was gone—no parting look, no sign of gratitude. Their leader lifted a brick, wrathful now.

I rushed him, and on the ground my hand found the brick he had dropped in our fall. I raised it and slammed it down against his face; I raised it, slammed it down; raised it, slammed it down—with each blow his face was less human, more meat and dark fluid. Behind me, I heard his friends making their way down the alley, no doubt to home where they would contrive stories to explain their injuries. The man's chest was still moving beneath me, and I wondered if that was a good thing. Oughtn't I to end this monster's ability to do again what he had attempted here today? But the question remained unanswered, as I then heard the soldiers returning to their leper captives. I did not want to risk another run-in with General Schmidt.

The last time had not been under pleasant circumstances. I'd been snatched up by his men, and dragged off to an interrogation room where high-watt bulbs were trained at my eyes and I was asked a series of questions I either could not, or would not, answer. I kept demanding to see my brother. "Schmidt," I'd say as they hollered at me and struck me with stones wrapped in wet cloth.

Two grueling hours later, they must have figured out who I was, because Schmidt came striding in with his imperial air. He took in my battered face.

"Nikolas," he said. "I can't go on protecting you forever."

I grinned and asked, "How's mother?"

He turned away then, showing me the side of his face. "Kristina is sick," he said, persisting in his habit of calling Mother by her Christian name. "She wishes you'd come visit her more often. I won't tell her what you've come become."

"Nor will I tell her about you, Marcik."

"That's not my name." He stood and began pacing the room, turning sharply on his heels each time he reached a wall. "You're a brilliant man, Nikolas, the genius of the family. We could use you on our side."

"I prefer my soul intact, thank you."

He grabbed me by the shoulder, pinching hard at the tendon between shoulder and neck. I might have whimpered. "You continue like this," he said, "and there will be nothing of you left intact."

Now, seeing soldiers in the distance, I ran down the alley, leaving my victim to live, though with the scars of his misdeeds tattooed into his face forever. As I ran, I damned myself for a fool at having left those lepers at the mercies of the soldiers, though the joy of violence was still in me and I couldn't suppress my smile.

I turned the corner and was nearly to the Saint Leocadia Avenue entrance to the Underground, when I saw a quivering mass on the sidewalk. It was the deformed man-child I'd saved. He looked horrible, forehead split like ripe fruit and the skin of one eyelid ripped and ragged.

"What happened?" I asked, as if I needed an explanation. Those men were riding the wave of patriotic idiocy. And if it had not been them, the bone fiends looking for an easy score might have done the job, or the insane Mayor Adams' administration had turned out of the asylums when Marcik and I were children. Remembering those days, I had the beginnings of an idea.

"Where are you from?" I asked. He grinned, revealing shockingly pink gums. His cheeks were rose-colored; his eyes shone with childlike brightness beneath the blood. "Do you speak? Can't you tell me where you live?"

He nodded and leapt to his feet. He knelt in the dirt and with a piece of wire began to draw an elaborate system of boxes and lines. Soon I understood it was a map, charting the streets of the district in beautiful, unnecessary detail. When he began in on the trelliswork of the house where I'd found him and his antagonists, I laughed out loud. "You live there?"

He pointed backward, over his shoulder, a gesture I determined to mean the past. "Your family used to live there? How many of you?"

He pointed to himself, held up his palm, fingers splayed. Five including himself. "Where are they?"

Hands behind his back, cuffed, an arm grabbing his neck, tossing him into the back of a wagon. Lepers? Himself uninfected?

"Don't you speak at all? What's your name?"

He opened his mouth, stuck out a tongue scored with dozens of razor cuts. When he tried to speak all that came out was a saliva-choked grunt. He looked around, saw a storm drain, and reaching down into the urine and the scum, fished out something slick and wriggling. He popped it in his mouth. He grinned, proud as an infant who's just wet himself.

"Slug?" I asked. "Your name is Slug?"

He jumped to his feet, and before I knew what was happening, he had me in a ferocious embrace. He spun me around and set me back on my feet, and when I'd recovered I asked him if he would like to come see my underground home—if he would like a new name, one to inspire fear instead of scorn. He jerked his head up and down violently, letting out little happy squeals.

What will Katya make of this? I thought.

April 13th

A continuation of last night's events: when we arrived back at the Underground, Katyana was waiting for us—or for me, at least, though if she was surprised by my new friend she did not show it. I turned to hide the bloodier side of my face. She looked to me, to Slug, then back to me.

"This is Slug," I said. "Our newest member."

Slug approached her and extended his hand, and with a shy turtle-like twisting of his head, he avoided meeting her eye. I wondered if he was frightened by her porcelain mask. I myself scarcely noticed it, but I suppose the uninitiated must find its smooth, expressionless surface surreal.

"I'm very pleased to meet you," Katyana said, all faux ladylike decorum. Slug scampered back and hid behind me. He peeked out, ducked back, peeked out again. "Is this another one of your little projects?" she asked.

By now the other four had come out and were standing expectantly at the tunnel's entrance. I turned to see what Slug was doing, and Katyana gave a small cry and hurried to my side. "Nikolas. Your face."

"I'm fine." I pushed her off, but gently, so that she could see I wasn't really angry. Without the others present, I would have enjoyed her doting, but just now I had my role to keep up.

"Take care that he gets set up properly," I said.

I thought she had not heard me, but she turned to the others and, in a tone both distracted and authoritative, instructed them to set Slug up in the pump room. They grumbled somewhat at being ordered around by Katya, ostensibly their equal, but I gave them a look that brooked no argument. When they were gone, she took my hand. "Come with me."

She led me to our bedroom, such as it is, and set me down on our bed, a hospital cot stolen from the now defunct Joshua Asylum. She opened my medical bags, found a swab and disinfectant, and began dabbing at the mess of my cheek. I winced.

"Does that hurt?"

"Not so much," I said.

"I don't think anything's broken." She traced a loving finger down my jaw, along the old scar from when Marcik and I were children. "But Nikolas, you really must be more careful."

"They weren't soldiers."

"Still, anything could have happened. You must promise me— if not for my sake, then for the revolution."

I could not deny her request, couched as it was in the language of the cause. And besides, didn't I enjoy her ministrations? "I promise."

But later, long after Katya had gone to sleep, I lay in bed staring up at the exposed pipes of the ceiling. They looked like the arms of some giant sea-creature, prepared to strangle us all. In the dark, I put a hand up to my face and touched the new stitches, then the older scar beneath. I thought about the past, and how despite how far we come, we can never escape its tentacle-arms.

I was eight, Marcik ten. Father had died in the Barbarian War, and it was just the three of us now—Mother, Marcik, and I. Marcik and I shared a pallet smaller than the one Katyana and I now sleep on. We breathed each other's air, guessed at each other's thoughts, and stepped gingerly over each other's boots and moods. At times it was comforting, but mostly it was stifling. I was the younger brother—and I knew even then that I was the braver, the stronger, the smarter; though Marcik's being two years older afforded him the official title "man of the house." When Mother needed something from the market, I had to accompany Marcik, because she trusted me to get it right, but it was Marcik who carried the money and did the purchasing. "It makes him feel older," Mother said.

And it was I who had to hold Marcik when thunder rumbled on the horizon, or when the insane roamed the streets at night, piercing our walls with their tinny laughter—but next morning he was all orders-given and orders-obeyed, a natural soldier before he ever became one.

One evening, as Mother was serving up the pickled cabbage heads whose smell I'd grown to loathe, Marcik came bursting in, nearly stripping the door from its rotting hinges. He had a paper and was waving it like a captured flag. For a minute, I thought it might be an exam from primary. I felt a twinge of annoyance: there were already ten or twelve such exams plastering the walls—*Satisfactories* mostly. My *Outstandings* were received with a perfunctory pat on the head and shoved in a drawer to mold. I was set to be a doctor, while he was still engaged in boyish games. I watched Mother to see if she would scold him for being late.

"Carnival's coming," Marcik said. "May we go, Kristina? May we?"

"Let me see." I grabbed for the leaflet, but he ducked behind the sewing table. I struck a spool of thread with my elbow and it went unraveling across the floor. Mother bent and gathered it up. She stood between us and laid her hand on Marcik's shoulder. He grinned at me.

"I'm afraid that's impossible."

He pouted. "But it's only five pence."

"Unless . . ." She turned to me. "I know you were saving for that watch, Nikolas."

"Compass." I had been planning to slip away one night—past the infantry standing watch at the borders of Joshua City, where trenches had already been dug for the Great Wall—to see what was left of the hell-swept planet.

"It would mean so much to him." She gave me her adult look, the one that said *Humor him. For me.* Marcik studied a crack in the ceiling. He wanted to say something, but knew it would not be to his advantage. I swallowed and nodded yes.

"What do you say to your brother, Marcik?"

"Thank you," he mumbled.

She drew him around to face her. "Look him in the eye."

"Thank you, Nikolas." His glance slid off me with an oily quickness, and he went to the bedroom looking for all the world as if he had been punished. Mother squeezed my hand and smiled at me.

The following morning, we were off in our Sunday best. The carnival was ten blocks away, in an overgrown cricket field. The ticket-taker seemed unsurprised to see boys our age, though I did detect a strange, carnivorous glint in his one good eye when I asked directions to the Puppet Palace. The other eye was made of glass, a milky thing that wandered in a dark socket. Marcik stared dry-mouthed and refused to give him the ticket until I pinched his arm. He hit me and I elbowed him off.

Marcik wanted to test out the firing range, so we did that, taking aim at targets no bigger than teaspoons. He could barely shoulder the rifle. We were out another five pence, and for our troubles were awarded a second-rate inkstand. Then he wanted to see the Mermaid Lady, who turned out to be an ordinary, not even pretty, woman in a sequin dress with papier-mâché fins. Finally, wearying of these gaudy amusements, as well as the pretence that Marcik was in charge, I told him we were going to the Puppet Palace. I expected him to argue, but he simply shrugged, perhaps not wanting to let on that he was scared.

But at the door to the Puppet Palace, he hesitated. The grinning maw of the Puppeteer hung over an archway draped with strings, so that it seemed we might become actors in the grisly drama ourselves. I grabbed him by the ear.

"Don't be a baby." Now that we were here, I was determined to enjoy myself. We'd spent over half the money I'd saved that summer, and the puppet show had been the chief attraction for me when I saw the leaflet. I silenced Mother's voice in my head. "It was you who wanted to come to this stupid carnival."

I pushed him down a shadowy corridor into a crowded, musty room. Rows of rickety chairs were set up before a box-frame stage. The light was dim but not menacing, and the Puppet-Box was unimposing. I prepared to be bored. The lights dropped off and a cavernous voice filled the stands.

"Ladies and Gentlemen!" the announcer began. "Creatures big and small! What you are about to witness will shock and amaze, horrify and thrill! It is not for the faint of heart. Those without courage are advised to leave."

I looked at Marcik, who was gripping the arm of his chair. The lights dimmed further and a red glow emanated from the cracks between the floorboards of the stage. Despite myself, a cool track of nerves ran along my arms and back. The sensation was pleasant, this mild fear I knew to be unattended by actual danger. The question of why people would pay for this sort of entertainment struck me briefly. It didn't come to me in those terms of course, but now I marvel at the price people are willing to pay in order to be scared, to be reminded of their imminent and perhaps horrific deaths. It is as if they are frightened of the truth, but at the same time want to experience it. Men who can face nature's laws head on and deal with their consequences are a dying breed.

The Puppet Master appeared, a stooped figure in a robe and pointed black hood like an executioner's mask. He addressed the audience in a hiss, his mantis-like head swiveling in its hood. Marcik was halfway out of his seat, looking around toward the exit.

"Sit down," I whispered. "I'm not leaving."

Marcik hunkered back in his seat.

"It is said by races older than ours," the Puppet Master was saying, "races who possess a knowledge beyond the reach of our feeble science, that the Puppet Master may control more than what lies at the end of his strings . . . that he may, in his tugging manipulations, get at something in the very soul of man—a Puppet soul within us all—and in doing so wield *absolute control.*"

I allowed myself a glance to Marcik and enjoyed his palpable terror. It served him right, acting like my better. Some man of the house he was. Couldn't even watch a puppet show without pissing his britches.

The Puppet Master ripped off the hood. It was the ticket-taker from earlier. The eye had been removed and all that was left was the socket. He stared directly at us, and there was a dizzy moment when I felt I would be sucked down into that hole. His head swiveled on to other audience members, but the image of that meaty absence was seared in my imagination.

"Does he tug at you?" the announcer asked. I had nearly forgotten he was in the room. Marcik made a sad little spasm at the sound of his voice. I put my hand on his arm to reassure him, though I ought to have let him suffer alone. He recoiled and made for the exit. He stumbled out, trying to retain some composure. I considered following him, already envisioning the real dangers outside. At the same time, I was pleased. It was as if I had known Marcik would bolt and I would have the slow joy of being alone with the Puppet show, and I even perhaps hoped he might be kidnapped or lost in the carnival forever when I didn't go out after him. I forced the image of Mother from my head and watched the Puppet Master manipulate his puppets into a wonderful play.

About half an hour later, I found Marcik sitting on a discarded plank of wood, just outside the entrance to the Puppet Palace. He was no longer crying, but his face was streaked and his eyes puffy. When he saw me, he came lunging in a fury of snivels and balled fists. We fell back against a tent post, and I felt something metal scrape down the side of my face. I curled up on the ground and eventually he tired of hitting me. He stood and wiped his nose. He looked at the gash down my face and at the blood I could feel warmly pouring forth. But I looked at him in perfect calm. His tears proved who was who between us.

"I'll hate you," he said. "I'll always hate you." He kicked me one last time and then ran off, into that city of bells and whistles, drunk bodies, and light. I stood and brushed myself off, wondering how I would to explain all of this to Mother as I ran after him.

April 15th

After my behavior today, I worry that Katya is still angry with me, but I know she will forgive me even this. I held a meeting with the others to properly introduce them to our newest member, the seventh head to make the body complete. It is fitting that his name is Slug. We are all less and more than human here: the Seven-Headed Lions, Slug slithering in his gutter, and now the most dreaded creature of all, the Puppet Master. A shadow to keep the children awake at night, a special message to my brother, the enforcer. We will not lie down, and neither will anyone else—not while the insane roam the streets, not while the lepers are herded into the backs of wagons. I knew nothing of Slug, but that did not stop me from telling his life story, which if not strictly true, ought to have been. Katyana stood in the back, her shoulders tense, her expression inscrutable beneath her mask.

"My brothers," I began, "carriers of the torch of New Jerusalem, tonight we welcome a new member. What you see before you, this sad sack of fear and downtroddeness, was not always this way. Once he stood proud, walked the streets with bright and clever eyes, son of two, brother of six, comrade of all. But his house was ravaged, his family snatched up and taken to the leproseries—the so-called treatment centers for those General Schmidt deems a threat to good citizens. Well, what is a good citizen? One who looks away or one who stares suffering straight in the eye? After today, they will not be able to look away any longer. I present to you, the Puppet Master."

Slug, who had learned his cue well, slipped on his holocaust cloak. Black from head to toe, his face buried in the hood, he presented an awesome spectacle. Even I forgot for a moment the pathetic flesh the disguise concealed. He ducked behind the curtain of a puppet box, began manipulating two dolls—a dapper devil and a beautiful, pale angel. I looked to Katya, but she shook her head.

Slug went on moving the puppets. The devil beckoned to the angel, but she had already turned her back. She sat in a corner of the puppet box, her shoulders slumped in sad reproof. The others watched with childlike glee, but they were nothing to me. Katyana stepped forward and grabbed Slug's wrist. He dropped the puppets and shrunk from an imagined blow.

"Nikolas," she said to me.

"Don't touch him," I said, though she'd already let him go. He was picking the puppets back up and brushing them off lovingly.

She shook her head at me and walked from the room. I followed her into the antechamber, where I grabbed her roughly. "You are always free to leave," I said. "You know that, don't you?"

She pushed me away and said, "I wasn't hurting him."

"I know."

"But maybe you were. It's more about you than them."

"You like me like this." I pulled her against me. I kissed her on the lips of her mask, then lifted the mask itself and ran my finger over her perfect chin. "You can't get me out of your blood."

She yielded in my arms. Her free hand reached to the table where the studded whip lay coiled in the lantern light. I bent over the table, raised the shirt on my back. "Whip me."

"You'll do what needs doing?" The whip fell home. The sharp heat spread from my ribs to spine. "You'll set him free?"

"Whip me," I said. "Make me warm." In the dark folds of a curtain in the corner of the room, I thought I saw a pair of watching eyes.

April 16th

I might have written more yesterday, but from Katya's shifting and sighing, I sensed that the candle I wrote by was keeping her awake. It was a delicate truce we'd established, and I was loath to disturb it. I set down my notepad and stood over the cot for a moment, watching her sleep. She'd removed her mask and her eye glowed in the moonlight. Her cheeks were a jungle of scars. Still, I liked her best like this—uncovered and unprotected.

I went into hall, threading around the slumbering bodies on the floor. I followed a trickle of water (a leak in the roof? the lingering hostility between Katyana and me?), and beyond that a confused muttering, maybe laughter. As I passed the pump room where I had installed Slug, I noticed light angling out. I eased back the door.

Slug was hunched over the puppet box, manipulating the strings and talking in a low voice. Yes, *talking*, though I couldn't make out the words. His back was to me, but there was a warped mirror leaning against the wall. In it I could see the angel and devil. Slug's whisper grew distinct.

"'Ladies and *gentle*men.' Not 'ladies and men.'" On the table in front of the mirror was a rusty straight razor; I often used the room to shave. Slug's glance seemed to go toward this table, though in reflection it was difficult to be sure. He picked up the puppets and rubbed them against each other, in a wild, copulating dance. "'Yes, pretty Katya. Whip me. Make me warm.'" He looked around nervously. "Nikolas will be mad. 'Dumb Slug,' he'll say. 'Can't learn his lines.' 'Ladies and men.' No, 'Ladies and *gentle*men.' Puppet men. Dumb Slug."

He picked up the razor and before I could stop him, drew it slowly, almost lovingly across his tongue. I stepped inside and grabbed him by the shirt collar.

"So you talk, do you?" He shook his head fiercely, and he shrank from expected blows. "Come outside."

He followed me up the ladder, whining like a sickened dog, and I felt a rush of sympathy for him nearly sufficient to stop me. I raised the manhole cover and when I was satisfied no one was watching, I pushed him out ahead of me. It was not dark out. In recent years, the night sky of Joshua City has gone a washed-out, chemical green—a sickly, unearthly color set to hem us in, to smother us in the quietest way. Slug crouched shivering in the glow. "Nikolas," he said.

"Go home," I said. He didn't move. "You heard me. Leave."

He stood and took two steps forward, his arms outstretched, palms first. In his hands was the razor. He offered it to me. I stared at his unlikely gift. "Nikolas," he said, "Slug love."

On the ground was a length of metal, something from the old railroad bridge, and now I picked it up and swung it at him. He hopped back. "Don't make me do it."

He turned and walked away, stopped, looked back at me. I waved the railroad tie. He moved on, bare feet dragging in the dust. I dropped the railroad tie and ran after him. But he was already scampering away through the foundation of an old building, over a mound of bricks and used vials, on all fours, into the shadows. After a while, I made my slow way home, to what I call home, not looking up from the ground. The thought of Slug's being out there in the streets of Joshua City made me angrier with myself than I had been in years. I looked up at the sky again. Stifling yes, but beautiful also—how I imagined tropical water must be. I wondered if I'd ever get out of Joshua City, or whether I even wanted to. I thought about the compass I'd wanted as a boy, as if there existed a navigational tool that could guide me now.

I heard footsteps behind me and quickened my pace to avoid an attacker, but then I recognized Slug's shuffling gait and smiled to myself, relieved at having been saved from my own failings. I slowed, allowing Slug to keep up with me. I left the manhole cover half off after I entered the Underground. Hiding in the shadows, I was pleased to watch Slug make his way down the ladder and back to his small quarters where Katya had ordered his bedroll to be made the first night of his addition to the family. I wondered how I would explain myself to her. I knew that if I said it true and good and right, she would hear the truth behind the truth we had always known.

Tantra Bensko

Notes From the
Nipple Saint

These are the pages I am leaving for you squirrels in the rock terraces. I know you squirrels can't read English. It is a hard language, anyway, the spelling being especially strange. But there's something about the little holes in between the rocks. You little guys running around looking so lovable. I want to communicate. And I know there is a kind of communication that goes beyond words. I know the imprint of the thoughts lingers on the pages. I knew for sure that it existed when my parents were going to put out mousetraps. I wrote notes for the mice, saying: "Flee! Flee for your lives! This is the time, right now, before Mama and Papa kill you." And that was the end of the mice. They can read what my thoughts are on the paper. I know it. I tried it a couple other times. One time it worked. The other time it didn't: I don't know what to think of that. But I haven't given up hope.

That's how I got started with poetry. I wanted to say something beautiful enough, profound enough, to put out for you squirrels in your holes in the ground. And I could never think of anything great to say outright. So I started putting poetry in the holes between the rocks, on little pieces of paper. They got shorter, more like haikus, more perfected, and eventually, I got to the most Zen stage of nothing, just blank pieces of paper, acknowledging that there is nothing I can say that is truly worthy of the reverence of nature, that is not mundane to some degree.

· ·

So, now I want to say something. I have learned something today. I found a magazine at Unclaimed Baggage. I know no one around here reads this sort of thing. I mean, there aren't even any book stores in Xoxell. Or at any town around here within an hour drive. But someone traveling through somewhere, on a bus or a plane or a ship, didn't pick up his bag, and this magazine was in it. I think you squirrels might understand this. Because if you can read notes... well, if mice can read notes, and I KNOW you are as smart as little mice... then you will be interested. The book was about a woman in Russia named Rosa who could read with her fingers above letters, could feel the vibrations of the colors. Red gives off a lot of heat. That makes sense. I can see how that would work. It said ten percent of people who tried could do it. It also talked about two sisters in China. The Wang sisters, who could read with their armpits. This has left me thinking. Ok, squirrels. Later.

I have tried feeling reds with my hands posed above the paper, and it is as easy as pie. The red surfaces give off a kind of heat, the orange a little less, the yellow some, but I could feel nothing from the cool colors, like green and blue. Nothing special about being able to that. You can just feel it. I have already learned how to feel shapes.

I shaved my armpit hair. I could feel the shapes with my arm pits. Indeed. I see a future in it. But I don't want to be a copycat. I feel I can learn to be as famous as the Wang Sisters or Rosa K. I can get on TV, which is what I need. I need to make some money. And I know I'm unique. I want to be famous and I think this is it. Armpits and hands have been done. I think about what would really get attention. And I have to admit the obvious. I hope this isn't offensive to you squirrels. I mean, I don't know if you have the same obsession with breasts as we do. But check it out next time you see me and you can probably tell that mine are noticeably big. Very nice. Very round. Big red nipples that stick way out. And they are set off when I am naked, by the extreme red of my hair, that extends just to the nipples. I think it's inevitable. That is what I need to learn to read with. I know I can do it; I just have to apply myself.

Squirrels: I love you. Please don't think I'm being cheap. I want greatness. I want to make money too to support my father. He took care of me and has made sure I never starved in all my 25 years, and I want the best for him, but I've been cultivating desperation, lately. There just aren't jobs out here other than stupid restaurants, the library that just has romance novels and science fiction pulp paperbacks. The denture store. The junk yard. The gas station. What can I do? I need to do something. I can't leave, 'cause Papa needs me. But I could travel briefly, make money, and come back. I could go to California and be on the TV shows where they show people with special gifts. I could make a lot of money if I could learn to read with my breasts. Or my nipples, if I wanted to specialize. I know specialists make more money. Get more respect.

Well, squirrels. I did it. It's impossible to make out words, though, at least so far. If it were just one breast, it would be OK. I could do it. But I need to have the paper go under both naked breasts or it doesn't have the effect I need. And already, just practicing that for a few days, I got caught by my cousin coming up to the door, and I had to explain it. I guess I could do it behind closed doors all the time, but I'd never hear Papa to tell if he was gallivanting down the hall without his walker.

I'm thinking maps. I can read maps, show off that particular skill. But why? It seems like there should be a reason. I can read them, but so what? Anyone can memorize a map. It has to be something else… A treasure map. A hidden treasure. But how can I do that? I think the only way is by planting a treasure somewhere. Yet… Is that cheating? Is that greatness? Would that get people's hopes up? Get them going to look for it and then maybe, unless I am really great with my mind, it might not be there. Hmm. Any ideas? Let me know in my dreams, tonight, ok, squirrels?

..

A treasure map made of blood. That would be easiest and most
artistically dramatic. I could plant some treasure. Blood would have
to be easiest to read. I would be the nipple saint. People would
make gold leaf icons of me holding maps dripping with blood to
my breasts, my bodice or my corset, red velvet, with trim, not coming
up to my breasts, my milk white skin glowing out of enamel on
wood. The icons would have rounded tops that come to that little
point, maybe have candles burning in front of them. They would
find the treasures of their ancestors. Can I do it? It has to be real. I
have to learn more than what I can read with my nipples. I have to
be a nipple saint.

I practiced for three days with lots of little things. Trying to dowse
where my contact lens fell was the best, because when I made a map
of the house in red crayon, my breasts sort of went down like a
dowsing rod over the toilet in the map. And when I pulled on the
toilet paper, there the contact was, which had ended up on the bottom
of the toilet paper roll. Halleluiah! Praise nipples!

    I tried it yesterday with a map made of blood, in the outside
world, and it worked. I could tell. My mind went into a kind of
spasm of heroic euphoria. I could tell Mathew where he could pan
for gold and find it. I knew it was right. We practiced by looking for
where his kittens had gone to sleep, and they were under the couch,
which I found on the map, and they were under the couch. He told
his church about it. Old Mathew Watts. He old his wife, who didn't
believe it, but that's because I was naked before him. I was a vision
of beauty and magnificence compared to his wife, a normal woman
with small breasts. Of course she didn't like it. I think it says
somewhere in the Bible not to be vain like her.

I am now getting a name for myself among the holiness. They start
speaking in tongues and shaking up and down, stamping their feet,
and making their heads go sideways all jerky. I don't know if they
get into the icons with gold, and curves and spikes, but that's what I

want. With crackle paint to make it look olden. Lots of red. I need to be wearing red velvet, with the dress pulled down below my breasts. Very white breasts, with red nipples. Maybe I should rouge them, or just let the blood from the maps rub off on them a little, run down, smudge, make them really stand out and look like maybe they are crying tears of blood. I can see it. Can you? Does it mean anything to you to see such beauty?

Can you imagine the fiery emotions it could engender? Do squirrels lick each other's nipples for fun?

I am now being canonized, or the equivalent in the holiness church on the corner. They have brought three maps to me and I have been able to tell them where to look. Only one has found the treasure. But that was a miracle and what more do you expect? The guy knew his father had buried money in the yard before he died, but after all these years, he hadn't been able to find it. To do that, I tuned into a kind of halo of my mind, a part of myself that Knows. I don't know if you guys do that. I feel like everyone can do it. And that will be my message once I get famous and make enough money to support Papa and me. To buy cornbread and pasta with some pesto sauce like we had one time in a restaurant. I won't sell this place. I'll be your friend always. I'll but you some…nuts? Is that what you would like? Chestnuts. Pine nuts. Brazil nuts. We always called them nigger toes, but that isn't done these days. Well, around here it is, but that doesn't count.

I know the other two men may have to wait awhile before they can go out west to pan for gold. But only one finding the treasure is enough proof for now. I feel a kind of light-headedness in knowing it worked. In knowing I tuned in to some part of myself that is divine. Some part that knows everything if I only let it. But no one would have ever cared if it weren't for reading the map with my nipples. If it weren't for the treasure. I want to do something more pure. I want to read in the dark, looking for something that doesn't make someone rich. For something that means more. That makes my halo glow in the dark. For the wives as well as the men. One day. Once I can buy Papa all he needs. Papa has been so good to me. And I'm all he has.

Squirrels, what do you think? Should I plant treasure? Should I wear a corset? Should I paint some icons and pretend they are by someone else? Or should I meditate? Should I drink only water, and no food? Give up sleep and wear something that hurts? Like barbed wire around my breasts. Should I paint my nipples red? Should I make it look like they are bleeding, a kind of stigmata? Or should I be true? Should I go into a state of apotheosis? Should I pray? Should I glow? Can I do it? I know that's what you want. The real thing. Otherwise, I won't be worthy of you. I will do it. I know I can. I can. I will.

This has been the hardest week ever. I am scratched all over. I have the poison oak rash. I have gotten burned. I have only dreamed while I'm awake. And still, I don't know where the treasure would be. The gold could be found. I think I need to look for something else. Maybe find out if the men's wives are cheating on them, and how. If they are, and they are looking at my breasts that dowse from their wives' hankies or something, and I say yes, they will get excited. They will want to pay me. They will want to get revenge on their wives and be extra nice to me. I just don't know. I just don't know. I want to sleep. I am hungry. I want some fried okra. Some creamed corn. Some tomatoes from the garden.

I could read faces with my breasts. I could predict. They are already forgetting about me at the church, and I need my fame to spread far and wide. If I could read the Bible with my nipples, that might be the best. Those Bibles that are written in red. That might cut it down to only the Christians. Hell, maybe even no Christians could handle that. I definitely don't want Satanic patrons. But in the meantime, I practice every day. I rub my breasts with barley meal, keep them sensitive, exfoliated. I drip water over them. I massage them with milk. Once, I tried rose petals, which was lovely. But it's getting a little late in the season. I luckily have breasts so big I can bring them up to my nose to smell, smell that rose water. I wish I could read food with them, it's been so long since I ate, with this damn fast. But what could I tell from that? I could read books, but only if they were printed in red. But shapes are so much easier. It has to be something useful. I could read cards. Tarot cards. Tell people's future. Am I any good at it? Only God can tell. I'll practice with you. I'll see if I can tell if you will eat the food I put out for you tomorrow. A right answer, and I'll keep trying. A wrong answer, and why bother? I must follow my God given talents.

Whiskey labels! That's easy! Not many words. I can do that. And the visual effect would be stunning. I think it's the whiskey I drank today that made me think about that, especially after not eating for so long on my purification fast. But why not? Catholics. don't care. I love you little squirrels. I love you to death. I just wish you'd eaten the nuts.

Today, I read some words from the Bible to the deacon of the church. And he told his friend at the church that splintered off. And he had me do it too. I told him it had to be red cause that's the color of Jesus's blood. He liked that. He took lots of pictures. I think I am going to be a hit. He said he'd discuss it with the pastor.

Well, that didn't happen, but his friends came over for a demonstration. I had them pay me first. They took pictures too, and then a video. I think I found my niche. There was one of those tassels in the Bible and they made use of that. I kind of liked it. It was a little bit risqué. A little bit of a thrill. Not only for them this time. But for me.

I advertised in the paper for doing this and I got a big following already. Someone named Herbet is painting my picture! I can't believe it! Reading the Bible with my breasts, in gold crackle, and paying me. Someone else said he had a special offer. I don't know what it is yet. He said he'd invite me to dinner and talk about it.

· ·

He wants me to read the Bible with my nipples while peeing. And I suggested the whiskey before, so he decided to combine it. I think if it works out, it will be one of the best paying jobs anyone around here has had. He has to take pictures first to paint from. He got me to sign a form. I don't know what he's going to do with it. I hope it fits the saint I feel myself becoming. They don't understand how much work this is. I can feel my eyes roll back in my head when I do it. If only they could see it, but the blindfold I wear keeps it private. My own private saintly action.

The photo session went off well. I feel I am accomplishing something. He said he thought someone would probably want me to appear on TV sometime. Late night, though. I want it to be good. I want to be able to read longer verses. I need to practice. I need to blush. I need to feel the fire and the blood in my skin so I can match the heat of the words in red. The words some feel are the words of God. I don't know about that. But I feel I have found what I have been made for. And I am so glad you can share it with me all along. I love you squirrels. I love God. I love my breasts. And I love way I can feel the halo of love around my head and around each nipple exultant.

Pinckney Benedict

The Beginnings of Sorrow

Whoo-oo-oo-oo-hooh-hoo-oo! Oh, look at me, I am perishing in this gateway.
. . . I howl and howl, but what's the good of howling?
—Mikhail Bulgakov "Heart of a Dog"

Vandal Boucher told his dog Hark to go snatch the duck out of the rushes where it had fallen, and Hark told him *No*. In days to come, Vandal probably wished he'd just pointed his Ithaca 12-gauge side-by-side at Hark's fine-boned skull right that moment and pulled the trigger on the second barrel (he had emptied the first to bring down the duck) and blown the dog's brains out, there at the edge of the freezing, sludgy pond. But that unanticipated answer—any answer would have been a surprise, of course, but this was *no*, unmistakably *no*, in a pleasant tenor, without any obvious edge of anger or resentment—that single syllable took him aback and prevented him from taking action.

Vandal's old man, now: back in the day, Vandal's old man Xerxes Boucher would have slain the dog that showed him any sign of strangeness or resistance to his will, let alone one that told him *no*. Dog's sucking the golden yolks out of the eggs? Blam. Dog's taking chickens out of the coop? Blam. Dog's not sticking tight enough to the sheep, so the coyotes are chivvying them across the high pastures? *This dog's your favorite, your special pet? You wish I would refrain from shooting the dog? Well, sonny, you wish in one hand and shit in the other, see which gets full first.* Blam. Nothing could stop him, no pleading or promises, and threats were out of the question. But that was Xerxes in his prime, and Vandal wasn't a patch on him, everybody said so, Vandal himself had ruefully to agree with the general assessment of his character. So when Hark said *no*, Vandal just blinked. "Come again?" he said.

No.

Well, Vandal thought. He looked out into the reeds, where the body of the mallard he had just shot bobbed in the dark water. That water looked cold. Hark sat on the shore, blinking up at Vandal with mild eyes. It would have struck Xerxes Boucher as outrageous that the dog should balk at wading out there into that cold, muddy mess, the soupy muck at the pond's margin at least shoulder-deep for the dog where the dead mallard floated, maybe deep enough that a dog—even a sizeable dog like Hark—would have to swim.

But damn it if, on that grey November morning, with a hot thermos of his wife's bitter black coffee nearby just waiting on him to drink it, and a solid breakfast when he got home after the hunt, and dry socks—Damned if Vandal couldn't see the dog's point.

"Okay," he said. "This once."

He was wearing his thick rubber waders, the ones that went all the way up to the middle of his chest, so he took off his coat—the frigid air bit into him, made his breath go short—laid the coat down on the bank, set the shotgun on top of the coat, and set off after the mallard himself. The waders clutched his calves as the greasy pond water surged around his legs, and his feet sank unpleasantly into the soft bottom. He considered what might be sleeping down there: frogs settled in for the winter, dreaming their slick wet dreams; flabby catfish whiskered like old men; great knobby snapping turtles, their thick round shells overlapping one another like the shields of some ancient army.

They were down there in the dark, the turtles that had survived unchanged from the age of the dinosaurs, with their spines buckled so that they fit, neatly folded, within their shells; and their eyes closed fast, their turtle hearts beating slow, slow, slow, waiting on the passing of another winter. And what if the winter never passed and spring never came, as looked more and more likely? How long would they sleep, how long could such creatures wait in the dark? A long time, Vandal suspected. Time beyond counting. It might suit them well, the endless empty twilight that the world seemed dead-set on becoming.

Vandal didn't care to put his feet on such creatures, and when his toes touched something hard, he tried to tread elsewhere. The pond bottom was full of hard things, and most of them were probably rocks, but better safe than sorry. He had seen the jaws on snapping turtles up close, the beak on the skeletal face like a hawk's or an eagle's, hooked and hard-edged and sharp as a razor. Easy to lose a toe to such a creature.

When he reached the mallard—it was truly a perfect bird, its head and neck a deep oily green, unmarked by the flying shot—he plucked its limp body up out of the water and waved it over his head for the dog to see. "Got it!" he called.

Hark wasn't paying any attention to him at all. He was sitting next to the tall silver thermos and gazing quizzically at the coat and, cradled on the coat, Vandal's shotgun.

"I told him to go get the duck," Vandal said to his wife, who was called Bridie. Then, to Hark, he said, "Tell her what you told me."

No, said Hark.

Bridie looked from her husband to the dog. "Does he mean to tell you no," she asked, working to keep her voice even and calm, her tone reasonable. "Or does he mean he won't tell me?"

No, the dog said again. It wasn't like a bark, which Bridie would have much preferred, one of those clever dogs that has been taught by its owner to "talk" by mimicking human speech without understanding what it was saying. "What's on top of a house?" *Roof!* "How does sandpaper feel?" *Rough!* "Who's the greatest ballplayer of all time?" *Ruth!*

DiMaggio, she thought to herself. *That's the punchline. The dog says* Ruth! *but really it's DiMaggio.*

Vandal laughed. He was a big, broad-shouldered, good-natured man with an infectious laugh, which was one of the reasons Bridie loved him, and she smiled despite her misgivings. The dog seemed delighted with the turn of events too.

"That's the sixty-four dollar question, ain't it?" Vandal said. He clapped Hark on the head in the old familiar way, and the dog shifted out from under the cupped hand, eyes suddenly slitted and opaque.

No, it said.

Much as she loved Vandal, and much as she had hated his bear of a father, with his great sweaty hands always ready to squeeze her behind or pinch her under her skirt as she was climbing the stairs, always ready to brush against her breasts—glad as she was that the mean old man was in the cold cold ground, she couldn't help but think at that moment that a little of Xerxes' unflinching resolve wouldn't have gone amiss in Vandal's character, in this circumstance. She wished that the dog had said pretty much anything else: *Yes*, or better yet, *yes sir.* Even a word of complaint, *cold, wet, dark. Afraid.* But this flat refusal unnerved her.

"He takes a lot on himself, doesn't he? For a dog," she said.

"Talking dog," said Vandal, his pride written on his knobby face, as though he had taught the dog to speak all by himself, as though it had been his idea.

Hark had begun wandering through the house, inspecting the dark heavy furniture like he had never seen it or the place before. Not exploring timidly, like a guest unsure of his welcome, but more like a new owner. Bridie thought she saw him twitch a lip disdainfully as he sniffed at the fraying upholstery of the davenport. He looked to her for a moment as though maybe he were going to lift his leg. "No!" she snapped. "Bad boy!"

He glanced from her to Vandal and back again, trotted over to Vandal's easy chair with his tail curled high over his back. He gave off the distinct air of having won some sort of victory. "Come here," Bridie called to him. She snapped her fingers, and he swung his narrow, intelligent head, looking past his shoulder at her.

No, he said, and he hopped up into Vandal's chair. Bridie was relieved to see how small he was in the chair, into which Vandal had to work to wedge his bulky frame.

There was room for two of Hark in the seat, three even, so lean was he, slender long-legged retriever mix. Vandal nodded at him with approval. The dog turned around and around and around as though he were treading down brush to make himself a nest, in the ancient way of dogs. In the end, though, he settled himself upright rather than lying down, his spine against the back of the chair, his head high.

"Xerxes wouldn't never allow a dog up in his chair like that," Bridie said. And was immediately sorry she had said it. Vandal had adored and dreaded his brutal, unstoppable old man, and any comparison between them left him feeling failed and wanting. *Xerxes, Xerxes. Will he never leave our house?*

"Xerxes never had him a talking dog," Vandal said. He handed the dead mallard to her. Its glossy head and neck stretched down toward the floor in a comical way, its pearlescent eyes long gone into death. It was a large, muscular bird.

"Not much of a talking dog," Bridie said. She turned, taking the mallard away into the kitchen when she saw the flash of irritation in Vandal's eyes. She didn't look toward Hark, because she didn't want to see the expression of satisfaction that she felt sure animated his doggy features. She wanted to let Vandal have this moment, this chance to own something that his father couldn't have imagined, let alone possessed, but it was—it was wrong. Twisted, bent. It was a thing that couldn't be but was, it was unspeakable, and it was there in her living room, sitting in her husband's chair. "Not much of one, if all it can manage to say is *no*."

Hark reclined in the easy chair in the parlor. The television was tuned to the evening news, and the dog watched and listened with bright gleaming eyes, giving every appearance of understanding what was said: Wars and rumors of wars. Earthquakes and famines and troubles. None of it was good at all, it hadn't been good in some little time, but none of it seemed to bother him in the least. He chewed briefly at his own hip, after some itch that was deeply hidden there, and then went back to his television viewing.

Vandal sat on the near end of the davenport, not appearing to hear the news. From time to time he reached out a hand to pet Hark, but Hark shifted his weight and leaned away, just out of reach. It was what Bridie had always striven to do when Xerxes went to put his hands on her but that she had somehow never managed, to create that small distance between them that would prove unbridgeable. Always the hand reached her, to pet and stroke and pinch, always when Vandal's attention was turned elsewhere.

And them living in Xerxes' house, and her helpless to turn him away.

About the third time Vandal put his hand out, Hark tore his gaze from the TV screen, snarled, snapped, his jaws closing with a wicked click just shy of Vandal's reaching fingertips. Vandal withdrew his hand, looking sheepish.

"No?" he asked the dog.

No, Hark said, and he settled back into the soft cushions of the chair, his eyes fixed once more on the flickering screen.

Over Bridie's objections, Hark ate dinner at the table with them that night. Vandal insisted. The dog tried to climb into the chair with arms, Vandal's seat at the head of the table. Vandal wasn't going to protest, but Bridie wouldn't allow it. She flapped the kitchen towel—it was covered in delicate blue cornflowers—at him, waved her hands and shouted, "Shoo! Shoo!" until he slipped down out of the chair and, throwing resentful glances her way, slunk over to one of the chairs at the side of the table and took his place.

He ate like an animal, she noted with satisfaction, chasing the duck leg she had given him around and around the rim of the broad plate with his sharp snout, working to grasp the bone with his teeth, his tongue hanging drolly from the side of his mouth. Always, the leg escaped him. Each time it did, she put it carefully back in the middle of the plate, and he went after it again. From time to time he would stop his pursuit of the drumstick and watch Bridie and Vandal manipulate their utensils, raise their forks to their mouths, dab at their lips with napkins. His own napkin was tucked bib-like under the broad leather strap of his collar, and it billowed ridiculously out over his narrow, hairy chest. Vandal watched this process through a number of repetitions, his brow furrowed, before he put down his knife and fork.

"You can't let a dog have duck bones like that," he said. "He'll crack the bone and swallow it and the sharp edges will lodge in his throat."

Good, Bridie thought. *Let him.* The dog stared across the table at her, his face twisted into what she took to be an accusatory grimace. Hark had always been Vandal's dog, never hers, and she had never felt much affection for him, but he had always seemed to her to be a perfectly normal dog, not overfriendly but that was normal in an animal that was brought up to work rather than as a pet. Restrained in his affections, but never hostile. Lean and quick and hard-muscled, with the bland face and expressions of his kind. And now he looked at her as though he knew what she was thinking—an image of Hark coughing, wheezing, hacking up blood on the kitchen floor swam back into her consciousness—and hated her for it.

Was there an element of surprise there too? she wondered. He hadn't known about the bones. An unanticipated danger, and now he knew, and she could sense him filing the information away, so that such a thing would never be a threat to him again. What else was he ignorant about?

Bridie had never disliked Hark before, had never disliked any of Vandal's boisterous, happy-go-lucky hunting dogs, the bird dogs, the bear dogs, the coon dogs, all of them camped out in the tilting kennel attached to the pole barn. They shared the long, fenced run that stretched across the barnyard, and they would woof and whirl and slobber when she went out to feed them. Dogs with names like Sam and Kettle and Bengal and Ranger. And Hark. Hark the waterdog, a little quieter than the others, more subdued, maybe, but nothing obvious about him to separate him from the rest of them. They were Vandal's friends and companions, they admired him even when Xerxes fed him scorn, and they were kind to him when even she herself wasn't. She didn't fool with them much.

Something had come alive in Hark, something that allowed him, compelled him, to say *no*, and now he was at her table when the rest were outside in the cold and the dark, now he was looking her in the eye. That was another new thing, this direct confrontation; he had always cast his gaze down, properly canine, when his eyes had locked with hers in the past. He'd regained his earlier cocksureness, and the impression of self-satisfaction that she had from him made him unbearable to her.

Vandal was leaning over, working his knife, paring the crispy skin and the leg meat away from the bone. "Here you go," he told the dog, his tone fond. Hark sniffed.

"If he plans to eat his food at the table like people," Bridie said, "then he better learn to pick it up like people."

Vandal stopped cutting. Bridie half-expected Hark to say *No* in the light voice that sounded so strange coming out of that long maw, with its mottled tongue and (as they seemed to her) cruel-looking teeth. Instead, he nudged Vandal out of his way and planted one forepaw squarely on the duck leg. *He understands*, Bridie thought to herself.

The plate tipped and skittered away from him, the duck leg tumbling off it, the china ringing against the hard oak of the tabletop. The dog looked perplexed, but Vandal slid the plate back into place, picked up the drumstick and laid it gently down.

Just as gently, Hark put his paw on the leg bone, pinning it. He lowered his head, closed his teeth securely on the leg—the chafing squeak of tooth against bone made Bridie squint her eyes in disgust—and pulled away a triumphant mouthful of duck. He tossed it back, swallowed without chewing, and went after the leg again.

"Good dog," Vandal said. The dog's ears flickered at the familiar phrase, but he didn't raise his head from the plate. Bridie bit into her own portion. Duck was normally one of her favorites, but this meal filled her mouth like ashes. Vandal stopped chewing, leaned down close to his plate, his lips pursed as though he were about to kiss his food, his eyes screwed nearly shut. He made a little spitting noise, and a pellet of lead shot, no bigger than a flea, pinged onto his plate, bounced, and lay still.

After supper, as Bridie retted up the kitchen, Vandal sat cross-legged on the floor in the parlor, the shotgun broken down and spread out on several thicknesses of newspaper on the floor before him. A small, smoky fire—the wood was too green to burn well, hadn't aged sufficiently—flared and popped in the hearth.

Hark sat in the comfortable chair, and his posture had become— she felt sure of this—more human than it had been previously. He was sitting like a man now, a misshapen man, yes, with a curved spine and his head low between his shoulders, but he was working to sit upright. He looked ridiculous, as she glanced in at him from where she was working, but she felt no impulse to laugh. Was he larger than he had been? Did he fill the chair more fully? While she watched, he lost his precarious balance, slipped to the side, thrashed for a moment before righting himself again.

The television was on, the usual chatter from the local news, a terrible wreck out on the state highway, a plant shutting down in the county seat, a marvel on a nearby farm, a Holstein calf born with two heads, both of them alive and bawling, both of them sucking milk. *Who could even take note of something like that in these times*, Bridie wondered to herself as she worked to scrub the grease from the plates. The next day it would be something else, and something else after that, until the wonders and the sports and the abominations (*how to tell the difference among them?*) piled up so high that there wouldn't be any room left for them, for her and for Vandal, the regular ones, the ones that remained.

A talking dog? Was that stranger than a two-headed calf? Stranger than poor old Woodrow Scurry's horses eating each other in his stables a fortnight earlier? Every day the world around her seemed more peculiar than it had the day before, and every day she felt herself getting a little more used to the new strangenesses, numb to them, and wondering idly what ones the next day would bring.

How you use? They were Hark's words, clumsy and laughable, coming to her over the din of the voices on the television. There was another sort of show on, this one a game of some type, where people shouted at one another, encouragement and curses. *That thing,* Hark said.

"So," Vandal said, "you can say more than *No.*"

How you use that thing, Hark said again. A demand this time, not a question.

The shotgun, Bridie thought, and she dropped the plate she was washing back into the sink full of lukewarm water and dying suds and hurried into the den, drying her hands on a dishtowel as she went.

"Don't tell him that," she said.

Vandal looked up at her, startled. Just above him on the wall hung a picture that his mother had hung there as a young woman.

She had died young. In the decades since it had been hung, the picture, it occurred to Bridie, had taken in every event that had occurred in that low-ceilinged, claustrophobic room. It depicted Jesus, a thick-muscled Jesus, naked but for a drape of white cloth, getting his baptism in the river Jordan. The Baptist raised a crooked hand over his head, water spilling from the upraised palm.

Vandal was fitting the barrels of the shotgun—which had been his old man's but which was now his, like the house, like the farm— back into the stock. The metal mated to the wood with a definitive click. "Why in the world wouldn't I tell him?"

Bridie was at a loss for a cogent answer. It seemed obvious to her that Vandal ought not to impart such information to the dog just for the asking, but he didn't share her worry at all, it was clear. How to explain? The dog looked at her with, she thought, an expression of feigned innocence. "A dog ought not to know how to use a gun," she said.

Vandal chuckled. "He doesn't even have hands. He has no fingers."

"So why tell him how a gun works?"

"Because he wants to know."

"And should he know everything he wants to, just because he wants to know it?"

Vandal shrugged. Bridie felt heat flooding her face. How could he not understand? He thought it was terrific, the way the dog had decided to talk, the way he could sit there with it and watch television, the way it asked him questions, the way it wanted to know the things that he knew. He was happy to share with it: his table, his food, his house, his knowledge. He was treating the dog like a friend, like a member of the family. Like a child, his child.

"What he wants is to have hands. What he wants is to be a man. To do what you do. To have what you have."

She caught Hark gazing at her intently, his eyes gleaming, hungry, his nose wet, his broad flat tongue caught between the rows of his teeth.

"What's wrong with that?" Vandal wanted to know.

He is not your boy, she wanted to tell him. He is not your son. He is a dog, and it's wrong that he can talk. You want to share what you have with him, but he doesn't want to share it with you. He wants to have it instead of you.

The dog wrinkled his nose, sniffing, and she knew suddenly that he was taking her in, the scent of her. A dog's nose was, she knew, a million times more sensitive than a man's. He could know her by her scent. He could tell that she was afraid of him. He could follow her anywhere because of that phenomenal sense of smell. In prehistoric times, before men became human and made servants out of them, Hark and his kind would have hunted her down in a pack and eaten her alive. Her scent would have led them to her. Hark's eyes narrowed, and her words clung to her jaws. She couldn't bear to speak them in front of the dog. She blinked, dropped her gaze and, under the animal's intense scrutiny, fled the room.

Behind her, Vandal spoke. "This here's the breech," he said. The gun snicked open. "This here is where the shells go." The gun thumped closed.

Vandal always wanted her after a meal of game meat: duck, venison, bear, it didn't matter what. It was something about the wild flavor, she thought, and the fact that he had killed the food himself. It made him happy, and when he was happy he always came to her in bed, his hands quick and his breath hot. He was at her now, pushing up her nightgown, slipping the straps off her shoulders, throwing one of his heavy, hairy legs across hers. She shoved at him.

"Don't," she said. "He'll hear."

After supper, after television and the lesson about the gun—he could name all the parts of it now, Hark could, and his speech was becoming rapidly clearer, the words coming to him swiftly and easily; and maybe that was true of his thoughts as well, slipping like eels through that clever brain in its dark prison in the dog's skull—Hark had refused to go outside to sleep in the kennel. He had simply braced his legs at the house's threshold and bared his teeth and muttered at them, *No*.

"For God's sake," Bridie had said to Vandal.

"What's the harm?" Vandal had asked. Plenty of people, he had told her in a patient voice, owned dogs that lived indoors.

"Not you," she said to him. "Never you."

No, he agreed, he'd never owned an indoor dog before. Xerxes wouldn't allow such a thing.

Xerxes. He couldn't understand what was happening to him, to them, because of Xerxes and the shadow he cast, even from the grave. Vandal had always wanted an indoor dog, a pet, and Xerxes wouldn't hear of it.

So Hark became an indoor dog, sleeping in the parlor. Bridie had tried to lay down a couple of old rag rugs on the floor for him, but he had just stared blankly at her from the chair, and she had left him there rather than risking having to hear that flat refusal another time.

"He won't hear anything," Vandal said. Bridie knew how sharp a dog's hearing was. Vandal knew it even better than she did, but he was saying what he imagined she needed to hear, because he wanted to get hold of her. A dog's hearing was like its sense of smell, a million times or more what humans are capable of. "He's downstairs. He's probably asleep," Vandal said. He nuzzled her, took the lobe of her ear between his teeth and nipped. He slid her nightgown down to her waist, his hands on her breasts, his palms and the pads of his fingers tough with callus. Her breathing quickened as he pushed her hard against the mattress and pressed her legs apart. "Who cares if he hears us?"

"I care," she said. She knew that Hark would not be asleep, not on his first night in their house. In his first moments alone and unguarded in a human place. He might not even be in the parlor anymore. She pictured him creeping down the hallways, clambering up the stairs, sloping through their rooms, looking at everything, that keen nose taking in the odors of the house and its denizens, possessing them, filing them away. He might be climbing up on Xerxes' bed—the guest bed, she corrected herself, Xerxes was gone—right now.

"We'll be quiet then," Vandal assured her, and she meant to protest, but he put his hands under her hips and lifted her, and she groaned and opened to him. He gave a sharp cry of delight. She shushed him, but he continued to exclaim as he moved against her, his voice growing louder with every fierce thrust of his hips, until he was calling out wordlessly at the top of his voice. By then she was far gone too, her voice mingling with his, and under it all the sharp metallic crying of the bedsprings.

In the night, while Vandal slept, Bridie considered Xerxes. X, as he had told her to call him, all his friends called him X. He had many friends on the neighboring places and in town, the men he hunted with, roistered with, brawny old men like himself who had fought in one war or a couple, men who took no shit from anyone. Terrible X, Mountain-Man X, X the Unknown and Unknowable, his eyes on her always, his hands on her too whenever Vandal was out of the house, when he was out hunting or tending to his dogs in the kennel. Sometimes when Vandal was in the house, too, sometimes when he was in the same room. X wasn't afraid, he wasn't afraid a bit.

Be quiet, he would say to her.

She never told Vandal because she was afraid of what he would do. What was she afraid of, exactly? That he would confront Xerxes, Daddy Xerxes, Daddy X as Vandal called him. Was she afraid that Vandal would challenge Xerxes, fight him, shoot him, kill him? Or was she afraid that he wouldn't? She could imagine no happy outcome to her revelation, and so she chose not to make it.

"No," she would tell Xerxes as he pawed her, plundered her. He didn't even hear her, she didn't believe. She might as well have been speaking another language, or not speaking at all. "No."

When a brain stroke had taken him one wonderful day—he had cornered her in the parlor, was squeezing her breasts, crushing her to him, one great hand pressed hard in the middle of her back so that she couldn't escape him—she had simply stood away from his stumbling, twitching, stiffening body, had watched him topple over like a hewn tree, had watched him spasm and shudder on the floor, his mouth gaping, hands clawing at his own face, one of his eyes bulging grotesquely, rolling upward independent of its twin to take her in where she stood.

She stared back into the rogue eye, in which the pupil was contracting, swift as a star collapsing, until she realized that X's gaze was no longer fixed on her, but on something behind her, above her. She was seized with an awful terror, and the effort of turning left her shaken, exhausted. Nothing. Nothing but the picture on the wall, which was as it had always been since the hand of Xerxes' wife had placed it there: Jesus and, standing over him, John, the Baptist, clothed all in ragged unfinished animal hides. She turned back to the dying man before her.

The eye reeled farther, impossibly far—it was funny to see, really, or would have been in any other circumstance—to fix on the ceiling, until finally the iris and the pupil disappeared altogether and the eye turned over white.

She leaned down to him, breathing hard from the fright he had given her over the picture, and put her mouth right up against his thick cauliflower ear, its whorls filled with stiff grey hair like the bristles of a boar-hog. This time, she wanted to make sure that he heard. "No," she told him.

Some folks, the voice said, *have too much life in them to die all the way.*

Bridie snapped awake, sure that the words had come to her in X's voice. That gruff commanding voice, weirdly distorted with wolf-tones and as full of echoes as though it were being broadcast from the moon. *How else should the voice of a dead man sound?* she asked herself. *He's come a long way back to say what he has to say to me.*

The gruff voice, and an answering sound, staccato: Hark's mirthless laughter. The sound of it chilled her. She had never cared much for loud laughter. The bared teeth, the closed eyes, the contorted features of the face, the shuddering, it all looked too much like pain to her, like convulsions or madness. She herself always laughed behind her hand, her eyes down. The voice went droning on below. It sounded like it was giving advice, and Hark's laughter had stopped. She could picture him soaking in whatever notions Xerxes was giving him.

"He's watching TV." Vandal's voice at her shoulder startled her. His eyes glinted in the weak light that filtered in through the window, the moon's final quarter. His good straight teeth glittered. He slid his hands to her breasts, kneaded her flesh. He wanted to go again. "He ain't paying any attention to us, is he?"

"How did he turn it on, Vandal?" she asked him. Another voice was speaking now, this one lighter, quicker, with a peculiar accent. She couldn't make out the words. Was it Hark's voice? Was he having conversation? Vandal urged her over prone, prodded her up onto her elbows and knees. His hands were shaking. He was as eager as a teenager, and rough, too rough. She liked him when he was sweet, and mostly he was, he was sweet, but there was no sweetness in him now. Nothing was strange, nothing was outside the realm of possibility. The television was talking to the dog, and the dog was talking to the television. She pressed her face into the smothering whiteness of the pillow, which smelled to her of her own soap and night sweat. Nothing was too strange to happen anymore.

The next day, as he went out the door, Vandal told Bridie that he'd gone colorblind. Hark was sitting in his place at the table, waiting on his breakfast to be brought to him. He looked from one of them to the other with eager eyes.

"You mean you can't tell red from green?" She'd had an uncle with the same problem. Except for dealing with stoplights and some problems matching clothes, it hadn't seemed to bother him much. As far she knew, though, it was a problem he'd had his whole life, not something he'd acquired.

Vandal waved a hand in front of his face, as though he were demonstrating actual blindness. "The whole ball of wax," he told her. "It's all shades of grey out there."

"You've got to see a doctor," she said to him. "This ain't natural."

"Natural," he said. "Ha. I wouldn't know natural these days if it came up and bit me in the ass."

"Seeing colors. That's natural."

"It's winter coming down," he said. "Just winter, and the color goes out of everything. It just looks like it's all an old movie."

She shook her head, and he drew her to him with a hand on her waist, another in the middle of her back. He pressed against her, and she felt the warmth that spread out from him, felt his hardness. His need for her was palpable, and it made her sad and excited all at once. She peeled his hands from her body because the dog was watching, too avidly. There was something in Vandal's touch that wasn't just for her, and wasn't just for for him either, it wasn't just selfishness. There was something in it that was for the dog too, and she couldn't stand that.

Vandal withdrew. "Who has the money for a doctor?" he said. "Who has the leisure?" His brow was furrowed. Already his thoughts had turned from her to his work. Seldomridge, their neighbor to the east, had called to say that a half dozen of his cattle were dead in the night, no telling what had killed them but the condition of their bodies was very strange, and could Vandal bring over the skid-steer and help him plant them? It was a full morning's labor lost from their own place, but there was no way a man could refuse to help in such a situation. No time to worry about little things like the color of the world going away.

His expression cleared briefly. "It's the winter time. That's what's got everything all turned around. Come spring and the color will come back. You watch."

After Vandal left the house, Bridie shooed Hark down off the chair and away from the kitchen table, hustled him out the door with gestures and cries. She made as if she might kick him, and he went, but she could tell by the set of his shoulders that he knew no blows were coming, and he went at his own pace. She kept waiting for him to tell her *no* as she drove him across the yard toward the dog run.

She had decided upon rising that morning what she would do if he refused her, if he refused to do anything she told him. She was expecting it, she was waiting for it, she was even hoping for it: reason to take down the choke collar that Vandal kept for training and slip it over Hark's head and cinch it tight as a noose around his neck. Watch the chain links cut into his thick pelt and the delicate flesh of his throat. Force him to do what she wanted. Hiss her orders into his sensitive ears. Show him what a dog was, and what a human was, and what the proper relationship between them should be.

And if Hark grew angry, lashed out, bit her? Then she should show Vandal the marks on her skin, and he would understand at last how utterly wrong the situation was, how obscene, and he would do what was necessary. She allowed the ball of her foot to come in contact with Hark's rump—was she tempting him?—but he just hurried on ahead, as though he were suddenly eager to enter the dog run. His tail was up and switching when the steel latch of the kennel door clanged down behind him.

That's that, she thought as she went back into the house. The day stretched out in front of her. Plenty to do, as always, and no Vandal, no Hark, no Xerxes to keep her from it. *That's it for him, returned to the place of his beginnings.*

All day, the voice issued from the kennel. Answered at first by the growling and defiant barking from the other dogs, and then their cowed whimpering, and then silence. They were good dogs, obedient dogs, conditioned to a man's voice. It pained Bridie to think of him out there among them; but what else to do? She had hopes that their good, simple natures would remind Hark of what he had used to be, what he ought still to be.

Better out there than in here anyway, she thought. *A kennel's the place for dogs, and what happens out there is no worry of mine.*

It was dusk, getting on toward night, when Vandal arrived home again, the skid-steer up on the flatbed, his shoulders slumped with weariness. "It's bad over at Seldomridge's," he told her. "Worse than he said." He washed his hands vigorously under the hot water tap, skinning them hard with the scrub brush and the Lava soap, lathering himself all the way up to the elbows. His face was pinched and drawn-looking.

"It's bad over here too," she said. He didn't seem to hear her.

"I'll be back over there tomorrow," he said. "After that, it's no more cattle at Seldomridge's." He looked around the kitchen, ducked into the parlor to check in there. "Where's he at?" he wanted to know.

She gestured out the window toward the silent kennel, and his face hardened. "I had work to do too, you know," she said.

"I didn't say nothing." He was already in motion toward the door.

"I didn't have the time to babysit your new pet," she called after him. His pet. His changeling child. She watched his large, awkward figure cross the yard and enter the chain-link run, kneel down just inside the gate. Her heart quailed. All afternoon the silence had worn at her. It worried her as much as the voice had done. More. A kennel was never a silent place, always some kind of choir going out there, a tussle, an alarm over a rabbit or over nothing. The jolly voices of dogs. Vandal was bent over something, shaking his head, mumbling, his shoulders bowed.

She strained in the failing light to make out what he was doing. She had a moment in which she imagined that the normal dogs had torn the strange one to pieces, and her heart leaped. *It will be my fault, just like the death of Xerxes*, she thought, *and he will never forgive me, and I will bear the blame gladly.*

And then he was coming back to the house, Hark slinking along at his side. When they entered the kitchen together, Vandal's face was wreathed in a great smile. The smell of dog, hairy and primeval and eye-wateringly strong, struck Bridie like a blow. Hark trotted into the parlor and climbed wearily onto the davenport, where he lay draped like a rug, his sides heaving.

"Tell her what you told me," Vandal called in to him. No answer. "Tell her what you been doing all day, while we was working."

Humping, came the voice from the living room, muffled against the davenport's cushions.

"Did you hear that?" Vandal asked her.

"I heard," Bridie said.

"Made them line up for him, and then he humped every one of those bitches out there, one right after the other. He's the king of the dogs now, I guess."

"I guess," Bridie said.

"We got to make sure he eats good tonight," Vandal said. "He tells me he wants to do it all over again tomorrow."

When Hark started in to walking on his hind legs, Bridie told Vandal that he couldn't spend his days in the kennel anymore. "I thought you wanted him penned," he said, "to keep him out of your hair."

"It's not right," she said, "a thing that goes on two legs and a thing that goes on four." She couldn't bring herself to call Hark a man. He wasn't a man exactly, not yet anyway. He was like a tadpole, Bridie thought when she looked at him, something in between two other things and not really anything in itself. He was neither man nor dog, and he was both, and he was awful. Nothing could exist for long in that middle condition, she didn't believe. It was unbearable.

"We've got to put him in some clothes too," she said, "to get him covered up." He went around in an excited state half the time, and the sight of him, slick and red, sickened and haunted her.

"Can he wear some of mine?" Vandal asked.

Probably, Bridie thought. He was getting more man-sized and more man-shaped with every day that passed. *And it's probably exactly what he wants to do too.* But she said, "I think we should get him some of his own." *Some coveralls*, she thought, *and a tractor cap to cover that low sloping forehead and the bony ridges above the eyes.*

The more like a man he became, the more he horrified her. She wondered if there was a point at which she would simply be unable to stand his transformation any longer, and what would happen when she reached it? Would she start screaming and be unable to stop? Would he simply turn into another man who lived in their house, like a vagrant brother or an unsavory cousin? Like Xerxes. Would such a creature be possessed of a human soul? Would it be murder to kill him?

After a couple of wobbly practice laps around the pasture field in the truck with Hark behind the wheel, Vandal yelled at him to stop the vehicle. "There's no way you can drive on the road," Vandal told him. Hark's head barely poked up above the steering wheels, and his thin legs wavered uncertainly over the pedals. He glared at Vandal. Bridie, who was watching, silently applauded. She was glad to see Vandal denying him something, anything. "You'd kill somebody, or die yourself."

You take me, Hark said. There was very little he couldn't say these days. Occasionally he struggled for a word, a phrase, but mostly his speech was fluid. At times his voice could be silky and persuasive.

He had taken to answering the phone when it rang, which was not often, and even to initiating phone calls in which he carried on long, secretive conversations with they knew not whom. There was no one outside the house, outside the farm, that they could imagine him knowing. When they asked, he simply told them that he was *finding out.* "Finding out what?" they inquired. *Finding what's out there,* he said. "What's out there?" Vandal had asked him. *You wouldn't believe me if I told you,* Hark said, staring straight at Bridie. *But you'll know before too long, anyhow. It'll soon be more of me and mine out there than you and yours.*

In the truck, he repeated his demand. *You take me, if I can't drive.*

"Take you where?" Vandal wanted to know.

Into town, Hark said. When Vandal just kept looking at him, he continued. *To get . . . fuck.*

Vandal laughed. "You want to get laid?"

Hark shrugged his narrow shoulders. He wore a youth-size denim work shirt and a pair of Levi's, procured at the Rural King store out on the county line, and they fit him reasonably well, adding considerably to the illusion that he was just a slightly misshapen boy or small man. Sunglasses and a one-size-fits-all John Deere cap helped to obscure his hairy forehead and his unnatural eyes. *Everything wants to fuck,* he said.

Vandal shut off the truck's ignition, pulled the key, and climbed out of the truck's cab.

You won't let me go in amongst the bitches no more, Hark said. His voice was less peremptory now, pleading. *It ain't right, keep me from what I want. What I need.*

"You think you'll find women in town to sleep with you?" Bridie called. "A thing like you are?"

Hark laughed, a short bark that went strangely with his hominid appearance. *There's them in town as would be glad to be with me any way I am. Any way I want.*

"That's why we stay far from town," Vandal said. He stalked away from the truck, his face dark and angry, and marched into the house. Hark stayed where he was, behind the steering wheel, glaring balefully through the dirty windshield. The glass was spiderwebbed with fine cracks.

"Get out of there," Bridie said to him. "You're not driving nowhere."

I belong in town more than you do, Hark said without looking at her. *You know it's so. More and more every day. You got no right to keep me out here with you, amongst the cows and the crows.*

She pictured him among people, in some smoky place where she herself would never go, a cigarette tucked in the corner of his mouth, his hat tilted back on his head because he was unafraid of his own peculiar nature, his long teeth gleaming in dim light, his eyes slitted, one of his paws (*his hands,* she corrected herself, *they are much more like hands now*) on the thigh of a giggling, sighing girl beside him. But was she a girl, exactly, this creature in the vision? Wasn't she just a bit too large to be a normal sort of girl, too sleek and well-fleshed, her hair thick and coarse down her neck, her nostrils too wide, her eyes broadly spaced, on the sides of her head, almost? *A pony,* she thought. And the heavily-bristled, barrel-bodied man across the table from them, snorting with laughter, little eyes glittering with nasty delight, his snout buried in his plate . . .

"Probably you're right," she said, and she followed Vandal into the house, leaving Hark where he was.

He found his way into the liquor not long after that. The bottles had belonged to Xerxes. Vandal was strictly a beer man, and Bridie didn't drink at all. It was a holdover from her upbringing, which was hardshell Baptist. Much of that way of thinking and living had left her in the years she had been gone from her parents' house, which had been at once a stern and a gentle place, but her dislike of hard spirits had stayed with her. She found him in the living room, as usual, fixated on the television screen, which was announcing yet another series of nightmares. His eyes were glazed, a half-empty bottle of Knob Hill on the TV tray at his elbow, and he blinked slowly when she entered the room, so that she knew he was aware of her presence. His breathing was loud and stertorous.

This ain't happening just here, you know, he told her. He nodded at the TV, where hail was pelting down from a clear sky, smashing windows, denting the hoods and roofs of cars, sending people scrambling for solid cover, flattening crops. Birds of every description were dropping dead into the streets. *It's happening everywhere.* He burped lightly and covered his mouth with his hairy palm. His tone had sounded mournful before, but now he giggled.

Bridie understood that he didn't mean their own situation, not exactly, not a dog turning into a man, not just (her thoughts turned away, but she forced them back: she had to look at everything that was happening, and not just a part of it) a man turning into a dog, or at any rate something less than a man; but other, equally terrible things, inexplicable things, things that had never happened before. And she knew that he also meant, *There is no stopping them.*

She sat down across from him, close enough that she could touch him. He took his gaze from the television and looked her full in the face, and his eyes were soft and brown, much more like the dog she remembered, and not antagonistic. There was pain written in them— did it hurt, to become a man?—and fear. For the first time, the sight of him didn't fill her with disgust. He sniffed.

It's the foller-man as gets bit. It's the foller-dog as gets hit. His voice was a kind of singsong. Playful. He took another swig from the bottle, waiting on her response. If he had not been what he was, she might have thought he was being flirtatious.

"What's that mean?" she asked him.

You tell me.

She thought a moment. She believed that she had heard a rhyme like it somewhere before. Her girlhood, maybe. A cadence for jumping rope. Was it some kind of a riddle? *The foller-man.* She thought of the head of a snake, then, the dead eyes and the mouth wide, the fangs milky with poison; and she had it.

"It's always the second man on the trail that gets bitten by the snake," she said. Hark nodded, and his head moved so slowly that the gesture seemed wise. "The first man wakes the snake up, and it strikes the second man in the line."

And the lead dog, he said, *judges the distance to get across the road before the car comes. But the dog that comes along just a second later, trailing the first one like he always does, he. . .*

"Gets hit," she said.

Is it a joke? he asked. *That the first one plays on the second one?*

"Not so much a joke," she told him, "as just not giving it any thought. Always looking forward, and there's no looking behind."

I never want to be no foller-dog anymore, he said to her. *Nor no foller-man neither. I'm going to be the firstest one along every trail, and the firstest one across every road.* He took another drink, and the level in the bottle dropped appreciably. He coughed and sputtered. *From now on in,* he said.

In other places, some not so very far away, the television informed them, the dead were said to be rising up from their graves. The recent dead, and the long dead: it didn't seem to make any difference. The ones who came back to life most often found their ways back to their homes, their families, back to those who loved them, and when they found somebody who recognized them—assuming anybody was left who did—they cried aloud at the wonders they had seen in the great lightless cities that they inhabited after death.

Would resurrected people have the vote, the television wondered?

Hark closed his eyes and sighed. *Some folks just have too much life in them to die all the way, I guess,* he said. He looked so sad when he said it that she felt a sudden stab of unexpected sympathy for him, and sorrow.

They took to having conversations, short ones, usually, that ended in unsatisfying confusion, because she didn't know the right questions to ask, or he didn't know the right words to tell her what she wanted to know. Sometimes, she swore, he held back his answers, wanting always to get more than he gave. When he asked her about the wider world, outside the borders of the farm, outside the boundaries of the county, she found that she didn't know very much—only what she saw on TV, really, and he saw as much of that as she did; more, in fact—and he quickly became contemptuous of her. Always, though, their exchanges came back to a single question:

"Why wouldn't you go into the water that day?"

There was something waiting for me in that pond.

"What was waiting?"

A spirit. There was a spirit on that water, and it wanted me to come in there with it. The spirit wanted me, the spirit and the water both.

"You were afraid the water would change you?"

I was afraid it wouldn't. I felt the change coming on me that day, and I had the fear that the water might take it off and leave me what I had always been. I wanted to be something else.

"The change didn't feel bad to you? It didn't hurt?"

It felt— exhilarating. He sounded pleased with himself that he had come up with that word, but his face was impossible to read.

Hark was still drinking and watching TV, and the liquor was holding out longer than Bridie had thought (had hoped) it might. Vandal had taken to spending long stretches away from the house, out walking the fields or shuffling about in the granary, sitting alone in the loft of the silent barn, watching over the place as it fell fallow without his labor.

Sometimes he went into the kennel, and she didn't care to ask him what he did there. He didn't touch her in their bed at night anymore, wouldn't undress where she could see him. Under his clothes, he seemed to have shrunk, and his gaze, whenever it fell on her, was cool and distant. At that moment, he was upstairs, asleep in their bed. He slept ten hours a night, sometimes more, and still he seemed always to be exhausted.

Hark dropped an empty bottle and it rolled across the parlor floor and disappeared under the davenport. *It could be,* she thought, *that Xerxes had him a stash that I never knew about. But how did he find it?*

"Hark?" she said.

Ain't my name.

"What?" she asked.

Nefas. That's what you call me now. That's my name now. Not that word you give me, that nothing. That Hark.

"I'm not going to call you — "

Nefas! he shouted. His teeth, still pointed, flashed at her. *Baphomet! Marduk, Shahar, Enkidu! Call me by my God-damned name!*

Her hand flashed out, and her open palm cracked against the sharp bones of his face. The sting of the blow traveled up her arm, to the center of her chest, and her eyes filled with tears, but she swung again, savagely backhanded him so that spittle flew from his gaping mouth. His right eye closed and his head twisted to the side. She thought that she wouldn't be able to stand the throbbing of her hand. Her fingers; had she broken them?

He flew at her with a snarl, and the momentum of his small, furious body took them both to the floor. He put his teeth on the swelling of her throat just below her jaw, and his breath was hot against the skin of her neck. *He will kill me now*, she thought, and the flaming agony of her arm, and Hark's noisome weight—or Marduk's, or whatever he cared to call himself, Nefas—on her, and the events of these last days, made that idea not at all an unwelcome one.

Instead, he began to squeeze her breasts with both his hands, and his breathing quickened as he fumbled to open her blouse. He pushed a knee between her legs and worked to part them. *This is how he did it,* he said.

"No," she said.

He gave a throaty little chuckle. There was real amusement in the sound. *It's all fine and dandy to tell someone No,* he said. *But the question has to be: Can you make it stick?* The stench of whiskey filled her nostrils. His teeth and his lips moved from beneath her chin to the hollow of her throat, and from there to her breastbone. He pressed himself avidly against her.

She willed her wrecked right hand into motion, her fingers and thumb searching for his eyes, her palm forcing his blunt head up and back. The stubble on his cheeks rasped against her like sandpaper, and she cried out with the pain and horror of it. She didn't want to hurt him. She had never wanted to hurt anyone in her life.

She caught sight of the picture of the baptism on the wall, hanging high above her—*I am where Xerxes lay*, she thought, *and this is the angle he saw it from at the last*—while her left hand went seeking, almost on its own, along the wall. In the picture, a great crowd of grey figures, cloaked like ghosts, filled the background, lining the far bank of the river. Seen from a distance, it was possible to take them for clouds, or a line of distant cliffs. *How is it I never noticed them before?* she thought, as Hark (*Nefas!*) fastened his eager mouth on her nipple, as her left hand found the set of fireplace tools that stood on the hearth and brought them all clattering down. As her left hand got purchase on the pair of iron log tongs and whipped them around in a hard arc.

The tongs took him up high, on the temple, and his suckling mouth fell away from her, his limbs spasming. She struck him again, on the shoulder this time, and he screeched and tumbled off of her, scrambling to escape, his limbs scrabbling against the floor. He was like an injured insect. She stood and went after him, straddling his body, thumping him on the back of the head, the spine. He squealed, and she wondered if Vandal might hear the sound and come to investigate. "Your name is Hark!" she shouted at him. Her blows rained down on him.

Nefas, he managed to gasp out.

"You will come when we call!"

Enkidu.

"You will do what we say."

Hark scuttled into a corner of the room, behind the easy chair, where Bridie had a hard time getting at him. She stood with the tongs upraised, waiting on a good moment to strike him again. When she saw his eyes on her, she tugged her blouse closed with her injured hand. A couple of the buttons were missing. Crouched in the corner, his spindly arms crossed over his head for protection, Hark indicated the picture with a lift of his snout.

Okay, he said. His ribs were heaving, and blood stained his shirt and his pants. *You got the upper hand of me. You going to make me get down on my knees and worship him the way that you do?* he said. *Bow down to your water man, your dead man? Your foller-man?*

Vandal lay next to her in the dark, moaning softly, his legs kicking from time to time beneath the bedcovers. He faced the wall, and when she touched him, she could feel the puckered ridge of his backbone. He had always been a thickset man, but now it was as if the flesh was melting off him, leaving his body a skeletal landscape of edges and hollows. She envied him his sleep. She had taken some aspirin, the last in the house, but her right arm continued to pain her terribly.

"What if we're imagining all this?" she asked Vandal's back. She kept her voice low, because she didn't really want to wake him. She hoped, somehow, that he might awake on his own, and be as he had been before. He shivered and whimpered at the sound of her voice. "What if he never talked or changed at all? What if we're dreaming it?" she asked.

Dreaming the same dream, he said. She closed her eyes at the sound of his voice, which was no longer his, little more than a buzzing or gurgling deep in his throat. Eyes open, eyes closed, she found that it was the same darkness all around her.

"Maybe I'm just dreaming it," she said. "Alone."

Vandal made a small snorting noise that she took to mean assent, and went on, like a being in a fairy story, with his impenetrable slumber.

Deep in the night, when she could not tell how long she had been asleep, the voice came to her from outside her bedroom door, whispering in like wind through the crack at the threshold: *The strong will do what the strong will do. And the weak will bear what they must.*

When he surprised her in the kitchen, she understood that this time there would be no lucky hand on the tongs, no surprise blow to the head. He wasn't drunk. He was ready. Nefas (she had come to think of him that way—he wasn't Hark anymore, and it seemed foolish to keep calling him by the vanished dog's name) had grown at least as large as she was, and nimbler, and far faster and stronger, with a beast's terrible speed and strength, and a man's cruelty. If she tried to hurt him, he would hurt her far worse in return, she knew. In some deep part of him, she thought, he hoped that she would fight him, because he very much wanted to hurt her.

Her right arm was immobilized in a sling that she had rigged up for it out of a couple of dish cloths, her fingers bruised, the joints blackened. She had a fever. Vandal was still upstairs, in the bed that was now far too large for him. He slept around the clock, wasting away. She would not have been surprised, upon going into the bedroom, to find him gone altogether.

If I had a pot of water boiling, she thought. *If I had a skillet full of sizzling grease, I would fling it in his grinning face.* There was nothing hot. He had placed himself between her and the great wooden knife block. He wasn't stupid. He had the shotgun in his hand, pointing clumsily downward, at his feet.

She found herself hoping that Vandal wouldn't awake, ever, that he would simply sleep through what was coming, for her, for him, for all of them. She hoped that he could go on forever dreaming for himself a world where the sunshine was bright and golden as in the old days, and untamed birds crisscrossed the sky in their lopsided Vs, and cattle drifted in friendly bunches across the pastures, and game, unending phalanxes of game, deer and clever squirrels and bear and swift, wily turkeys that could be hunted and brought down but which did not die, which lent themselves again and again to the eternal chase—she hoped that, in his dreams, all of these filled the emerald mansions of the limitless forest.

God be with you, she thought, and then Vandal, like Hark, was gone from her thoughts.

Nefas set the shotgun carefully on the floor behind him and put his hands on her shoulders. His touch was heavy but not painful. His hands were broad and short-fingered. "Please," she said.

Call me by my name, he said.

"Nefas," she said, choking on the word. "Please."

He leaned into her, cradled the back of her head with his hard palm, sniffed deeply at her hair. *Call me by my name,* he said.

She struggled to remember what he had said she should call him. Why did he need so many names? She couldn't recall them all, and she was terrified of what he would do to her if she couldn't name him properly. Her memory leaped. "Baphomet," she said. "Marduk, please."

He bit the lobe of her ear, hard enough to draw blood, and she cried out. She struggled to free her arm from the sling but it was caught fast. *Call me by my name,* he said, his mouth against her ear. His breath was moist, his tone simultaneously intimate and insistent. He cupped her right breast as though he were weighing it, as though it were a piece of fruit that he was considering buying. His weight against her drew agony from her wounded hand, trapped between her body and his.

"Enkidu," she said. She knew that she could not, must not, resist him, and she steeled herself to surrender. Why, she wondered, was it not possible simply to die? To her astonishment, her uninjured hand, her left, hefted a cumbersome iron trivet from the stovetop. It had belonged to Vandal's mother, and Bridie had never cared much for it, but she had kept it for the sentiment she imagined it provoked in Vandal.

She raised the trivet over Nefas' shaggy head. The fingers of her left hand were bloodless, she was holding it so tightly. He followed its ascent with his eyes, but he did not take his mouth away from her ear. He made a sound that she thought might be laughter. His hand went to the skirt that she was wearing, and he tugged the hem up to her waist.

Shall we fuck each other, or shall we kill each other? he asked. It didn't sound like he much cared which. Both were fine with him. With one of his feet he hooked the shotgun and slid it forward, where he could get a hand on it quickly.

"This doesn't have to happen," she said.

No? he asked. His hands were busy, unbuttoning, unclasping. She was nearly nude, and still her hand stayed poised over his skull. The trivet had a number of pointed projections. It had always seemed a peaceable thing, domestic, sitting patiently atop the stove, but in her hand it had taken on the look of some exotic piece of medieval weaponry. He shucked his baggy Levi's, and the buckle of his belt clattered against the linoleum. *Seems to me it's happening already.*

Spare me, spare me, she thought, but she didn't say it because a creature like him wouldn't spare her anything. He was toying with her. He had come an unspeakable distance and waited an unthinkably long time for the pleasures he was planning to indulge. "You were a good dog," she said. "Can't you be a good man?"

He considered a moment, drew fractionally away from her. Her skin where it had touched his was hot, and the small space between them felt deliciously fresh. The trivet was growing heavy, her hand was trembling with the effort of holding it over him. Nefas jerked a thumb upward, and his hand brushed the metal. He could have taken it from her if he had wanted, but he let it stay. *Is he a good man?* he asked her.

She had to struggle to work out who he might mean. Vandal, asleep in the master bedroom overhead. "He was," she said. "I don't know what precisely he is now."

You think it's only me that gets to choose, he said. *He chooses too. Every minute he chooses.*

Vandal, upstairs, choosing oblivion.

You choose too, just as much as him. Just as much as me. He tapped the trivet with a dense fingernail, and it rang like a bell. *You're choosing right now. What is it you're choosing?* "Not this," she said, indicating his nakedness, and hers. His eyes roamed over her body, and she had the impulse to cover herself, but she resisted it. It took her a great deal of will to open her fingers; wearily, she dropped the iron trivet onto the counter, where it thumped and rolled and left a small scar. "Not this either," she said. Unable to suppress a whimper of pain as she did it, she shucked the sling and flexed the stiffened fingers of her hand.

Nefas returned his gaze to her face. *He ain't fucked you in a while now,* he said. *And you don't want to fuck me. You just planning on doing without it for the rest of your life?*

"That might not be such a very long time," she said. "With the world the way it is."

And yet it might, he said to her. *That's one choice as is not left up to us.*

Stifling her disgust, she reached out and took him by the hand, his broad palm in her swollen fingers. She drew him gently to her, not in the way of a lover, but as a mother might. An expression of shock, unmistakable even on his inscrutable face, crossed his crude features. Slowly he came to her, almost against his will. She gritted her teeth and shut the feel of his hairy hide away from her. He laid his bony head on her bosom, and she embraced him.

With surprise, she felt how meager he was, how slight his frame. *He's made out of a dog's bones, and he's got a man's mind,* she thought. There was no joy in him anywhere, she could feel that plainly, none of the kind of blind infectious joy that even the least of dogs possesses in abundance. "Why do you think he gave his place up to you?" she asked, meaning Vandal. She could see now that that was precisely what he had done. Slipped away from her, away from the world, and left this twisted creature in his stead. "Being a man isn't what you think it is."

Hark began to cry. His hot tears slipped over her breasts. "I've got my teeth in it now," he said. "I can't ever go back. I don't much want to go forward, but I know for sure I can't go back." He put his arms around her and she stiffened in his embrace, but the lust had passed through him for the moment and left him innocent. It would come back, and the old struggle would rise up between them again; and how it would end she didn't care to contemplate. For the present, they could manage to stand together this way, skin to skin and inextricably linked.

Nefas cocked his head. *I can hear him, you know,* he said. *Always hear him.* His voice was quiet. *Listen to him as he comes this way. He's pretty near.*

"Who?"

Him. Him as sent me on ahead.

She recognized the quality of his fear. It wasn't fear for himself, she realized, and the knowledge clutched at her. "Who can you hear?" she demanded. She struggled to keep her own voice even.

I figured you knew, Nefas said. *I figured you knew all along.* He looked up at her with wide eyes. *He's coming along on my heels, but he ain't your foller-man. It's nothing like that. I don't believe he's any sort of man at all.*

Terror bloomed in her, and her vision dimmed. "X?"

He wanted me to tell as soon as I could talk proper, but I found out I wanted you, so I didn't say it.

"Didn't say what?" she asked. "What were you supposed to say?"

He wanted me to tell you that he don't care about what you said. He supposes he should hold it against you, but he don't plan to pay it any mind at all.

The house felt very small and fragile in that moment, and she felt small and fragile inside it, holding onto this creature, this hairy thing that wasn't her husband, that wasn't her dog either. The world was drawing in around her, the broad fields folding up to the size of handkerchiefs, the once-straight fences crowding and jostling themselves crooked, the barn and the granary and the machine shop butting up hard against the house and the dog run and the kennel, the woods and tangled marshes infiltrating the cleared spaces, humans and beasts colliding, the dead and the living spilling over each other; order failing, pandemonium as all the things that had been separate for so very long came rushing together, splintering one another like ships driven before a storm, until there was no way to know what was one and what was another.

Probably, Bridie thought, this has happened at other times, perhaps countless times before, perhaps every age came to its close in just this way, with no one left alive to tell the tale. Her mind went to the pond, and to the turtles huddled under the shivering surface of the water. *Them*, she thought. *They are the great survivors.*

The house was drawing everything into it and down, like a great whirlpool—all the abhorrent things, all the terrible marvels. Bridie stood at the heart of the catastrophe, and so alone was able to see it for what it was: the end of one thing, and the beginning of another that was infinitely worse.

Perhaps, she thought, Nefas could serve her as a guide, she thought, a scout among the ruins, blend of senses and mind that he was, a genius of sorts, and utterly unique. It might be possible for her to lose herself in the shrieking bedlam, to hide herself away in the ruins, but for how long? The world's collapse might never end, and X would never stop his returning. "Can you smell him?" she asked. From outside, a whispering as from the tongues of a thousand snakes.

He shook his head. *Not yet. But soon.*

"Will you take my part?" she asked.

His eyes were wide, and he was shivering against her. *You don't have the least idea what you're asking, or who you're asking it from*, he told her. He shrugged and pulled her closer, and she felt him decide in her favor. He leaned down and scooped up the shotgun, and his grip on it looked so clumsy and unpracticed that she almost laughed. She had the impulse to take it away from him, but she chose instead not to insult his pride. The understanding between them was brittle enough. "I'll do what I can," he said.

They clung to each other in the midst of the hissing, swaying chaos, murmuring useless reassurances as twilight consumed the kitchen. And Vandal, curled deeply into himself, slumbered away in the upper bedroom, twitching from time to time as dreams of the world, full of infinite life as it had never been, and as it would never be, flitted beautifully across the thin translucent scrim of his mind.

Surreal South'09

Cover artist **MINNA SVENSSON** is a photographer and mixed media artist who enjoys working with digital art and collages. With her witty, playful imagery, Minna creates whole universes of mystical fables, often of the eerie, little, bizarre kind. She finds paradoxes utterly fascinating and likes to play with these in her work, which gives her a unique style that floats around somewhere in the borderland between fairytales and horror stories. At the moment Minna is studying art and film in Gothenburg, Sweden. In the future she wants to explore all the wonders of this world, expand her artistry, and live in the South in an old ghost house with a front porch. To see more of Minna's work visit: www.obsceneteaparty.com or contact her at: kuchimallan@gmail.com.

Photo by Christine Lumans

ALEXANDER LUMANS was born in Aiken, South Carolina, and is a graduate of the MFA Program for Fiction at Southern Illinois University Carbondale. His fiction has been published in *Clarkesworld* and *The Versus Anthology* and is forthcoming in *Greensboro Review*, *StoryQuarterly*, *Gargoyle*, *Southern Indiana Review*, and the anthologies *Writer's Voice 2009* and *Press 53 Open Awards 2009*. He was awarded scholarships to attend the RopeWalk Writer's Retreat Mastersclass and Retreat in 2008 and 2009, respectively. He won First Prize in the 2009 Press 53 Open Awards in Genre Fiction for his story, "Haruspices," and an Honorable Mention in Press 53's 2008 Competition. He has also been nominated for the 2008 AWP Intro Award as well as for the anthology *Best New American Voices 2009*. He now lives in Boulder, Colorado.

Story note:
Research for this story led me to the basement studio of a local taxidermist/budding fishing lure manufacturer. Before he could get into showing me how to skin and mount a bass, I managed to impale my finger on one of his Muskie hooks he had hanging from the basement's rafters. He took me to get fixed up at the nearby emergency room (in the hospital where he'd been born). He never got around to explicitly teaching me anything, but he did give me a Ziploc of frozen squirrel meat. He also let me keep the hook. It hangs over my desk to this day.

Photo by Troy DeRego

BECKY HAGENSTON's collection of stories, *A Gram of Mars*, won Sarabande Books' Mary McCarthy Prize in Short Fiction and the Great Lakes Colleges Association New Writers Award. Her stories have appeared in the O. Henry anthology as well as *Southern Review, Black Warrior Review, Freight Stories, Crazyhorse, Mid-American Review, Gettysburg Review*, and many other journals. She lives in Starkville, Mississippi, where she is an Associate Professor of English at Mississippi State University. "Anthony" will appear in the forthcoming collection, *Strange Weather*, which won the 2009 Spokane Prize and will be published in 2010 by Eastern Washington University Press.

Story note:
I originally thought this story would be entirely in Nia's point of view, that Anthony's presence would make her family stronger, and that he would eventually go away. But Anthony turned out to be as compelling to me as he is to the other characters, and he took over the story in a way I hadn't expected. It's always exciting when a story takes you in a direction you didn't see it heading, and that's what I loved about writing this one.

Photo by Michelle Brooks

DANIEL MUELLER's collection of stories, *How Animals Mate*, won the Sewanee Fiction Prize and was published by Overlook Press. His fiction has appeared in *Playboy, Story, Story Quarterly, Mississippi Review, Another Chicago Magazine, CutBank, Prairie Schooner, Cincinnati Review, Gargoyle, Orchid*, and elsewhere. He is the grateful recipient of fellowships from the National Endowment for the Arts, Massachusetts Cultural Council, Fine Arts Work Center in Provincetown, Henfield Foundation, University of Virginia, and Iowa Writers' Workshop. He teaches on the permanent creative writing faculties of the University of New Mexico and Low-Residency MFA Program at Queens University of Charlotte.

Story note:
True story. On August 16, 2006, retired Albuquerque city employee Gary Hoffman *thought* he'd hit it big when the nickel slot machine he was playing at Sandia Casino said he'd won $1,597,244.10. He even received a marriage proposal during his short-lived celebration.

Photo by Adam Zion

HEATHER FOWLER received her M.A. in English and Creative Writing from Hollins University. She reads and writes—quite a bit. Sometimes, she teaches about reading and writing, most recently at the UCSD Literature Department. Among other venues, she has recently published stories in: *Night Train, Underground Voices, A cappella Zoo, KeyHole Magazine, Trespass, SubLit, WordRiot, Dodzplot Flash Fiction, Storyglossia, Temenos, Mississippi Review Online,* and *Frigg: A Magazine of Fiction and Poetry.* "You Are One Click Away from Pictures of Nude Girls" was listed as a Notable Story of 2008 for the storySouth Million Writers Award.Visit www.heatherfowlerwrites.com for linked-in work, a full bibliography, and a list of current events.

Story note:
This story emerged from a combination of my frustration with those aggressive porn sites that seem innocuously arrived at, yet impossible to exit—and the idea that so many men are lonely or long for a woman they will never obtain—while ignoring the strong beautiful women who are already near them. It is also the story that I've privately referred to, for some time, as my lovingly-reframed-sex-positive-c-word-manifesto story, or, otherwise, just the c-word manifesto piece.

Photo by Chris Blanz

J.T. ELLISON is the bestselling author of the critically acclaimed Taylor Jackson series, including *All The Pretty Girls*, *14*, *Judas Kiss* and the forthcoming thriller, *The Cold Room*. A former White House staffer, she moved to Nashville and began research on a passion: forensics and crime. She has worked extensively with the Metro Nashville Police, the FBI and various other law enforcement organizations to research her novels. Ellison lives in Nashville with her husband and a poorly trained cat. Visit www.JTEllison.com for more insight into her wicked imagination.

Story note:
"Chimera" came to me in a dream. A very, very bad dream. I was watching the movie *Constantine* with my father right before bed, and the movie came to life in ways I could never imagine. The demon came for me. I knew, with the absolute clarity that comes from your unconscious, that this had happened before, and if I screamed, he would go away. My poor parents were awakened by the bloodcurdling shrieks echoing through their house. My father rushed outside, positive a young woman in the neighborhood was being murdered. Finding no one, he came back to the house, realizing at last that it was me. I've never screamed aloud from a dream before. Even though I've captured the demon, and put him on the page where he can't ever hurt me again, I still sleep uneasy in that room.

Photo by Michelle Seymour

JEDIDIAH AYRES received his diploma from Fayetteville High School in Arkansas and cut his hair for a minimum-wage job. He has never won an award or been nominated for one.

Story note:

"Miriam" is essentially recycled from a screenplay that I wrote. The character, whose back story this was, changed and her scene was cut from the movie, but I was fond enough of Miriam to give her another shot in a short story.

Photo by Chris Glass

JESSICA GLASS holds a Masters of Fine Arts from Queens University of Charlotte. She has been writing stories since she first learned to put letters together into words (think "The Babysitter From the Black Lagoon"), but this is her first publication. She is happily anticipating unemployment as her sinking ship of an employer goes the way of the recession. She and her husband and new baby son live in Virginia with a passel of unruly pets.

Story note:
This story was inspired by a Dresden Dolls song by the same name. I started thinking about the concept of a mechanical coin-powered automaton, what it would look like, how it would interact with humans. We're talking about a much more sophisticated machine than your run-of-the-mill C-3PO. The question is further complicated by the uncanny valley hypothesis, a fascinating psychological phenomenon in which humans display empathy toward a nonhuman entity until a certain threshold of familiarity, or similarity to human appearance and behavior, is reached, at which point the human response plunges into revulsion. When a creation is only slightly humanlike, we're more than willing to bridge the gap emotionally; but when it is so lifelike as to appear human, we tend to focus on the tiny details that still separate us. I wanted to write about the conflict inherent in a relationship between a human and an incredibly humanlike machine. And the story was born.

Photo by Young Jean Lee

JOHN MCMANUS is the author of the novel *Bitter Milk* and the short story collections *Born on a Train* and *Stop Breakin Down*, all from Picador USA. In 2000 he became the youngest-ever winner of the prestigious Whiting Writers' Award. He has been the recipient of a James Michener Fellowship at UT-Austin, as well as fellowships at the Camargo Foundation, Caldera Arts, the Robert M. MacNamara Foundation, and the Corporation of Yaddo. His short fiction has appeared in *Ploughshares, The Oxford American, Tin House, and Columbia.* Born in Knoxville in 1977 and raised in Maryville, Tennessee, he lives in Virginia and teaches in the MFA programs at Old Dominion University and Goddard College.

Story note:
I thought of this story around mile twenty-two of the Baltimore Marathon last fall. If it seems lacking in its glycogen store, that's probably why.

Originally from a small town in south Georgia, over the last fifteen years JOSH MCCALL has lived in El Paso, Texas; Juárez, Mexico; Norfolk, Virginia; Brooklyn, New York; and Mérida, Mexico. Currently he's an MFA student at Florida State University. In 2006 he published *The Blackout Gang* (Razorbill/Penguin USA), a young adult novel, and has since completed work on a second novel. "The Ballad of Scrub and Shelly" is his first short story publication. Visit www.joshmccall.com.

Story note:
I started this story after watching *The Five Obstructions*, by Lars Von Trier and Jørgen Leth. I was intrigued by the idea of creating obstructions or obstacles and forcing yourself to write around them. I tried to get a couple of writer-friends to play along. They refused, so I went at it alone. I won't say which parts of the story were the original "obstructions," except to note that there were two and the bear wasn't one of them. I grew up working summers on a tobacco farm, and the wife of the farmer was constantly telling me to "watch out or that bear's gonna get you." What she meant was heat exhaustion, but I thought it no accident that she called it a bear.

JOSH WOODS is Editor of *The Versus Anthology* and a recent Assistant Editor of *Crab Orchard Review*. His fiction appears in *XX Eccentric: Stories About the Eccentricities of Women*, *The Versus Anthology*, and *Press 53 Open Awards Anthology*. His non-fiction and book review works have appeared in *The Susquehanna Review*, *UE Magazine*, and *Crab Orchard Review*, and he was the winner of the 2008 Press 53 Open Awards in Genre Fiction. He is currently an Assistant Professor of English at Kaskaskia College, and he hails originally from Henderson, Kentucky.

Story note:

As the title of this piece indicates, this is actually a group of excerpted entries from my novel, *All Hell*, which is in encyclopedia format. A few notes on origins: The Henderson in this is based on my very real hometown Henderson, as is my delusional version of the town's history; the character Jack is heavily inspired by one of my very real best friends, Nathan Gilliam; my Elohim and my Yahweh grew out of legitimate yet esoteric interpretations of Biblical material, thanks to Harold Bloom; and the occult symbols, as well as my version of the Tree of Life, are very real as well, so gaze upon them at your own risk. I must thank Pinckney Benedict for helping me find the gall to write such a thing.

Photo by Douglas Miller

KURT RHEINHEIMER's stories have appeared in many magazines, ranging from *Redbook* and *Playgirl* to *Glimmer Train* and *Shenandoah*, and have been anthologized in four volumes of *New Stories From The South: The Year's Best*. His story collection, "Little Criminals," published by Eastern Washington University Press, was a finalist for the Virginia Fiction Book of the Year in 2006. He is the winner of several national awards for fiction, including the Lawrence Foundation Prize and the Wordstock Prize. A follower of the Baltimore Orioles since their rebirth in 1954, he fancies himself the very best fan they have ever had. His love-letter essay on the topic appears in the book *Scoring From Second: Writers on Baseball*. Kurt is editor in chief at Leisure Publishing in Roanoke, Va., publishers of magazines including *Blue Ridge Country* and *The Roanoker*, as well as the Virginia Travel Guide. He and his wife Gail have been known to hike every weekend; last summer, they completed the 546 miles of the Appalachian Trail in Virginia—done all in day hikes over several years.

Story note:
It took many years after my sister's death for me to even broach trying to tell her story, which became the last piece of a story collection based on my family. In retrospect, I think casting "How To Get Sick" in second person not only helped establish the terrifying strangeness of the illness, but also allowed me wade into the tragedy with at least that little protection.

Photo by Miriam Berkley

KYLE MINOR is the author of *In the Devil's Territory*, a collection of short fiction. His story "The Truth and All Its Ugly" appeared in the inaugural *Surreal South*, and other recent work appears in *The Southern Review*, *The Gettysburg Review*, *Plots with Guns*, and *Best American Mystery Stories 2008*.

Story note:
"Dressing the Dead" is written as tribute and homage to the American poet Frank Stanford, and contains several out-of-context lines from his posthumous collection *The Light the Dead See*, which is recommended to all readers.

Photo by Jay Fram

LAURA BENEDICT is the author of the novels *Calling Mr. Lonely Hearts* and *Isabella Moon*. Her essays and short stories have appeared in *Ellery Queen Mystery Magazine* and a number of anthologies. She lives with her husband, two children, two dogs, and the occasional intrepid bobcat in rural southern Illinois—a lonely, enchanted sort of place that offers excellent inspiration for writing thrillers. Visit www.laurabenedict.com to get to know her better.

Story note:
In 2006 a young Virginia family was brutally murdered during a home invasion. While none of the characters in this story is in any way meant to resemble that crime's real-life victims or participants, "Five Revelations" is an attempt to exorcise my soul of the pain that comes from knowing humans are capable of such evil.

Photo by Emma Dodge Hanson

LEE K. ABBOTT is the author of seven collections of short stories, most recently *All Things, All at Once: New & Selected Stories* (Norton, 2006). He's been published nearly everywhere: *Harpers, Atlantic, The Georgia Review, The Kenyon Review, The Southern Review* among them. His work has been reprinted semi-regularly in *Best American Short Stories* and *The Prize Stories: the O'Henry Awards*, as well as the Pushcart Prize volumes. He teaches in the MFA Program at the Ohio State University in Columbus.

Story note:
"Youth on Mars" is another effort to see what results when Mad Max meets Walt Whitman. Moreover, it's another of my trash-compactor stories, a place to put all those lines and images and "moves" that found no home elsewhere.

Photo by Sam Beachell

MELANIE DECAROLIS descends from one of the pioneering families of Pinellas County, Florida, was named for the supporting heroine of *Gone With the Wind*, and owes her very existence to a couple in Little Rock, Arkansas who are not her parents. She lives in Boston, where Yankee is a cuss word, used most fervently from April to October.

Story note:
This story showed up in my life during a really evil four-month period when I was dealing with a broken job situation, a broken friendship, a broken heart, and a broken leg. Only two of these were related. The muses must have taken pity on me, because they sent the story to me in a dream, literally. Other than moving the setting to Defiance, Iowa (the gas station is an hour east of Omaha) and one woulda-really-been-a-badass-scene I was too lazy to write, this is exactly how it happened.

Photo by Megan Garriga

MICHAEL GARRIGA is a PhD candidate in Florida State University's creative writing department. His work has appeared, or is forthcoming, in *New Letters, Black Warrior Review, storySouth, Louisiana Literature,* and *The Versus Anthology.* He currently teaches writing in Valencia, Spain, where he lives with his wife, Megan.

Story note:
I consider this story a morality tale really, a kind of shout to would-be revolutionaries, warning them against the use of zombies in their coups, because after all, zombies are even less reliable than we've been led to believe.

Photo by Catherine Pierce

MICHAEL P. KARDOS grew up on the Jersey Shore and now teaches creative writing at Mississippi State University. His fiction appears in *The Southern Review, Prairie Schooner, Gulf Coast, Crazyhorse, Prism International, Blackbird,* and elsewhere.

Story note:
I once lived in an apartment building with a baby directly upstairs that screamed all day and all night. I mean, it was really weird. The way the baby's parents dealt with the noise was to turn up their stereo super-loud. This made it hard for me to get my writing done. Around this time, there was a rabbit that seemed to be keeping vigil on the lawn outside my entryway door. He stayed there for weeks, and would let me get pretty close to him before hopping away. He seemed like a nice rabbit. Anyway, these small details from my life were occurring around the time that I was reading *Grimm's* fairy tales. It all sort of fell into place.

Photo by Flora D'Souza

A PhD candidate in comparative literature at University of Illinois Urbana-Champaign, **OKLA ELLIOTT** also holds an MFA in creative writing from Ohio State University. He was a visiting professor of literature and creative writing at Ohio Wesleyan University for the 2008-2009 academic year. His non-fiction, poetry, short fiction, and translations appear in *A Public Space*, *Indiana Review*, *The Literary Review*, *The Los Angeles Review*, *New Letters*, *North Dakota Quarterly*, and the *Sewanee Theological Review*, among others. He is the author of two chapbooks, *The Mutable Wheel* and *Lucid Bodies and Other Poems*, and is co-editor, with Kyle Minor, of *The Other Chekhov*.

Story note:
This story is a radically condensed version of a project Raul and I have been working on since 2005. In that time it has undergone several changes in form, content, and scope—from a musical, to a play-film-musical hybrid we dubbed the *Platypusical* (in honor of that animal's ambiguous genus), to a screenplay, to its present form: a novel of slightly over six hundred pages titled *Joshua City*. (con't on page 350)

Photo by Celina Hokeah

Oscar Hokeah is Kiowa/Cherokee born and raised in Oklahoma. He is a recipient of the Truman Capote Scholarship Award, and the Native Writer Award through the Taos Summer Writers Conference 2008. He has short stories published in *Red Ink Magazine* and *Yellow Medicine Review*. He is a senior in the BFA program for Creative Writing at the Institute of American Indian Arts in Santa Fe, New Mexico. He enjoys long conversations about postcolonial theory on non-native literature, and he spends his evenings curled up with various articles on processes of decolonization. What he considers the perfect day: Five a.m. at the coffee shop with an even blend of fair trade coffee, as he sits behind his laptop with a short story in front of his eyes. He is currently working on a series of short stories based on his life growing up in modern Kiowa and Cherokee communities in Oklahoma. He is friendly, polite, but reclusive, and sometimes he is seen at the powwows gourd dancing or grass dancing. If you see Oscar Hokeah in public feel free to approach this young man of thirty-three years and say hello.

Story note:
Saynday is a traditional Kiowa hero, often depicted in children's stories, but in "Saynday's Parade" our hero saves us from ourselves. *Pobs* is short for the Kiowa word *Pobby*, which means brother, so in essence *Pobs* means *Bro*.

Photo by Eleanora Benedict

PINCKNEY BENEDICT grew up on his family's dairy farm in the mountains of southern West Virginia. He has published two collections of short fiction (*Town Smokes* and *The Wrecking Yard*) and a novel (*Dogs of God*). His third collection of fiction, *Miracle Boy and Other Stories*, will be published by Press 53 next spring. He currently serves as a professor in the English Department at Southern Illinois University in Carbondale, Illinois.

Story note:

"The Beginnings of Sorrow" evolved out of my long-standing fascination with werewolf tales, from the Roman soldier in Petronius' *Cena Trimalchionis*, for example, up to the fairly recent (and terrific) film *Dog Soldiers*. I wanted very much to write a werewolf story in reverse, one in which a dog painfully and protractedly becomes a man. Setting that story on a failing farm in the Appalachian highlands seemed natural to me, as did the rapid disintegration of the world outside the farm, communicated as it is by television: a fantasia on the hermetic environment in which I was raised.

RAUL CLEMENT lives in Greensboro, North Carolina, where he attends the University of North Carolina at Greensboro and plays in the indie-new-wave band LA Tool and Die. His short fiction, nonfiction, book reviews and interviews have been published in *Mayday, Chaffey Review* and *Main Street Rag*. He is currently working (with co-author, Okla Elliott) on a novel, *Joshua City*, a Brechtian, po-mo/sci-fi monstrosity replete with lepers, revolutionaries, and Siamese triplets who can see the future.

Story note (con't from page 347):
This world, replete with lepers, revolutionaries and Siamese triplets who can see the future, centers around Joshua City—a post-apocalyptic nation-state where water is a luxury, the film industry is a vehicle for government propaganda, and trains are deified. The difficulties in compressing such a complex world into a 4000-word short story are legion; in order to do so, there have been many necessary truncations, elisions, and omissions. The product, we hope, however, will at least give readers a taste of what *Joshua City* has to offer.

Photo by Savannah Stanley

SHERYL MONKS holds an MFA in writing from Queens University of Charlotte. She writes stories from her home in Hamptonville, North Carolina.

Story note:
When I was nine years old, my mother took my siblings and me to an amusement park in Lakeside, Virginia, where we watched Conway Twitty in concert. After the show, we walked up front, and my mother brazenly called to Conway, who stood upstage, speaking with his band mates: "The girls at the beauty shop think you wear a hairpiece." Conway turned and looked at my mother, then walked toward us at the edge of the stage, bent to his knees, and bowed his curly head. "See for yourself," he said. Mom reached up and tugged on his hair. Kazzam! It was my first magic show.

STEVEN A. PATTEN MD is a native of Atlanta, Georgia—a Grady-Baby, born in 1958 to Edward Roy and Katherine Smith Patten. He attended The Northside High School of Performing Arts. He received a BS in Biomedical Engineering from Vanderbilt University and a Doctorate of Medicine from Emory University and interned at Georgetown University. He is currently a graduating senior at Queens University of Charlotte's MFA in Creative Writing program. He has been a finalist four times for the *Glimmer Train* Literary magazine's contest for Short Stories, twice making it to the top 25 finalists category. His work has been published in *AnLage* and the *American Anthology of Poetry* and *the Journal of the National Associate of School Based Healthcare*. He maintains a practice in Internal Medicine and Geriatrics in Atlanta and lives with his wife—Karyl a dentist, their four children—Katherine, Celeste, Thomas and Steven C., two dogs, two fish and one Chinese Dwarf hamster—Petey, Jr.

Story note:
This story grew out of my fascination for a news item about a state trooper who was fired for letting off a speeding porn star in exchange for sexual favors which he took pictures of (I guess to show the guys) and my continued interest in dreams and what it takes to sculpt a living psyche.

TANTRA BENSKO's great grandmother, a close relative of Jimmy Carter, was the first settler in an "oddscure" region of rural NE Alabama said by the denizens to be "world famous around here." The land was passed down to the relatives who created a vivid reality that contributed to Tantra's sincere absurdity. Tantra has an MA in English from Florida State and an MFA from Iowa's Writing Program, taught writing in Universities for 6 years, has been published in magazines such as *Fiction International, Carolina Quarterly, Sun Dog, Chattahoochie Review, Southern Poetry Review, Florida Review, Mississippi Review,* and many more. She promotes a genre she calls Lucid Fiction, with articles about it in magazines including *Unlikely Stories,* and *Retort.* She is an artist as well. And she likes to wear bizarre costumes, particularly in large groups for fun. She likes to pretend to be various animals with her boyfriend. Sloths, duck billed platypus, and ticks are some of their favorites. She participates in making surreal comedy movies and experimental music with Paul C. Wilm in Alabama, playing heavily on characterizations suggested by the South, and fueled into hilarious intensity as a reaction to spending long periods of time there with her father, who at age 86 began writing brilliant literature himself. She raised her son on Dada and their life is one big Exquisite Corpse. www.freewebs.com/tantrabensko

Story note:
"She taught herself to read with her skin, picking up subtle differences in heat in the ink on the page. The red of the Bible's ink was easiest to pick up, and brought in the most support."

LaVergne, TN USA
10 December 2009

166554LV00003B/12/P